Addison Jones grew up in California. She is the author of four novels and a collection of short stories, all written under the name of Cynthia Rogerson. Her short stories have been broadcast, anthologised, shortlisted and included in literary magazines. She holds a RLF Fellowship at Dundee University, and supervises for the University of Edinburgh's creative writing programme.

WAIT FOR ME, JACK

JACK

Addison Jones

SANDSTONEPRESS
HIGHLAND | SCOTLAND

Published in Great Britain by
Sandstone Press Ltd
Dochcarty Road
Dingwall
Ross-shire
IV15 9UG
Scotland.

www.sandstonepress.com

The publisher acknowledges support from
Creative Scotland towards publication of this volume.

ISBN: 978-1-910985-38-0
ISBNe: 978-1-910985-43-4

Cover design by Ami Smithson at Cabin
Typeset by Iolaire Typography Ltd, Newtonmore
Printed and bound by Totem, Poland

*To anyone who wonders if they
married the wrong person*

Acknowledgements

I am grateful to my parents for too many things to include here. Also: my husband, Peter Whiteley, for his constant encouragement and for the title; my editor, Moira Forsyth, for noticing all the bloopers; my brother and sister, Mike and Carolyn Jones, for their astute input; Clare Atcheson for her wise cracking wisdom.

I am also indebted to the following people for the time they took to answer my questions, and in some cases, for listening to or reading parts of this manuscript and offering suggestions:

Ernie Stanton (China Camp)
Mairi Hedderwick
Anne Modarressi Tyler
Maggie Macdonald
Michel Faber
Anne Macleod
Janey Clarke
Jane Glover (de Young Museum)

I am especially grateful to my brother's childhood friend Bob Thawley and his wife, Marion, for pointing out all the places I made huge mistakes in geographical terms. This particular marriage could not have occurred anywhere else, but I have not lived in California for almost forty years.

'It is never easy to make marriage a lovely thing.'
Dr Marie Stopes 1918

Billie Makes Coffee for Jacko

Friday, February 12, 1950 San Francisco
12:10pm

The way Billie looks at it, there are two kinds of lives. The kind you're born and raised to live and the kind you're not. Which is virtually any other life, anywhere, with anyone. Or no one.

(She's typing while she's thinking. She can type eighty words a minute without looking at the keys.)

She was raised to live in the valley, somewhere like her hometown of Redding. Like their mother, marry young – a farmer or a brewery man or a trucker. Hang on to him if she could. Eat a million Sunday dinners at her in-laws, have lots of babies, look after her mother as she got older, and sometime later, get fat, play golf and die. Not very terrible, not at all. You could get up in the morning and know pretty much how the day would pan out, and all the years ahead, as clear as a straight valley road. Instead she's living the other kind of life here in San Francisco. Not safe, not known, and no guarantee about how she'll end up. A wild, crumbling, twisting cliff track. She can almost see the bridge she's burned. She can smell it. A thrilling, charred smell.

Billie's still typing, meanwhile. She yanks the letter from the typewriter, slips it in the out tray and inserts another piece of paper. Recommences typing. Her cherry red lips press with concentration. Now she's thinking about her date tonight. Will he be the one? Terry. No, Timmy. Tonight, anything is possible. He very well might be the one, who knows? She enjoys the fact of her own unknown future. Like having a ticket to a foreign country, an exotic place she's only seen on postcards, sent by people who scribble indecipherable messages. Tragedy? Ecstasy? She's never had a passport, never even seen one, but she pictures it tucked away in her purse anyway. Poised for departure, her heart aching for the big unknown.

Jacko leaves the building for lunch. He's peeked at the cafeteria and decided it's lousy. Old people, fat and ugly people, and it stinks of cabbage. In fact, now he thinks of it, the whole set up is a little stuffy. The furniture, the clothes, the job itself – call it anything you like, the bottom line is writing stupid lies about stupid products for the benefit of stupid buyers. Nothing and nobody with any taste at all. Not a soul he'd like to drink beer with. Oh sure, it's good money, but for crying out loud, what's a man like himself to do? Bury himself in a place like this for years? He's walking swiftly, feeling lighter with every step he takes away from Perkins Petroleum Products. Maybe he won't go back.

Mr Tidmarsh comes round after lunch. Introduces himself to Jacko. Slaps him on the back, asks him how he's coping.

'Great to have you on board, soldier!'

Jacko bets he always gives the ex-servicemen the back-slap, never the other men.

Then he says:

'You've met Billie, yeah? No?'

'No.'

'Billie, come shake hands with Jack MacAlister,' he shouts across the room to her. 'Fresh out of college. First day copywriting. The new boy, eh, Jack?'

Another backslap, followed by an arm punch. Jacko flinches. His dad was Jack; he is not, and never will be, his dad. He is way more than *Jack*, Goddammit. At least another syllable. But the correction can wait till Monday.

'Find a nice place to eat lunch, Jack?'

'Yeah.'

And finally, over comes Billie from her desk, and she says, 'Hey.'

'Hi,' says Jacko.

They don't shake hands. Hardly look at each other. Both look, instead, at Mr Tidmarsh.

'Billie, make Jack a coffee, will you honey?'

'Oh, I don't want a coffee. Thanks anyway,' says Jacko.

'I don't mind,' says Billie coldly.

'Okay then,' he says. If she's not going to even smile, then she can damn well make him a cup of coffee. 'Black, with sugar.'

There's a line at the coffee maker and Mr Tidmarsh is gone when she gets back with Jacko's coffee.

'Thanks.'

'Okay.'

She returns to her desk slowly, with a wriggle in her walk he decides is for his benefit. He looks at her the way he looks at almost every girl. Checks her out. Just the right height. Small hands and feet, medium tits, darling legs with sweet knees peeking out when she sits. Interesting eyebrows. He didn't know eyebrows could be sexy. And hair, swear to God, just like Marilyn Monroe. That same butter yellow, that same way of falling over half her face. Her voice too: little-girl whispery. Then he goes about his business again. Arranges the pencils neatly, the pad with the lists of products. His ashtray, his Zippo lighter. Lights up a Viceroy and goes back to the minuscule photographs of the products in the catalogue. It's a huge volume with thin pages, like a phone book – as he flicks through he sees artificial legs, toilet seats, shower curtains, hula hoops. Tries to visualise them individually, be interested in them. Think of ways they could sound more enticing. It's hard because forcing himself to care is exhausting. Caring eventually trickles in, but then, ironically, for the sweet-kneed Billie he pretends it's old hat. Yawns loudly and stretches between bouts of concentration, and of course, this results in genuine boredom again.

He's young and single; there's a girl with sexy eyebrows on the other side of the room. Caring about petroleum products would be unnatural. He makes a list of questions he needs to ask someone, which soon dwindles into a to-do list, then some sketches of the desk he wants to build this weekend, and finally, in the margin, a doodle of Lizbeth's breasts. They are anatomically accurate, though based on imagination only. She'd always teased him, then giggled like mad when he started unbuttoning or unzipping. Strangely this never made him fall out of love. Or perhaps, not so strangely. Bared breasts might

4

have killed it. Anyway, Lizbeth is in Paris and it's over. Though suddenly, now, sitting in his new office, he doesn't believe it will ever be over. Even if he never sees her again.

There sits Jacko, feeling a bit old at twenty-four, in a cloud of his own smoke, his mouth dry and his energy wilting. Life is not turning out the way he'd anticipated.

Billie's considered and dismissed half a dozen boys she knows, and she's still typing. *Clickety clack, clickety clack*. None of them will do for a serious boyfriend, much less a husband. How about that new boy, Jack MacAlister? Cocky, that's for sure. Actually, he reminds her a little of James Dean. Dangerous, even though he looks about twelve. Had she smelled beer? Bit daring, drinking at lunch on the first day of work. And no real smile for her. Just a smug look that said: *Oh yeah, I know. You want me.*

Not likely, thinks Billie Mae Molinelli. She's never had to chase a boy, there's always been a line of them just waiting for a chance with her. But he has nice eyes, blue and smart, and the cutest cowlicks. One on the crown of his head and one just above his forehead. (Not dark with cheap oil, thank goodness. Oily hair is what valley boys have.) She can't remember why, but Billie has always had a soft spot for boys with unruly hair. And is Jack's V-neck cashmere? It looks so soft hanging over the back of his chair, and as yellow as...well, as the Butterfinger sitting inside her bag right now. Gee whiz, she's hungry.

The rest of the afternoon passes, with Billie typing and Jacko scribbling. Suddenly, it's five o'clock.

'Okay?' Mr Tidmarsh asks Jacko, on his way out. 'See you Monday?'

'Yup. Monday.'

Jacko pulls on his V-neck. He's never seen the point in keeping good clothes for special occasions. His dad did that, and see where it got him. A life in slob clothes, and a brand-new suit for the coffin. Billie finishes her typing. Loops her sweater around her shoulders, puts on some lipstick. Squints at herself in her compact, as if she's alone.

'Bye,' she says nonchalantly to Jacko, and sails past his desk.

'Bye.' He clicks his new briefcase shut carefully, as if there's something important inside, and follows her down the stairs to the street into the February sun. A wall of light and cool air. She stands on the sidewalk outside, putting a cigarette in her mouth. Without saying anything, as if they've known each other for years, Jacko pulls out his Zippo and flicks it under her cigarette. She smiles her thanks, and inhales. They are almost the same height, so their faces are near. They don't look at each other. She begins to walk away, giving him a little wave. He lights his own cigarette, heads in the other direction, then quickly swivels and follows her. He has to walk fast. When he is a little ahead, he turns to face her and walking backwards, says, 'Hey, what you doing for dinner? You like Chinese?'

Billie doesn't stop walking, just half smiles, pityingly. He's spunky, have to give him that. Poor guy. Dumped last week, she bets. He reads her look, almost says: *Hey, just kidding*. Instead says:

'Could have a few drinks first. It's early. We could go to North Beach. Vesuvio. There's always some good music on Friday nights. Some great sax player's been there every Friday this month.'

'Oh, no thanks. I'm meeting someone.'

Something alerts him to something unpleasantly familiar. What is it? Her vowels? Her way of walking, slightly flat-footed? But she's wearing very classy shoes, and she's not wearing her hair in bangs. He notices things like this. No, she's not a bit like the farm girls he grew up with in Sonoma. There is nothing wrong with this girl.

'You got a date?'

'Yeah!' She laughs a little. *Of course a date!*

So he smiles crookedly, hoping his smile hints at a wealth of untold jokes. Jokes she'll never hear now, the stupid girl. He boldly gives her the once over and says:

'Well, have fun then!'

He turns on his heels and leaves her in his wake. Strides down Market Street. The sun is glinting off the sidewalk, even the bubble gum glows. The whole place is exploding in light. Billie's hair, glinting gold. Goddammit! If he were in private, he would hit himself hard. *Damn, damn, damn.* Nothing like starting a weekend by making a fool of himself. He takes a deep breath and expels the humiliation. He's Jacko MacAlister, Goddammit. No girl is going to ruin his Friday night.

Billie, meanwhile, strides along a few more seconds, oblivious to everything but the loveliness of the evening, the prospect of her date later, the compliment of that new boy asking her out. Then she glances up to see him about to disappear round the corner of Pine Street, into the shadow of the Bank of America building. Lean, neat, an easy athletic gait, arms swinging like a man undefeated. Into the shadows he goes, and his shoulders are half gone, and his torso and legs too. A beat of a second more, and he will not be visible.

'Hey!' she shouts, but he is too far to hear.

Then she begins to run because something inside is lurching towards him, as if the sight of him is something she cannot live without. No idea why, or what she'll say to him if she catches him. And when she opens her mouth to shout to him again, he turns around with a look of pure smart-ass delight.

SIXTY-THREE YEARS LATER

Jack Makes Hot Chocolate for Milly

Jack MacAlister sat at the table taking pills. Statins, of course, for his cholesterol. And blahblahblah for his blahblahblah. So many pills he had to concentrate and order his throat to swallow, not regurgitate.

'Jack!'

Jack kept swallowing pills, squinting at labels.

'Jack! Jack!'

'What? What is it?' he growled. He'd been in a bad mood for so long, he couldn't remember not wanting to strangle his wife. And he did love her, he did, damn it. Not that he often told her straight-faced. Here she came now, he could hear, he could even feel the vibrations of her clanking mechanical progress down the hall. The sight of her oppressed him for all sorts of reasons. She was not a pretty sight, with those continence things poking out of

9

the top of her pyjama bottoms, and the stink of urine and today – yes, a whiff of shit. Her hair (no longer butter yellow – when had she stopped dying it?) was scraped into a ponytail tied with a rubber band. Her breasts were clearly visible when she leant over, because the top button popped off long ago and neither of them cared enough to find someone to sew it back on. There they swung, sad empty sacks.

'Have you let the dogs out, Jack? I haven't seen King since breakfast, and you know Jaspy could be anywhere.'

Her voice was cranky too. Her husband was so lazy, so selfish. He didn't care about anyone but himself. Mister I'm-all-right-Jack! Look at him, just sitting there in his boxers and T-shirt, having breakfast while the dogs were God knows where. You could see his balls, for pity's sake! Disgusting old man.

'The dogs are dead,' said Jack with some satisfaction.

'Oh!' said Milly, remembering with a thump. 'Darn it!'

'The dogs died ages ago. Darling.' And then, as if to punish her: 'Jaspy was hit by a car and dragged half a block. King was put to sleep. Cancer.'

'Oh dear.'

'Well. They were old.' He felt guilt at her stricken face. Also, weirdly, genuine grief. Weird, because he'd hated the damn dogs. Hair everywhere, middle of the night barking, and a cloud of dog stink every time he opened the car door. The dogs had always been hers, not his. A series of drooling parasites dating back to the time Milly had been Billie; his terrible crime had somehow entitled her to dogs. Hell! But he felt momentarily close to tears, remembering the dogs and the way they used to act so glad to see him every time he came in the front door,

10

even if he'd just been to the garage. And, oh no, here came actual tears, washing down his cheeks. The doctor had warned him to expect mood swings and tearfulness. Strokes make you cry like a baby. Though he'd never credited his own crying babies with a genuine reason to cry, now he wondered.

'Oh dear, dear, dear,' fussed Milly. 'I knew the dogs were dead!' Then, frowning: 'Are you crying again? Silly boy. Cut it out, Jack,' she said softly, as she moved noisily to the kitchen.

The tears obeyed; as quickly as they'd welled, they vanished. He went back to his pill popping. An idea occurred to him, while she and her whiff moved past. He held his head still to prevent the idea from sloshing out his ears, nose or mouth. He wasn't sure how his thoughts leaked out, but those were the obvious places.

'Jack.'

'What?' Irritated again.

'What day is it, Jack?'

'Monday,' he replied with grim authority, and he glanced at the wall calendar automatically – before he retired, that used to work. One glance and he'd instantly known what day he was in, but what was the point of a calendar now? There were no recent or imminent events, like work meetings or parties, to anchor him to one particular day. He looked at the *Chronicle* and saw that today was actually Tuesday, but he didn't correct himself. She'd never know, or if she did, she'd forget in three seconds. Who cared what day it was, anyway?

More than ever, he felt time was the problem. He was leaking not just thoughts, but time, and his life was in disarray as a result. His desk was littered with overdue bills, but hadn't he just signed the checks to pay them yesterday? Perhaps it was not just himself becoming less solid and certain; perhaps the entire universe was slowly slipping its moorings, like the time his sailboat drifted from the dock into the bay. Perhaps time itself had run amok. That was more bearable, so he held on to this image. A sinking ship meant they were all in the same boat. Lots of company. Good.

'Monday. Good. A beautiful day!' she announced, flicking the kitchen venetian blinds open by turning each individual slat. Like the missing pyjama button, this had become normal. They used to talk about repairing or even replacing the blinds.

'It feels humid again,' grumbled Jack, not looking up from his pills.

There was that feeling to the day. Oppressive, noisy with birds fretting about the air pressure.

'It is another beautiful day!' corrected Milly forcefully. He glanced up, and there it was. Her stubborn face. The fiercely cocked left eyebrow.

'Beautiful!' She spat the word at him.

Jack ignored her, focused on the pills. Hadn't he already taken that pink one?

'You're just tired,' accused Milly. 'Why do you stay up so late?'

He remembered last night vaguely. His reluctance to end the day – well, of course. How many more days did he have? He wondered why Milly always wanted to rush to the end of the day, closing blinds early, going to bed by nine.

'Me, tired! I'm not the one getting up in the middle of the night to eat yoghurt! And God knows what else. Didn't we have a whole loaf of raisin bread? Milly?'

12

She ignored him, brushing crumbs from the counter to the floor for the dogs.

Jack and Milly were lucky. They could see Mount Tamalpais from their living room window, San Francisco Bay was half a block away, and their street was leafy and quiet. Once there'd been a chicken farm right here. Milly liked to remember this fact. A time when their house was just a marshy field full of hens and rickety sheds. Other houses were close, but it still felt private here. Their world had only them in it. And the ghosts of King and Jaspy.

'Sam! I mean Jaspy! I mean Jack! Jack!'

Names felt like random odd socks to Milly. She knew they each belonged to one particular other, but she was in a hurry, darn it. She grabbed the name that came to her easiest, and sometimes that happened to be the name of a child or a dead dog.

'Jack! Do you hear me?'

Jack was almost done. Two more pills, and that would be that. His plan was hatching now, and he almost smiled. Funny how having a project – any kind of project – was so cheering. The day ahead beckoned, and he swallowed the last pills with mango juice. It tasted sweet and cold: delicious. He hadn't noticed this earlier. In fact, everything was shifting now. It was almost imperceptible, but there it was. Everything had a tingly halo around it, even the sound of the morning radio, the appearance of his wife, the smell of the burnt toast. The house itself was vibrating with foreknowledge.

Today will be different.

For years now, Jack had been conscious of a waiting sensation. All day, every day, he'd been waiting for their lives to get back to normal. Never mind that his old life drove him half crazy, the way the checkbook never balanced, Milly cooking meatloaf three times a week, the dogs never doing what he told them to do. That was normal, and normality was what he yearned for now. Having a plan, no matter how bizarre the plan, tasted like normality to Jack. He was in control again.

'Jack!' she shouted again. That man was so deaf.

'Whath ith it?' His tongue was suddenly furry and swollen, and the words came out thick as molasses.

'Where. Are. The. Dogs.'

'The thog's er thead, Milly.'

'What's wrong with you?' she asked. He asked himself the same question. Was he drunk? He had to concentrate, remember if that amazing martini he made recently was as recently as five minutes ago. No, no, it was just more post-stroke crap. He took a deep breath and corralled his tongue. So annoying. You think you're in an ordinary day, then wham. Some days he drooled. Some days his left eyelid only opened halfway till lunch time.

'I thaid. The thogs. Er thead.'

'Oh! I knew that!' Angry at herself again.

'Courthe you thid, tharling. I knew thath thoo.'

'I just told you that! You always have to be right, don't you?'

Jack smirked and sighed. The woozy feeling hovered about an inch from his skull. Would it descend and engulf him? Some days he woke inside this cloud of fug, other days merely slipped into it, then out. Like a seal bobbing in some waves, gasping for oxygen. Now and then he still got rushes of energy, when he thought all things were still possible, if he could just get his teeth in and shave. He'd buy a new hat. A nice grey Fedora, or a soft brown trilby. Nothing like a new hat to perk a man up. Then he'd go to

14

the Montecito Travel Agency and walk out with a plane ticket tucked into his wallet. If the damn agency was still there – last time he looked, not only couldn't he find it, but the teenage boy he asked had never heard of it. And come to think of it, did men wear hats any more? On what day had men stopped thinking they looked great in hats? He sighed again, remembering how putting on a hat used to make him feel ready for anything.

'I guess that means I don't have to feed the dogs then.' She sighed.

'I guess not. No more feeding the dogs.' No lisping this time, whew! Come home to Daddy, tongue.

'As if you would. Even if they were alive, I mean. As if you ever did.'

Then a giggle snuck into their eyes, but they didn't give it away. No, no! It was automatic, this withholding of pleasure from each other as long as possible. The smiles resided quietly in the corners of their softly puckered mouths. Their yellowing eyes.

'Hey, you think it's easy being perfect? It's lonely, I tell you, lonely as hell out here,' said Jack, staring her down, and she surrendered at last. That old girly giggle.

Bless her; it was so easy to make her happy. And wasn't that forgetfulness of hers also a blessing for him? She forgot all his misdemeanours hourly, and kept sliding back to her original adoration of him. In her brighter days, she could sulk for entire weeks. Once, when she was about twenty-five she didn't speak to him for almost a month.

But wait. Her face was changing again. He could watch her thoughts flit through her mind as easily as if she was speaking out loud. *Oh no, here we go again*, he thought. The cocked eyebrow, the look.

15

'Did you return Elisabeth's call?'
'You never said she called.'
'I told you, Jack. Three times, I told you.'
'Are you sure?'
'Would I lie?'

Thinking about his daughter, the great idea drifted off. He'd had the idea before; it was a fantasy, a comforting dream. He'd even attempted it once and failed. Besides, his bowel movement was calling, and all other thoughts (even about his daughter) were shunted to the side. Who could have predicted that one day the high point of his day would be a crap? Perversely, it could also be the most hellish part of the day. Excruciation followed by bliss. An accomplished bowel movement was like the first time he sat in the driver's seat and really opened up the Singer, hit a hundred miles an hour. The Singer scream. One thing was for sure: bowels were king. Jack never *ever* messed with them. Off he toddled to the bathroom, like a sinful Catholic to confession. He took the newspaper and then picked up a pen in case he had to resort to the crossword.

So another morning was lived through. It was hot already. The windows throughout the house were open, but there was no breeze.

Jack's Glenmorangie glass from last night, his wine glass and his martini glass, were stacked in the decrepit dishwasher with the breakfast dishes. With great difficulty, clothes were dragged on for the millionth time, teeth were inserted, tears were cried, ringing phones were answered.

'Hello, daughter!' Jack said, in his usual affectionate but ironic tone. She was his only daughter – set against his five sons (if you counted Louise's boys and his son

16

with Colette, and he did). Right now, he loved having a daughter so much, he used the word with gusto. The boys were so much less...well, satisfying. He found their lack of achievement humiliating, and their overachievement threatening. A daughter could be flirted with, and flirting was Jack's hobby.

'Yes, yes,' he was saying to Elisabeth. 'No, the doctor said I'm plant now.'

'What? I did not. I said I'm fine now. Why would I say I was a plant?'

'No, it was not another heart attack, it was another stroke. A mini-stroke. A micro-mini. An episode is what he actually called it. Ep. I. Sode. Like *The Simpsons*. Don't worry.'

The sheer effort of speaking clearly was making him sweat, making his chest hurt, and also there was a strange new sensation in his left buttock. Not quite pain, but distracting. Irritating!

'No, the hospital was not a pleasant place. What? No, I checked myself out yesterday. Called a taxi.'

'What?' The novelty of a daughter was starting to wear off again. The boys were never this nosey. In fact, it was quite appealing, the way they mostly just ignored him.

'Your mother is fine.'

'Fine, I said! Aren't you, Milly?'

'Oh, she's not here now. Creepy how she just disappears.'

'Yes, yes. We are both taking all the right pills.'

'Yes, we did. Thank you very much, daughter. Clever idea, having the days of the week on each little pill compartment.'

'Yeah, yeah. No, I am not being sarcastic. I haven't thrown it away! Going to start using it next week.'

Who did she think she was, Florence friggin Nightingale? Then, because this kind of thinking always led to remorse:

'Listen honey, why don't you come for dinner soon? Bring the kids. Bring your grandkids! Tell your brothers. Tell everyone, I'll barbecue.'

'Tomorrow?' Too soon! The floors needed to be mopped and the bathroom fumigated. 'Tomorrow's not good. Can you come later in the week? Friday maybe?'

'Because I'm busy tomorrow, that's why.'

'Busy doing stuff.'

'Stuff, I said! You think you're the only one with a life? I have a life, okay?'

'No. Not just solitaire on the computer. Yeah. Friday it is, then. Goodbye, Elisabeth. Goodbye! Goodbye!'

He hung up with a mixture of anxiety and irritation and something else he could never put a name to, but made his throat feel funny. Damn her! Just his luck to have a conscientious daughter. Strange how he was afraid of his kids finding his house in a mess. When did that switch round? But then they had the power to pull the plug. No one ever told him how just plain humiliating it was when you got near death. Just when you could least deal with it, there it was, slap bang on your doorstep. Like a continual day of being caught shoplifting condoms, of losing erections, of wet farting on a first date. No two ways about it, getting this old was basically one helluva hangover without the memory of a fabulous night before. His incompetent scatterbrained daughter telling him what to do was the final blow.

He was jealous of his neighbour and old friend Ernie, who was the same age. None of his kids gave a damn. And his wife, Bernice, still cooked great dinners, every damn night. And still drove. Probably still gave him blow jobs. He bet she never asked Ernie what day it was, or demanded he buy Tena Pull Ups at Walmart, that cavernous hell. But then he remembered a conversation from last week, or last year – it was hard to tell – and Ernie had said, You always think my marriage is perfect. That we never fight. Are you insane?

'Elisabeth! Get down from that table right now!' Milly suddenly barked to her four-year-old daughter, who for a moment was visible, in those soft pink Oshkosh dungarees she'd loved so much about sixty years ago. Then, because her shout had dispelled the child, Milly smiled goofily, embarrassed.

'Jack? Jack?' Hoping he hadn't heard her crazy shout. 'Good,' she said aloud to the empty room. He must be in his office still. 'That man is so deaf!' And then she giggled, because what had just happened struck her as hilarious. She made herself laugh again! What excellent company she was. She giggled on and off for a good five minutes, because even the fact of her laughter struck her as funny now. The way it hiccupped a bit, just like her grandmother's.

No two ways about it: Milly was a bit dippy. Even she knew it. There'd been no dramatic dip into dippy-ness, no particular day or event that led her family to frown and say: Oh no! Milly is off her head! But here it was now, craziness as solid a part of herself as her cocked left eyebrow and her yellowing toenails. Her mind was like a weather report. Cloudy intervals, with occasional clear warm afternoons. Now and then green clouds with polar bears riding them.

Still, the bigger truth was that, crippled or not, senile

or not, Milly remained the guardian of this house. Punctual and reliable in the extreme. Morning and night: unlocking and locking doors, opening and closing each venetian blind. The bed sheets were only changed by her, and only she knew when it was time to buy more toilet paper. She was pretty certain they had never run out of milk. She'd been the guardian of this house for over fifty years. It had been a new house then, so if the house had a consciousness (and in her opinion it did), it belonged utterly to Milly. No other mistress haunting the corridors. It would obey no other queen. If you could marry houses, Milly would have divorced Jack years ago.

Jack turned on his computer and began a game of solitaire. Milly walked down the long hall to the bathroom. A journey of seven minutes, but her bowels were her friend, so actual toilet time was a fraction of her husband's. Then she returned to her chair in the living room. A three-point turn in order to drop her bottom on the seat. Her kids wanted her to get a wheelchair. What did they know? In this respect, they were the enemy and she ignored them. Heaven's sake, it was only those old broken bones. She spent the rest of the afternoon keeping Jack on her radar by noise and intuition. Garage? Bathroom? In some floozy's kitchen drinking gin? No, no, that had only been a short phase, long gone. Jack was a faithful man, a good man, with a bit of mid-life nonsense on his CV. Now... had he eaten his fruit, taken his vitamins, put on clean socks?

The dogs were also on her radar – she kept glancing down to the places where they used to sleep, and where their food dishes had been. She did this in the same reflex way she'd checked her babies were breathing, and later, that they were still in the yard, or still in their rooms. For years after the youngest left home, she'd kept waking at night and panicking, till she remembered their new addresses and phone numbers safely stored in her address book. A radar out of range of its objects, she couldn't stop reaching out for her children in a visceral way, every minute of the day as if one of her organs – her heart? her thorax? – had developed searching tendrils. Darn those kids! They'd better be wearing sun cream today, look at that sun!

Milly kept her family safe. That was her job, and she could not stop doing it for love or money. This memory problem was a mere hiccup, an annoying blip. Like her vision dimming, but never badly enough to incapacitate. Like the way her left leg had slowly ceased to obey, but still let her get around on her own. She said *no* to taking her own limitations seriously. That way lay defeat, and she certainly didn't want pity. No, no, no. She was still needed, so tethered herself relentlessly to her charges. Or charge.

'Jack!'
'Jack!'
'Jack!'
'What is it?' Angrily. The computer was winning.
'I have four thirty. What do you make it?'
'Jesus, Milly.'
'I said, I have…'
'Four thirty. Four thirty, okay!'
'It's four thirty already?'

The days flew by so quickly, so painlessly. She really didn't know what all the fuss was about. Getting old was a breeze. After checking her watch once more, and telling herself she'd rise in thirty minutes to close the blinds, she sat in her window seat and re-entered her dreams. And what did she dream about for the next half hour? It was a patchwork of things around her and things that had happened – the gulls crying, the smell of eucalyptus, the classical FM radio music, all the birthday parties she'd ever given for her children, the cupcakes she'd made for PTA sales, the Halloween costumes she'd sewed, the trips to San Francisco for the sales, the way chocolate milkshakes tasted at Courthouse Creamery, the way the waitress used to give them the silver shaker with the remainder of the shake to pour out themselves. The coffees another waitress used to bring herself and Harold, even though they hated coffee. The splinters in her bottom from the deck that scary morning, with Jeff looming over her and Mister Rogers on the television. The taste of Jack's skin after a sail. (A small smile at this.) Harold's nose in profile, like a Roman. Her hand briefly in his, in the dark theatre. Then up popped that favourite pair of cream gloves she'd worn to church all the time, and where had the left one gone? Under a pew? And her wedding ring too, where had that got to? Thick gold band, with rubies inset. Oh, her throat swelled, remembering these lost loved items. Her children, her babies – she missed them too. Darling Charlie sliced into her chest, cold in his crib with the decals of Bambi. Then she kissed his forehead, bowed away from him and thought about the way her children were all so different. Like Jack, she included Louise's boys as her own children, and as an afterthought, darn Colette's son too. She spent whole minutes just contemplating their very different hair colours. A sudden memory of Sam in his Senior Prom suit, face freshly scrubbed with dabs of Clearasil on his forehead and nose. Oh, how those flesh-tinted dabs had torn at her! And that hat she'd bought

Elisabeth once, to wear to Easter Sunday Mass. White straw, and it had gone so well with her pink seersucker dress, hadn't she been a picture? Her heart swelled with pride now. Satisfaction for a day well executed. And wasn't that exactly how it had been, for all those years? Her moody children, her wayward husband – *just normal people, all of them* – with her on the podium waving a baton, conducting their lives into some semblance of order and safety and...attractive appearance. Oh, the thrill on the rare days when they all seemed to obey!

Even now, in her daydreams, she wanted to photograph those moments. To run and find her camera, but by the time she was ready the moment had passed. The ice cream had melted, the arguing had recommenced, the cloud moved over the sun.

It was strangely difficult to access any specific memory, but these unasked for memories just bubbled up. Her face was peaceful, slack. If she was homesick for those years of raising children, of handmade cards sticky with syrup, of Lego under the sofa, of midnight bedwetting, of those small bodies always pressed against hers, it was such a constant state she didn't interpret it as homesickness. In any case, homesickness, like love, took energy, and this was something Milly did not have a lot of. Despite centuries of literature and music proclaiming otherwise, Milly knew that love was *not* what remained when everything else was stripped away. What remained was an awareness that love had been. Milly needed every ounce of energy to get out of bed in the morning, and repeat the essential routines of daily life.

When she surfaced, it was exactly five o'clock.

First thought: Close the blinds.

Second: Where is Jack?

Third: Have the dogs been fed?

Fourth: Are the children all right?

Fifth: When will I see them?

These last two were wistful, thin thoughts, and evaporated within seconds. Not like numbers one, two and three, which were on a constant loop.

She rose slowly from her chair and closed down the house. Flicked each venetian blind down, switched on lamps, looked for dog food then remembered. Did the pepper grinder need more peppercorns already? Gosh darn it.

'Jack! Jack!'

'What is it?' *Still* losing at solitaire to the computer, in between naps in his chair. Computers cheated, obviously.

'Come here, please. I need you to open the pepper grinder.'

'I'm busy, Milly. In a minute, okay?'

'Oh, to hell with you,' she said, leaning on the table, the grinder in one clenched fist.

At the periphery of her vision were all the people who wandered her house from time to time. When she was anxious or angry, like now, they tended to creep a little closer to centre stage. (Not quite like her vision of four-year-old Elisabeth in her Oshkosh overalls, or the way she'd hallucinated her sister, Louise, for a few weeks, a million years ago.) She didn't know these folk. And no, they did not frighten her; they seemed a friendly lot, placidly walking around her rooms, intent on getting somewhere for some ordinary task. To the store for milk and bread; to the garden to pull weeds; to the hall closet for clean towels. Yes, she understood they couldn't exist, and, yes, she also knew not to mention them to Jack any more. He dismissed them as urinary infection hallucinations.

24

Secretly, she believed they might have an existence. She'd become fond of a few in particular, a small boy and a fat old woman. Some days she convinced herself the boy was her baby Charlie, grown seven years older, and the fat woman could be her long-lost sister, Louise, grown old. Loulou had always run to fat. They looked her in the eyes, unlike the others, so if they existed perhaps they had a fondness for her too. They didn't talk, but their presence was calming. Maybe they were in the future, and to them, she was the ghostly figure that couldn't rationally exist. Perhaps, she thought, her loneliness had pulled them out of thin air for company. Perhaps they already existed, and her eyesight had developed somewhat. As if the older she got the thinner the membrane between herself and an afterlife. They'd been around for about a year now, and were hardly worth noting any more. Part of the furniture, so to speak.

After they had dinner, microwaved macaroni cheese, Milly made the treacherous journey from table to dish-washer, while holding on to both her walker and an expensive plate. Sometimes she put items on the floor and gently slid them along with her feet. Sometimes she used her mouth for carrying things, like dishcloths and newspapers. But plates were just too heavy, not to mention slippery. She took the plates one at a time, and nudged the walker along with her lower arms and elbows. If Jack was asked how his crippled, partially sighted wife managed to set and clear the table, serve meals, make their bed, do the laundry, he would shrug and laugh like a naughty boy. *I have no idea!* he'd say gleefully, and it was true. He'd rarely witnessed her doing these daily tasks. He was a busy man, and anyway – what else did she spend her days doing? What bills had she paid? What job had she spent fifty years working at?

Milly, Jack often said, was getting away with murder.

The kitchen radio was on, as usual, and tuned to Classic FM – not because they particularly liked classical music but because it was a new digital radio, and they'd given up figuring it out. A rogue programmer had allowed an old Billie Holliday to slip in between Mozart and Chopin. *If I should take a notion, to jump into the ocean.* Milly inserted the last dirty dish – Jack's dinner plate – into the dishwasher, and then with a melodramatic arm gesture, as if sweeping away hordes of admirers, she said: 'Wa!' to the empty kitchen. The walking folk scattered instantly and disappeared like a spray of water on a hot sidewalk. What she meant by this odd syllable – by *Wa* – was a combination of *voilà* and *moi. Wa* meant: This is me! The best of me I've got. Take me or leave me, darn you.

Milly said *Wa!* a lot, but Billie Holliday had caused this particular *Wa.*

She'd always been susceptible to certain music. Classical music had no nostalgia for her; it was neutral, impersonal noise. But this! *If I go to church on Sunday, then cabaret all day Monday, it ain't nobody's business if I do.* She had no defence against this. She closed her eyes and recalled dancing. Like her grandchildren's fingers twitching in the correct sequence when they were imagining texting someone. Her day to day memory was poor, but her muscles had an excellent memory. The swing of her left foot now, the sliding, the twirling, the precise flying feel of her arms as they floated in the air to the sad defiant music.

I swear I won't call no copper, if I'm beat up by my poppa.

Her eyes squeezed shut. Pretending to dance always

26

brought a wave of sweetness and melancholy. Too much, and when the song ended, she was limp.

'Hey. Honey. Milly.'

'Jack! How long have you been standing there? Did you need something?'

'What were you doing?'

'Nothing. What do you mean?'

'I saw you.'

And this was when his great idea trickled back in. A good husband might flirt with other women, but he did not leave his wife. *Milly was his person.* He fell in love with her all over again, as if he'd just met her. Tears welled up.

'So?'

'Were you, sort of, dancing?' His voice cracked on the last word.

'What? Are you bananas?' A full face frown. Eyebrows, mouth, nose, jaw.

'You were, weren't you?'

After a pause, Milly said primly: 'I was *thinking* about dancing. I was remembering. But how did you know?'

'Just the way you shut your eyes. And you kind of rocked. A bit.'

'Did I?'

'And smiled too.'

Milly glared, then said: 'Oh, come here, you.'

'No, you'll hurt me. You'll tickle me.'

'Don't be silly. I am *not* the one who tickles.'

'You were a wonderful dancer, sweetheart.' In fact, he had vivid recall of all the men's eyes on her, while she spun round some ballroom – Larkspur Landing? That red dress with the orange sequins. New Year's Eve, 1951. Boy, he married a beauty all right.

'I know.'

'I was a terrible dancer,' he said.

'I know.'

The ballroom image wouldn't go away now. 'I don't know how you stood me, dancing with you.'

'Well! We didn't do it very often, did we?'

'No.'

'Come here right now, Mister Jacko MacAlister.'

'You're so bossy! All right then, Miss Billie Mae Molinelli. For one minute.'

She let go of her walker, he took her weight, and miracle of miracles – what was going on today at Classic FM? – the next song was 'In the Mood', Glen Miller.

Who's the loving daddy with the beautiful eyes?

What a pair of lips, I'd like to try 'em for size...

It occurred to Jack that Classic FM would never make a mistake like this; never play old jazz. Was it the radio's fault, or their own? Then it occurred to him that marriage might be a bit like dancing to radio music. You didn't know what song you'd get next. First you'd be with your partner, happily dancing and thinking – Yes, I get it, and it's good to be here. I know this kind of music. Look at us – just like everyone else! Then a song might start up that you didn't expect, and didn't much like. Maybe the sax player squeaked, the pianist sounded flat, and someone was singing the same three jarring lines over and over – so irritating! You'd keep dancing, but now you'd be thinking: Actually, this isn't much fun any more. Five minutes later, you'd think: This is hell. When will this song end? I can't stand much more of this. Then suddenly, there'd be an old much-loved song, like this one playing right now.

And I said: Hey baby, it's a quarter to three,

28

There's a mess of moonlight, won't-cha share it with me?

Such a relief to be on familiar ground again, it reminded you why you married in the first place.

They danced without moving their feet. At first he let her lead, and followed the swaying of her torso, let her hug him tight, rest her head under his chin. Hey, what the hell? She'd shrunk! That would explain her skin being so loose.

First I held him lightly, and we started to dance.
Then I held him tightly, what a dreamy romance.

'So,' said Milly softly. 'What will we do now?'

'What do you mean?'

She had to think a moment, how to explain herself.

'I mean, what happens next? What do we *do* now?'

It was still an oblique query, but he understood. What was there left to do, in the face of imminent death? It was so in tune with his own thinking today, tears welled up again. It was heaven, now and then, to be understood by his wife.

'Well?'

'I'm thinking, sweetie.'

'Well?'

'As long as we can keep dancing, Milly, I think that's what we should do. Dance.'

'But I can't dance, silly man.'

'Shush,' he whispered. 'Just dance.'

Pause.

'*If that's all there is my friend, then let's keep dancing,*' she sang into his chest. 'Remember that song, Jack?'

'Yeah. Shush, now.'

'It's such a corny song.'

'I know, I hated it.'

29

'Me too.'

When the chorus began, Jack took her left hand and held it to his chest, and led her in his own rhythm. *In the mood for all his kissing, in the mood for his crazy loving.*

And for a minute it worked. Then he missed a beat, and another, and she began to snort with giggles, which brought tears to her eyes. In his entire life, he'd never met a woman whose laughter could literally leak out of her eyes.

'Oh, forget it,' she said. 'I've got things to do.'

'Aw, come on, Milly. Give me another chance.'

'You're going to make me fall.'

'I love you, Milly.'

'I know.'

'No, I mean I really love you.'

'Okay. We're almost out of dishwasher tablets.'

She moved away from him, gripped her walker. He noticed the pee smell again, but this time it was not repulsive. All he wanted was to hold her again, but she was fussing with the butter dish now, trying to close the lid.

Jack suddenly remembered taking her to the Sutro Baths, that first summer. Her red bathing suit, the way her skin looked milky against it. It was the pool's last season, though no one knew that. Six salt water pools fed by the nearby Pacific Ocean, over five hundred changing rooms, and little refreshment bars scattered everywhere with names like Dive Inn. The high curved glass ceiling beamed down sunlight and bounced voices and splashes: a constant racket of delight. There were rings to swing from into the water, but what he remembered most was showing off his dives from the only diving board. He'd learned to dive by jumping off a rock into Sonoma Creek the summer he was fifteen, and he was proud. The way he used to cut cleanly into the water and surface like a seal. But at the Sutro Baths, with the bracing green Pacific below him, he remembered feeling awkward because she was watching in her red bathing suit. He worried he'd be clumsy, and then he worried that being worried would make him clumsier, because grace (he'd learned) had to be instinctive. But it was all right, and when he surfaced and looked for her face, there it was, smiling at him as if he'd just won an Olympic gold medal. Something so naked about her admiration. It was better than getting drunk.

He'd tried teaching her how to dive, but she was surprisingly inept. She kept freezing at the last second and bellyflopping. She laughed, but he could tell it hurt. Much later, because the pool was almost empty, she just sat on the diving board and swung her pretty legs. He was treading water below and they talked. Talked and talked, and treading water was so effortless he felt he'd never sink as long as he could keep talking to her.

'A matter of weeks, Jack,' his doctor had said yesterday, sitting by his hospital bed. 'Or maybe months, but not six. Have you looked into hiring a home care nurse? Or entering a care facility? Or hospice care? I can help arrange that.'

'Fuck off.'

'What?'

'My cough. It's getting better.'

Jack could have done without the light banter about summer vacations immediately after the diagnosis. Like discussing what a great party it was going to be, what a pity you weren't invited.

He poured a brandy and port, took it to the living room and turned the television on to PBS. Inspector Morse and Sergeant Lewis were sitting at the Oxford high table suspecting murderers, but Jack was visualising this: the children, all six of them plus their spouses, would arrive on Friday. The shocking discovery would be shared. They'd come straight in, no door knocking in this family. They'd notice how clean the house was and wonder if a cleaner had finally been hired. They'd walk around, calling: Mom? Dad? Grandma? Grandpa? Or in Danny, Donald and August's case: Jack? Milly? Anybody home?

After peeking into the other rooms, they'd peek into the master bedroom and at first they'd think they were asleep, all curled up. He was so enamoured of this scene, he edited it and replayed it, with different night clothes, times of evening, lateral poses. Perhaps the remnants of the wood fire would linger, covering any unpleasant odours. Stink would ruin the mood. Got to get it right. This reminded him of all those early imperfect ragged manuscripts, the ones he'd sensed containing a germ of genius. The way he'd tweaked them and carved them, chosen the perfect cover, the best quality paper, the right blurb for the back sleeve. Goddammit, he'd been the genius, not the author. Actually, the whole of life had been a rough draft, just waiting for his expert editing, his instinct for what people really wanted. If he'd ever got around to writing that damn novel, it would have been the best masterpiece in the history of literature. It would have, once and for all, pinned down his genera-tion. More intellectual than Dos Passos, more perceptive about women than Hemingway. If he'd had time.

He remembered the fiasco last autumn after his heart attack and just before he lost his licence.

'Come on, Milly,' he'd said. 'We'll drive out to Hawk Hill. You always love that drive.'

All the way there, he'd kept rehearsing how he'd put on her favourite CD, and his too. The Harry James Orchestra, *You Made Me Love You*. Then when they got to the bit of Pt Bonita Road where nothing lay between them and the Pacific Ocean, he'd say: Close your eyes a minute darling. I love you, Milly. You're the best. Then he'd close his own eyes too, and gun it. Shoot them both over the cliff, and sure it'd be scary and they'd probably scream, but then it would be over within seconds. He'd been very curious about what the car would do, mid-air. He hoped they'd remain in it, right side up. Not upside down. It would be terrible if one of them fell out of their seat while the other watched.

But at Corte Madera, Milly had started demanding they find a bathroom.

'Just do it where you are. That's the whole point of diapers.'

'I do not pee in my underpants, and I do not wear diapers. Are you crazy? Stop the car now!'

He'd finally stopped the car at a cafe in Sausalito, and ended up ordering coffee and carrot cake for them both. By the time they'd finished, the urgency had drained away and he'd driven them home again. Milly hadn't even noticed the cancellation of Hawk Hill. Just sang along with Harry James, happy as a clam, even prettily clapping her hands as if they were in a public place and people were watching.

Now Jack thought, Oh hell, why wait till Friday? The house was clean enough, damn it. At least the kitchen was. Let them think what they like. He waited till Milly left the kitchen and was making her way to the living room to watch the ten o'clock news.

(She used to be queen of the remote, till they got

Comcast. Jack had taken three months to get the hang of the new remote, and was now the undisputed boss of the television, which meant now and then Milly left the room in disgust. *Sex and the City* was a good one to send her skedaddling.)

Milly sat down and Jack made his way back to the kitchen. Opened the bottle of pills and shook them all onto the cutting board. Quickly found the rolling pin and some foil. Covered the pills and began crushing.

'Jack?'

'What?'

The kitchen and living room were a semi-open plan, so all he had to do was swivel his neck to see Milly sitting in front of the television. Her last evening watching television. His last, too. Quite nice to know; no more wondering when.

'What are you doing?'

'What?'

'I said. What. Are. You. Doing?'

'Nothing. Getting another drink.'

'The news has started, honey. I need the volume turned up.'

'I'm coming. Just a minute. How about some hot chocolate?'

'What?'

'I said, how would you like some hot chocolate?'

'I thought you were making a drink.'

'I meant a hot drink.'

He filled the kettle while he shouted to her.

'Well?'

'No thanks. It's summer. Who drinks hot chocolate in summer?'

'Oh, come on.'

34

'Oh, all right.'

The kettle began hissing. He scooped the ground-up pills into two mugs, added instant hot chocolate and returned to the living room. How long would the pills take? He'd kind of like to watch the last episode of *Brideshead Revisited* after the news. He'd seen it before, of course, but forgotten how it ended. His hands were shaking, and it took several seconds to find the volume control. He sat on the arm of his wife's chair and watched the world's stories, told by a man in a violet shirt and yellow tie. When had that become acceptable? The man was an obvious homosexual. How wonderful! He secretly, since Dulcinea Press, took some credit.

Milly leaned into Jack, caught sight of his hands speckled with sun damage. Looked at her own skin; her hands belonged to an old lady. As did the white hair she spotted on the sleeve of her blouse. No connection to who she was at all. She wanted to say: Okay, enough! Joke's over now. Back to my real self, please. She wondered who would die first. She sighed, because it would have to be him of course. He needed her, she mustn't leave him alone. She'd see him out, tidy up afterwards. This made her feel tired. Obviously, she had imagined dying. For years, now. There was no end to the lovely dropping sensation when she did this. Yes, of course she was grateful for her life, but the strain of being Milly was too much some days. Could death be a sensual experience? For Milly, maybe yes. As for what happened next, well, Milly had decided to *not* accept non-existence for either of them. It was too final and terrible. Goodness sake, why believe in something that made your heart hammer in the middle of the night? What was the point in *not* believing that souls were immortal and more – that some version of heaven was a possibility? If the end result was a true mystery (and so far as she knew, no one had yet proven anything one way or another) and death came no matter what you believed, why not choose to believe the more pleasant version? To her, atheists like Jack were simply masochists and puzzled her exceedingly. A bunch of intellectual fools, embracing anxiety for no good reason at all.

Milly was not worried about losing her husband, because worrying would be a waste of time. She'd never lose Jack. The tenacity of Milly's love was like the revolutions of the planets.

'There's the kettle, Jack.'

'What?'

'You are so deaf. I said, the kettle is boiling!'

'Is it?'

The last kettle boil, he thought. He watched himself think this.

While he carried the two mugs of carefully stirred hot chocolate, and while the news presenter talked of earth quake victims in Peru and single mothers in Brooklyn, and while two teenage boys raced cars outside this house, Jack felt a sudden loss of balance and a strange, almost anaesthetic tingling at the top of his arm. He dropped both mugs.

'Oh brother, Jack. What a mess! You sit down, I'll clean it up.'

But Jack could not move forward. Or talk. He thought: But it hardly hurts at all. How funny. And he was cranky – did he give permission for this sequence of events? What the fuck? That chocolate was going to stain the carpet. He just had it cleaned last month, damn it.

And now his knees were buckling, a weakness travelled

36

up his body and it felt almost nice to crumble up and sink.

'Jack? Jack! Darn it, Jack. Get up this minute.'

Jack was dying again.

'If you're messing with me, Jacko MacAlister...'

A sulk just rising to the surface, her eyebrow almost cocked, lips almost pouting. Two year-long minutes passed during which, behind closed eye lids, Jack watched a slide show of his life. It was so cliché, he smiled. A sort of *This is Your Life*, or a movie preview. The highlights, plus some other weird stuff. But this meant it couldn't be the end, right? Too corny to be anything as serious as death. But there they were, except not in chronological order, and some images of no particular importance at all. Colette's green dress with the low neck, the feel of that silky fabric. That green Hillman, and pouring water into the radiator on the old Highway 5, near some chicken farms. The chicken enchiladas with black olives he ordered when they'd gone to Cabo San Lucas at last. Pregnant Milly when she was Billie, in her bra and underpants, laughing so hard she sprayed her beer all over him one humid summer night. The wake behind the ferry, the taste of Chardonnay brisk on his tongue and Cheryl's hand in his. Then her hand became attached to buxom Lizbeth, and she asked him to dance. Shouted, dance with me! His mom was shouting at him about the ice chest, because he left the door open and all her ice cream melted. Jacko! I'm going to tell your father when he gets home. The phone call earlier today, with his daughter. The irritation. Then that same daughter as a newborn, the surprise of her. Charlie, limp and blue in that dinosaur sleeper, but this time when he shook him and shook him, Charlie opened his eyes and smiled. And then laughed, that infant chuckle. Then his sister, Ivy, and himself giggling, playing hooky from Mass, sneaking out St Mary's side door and running down the sidewalk to the store and stealing beef jerky. The taste of the jerky, tough and salty, softening on his tongue. And the jerky became the jerky from the store at Dogtired Ranch; washing it down with cold beer. Cold rain, raining on the night when Louise drove away to live with that weirdo, Coffee Enema Bob. It poured and poured till the fish pond flooded over. And the heat spell the summer the fish pond dried up and the tar on the road outside their house bubbled up. Sitting in the dirt and nudging potato bugs till they rolled into balls; rolling white bread into beads and the crust into a snail shape before shoving it all in his mouth; chewing the liquorice weeds that grew on the corner of Railroad Avenue and Verano. Telling Milly that Dulcinea was the perfect name for his publishing company, and her look of admiration. Opening a bottle of cold champagne on the deck, and a yellow jacket drowned in his glass, and Milly poured him another. The way the deck had aged, and the way it had looked in the beginning, so solid and smelling of resin. Three times, that deck had been renewed. The way he felt when he bought the house lot, choked with blackberries, and he'd sketched ideas for the architect in his yellow pads. As if he was God. But wasn't it the best house in the world?

It was enthralling to watch. The longer he watched the more his heart swelled, and he'd cry if he could. He was falling in love *with his own life*. His chest was positively swollen with love. Jesus Christ! Every minute, so dear, so familiar, so...particularly *his*. He'd definitely buy a ticket to see this movie, in 3D. And to hell with the expense, he'd get a giant bucket of popcorn and Coke too.

'Jack, that's enough now. Knock it off, Jack. Jack?' Defiantly and tearfully.

Milly closed her eyes tight, tight. Opened them, but did not look at her husband's face. Her mouth was twisted, as if tasting something repulsive. All her life, she had to wait till events were hours – days – old, before really comprehending them. She literally could not feel the truth of the present. And so part of her was still watching the television, waiting for the commercials to be over and the news to come back on. Thinking about how to clean that hot chocolate up, and about her granddaughter's twentieth birthday later this week. The plants in the bedroom that needed watering. The dogs that needed letting out before bed. Unless they were dead, of course. She wanted to turn the volume down again because the commercials were so irritating, but the remote control...well.

'Jack,' she said automatically, but stopped herself telling him to turn the volume off.

Then she clumped her walker frame to the wall socket, leaned over and pulled the television plug out, almost falling over.

'For heaven's sake!' she said with disgust, but then her voice frightened her, with no Jack to hear it. The movements of her own body scared her, with no Jack to witness them. The side of her facing Jack sensed a void now; her skin felt a chilliness. She made her way to him, quickly, as quickly as she could, with little whimpering noises, because something in her was lurching towards him. As if he was about to disappear from sight for ever, unless she could reach him in time. The ball was still in her court, right?

'Hey! Jack. Wait for me, Jack.'

There he lay, on his front, his face half hidden and pale. She didn't cry or make a sound, but her face crumbled. She looked the least pretty she'd ever looked, including the times she was straining to push out babies, and the time she'd screamed that she hated not just her husband, but her husband's guts.

I hate your guts!

The living room was suddenly jam packed with the ghost-strangers rushing silently to other rooms, except the fat old lady who might be Louise and the small boy who might be Charlie. The boy sat on the arm of the chair and the fat old lady was so close, Milly felt the gravitational pull of her soft bulk. There was a rasping sound suddenly, and she held her own breath to listen closer. Jack turned his head slightly and opened one eye. Milly screamed a tiny scream, and the room gradually seeped back. Fat lady and boy, gone.

'I'm calling an ambulance. Stay where you are, sweetie.'

'Don't.'

'What?'

'Don't. Call. Blance.'

'But...'

'Justa. Spode. E. Pi. Sode.'

Milly helped Jack lever himself up using her walker. Everything in his body hurt, but in a distant surreal way. Sensations were difficult to interpret. What was that throbbing in his chest...pain? Had pain always felt like this? Strange, strange, strange. An hour later, they were both in bed. Tuesday was finally done. It had seemed very long, yet here they were already, at the end, false teeth taken out again, remaining teeth brushed, non-existent dogs ignored. They snuffled their goodnights and curled up away from each other. Just a light blanket over them as the night was still warm. Buttocks comfortably snuggled against buttocks. They did not kiss goodnight. Milly's sleep was light and fragmentary, a smooth flat pebble skipping over turbulent water, but Jack's sleep was sudden and deep. He considered the view, then jumped off the diving board into the cold green Pacific, sunlight pouring down, and echoes filling his ears. As he exhaled for the last time, Milly turned towards him, unaware he was no longer dreaming, and she kissed the spot between his shoulder blades. She often delivered this belated kiss, and actually so did he. Sometimes.

Seven hours later, Milly woke.

'Jack. What time is it?'

'Jack!' in her most nagging tone. 'I said. What. Time. Is. It. Feels like we slept too long.'

'Jack! Oh God, Jack. You'd better not be. Wake up!'

She sat up in bed.

'How dare you! Did I say you could? You get back here right now, do you understand?'

Curled on to his side, Jack's mouth was pulled by gravity into a half-smile. Milly slumped, defeated. The birds outside suddenly seemed too loud, as if they'd entered the house. She carefully leaned over him to double check. Bastard! Then she got back under the covers, and without another thought went to sleep. She slept and slept and slept. Every time her mind approached consciousness, she slid back down under the safe dark cloak, where everything was as it had always been and she was asleep with her Jack who had driven her crazy most of her life and could not be allowed to leave it. His body was the only body her body knew. She'd never fallen asleep beside another man. His

Old Spice and scratchy chin were still there, but just silence where there used to be snores sounding like a rubber ball bouncing, and farts lasting minutes.

Eventually a painful need to urinate forced her to leave Jack alone in bed. She did not look at him. In fact, she had on her *You've really blown it this time, I'm not speaking to you* face and went to unlock the front door, flick each venetian blind open, collect the newspapers from the driveway, make herself a cup of coffee. She moved as creakily as ever, but efficiently. Then she went back to bed.

When she next woke, it was to the sound of crickets about three thirty in the morning, and as she calculated this fact, she realized she hadn't eaten for almost forty hours. She clanked and creaked with her walker, down the hall to the kitchen. At the refrigerator, she felt for the bacon, eggs, butter, milk and cheese and cooked an extravagant omelette, oozing with cheese and crispy bacon. She'd always had a greedy appetite. Then she dumped all the greasy plates and cutlery and frying pans into the sink for Jack to wash, because he'd been such a bad sport, staying in bed and missing this midnight feast. Typical. It was all right when he planned a party, but let someone else take charge and he just wasn't interested. And who did he think was going to clean that hot chocolate off the carpet?

She suddenly sensed the shape of her life, as if it was in the hall just behind her, over her shoulder. A physical object. There she'd stood in her life before Jack, and now here she stood, Jack-less again, as if those decades in between had shut up like an accordion no one wanted to play any more. She felt light, hardly knew herself. She was still angry, a bit. How dare he! She closed her eyes and saw him heading out the front door in some eternal weekday morning, yellow Brooks Brother's shirt, his old leather briefcase swinging. Kissing her quickly on the lips, tasting of coffee and smelling of Old Spice. *See you later, hon.* That old distracted goodbye of his seemed to echo over and over. It took so much for granted.

She curled up under the quilt on the sofa and drowsily watched the sky turn grey, then light grey, then a bold blue with birds, clouds, cars passing. She almost drifted back asleep, when the phone rang.

'Hello?'

'No, you didn't wake me. Not really. What do you want, Sam?'

'Oh yes. Your father's home.'

'No, I'm afraid you can't speak to him. Not right now, dear.'

'Because…because he's…well, because he's still in bed.'

'Elisabeth said he invited you to dinner Friday?' She frowned. Her daughter had always irritated her. The boys, never.

'He invited everybody? No, you don't need to bring anything. Just yourselves.'

'Look, Sam. I don't know how to say this, so I'm just going to say it. Your father's dead. He died in his sleep. Can you swing by today sometime, help me sort it all out?'

Milly took to sleeping on Jack's side of the bed, and with her head on his pillow she tried to imagine the dream that took him away so it could sneak her away too. She didn't know about the diving board at the Sutro Baths, but the letting go – she could rehearse that. And wait for it. Boy oh boy, then he'd catch it.

SEVEN YEARS EARLIER

A Decent Martini

Christmas Eve 2007, San Miguel, Marin County
2:42pm

What a week! Rain, rain, rain. Jack noticed newts and slugs everywhere suddenly. And mud – his car was a mess. Okay, they needed the rain. The hills were finally fully green, after a month of merely glimmering green, then retreating back to brown and gold. It was good to be able to flush the toilet again, any old time you wanted. But still – rain was annoying. It felt like he had to learn all over again how to keep dry – which shoes not to wear, which jacket was waterproof, and where the hell had he left that old umbrella ten months ago? Had he thrown it out? He'd forgotten how damp everything could get. Even the firewood.

Then that accident on Saturday. Idiot teenage boy, slowing down so quickly, before Jack had a chance to even think about finding the brake pedal. Between the

44

physically painful sound of metal crunching and Milly's hysterical yelling, he'd almost had another heart attack. Then Sunday afternoon they got home from lunch in Tiburon, and realised they must somehow have left her cane in the parking lot. Unless she'd thrown it out the window. He'd been too tired, too drunk to drive all the way back. He was hanging on to his licence by the skin of his dentures. And to top it all off, the Christmas card this morning from his sister, Ivy. Oh God, her infinitely sweet spider handwriting. It always reminded him of that endearing gap between her two front teeth.

> *Dear Jacko:*
>   *I been to a lot of funerals lately, and I don't want to hear about yours. Or wonder why you haven't written. So if you don't mind, I'm going to say goodbye now, while we can both write.*
>   *Merry Christmas! And goodbye. You been a good brother.*
>   *Ivy*

And then, scrawled at the bottom and up the margins:

> *PS. I'm 3 years older, remember. You don't need to fret yet.*

He knew it by heart. By God, that girl always knew how to get to him. Yes, Ivy, at eighty-three, remained *that girl*. The last time he saw her she was nineteen and climbing into the cab of a Mayflower moving van with her brand-new husband, bound for Summers County, West Virginia. Ivy had written to Jack all those years since. Short erratic letters full of dry humour and bad grammar.

45

Pithy snapshots of her life as it unfolded. She always seemed surprised by events, and reported new husbands and new dishwashers with equal amazement and many exclamation marks. As if to say: *Do you believe it? This really happened to your sister, of all people!!!* He used to imagine her one day writing: *Do you believe it? I friggin died today!!! What a hoot!!!* Her words in loopy curls, at first in fountain pen, then a black felt tip. Now and then, a typed letter. Never a word-processed letter, much less email, which Jack used all the time now. He wrote back about once to every dozen of her letters. His own tended to be longer, yet they never seemed to be getting to know each other better. Their relationship remained frozen, with him a sneaky shy nine-year-old, hiding her favourite hair clip so she had to chase him round the porch and tickle him till he damn near peed himself. Then she always pulled out something sweet from her pocket. Or beef jerky. They'd both loved beef jerky.

And now, this terse little message on a Christmas card of Santa hohoho-ing across the snowy sky. He almost wrote back to her, saying: *Hell no, that is not fair – you got to keep writing!* Whenever he thought of Ivy, his syntax went straight back to childish grammar. No more letters from Ivy? Life was just one annoying tragedy after another. He hadn't realised how much space Ivy took up. What on earth would he do about it? Monday, Tuesday, Wednesday, he pondered Ivy.

Everything was dropping away.

His sailboat, *Sweet Epiphany*, had been sold last year (or was it the year before?) to that whippersnapper with new money who couldn't even sail. He'd felt guilty, because he'd never quite given *Sweet Epiphany* the attention she deserved, and now it was too late.

Then his beautiful Dulcinea Press, finally declared dead once and for all at the board meeting last spring. It was easy to blame Amazon and discount deals at the big chains, but the truth was he'd simply misjudged too many writers, and over-estimated the reading public's good taste. He'd been planning on selling the business anyway; he was eighty years old for heaven's sake. But still. Those daily ferry boat commutes, that third-floor office on Columbus. Last time he locked up, it was spotless and empty as if Dulcinea had never existed. He had not been able to throw the key away, or return it. It sat in his desk drawer along with his father's watch, the one he'd received for thirty years of handling the Buena Vista wine barrels. Which, as Jack had been told countless times, was an art. There were right ways to empty barrels, fill them again, settle the wine, do the lees stirring and bung checking. Funny, Jack hadn't had any respect for his father at the time, but now as he humbly bowed out of his own business, a belated appreciation filled him. Life came round and bit you on the ass sometimes.

Jack and Milly lived on less now: luxuries like vacations, cashmere sweaters, oysters – all out the window. He'd noticed the house looking shabbier – as if it, too, was giving up. Hardwood floors that needed sanding and re-varnishing. Window frames that needed replacing. His old ten speed and his newer mountain bike, covered with cobwebs. His tools still neatly arranged, but rusty. And today, looking at the shelves of new books lining their hallway, they suddenly seemed not so new. Teetering towers of proof copies and manuscripts still lined the floor of their bedroom, but they were softly padded at the base with dog hair.

Everything was dropping away or getting stale. They

hadn't even bothered getting a Christmas tree this year.

After lunch, Jack announced:

'The rain's stopped. I'm off for a walk. Might pop by to see August, he said he'd be staying with his mom this week.' In an overloud, defiantly jovial voice, as he was putting on his jacket.

Milly asked, after a minute of marshalling her thoughts then forgetting to keep them inside her head:

'Should I be worried?'

Jack froze, then pulled his jacket tighter and gave her shoulders a quick squeeze. Amazing how her radar still worked.

'No idea what you mean, honey pie, but of course you don't need to worry.'

'Oh, I know. We agreed about that, didn't we. Tell August...tell him I love him!'

'He loves you too.' It was true, thought Jack. Who would have thought that could happen?

'Take the dogs, they need a walk too.'

'Do I have to?'

'Yes.'

'I hate the dogs.'

'No you don't. You just think you do.'

He put on his new shoes, desert boots that were identical to the desert boots he'd worn fifty years ago. They'd stopped making them, so it was a happy day, spotting these in a shoe store window again. When he looked down at his feet, there was nothing visible to say he was not his younger self. Then Milly pulled his face down and kissed him three times. Quick, dry pecks on his lips. And off he went with Jaspy and King pulling on their leashes, down the road to Colette. His son August might or might not be there, but Colette would make him a martini, and a decent one at that. There'd been a time when he'd woken every day salivating for Colette's martinis.

Jack felt naughty, though he'd not philandered for at least ten years, not since Tracey from the beach predicted correctly that he was a Leo and invited him to look at her vacation snapshots and they'd ended up on her ancient waterbed. Not a proud moment. Not his style, to sink as low as someone who believed in astrology, and water beds were so passé. He remembered Colette laughing over that episode, but also agreeing that it was humiliating. Then she'd told him about herself and the furnace maintenance guy, an equally undignified tale. They'd both agreed the only redeeming outcome was the relief of telling the stories to each other. And not telling another soul. They were confidantes. He was pretty sure they'd not been confidantes when they were sleeping together. Maybe the two kinds of intimacy didn't mix.

It was a good half-hour walk to Colette's, but the day was warm, or as warm as mid-winter could get here. Mid-fifties. Jack loved sunny winter days after rain. They made him feel young, energetic. Everything was rain-washed; his street glowed. The dogs stopped to sniff and dribble pee every few minutes, making Jack want to do the same. He knew more about prostates now than he cared to. Not a sexy subject. Sex, sex, sex. He reminded himself that not leaving Milly cancelled out all those old infidelities, but he still felt like Bad Jack MacAlister, walking to Colette's house. That Bad Jack, Poor Dear Milly's husband. So unfair that no one ever thought of him as Poor Dear Jack. Did they think it was easy being married to someone who took ten minutes to walk from the front door to the car? There he was, trapped in a house with a crippled wife who often made him feel cranky, sulky and sneaky. The Jack that Colette knew was light-hearted, affectionate, funny. Sexy, as well. Well, as sexy as an eighty-year-old man had a right to be. Colette knew the real Jack was a rat-pack kind of guy.

Both dogs decided to poop at the corner. There was bunch of dead buckeyes already there and the poops blended in. Jack had a quick look around at the empty street, then continued walking slowly, swaggering rat-pack-ishly.

He imagined a novel in which every chapter was the same man walking to the same woman, over three decades. Weather – that would be the thing to hang chapters on. The way even the air smelled completely different, month by month. Times of day had different smells too. Sometimes he felt like he was drinking the air, that it was entering his lungs through his stomach, that he breathed deeply sometimes because he was thirsty. He supposed breathing wasn't so very different to drinking, not really. Moods, as well as economies and planes in the air and boats at sea, could be affected by air pressure and moisture content. Air, since he read *Storm* by George Stewart back in '52, had never been just air. Maybe he'd begin writing that novel when he got home. Yes, now was the time. He had a good feeling about this one. The others had never felt this right at the beginning.

Jack took the long way, because thinking about this potential masterpiece distracted him, and he forgot his mission. In any case, the rhythm of putting his feet one in front of the other, of feeling the dogs pull on the leash, was soothing him in the old way. He took several slow walks around these streets every day. Since retiring, he found the house claustrophobic after a few hours. Each house he passed, he told himself a potted version of the history. Blonde kids with stingray bikes. German family, wife had hair to her waist. Cocktail hour always included wieners tooth-picked to chunks of pineapple.

Then he came to 10 Bay View, Ernie and Bernice's house. He sighed, not because Ernie was dead (he wasn't), but because Ernie always reminded him of his own youth and that made him nostalgic. He thought of their Saturday walks to the Sebastiani Theatre for the double feature, that summer before they'd started high school. They'd talked about girls and sung snatches of random songs, or walked in an easy silence, their muscles loose, their arms and legs swinging, the sun hot on their heads. An exquisite sense of anticipation all that summer. He wasn't sure if he'd ever been as aware of sheer potential since.

Ah, youth!

Then Jack passed two other houses that used to contain friends, and he saw them sitting on their deck chairs, lighting cigarettes, or pulling tabs on a Coors while tending the barbecue, or throwing Frisbees for the dog – God, all those Frisbees, and the never-ending fun of buying new ones. They moved, they smiled, they opened their mouths in recognition of Jack, and by the look in their eyes were about to say something slightly sarcastic, slightly funny and irreverent. They'd been his buddies, after all. They moved their mouths but nothing ever came out.

At the end of the street, there was Colette's third dead husband, opening his mouth to reveal his terrible teeth and cackling lewdly as if to say: *Jack, you checking out my wife again? You old dog!*

Jack didn't feel sad. He passed these houses too often, and the nostalgia was too familiar. He felt flat. But now for no particular reason (what had changed?) he felt his heart pumping quicker, and his steps felt less effortful. Thank God, he thought, here it comes again, that old renewal. He had two seconds' worry about his heart, then remembered the magic pacemaker in his chest, keeping tabs on things. And the stent. He was all loaded up with metallic magic. He wished he was still a smoker. This was a lighting-up moment.

'Jack!'

She stood in her doorway, a cell phone in one hand, wearing a paint-stained apron over jeans. Looking, with every atom, mid-stream some engrossing activity. Jack shivered with the thrill of being unimportant to a woman. And an ex-lover who had become unattractive! Colette was stripped down to the bones of her personality: sharp cheekbones, burning blue eyes, pale skin transparent as cling film. Even her protruding abdomen seemed angular somehow. She'd reinvented herself as a Room Improver, and resided entirely in her eyes and her brush-wielding hands. Her body existed to support these parts, and the rooms in her house were continually changing colour.

'Come in, man! Look at you, in shorts in the middle of winter. Merry Christmas!'

'It's not Christmas,' he said, untangling the leashes.

'Pretty damn near. Christmas Eve.' She gestured behind her, to the artificial tree with twinkling blue lights.

'No! Is it?' Jack laughed, a short barking sound. Time! He had to take his hat off to Time – what a sneak, what a scoundrel. It was exactly as Waugh had described it in *Jenny Kissed Me*. And it was so satisfying when Time didn't catch him out. He pictured the present he'd bought for Milly, wrapped and hidden under his socks. A watch. Her old watch was not broken, but she loved watches.

'Yes, of course, it's Christmas Eve, you silly old man. You know it is.' Then she squinted at him. 'How are you?'

Pause.

'Not good.'

'Okay. Tell me everything.'

He noticed the wrinkles around her pursed mouth. They reminded him of something distasteful, but he didn't want to think what. Regardless, he had an urge to kiss her right there on the doorstep, out of sheer gratitude for inviting him to speak his mind. A loud wet kiss. Colette sidestepped him, and almost skipped into the kitchen to get Jaspy and King a bowl of water. Light-footed and saucy, a bit like Ivy, actually. All his crush women were versions of his big sister, come to think of it. Including Lizbeth? Especially Lizbeth. Who may not even be alive, for all he knew.

'Is August around? He mentioned he'd be here for Christmas.'

'He'll be here tomorrow. Sit down Jack. I've got some news about August.'

'Not again.'

It was as if their son had entered the room anyway, with that look, half sheepish, half proud. Jack used to love that about August. Colette made their martinis and came to sit next to him on the sofa.

Meanwhile, Milly was sitting on the window seat she claimed for her own about five years ago. Like Goldilocks, she'd tried other seats, but this one fitted the best. She could look out of the window and see the path leading to the front door, as well as the main rooms of the house. She could watch television if she chose; the remote was on the table next to her. There was also a magazine nearby, ready to hold should Jack reappear. She tried not to gaze vacantly into space in his presence; she was too vain for that, and besides, he inhibited her space-gazing. Jack had never caught her picking her nose. That she knew of.

The mention of August, and therefore Colette, was still hanging in the air. She absent-mindedly turned on the television and clicked through dozens of commercials. 'Jingle Bells' and ecstatic children ripping paper. Somehow Christmas was here again, but she was prepared even if the Christmas ornament box remained in the basement. She'd ordered gifts by phone weeks ago, wrapped them and hidden them in her closet. She had not told Jack – not because he liked surprises or hated Christmas, but because she thought Christmas should be full of secrets. She had bought Jack a grey cashmere pullover from Brooks Brothers. Yes, they were living more frugally now, but she refused to consider lambswool.

There were also commercials about haemorrhoids and erectile dysfunction, enlarged prostates and incontinence pads and cures for arthritis. She smiled at the long list of dire side effects, intoned as if they were pleasant little nothings, like freckles occurring from prolonged exposure to the sun. She was never going to be as old as these people. Never so stupid as to get that old and sick. She stopped clicking when she came to one of those new reality programs, some kind of talent show. Ideally, she'd now open a pack of Junior Mints. She relaxed into the naughtiness of watching daytime junk alone, but after a while, the program seemed familiar in an unhappy way. All those vulnerable faces, those fevered eyes, those songs and dances they poured their hearts into. At least one of them cried every five minutes, unrehearsed, raw. It was hard to watch, and hard to turn off. It reminded of phase of her marriage. That same cruel pause before the verdict. Would he betray her? Leave her? Love her? Carry them to the next round? She'd tried so hard, but was it hard enough?

While a mile away Jack tasted a dry martini in silence because that honoured Colette's martini-making skill, Milly turned off the television, and her thoughts rolled this way and that. The windows looked out on trees, leafless and winter black. If a monitor was measuring her heartbeat, it would register mild fluctuations as the distant past threaded into the recent past. Today her thoughts all contained Jack, in one incarnation or another. She had been cursed by the fates, and married her true love. Her face was slack, but she was still a beautiful woman. She had a clear jaw line, and her neck had loosened but not turned to crepe. Her skin was moist and delicate. Her blonde hair had faded to white, not grey, since she'd stopped dyeing it. She would like to leave the chair, leave the house like Jack, of course she would, but just imagining the process was wearying enough. If she wanted to go out, she needed assistance getting down the gravel path. Then the complex manoeuvring into the car. Dropping down into the car seat, then lifting her left leg with her right hand as if it belonged to someone else. Hazards every inch of the way. Last time she went out she fell, despite the stupid cane. Elisabeth kept mentioning walking aids. *Get a Zimmer frame, Mom, it'll make your life much easier.*

'Forget it!' she said right now out loud, as if her daughter was present. Mild enough words, but in a venomous, determined tone. Know-it-all child, that Elisabeth. Anyway, she was not going to fall any more. She was not, darn it. Falling was very...irritating. There was pain of course, but worse was the humiliation of lying on the floor, sometimes with her skirt up to her underpants. Once she lay all afternoon in the backyard, by the leeks. Darn near froze to death. If only she'd been more careful driving Sam to the hospital forty thousand years ago. If only.

No, it was not worth going out. There was enough to deal with here, without taking extra risks. Every impulse, from picking up a dropped sock to a trip to the bath-room, was enacted in slow motion, with much strategic thinking. If, for instance, the kitchen phone rang and she was in the hall, she thought, twelve rings. It will be twelve rings before I can get to it. If the phone rang and she was in the bedroom, she said, 'Oh, nuts.'

No, this seat was fine, and she'd stop wanting things she couldn't have, like legs that worked and a faithful husband. She used to pray for things, but when she got them, they nearly always backfired so what was the point? She'd stopped trusting herself to know what she really needed decades ago. Now she was just grateful things were not worse.

Jack was grateful that Colette had finally stopped talking about August's child maintenance issues with his ex, but now she was talking about her latest plan to transform the guest bathroom. She could never just say *paint the bathroom,* it always had to be a metamorphosis or trans-formation. It was much more fun when they talked about life in general terms, or about his own past triumphs and travels. Why couldn't she ask him again about the time Dulcinea won Best Small Publisher of the Year? Or when his star writer came out of the closet? Why could they never refer, even obliquely, to the times they tore each other's clothes off? My God, had visiting Colette become boring? Another thing that had slipped away. He watched her puckered mouth move, and her words had a soporific effect. The gin and vermouth in his blood had begun dissipating, and he knew she'd not pour more. He roused the dogs and reattached the leashes. Apologised for their stink, and not for the first time expressed his wish that they would die soon.

'Give my love to dear darling Milly,' said Colette, without irony.

'Okay,' said Jack.

On impulse, perhaps because he looked like a sulky ten-year-old in his shorts and scabby knees and desert boots, Colette kissed him smack dab on the lips, just like his fantasy.

Jack toddled home with Jaspy and King, in a kind of trance. He was attached to home with an umbilical cord, and whenever nothing else was going on, whenever he was hungry, sleepy, bored by an ex-lover, home reeled him in like a trout. But was it really so involuntary? As he approached his house, his steps quickened. Suddenly, he could hardly wait to see his wife. Milly was many irritating things, but she was not work. He didn't have to be witty or smart around her. He didn't even have to make conversation.

It was early evening, and he noticed Christmas lights on trees in windows, and plastic Rudolphs pulling Santas on lawns. He remembered vaguely that his children and grandchildren would visit tomorrow, with a cooked turkey. In fact, August would probably come too, the cuckoo in the nest everyone adored. Billy would bring Maria and all ten of their children – being the only

MacAlister child to stick at Catholicism and marriage. Jack was surprised to find he was looking forward to this too, to having his house full of chaos, and Christmas paper and carols. Kids whining and babies crying, but loud laughter too. He'd light the fire, open that bottle of Chateau Buena Vista Réserve. He wondered if it was too late to get a tree. A real tree, not some damn fake thing. You needed the smell of pine, or there was no point.

Inside, at the sound of her husband's footsteps, Milly grabbed the *National Geographic* and miraculously lost twenty years: cheek muscles tensed, a smile in her eyes, back straight. A pretty marionette whose strings had just been pulled taut.

'Is that you Jack?'

'No! It's one of your boyfriends!'

Milly's stomach tingled with pleasure. Was this, Milly wondered, what love boiled down to? A physical symptom, like an infection or inflammation, that flared up now and then. Nothing that could be faked or imitated or summoned or ignored. She still wondered things like this, forgetting that she had wondered them many times before. Why did Milly still love her faithless husband? Maybe, she thought, it was simply because he still loved her. She was convinced she was beloved. Stomach tingles didn't lie. Or so she told herself.

Jack headed to his office and she got up to make dinner. They sighed, shook their heads slightly, and slipped back into their ancient way of being – aggravated and comforted in equal measure. As if he was an old armchair with a misshapen seat that she had push back in every time, and she was an heirloom table with one leg the wrong length so his cup of coffee was always spilling.

Outside, as the day wound down, the rain began again. It made a light steady patter on the roof, and because they hadn't cleaned the roof gutters for years, it soon overflowed and splashed down the sides of the wooden house with Jack and Milly inside, feeling cosy. Jack poured himself a large glass of Two-Buck Chuck. Every bit as good as any of those fancy wines he kept for company. All the money he'd wasted over the years! Milly began frying hamburger meat, and fretted about the ants. How did they get in the house? Not one thought of Christmas returned.

Jack Is Not Dead

July 16, 2002, San Miguel, Marin County
10:01am

Milly sat in the window seat between the front door and the living room. A habit she began yesterday, but already it felt like a tradition. It was hot, and predicted to hit ninety-five later. She wore a short-sleeved blouse and a cotton knee-length skirt, with Birkenstock sandals on her feet. She could get the phone if it rang and she could see who was at the door without getting up. She sat very still and looked at the book she held. Under her book, a small dictionary lay cradled in her lap. She frowned softly and concentrated. She read the same sentence over and over again. *He takes her hand and guides it to his cock.* She didn't understand. She hoped she didn't understand. Goodness, it was so hot! The book belonged to her husband, whom she much admired and respected, even if he drove her nuts, and it said Everyman's Classic Library on the spine. Surely it wouldn't be about – that. She tried to read on but came back to the same passage. *...guides it to his cock.*

She could not say *cock* out loud, even to herself. Actually, even the word *penis* repulsed her. There was no good word for it, she thought. Her boys – all four of them, counting Louise's two, and not counting poor Charlie who never got old enough to call his anything, and also not counting Jack and Colette's August, who probably found a more obscene word for it – had called their penises *willies* when they were little. A house full of willies! How hilarious they used to think it was, that Willy was called Willy (before he became Billy). They used to have peeing contests in the yard, and aim at each other when they lost. For at least ten years, one of Milly's daily chores had been to mop the pee-sodden area around the toilet. And sensitive serious Elisabeth actually learned to pee standing up, one summer.

A bee buzzed lazily in and she looked up in gratitude for the distraction. She followed its course through the open kitchen door, then lost it as it made its way into the hall. A diminishing drone. She felt a lovely numbness come over her. It had happened yesterday too, when she first relaxed in this chair. All her life, Milly had been rushing, rushing, rushing, then falling into bed with chores half done, lists half crossed out. And now suddenly it seemed her body was putting on the brakes. It wasn't even waiting for her conscious surrender. Every muscle was limp. She closed her eyes and entered – not sleep, because then she'd fall off her seat – but a half-sleep. Irresistible. Like sliding onto an air mattress and just floating away down river. Ah!

This was how Jack caught her when he returned from his doctor's appointment, new blood pressure instrument tucked under his arm. He froze. Was she sick? Certainly not drunk, anyway, no daytime martinis for his Milly, but she'd never been a napper either. Her mouth was open and her book was on the floor. She looked odd, but also relaxed and a tiny bit like she used to. Not angry, anyway. She snored a little, a soft feminine snorting. He picked up her book and decided not to wake her. The party wasn't for a few hours. He quietly walked past her, into his office. He was working more from home since his heart attack six months ago, and there was always a pile of manuscripts on his desk. He stared into space instead. Behind him, on the wall, were framed book covers, and photographs of his staff and some of the more successful authors. Old Andy Frances, holding his first bound copy of *Here I Am*. None of this could cheer him today because Dulcinea Press was going to the dogs. He had to offer his A-list writers less for their new books than they'd got for their first. He'd tried everything. Cheaper production materials, less on marketing, discount rates, more on marketing. Writers would write regardless, readers would read regardless, but publishers could not publish without money. He never could have predicted this downturn. It felt like a trick. This heat was giving him a headache. He had a sudden longing for fall. For fog and football games and sweaters.

A loud adolescent car horn woke Milly. She jerked her head up and frowned. She saw dusty footmarks on the rug that hadn't been there before.

'Jack! Are you home?'

'I'm here. Working,' he shouted behind a closed door.

'I wasn't sleeping,' she shouted back.

'I didn't say you were sleeping.' He left his office and

62

gave her back her book. 'Here you go, sweetie. Of course you were wide awake.'

'I only closed my eyes, is all. Where's the dogs?'

'I don't know.'

'You said you were taking them with you.'

'Did I?' He was always in the wrong about the damn dogs.

'They could be anywhere. Out on the road.' She glared at him. 'They could be dead right now!'

King and Jaspy came padding down the hall on their clumsy puppy paws. They licked her bare legs. She glared at Jack, but couldn't keep it up. It was one of those times. Since she hit her seventies, three years ago, these times were more frequent. Mercurial, that was Milly now. Mercury Milly.

'Listen,' he heard himself say. 'There's just time before the party. I'm sure it's open. Let's drive to St Mary Magdalene.'

'What for?' She couldn't make the connection. It was like the cock and hand all over again.

'Milly. Milly!' Boyishly reproachful. 'What happened fifty years ago today at St Mary Magdalene?'

She laughed out loud this time, not at his words, but his face. It was absurd. Wrinkled and wistful.

'Very funny, is it? Well, get your shoes on, then. Let's go.'

It was a forty-minute drive to Bolinas. The rounded hills were blonde, and the few trees hunched their branches, parched. As the road wound into the town, they both said 'Ah!' at the same time. The clapboard houses, the dusty sidewalks, Smiley's Bar and the old grocery store. Oysters in the shell. There was not much to say it wasn't 1952, aside from the style of cars and the price of oysters. Three

63

dollars each! The sky was delphinium blue, the town was stunned with sun. Even the seagulls were quiet, perched on fences and porch roofs.

The hillside steps were blinding white, leading to the small church. Jack took her arm going down. He'd brought her cane in the car, but she refused it as usual. Walking was a slow process, but neither commented. No people around. Would the door be unlocked? Yes, the heavy dark door swung inward and waves of coolness wrapped round them. Woke them up. They'd not been here for many years, but it was the same: the narrow stained glass windows letting in just enough light, the simple brown crucifix, the ashy cinnamon smell of incense, the white wooden walls. They stood in the aisle, her hand touching his sleeve. Then without speaking, they turned into a pew and sat down.

Whole minutes passed. They faced forward and so close they touched shoulders, arms, legs. Hands touching. This was not like them at all.

Milly wondered who she would have become if she'd married someone else. It was a fact that who you married altered you. And God knows, thought Milly, identity was a nebulous thing at best. Did it matter who you loved? It mattered very much how that person changed you. If she'd married too-nice Jimmy, she might have discovered her own potential for cruelty. If she'd married sexually ineffective Larry, she might have become a wanton woman. Shy, fat Harry might have made her outgoing and chubby, and low-earning Andy might have turned her into a career woman. With Timmy, she might be living in a mansion by now, with maids to do her beckoning. She might have become an aimless alcoholic, from boredom and a sense of unimportance. But she'd married

Jack. Here they were, and the people they'd become were not so bad. At any rate, they'd made some nice kids. And raised two others to be nice, and then August too. Six nice human beings in the world, thanks to them. Not to mention all those grandchildren. Yessiree!

Suddenly, she was relieved all over again that Jack was not dead. Since his heart attack, she'd stopped taking his aliveness for granted. Bliss, to feel him next to her. And bliss, to be out of the sun and off her feet. She'd forgotten why exactly they were sitting in this empty church. She was at peace, rare enough. Then it came to her, rising up from her contentment, and she thought, *Yes, I was here for a wedding and it was mine. I was late and I was worried about my deodorant not working and the flower girl tripped and fell.* She wondered if she still had any memento of that day – dried flowers or confetti. She doubted it – Jack was a terror for clearing stuff out. Her wedding dress had been thrown out when it began to decay, and in any case, Elisabeth would never have squeezed into it. Milly looked down at her hands and there was her wedding ring. It was her third one, she kept losing them, but it was on her finger and her finger had definitely been here at the wedding. Not to mention her entire body. And Jack, who was not dead. She looked towards a side window, sneaking a glimpse of his profile. He was an old man! The skin below his ear hung in a little fold, and his jaw was drooping. An old man, yet inside the old man was the young man she'd made promises to. Vows spoken not ten feet from where she sat now.

She'd meant to be such a good wife. To make Jack happy.

She sighed. Time spent sulking and snapping and shouting, it might amount to years now. To decades.

It occurred to her marriage might be like an imperfect haircut one just had to endure till it grew out, only it never really grew out. A haircut that looked good sometimes, in certain lights, and other days just plain ugly. She'd never found the right hairdresser, that was the curse of her life. Her fingers went up now, and she pushed the hair off her face.

Jack saw his young bride, she was right there at the altar. Clear as the old woman next to him. There he was too, and look how skinny he was! Goddammit, he was one handsome guy, and she couldn't be more gorgeous. What a couple of kids they were, but they'd felt so mature. Sure, they'd slept together, lots of times. They thought that meant they knew each other, but really they'd been strangers. Which had made their kisses constantly wonderful. He recalled her taste – lipstick and a whisper of all she was happy to give him. He bowed to them now, to their smooth-skinned, cherry-cheeked courage. About to tumble, eyes closed and all tangled up together, into the unknown.

But it was not that simple, because Jack could also see someone else. He visualised himself and another woman. They stood right now outside this church, perhaps looking at the view of the ocean. Lizbeth? Yes, well, why not. It *could* have been Lizbeth. A woman made happy by him, a little overweight and wrinkled, but all the lines were in pleasing places. He sighed happily, full of unlived lives.

About the same time, they both remembered the anniversary party. Their children had done all the organising: the food, invitations, the wine, the cake, but it would occur in Jack and Milly's home, so there were still tedious things to do, like checking for toilet paper, and clean towels, and floors to be mopped. Not to mention dogs fed and walked, then secreted away in the garage. And the exhausting task ahead of small talk and remembering names.

'I wish we weren't having a party,' whispered Milly, half to herself. 'I wish it was a normal day.'

'Me too, hon.'

The church receded even before they left it, their thoughts flying towards chores. Blinded by the sun as they walked slowly back to the car, they leaned towards each other. They felt wrong together, mismatched, a mistake taken too far. But from a short distance they looked like many couples did to outsiders – exclusive, close. From a greater distance, they looked like a single person.

It wasn't late – not eleven yet, but no time had been wasted. Ernie and Bernice and their diminishing group of friends – five in total – had been seated by 8:00, dancing by 9:00, drunk and gone by 10:00. A wild time, a good party. Even the arguments had been condensed, so from kick off to forgiving hug, they'd lasted about ten minutes. Sure, a few tears when dead friends were mentioned, but a lot of laughter of the loose, cackling variety. How hilarious, that they were the age they were. What a joke! It felt downright rebellious to be getting old and still swinging to Glen. They were quite sure their own parents never felt this young, this irreverent at seventy something. This proved they'd never die. How could they, right?

Now it was just family, sitting around the table. And though it was their wedding anniversary party, Milly saw that it was really nothing to do with them at all. The party had a life of its own, and was a memory in the making. Her and Jack's role had been to provide the circumstances for them all to remember each other. To have these times of loud overlapping conversations and spilled wine and kids' whining and laughter and blushes. Emotion so close to the surface, it got mixed up with the gravy and the way the coffee tasted. Her children had each other, and laughed at their parents. Knowing what she knew, that she'd not always be here, she was glad. Anyway, she'd never really got the hang of talking to grown-up children. Much easier when they were little.

The cake was in the middle of the table, a mess of lurid icing and crumbs. Under the table, the released dogs were happily licking, as if the floorboards had become edible. Ella Fitzgerald was singing about loving some damn man no matter what, but no one was listening – they were all talking at the same time. Jack opened another bottle, while Milly sat quietly, hands on her lap, looking bemused.

When a gap finally occurred, Elisabeth asked, 'So, Mom. Fifty years. What have been the best parts?'

'Me? The best parts?'

Milly stalled for time by fiddling with her napkin, wiping her mouth, taking a sip of juice from her wine glass. She was on her tenth juice. How had she got to this day? One thing had led to another, then another. Like moving from one house to another house, and she'd made the best of each house. Found the strengths, covered up the weaknesses. But she felt odd now, insubstantial. She felt like she'd been right here, in this day, all along. And she'd been in all those other places all her life too, headed to this day. All those times existed, somehow, simultaneously.

'Mom? Tell us what you enjoyed the most. Please!' asked Sam.

'Come on, Milly! Come on, Mom!' chimed the others.

Now, this room. Not anywhere else. These familiar dear people, looking at her. God, they could all use a good scrubbing, she couldn't help but think. And a haircut.

'I enjoyed raising you. All of you.'

She said this softly, doubtfully, and saw clearly the space they'd taken up in her life. That clump of years. That witnessing of babies metamorphosing into children, and then into unrecognisable adults. Of one baby who did not. That inheriting of two boys she'd only loved as an aunt before, then realising they'd somehow become her own. August was sitting next to her, so in her mind she scooped him up too, not because he was Jack's son, but because he was lovable and he was there.

'It's been...such a pleasure to raise you all,' she said, with more certainty. And looked sternly at the six children, one by one.

But they were all middle-aged people, like herself! Had they caught up with her and Jack? And who was that strange man, sitting next to Elisabeth? And that woman, her arm looped around Sam's shoulder? Oh yes, the new boyfriend and girlfriend. Odd words to apply to men and women in their forties, but yes, that's exactly what they were. And there sat Daniel, alone, and his wife God knows where. At least Donald was still with Charlotte, and Billy was still with Maria, thank God. But poor August was entirely alone again and looked neglected – wrinkled shirt, stubble-faced, a slackness to the way he sat. She knew most of her children thought it was pointless to devote a life to keeping a marriage intact, but she was proud today. Proud of her family gathering around the cake, with *fifty years* in pink icing inside a red heart. She felt she deserved a...well, an adult version of a Girl Scout badge. It had been such a long, bloody battle. This day represented a victory over all the forces of divorce.

But look at their faces. Still waiting for her.

'I have loved being your mother,' she said seriously now.

'Milly, honey pie,' slurred Jack. 'I think they mean the best parts of our marriage. As today is our fiftieth anniversary. Remember?'

A second of anger crossed her face, one eyebrow cocked. Some giggles from round the table.

'All good times,' she said. 'And I thank God you are not dead, Jack.'

At this, after three seconds of silence, everyone laughed.

'Here's to you, Mom,' they said, raising their glasses. 'Here's to love like yours.'

'Here, here,' said Jack, joining in. He may be mocked by his kids, but knew better than to let them know he cared. He'd had six glasses of wine. Love seemed irrelevant. It hardly mattered when compared to the fact of their tenaciousness. Hell, they hadn't killed each other, and that was a miracle worth celebrating.

Then August put another record on – he was the only child who loved the old music. Harry James oozed into the room.

'Not that old crap again!'

'Sure some of my old Stones albums are still there. Or Grateful Dead.'

'Put on something decent!'

'Leave it!' commanded Jack, and moved into the seat August had left empty, next to his wife. She was humming softly and Jack was swaying, and clicking his fingers. The music was as fresh, as cutting edge as ever. He couldn't shake the feeling that their generation had done something no other generation had ever done. He and Milly sat alone on their island of nostalgia. Jack kissed his wife on the side of her head, and then on her mouth. She kissed him back, and August took a picture of them with his phone.

The next day, Jack was mildly depressed and spent the day hiking. There had been a time he'd felt sorry for himself because his wife could not join him on hikes. The plan had been to be one of those couples who did everything together. He'd adjusted long ago, but today for some reason, he felt sorry for himself again. Not only that, Jaspy and King were very disobedient. Still puppies, but still. They kept running off and he had to resist the urge to not call them back. 'Fuck, fuck, fuck,' he kept mumbling to himself. He had drunk too much last night. It was so hot, the sky was white, too hot for blue. Everything looked ugly and dirty. He walked till his muscles ached and the sun burned the places not covered by his old hat.

Milly felt energetic and excited, as if in some delayed reaction to the prospect of having a party. She decided to clean out the hall closet. And the refrigerator. It was satisfying, throwing junk away and creating space. Temporary, of course, since she could easily visualise the clutter accumulating again. But still, it was satisfying.

FIVE YEARS EARLIER:

Killing Ants

July 14th, 1997, Dogtired Ranch, Mendocino County
2:13pm

Here they were again: Dogtired Ranch. Would this be the last time? There had to be a last time one of these times. It was a hellish drive, longer every year. They'd both wondered if last summer had been the last time, but here they were again. It seemed to Milly that last times always made that decision themselves. No warning, just the retrospective awareness.

It was good to be back, she told herself. Flies circling endlessly, yellow jackets buzzing all day and mosquitoes buzzing all night, beer tabs being ripped off. Coconut sunscreen and smoking barbecues. The sandy beach, in the curve of the river. Cold for swimming, but perfect for sunbathing. A timeless place. The sense that, despite all the noise and movement from the beach, all the laughter of the poker-playing men in the shade, the wives' overlapping gossip about their marriages and everyone else's marriages, the fourteen-year-old bikini-clad girls pretending to ignore the fourteen-year-old whooping-it-up boys, and above it all the children's giggles, screams, tears – despite all this *humanity*, time was not moving here at Dogtired. Or if it was, it was moving like maple syrup on a cold day. The only age group missing was the eighteen to thirty-year-olds. Dogtired was not for everyone.

They always booked the same log cabin, the same mid-July weeks.

'We always go to Dogtired in July,' Milly had told the checkout girl in United Market yesterday, as she stocked up on food for the trip. 'Every summer. It's an old MacAlister family tradition, every summer,' she'd repeated proudly, forgetting it had begun as a desperate measure the year her sister, Louise, fell crazy in love with Coffee Enema Bob (he swore coffee enemas cured everything including cancer), and gave her sons to her sister without a backward glance. That first summer had been hell. Four kids crammed into the back seat, and in front, Billy (when he was Willy) on her lap. Louise's boys had been so pale, so quiet. So polite. Milly remembered washing Danny's pee-sodden sheets daily. She'd felt as if they were all floating, and she was supposed to tether them to earth again somehow. They'd needed a miracle, and Dogtired had been it.

There had been a time when Milly had lain awake at night, fretting about the possibility of Louise's ex-husband emerging, stealing those poor boys from their beds. It made her slightly ashamed because he wasn't a bad man, but she'd imagined blocking the door with her body. Her dogs would attack his legs and her children would fell him with cast-iron frying pans. She never got further than that, never actually disposed of the body.

There had been a time she'd yearned for her sister to return, but then one day she realised she'd begun to dread such an eventuality. A secret dread. She'd have to act over the moon, but, oh, it would break her heart. The boys had become, by a process she couldn't understand, her own children. She could not lose them too, she told herself, then listened to the *too* and remembered poor cold Charlie.

Ah, Charlie!

Ah, Danny and Donald!

Ah, Louise!

Her sister could attract nice men, but had never learned the knack of appreciating them. Always chased the bad boys. Maybe a missing gene, certainly nothing she could help. Milly remembered racing down to the train tracks with Louise, their thongs (Were they called that any more? Hadn't thongs become string underpants?) slapping the sidewalk. Her sister was always going closer to the thundering freight train, and daring Milly to do the same. Louise's saucy hip and shoulder wriggle to the caboose man, and his amazed look. She always did that, no matter what the caboose man looked like. As if she was the Shasta County Homecoming Queen, served up just for him. She'd had a red gingham skirt that she wore all one summer, the summer she was fifteen – full from the tiny waist, made of the lightest material, so when she ran, or it was windy, anyone could see her underpants.

It had been almost thirty years, but Milly still couldn't think of her sister without a clear recollection of her own first reaction to the news. She'd wanted to shake Louise hard. Slap her. Typical no-class Louise. Louise had written postcards and letters over the years, asking for news of her sons, and for forgiveness. One of the early letters:

Billie: I'm sorry, sis, but I don't see how I can come back now. I'm a rotten mother. Obviously. Mom was a rotten mother too, we just didn't get it. Thought she was normal. She was hard, Billie. You don't like to think of all those times she was drunk and just didn't care. You don't even remember feeling scared! That time she fell in the kitchen and just lay there in a puddle of her own piss till we came in for breakfast. But I remember, and I see her in me. I'm OK, I'm not saying I'm a bad person. But I am not a decent mother. Danny and Donald are better off with you. I know you'll see the sense in this. But I got to say, I miss you more than I can say.

    Love, your stupid sis

    PS. I am crying as I write this. Just so you know it ain't easy.

She'd made it sound like her desertion was an act of self-sacrifice – and perhaps it was. Louise and Coffee Enema Bob had split ages ago. (*I don't know why no man is sticking with me, Billie. Or maybe it's me that's not sticking with them. Seems like Chuck did something to ruin me that way. He was too nice and I used up all my sticking power on him. Nowadays, I get so I can hardly sit still, once I'm done with a man. And he don't need to do much to start getting on my nerves. It's all my fault, I know that. I'm not dumb. Just impossible to live with.*) After mentioning various men and various communes over the years, she was living with a woman reiki healer in a trailer park outside Dubois now – though there'd been no letters or postcards for a while. More than two

75

years. Milly tried to picture her funny frizzy-haired sister cooped up in a trailer miles from the coast, but all she could come up with was her sister pacing the bedroom they'd shared in Redding, swearing in that sexy voice: 'Goddammit, Billie, if I don't get out of this hick town soon I am going to fucking explode.' Though when they'd moved to San Francisco, Louise hadn't settled. She had missed Redding and their mother.

It occurred to Milly that Louise wouldn't realise she wasn't Billie any more. For her sister, she was frozen as Billie – thirty-nine years old, blond hair still natural, figure still marginally intact, husband still faithful. Milly might never see her sister again, might not even be informed of her death. This made her feel guilty for wishing Louise would never return to claim her sons.

Ah, Loulou! Darn you!

Yes, it was never pleasant remembering how the Dogtired Ranch tradition began, and so she mostly didn't. Not while she chatted to the United Market clerk, and not now, while she organised their cabin the same way she'd always done: first putting the groceries on the sticky shelves, then making the bed up, then unpacking clothes. She noticed the absence of Mackie and Jaspy, but was relieved they'd decided to use a kennel this summer. Mackie was way too old, and Jaspy was way too young. Both were work. She wondered when August would turn up with those miniature twin girls of his.

He was moving into his own cabin right now. His daughters clung to him, sweat-soaked limpets with Asian faces. Their cabin was at the unpopular end of the ranch. It took years to be promoted to the best cabins. He walked through the wall of midday heat to his dad and

76

Milly's cabin, a daughter glued to each hip. At three, they were still light enough to carry. He was remembering his ex-wife's words that morning:

'I don't trust you one bit, August MacAlister. If anything happens to the girls at that stupid Dog place, I'm going to kill you.' Ah Lam had stood close to him as she hissed these words, so the children couldn't hear. Some of her saliva sprayed him. This had almost certainly been an accident, but still.

He arrived and stood on the porch.

'Hey, Milly,' he called. 'Hot, eh?' He unpeeled the girls, walked inside and opened a coke.

Milly had never wanted to meet, much less love this proof of her husband's adultery, but the love had come anyway that Sunday afternoon when Jack brought him home to meet his siblings, a skinny five-year-old with Jack's eyes and cowlicks. She'd kept her distance, but it turned out that loving August was as involuntary as loving Donald and Danny. He brought out her deepest maternal instincts because no matter how tall he grew, how old he got, he always seemed vulnerable. Growing up in a house with no siblings, a series of hedonistic step-fathers, a mother who could make martinis but not cook a hot dog without boiling the pan dry. In addition, though it hurt to admit it, he was the most beautiful child Jack had produced.

If only his mother hadn't moved into their town! Milly bumped into her at the grocery store, in the post office, at the beach. It helped marginally that Colette was now married again, was wrinkly like the chain smoker she was, and Jack's interest in her seemed entirely platonic. Poor darling August, having such a woman for a mother.

She held her arms open now, inviting his hug, which he duly delivered.

'How are you? Are you settling in okay?'

'Yeah, it's good. But hot, eh?'

None of the cabins had air conditioning. In fact, they had no electricity. Food and drinks were kept cool with blocks of ice in iceboxes.

'Where's Dad?'

'I have no idea.' Flat toned. Wasn't she enough? Jack Schmack. She headed to his daughters, both still in the doorway, edging her way round the room holding on to furniture. Her leg was bad today. It came and went. Heat and tiredness didn't help.

'Come in, girls! It's…it's me!' Jack was Grandpa, but she hadn't decided what they should call her. *Grandma* seemed a presumption, but would *Milly* seem to exclude them from the tribe of their cousins? Milly and Jack had seven grandchildren now, including Louise's.

'Milly, you should get a cane. It would be much quicker. Much safer.'

'I am fine the way I am,' she said, teetering as she closed the dangerous gap between a table and the doorway. A moment of no support. Would she make it?

August, pouring milk for his daughters, watched nervously out of the corner of his eyes. The girls stared at her with identical serious faces. Oh, this was all so ridiculous and predictable. The minute Milly pictured falling, she knew she would. Wham! A cloud of dust rose from where she fell. It was a soft, rolling fall. No damage, just that familiar indignity, and Milly lay there, giggling.

'Oh my!'

'Jesus Christ. Are you all right?'

Her laugh was like crying. A high-pitched, helpless, soft noise.

'I'm fine. Just give me your hand for a minute.'

August levered her up, and she swallowed her giggles.

'Where is Ah Lam?' she asked.

'Ah Lam's not here this year. We're not together any more. I told you.'

'Did you? Well, tell her we miss her,' stubbornly avoiding August's eyes. She'd only known this wife for a short time, but felt obligated to keep her present somehow, if only in her name spoken out loud. Goodness, it took her long enough just to learn how to pronounce it. She stared at him hard, then looked away when he looked at her.

'Well, it couldn't be hotter,' she said. 'I hope Ah Lam's not stuck in commuter traffic.'

August sighed, and the girls clung to him again, their hands sticky.

'Milly, mind if I leave the kids here for a little while?'

'Not at all.'

He disentangled himself from the twins and let the screen door slam. The girls glared at Milly. She'd never seen such dark eyes. They were all pupil. And their black hair was exactly the same length. Aside from their different clothes, they were identical. And so petite! Like dolls.

'Um...Miho?' Looked carefully to see which girl responded, but both girls continued staring. She smiled her biggest smile.

'Well, Miho and Chiew, what will we do with you? I know, let's make play-dough.'

It used to work, she was thinking. Playdough, the making of it and the playing with it, used to eat up entire afternoons. The salty, crusty texture, squished between fingers.

'Where's the flour?' asked one girl suddenly. Milly startled. They didn't look old enough to talk.

'And a bowl?' asked the other, looking round the room sceptically.

'Ah,' said Milly, remembering she had no ingredients for playdough. 'I'll tell you a story instead. Bring me a Coke please. And the cookies. Bring me that bag of cookies.'

The girls exchanged a fathomless look, did as they were asked and collapsed against her legs. She hoped they wouldn't make a break for it. She doubted she'd have the strength to hold on to them for more than a second. She looked at their bodies, soft limbed, tumbled together. She wanted them to like her but felt this was unachievable, so contented herself with observing their beauty.

Jack, meanwhile, was sitting by himself in the air-conditioned resort bar, having a Coors. He'd just reached that state of inebriation where he felt happiness – there was no other word for it – pouring in. He was revisiting the best parts of his life. That big European prize one of his authors won, and Jack had taken the stage too and bowed, and everyone had applauded. Lizbeth's alabaster shoulders, when she'd worn that green silk dress and moved into his arms to the tune of 'Moonlight Serenade'. Walking in to Paul Elder's Books with Milly (when she'd been Billie), on the corner of Sutter and Stockton on Valentine's Day. Choosing *Catcher in the Rye* by Salinger and then drinking cocktails in Vesuvio Café. He remembered wanting to ask her to marry him, and then drawing a love heart with their initials on the fly leaf instead. Not even telling her it was there – just giving her the book later. It was only their second date, after all. He had liked himself so much then. Several epiphanies hovered just outside these memories, close enough for him to taste them. Ah, wisdom! Acceptance of imperfection! Clarity! Life was good. He was about to order another beer, when the screen door slammed open.

'Hey, Dad.' August slumped on to the stool next to his father.

Jack's epiphanies evaporated and he sighed. The barmaid brought two Coors without being asked.

'Augie, how could you screw up your marriage so quickly?'

'Yeah, well. That's what I like about you. Always good for small talk.'

'Bullshit. I don't know what's wrong with you kids. Seems like you're all...marital wimps.'

'How about Billy and Maria? They just celebrated their tenth anniversary.'

'Ten years! That's nothing. Amateurs. What was so wrong with whatsherface?'

'Nada. It's me. Guess I'm a screw up,' he said, looking up and smiling like a child who had just been caught eating the frosting off an uncut birthday cake. Then softly, 'I know, I know. She's nice. A good mom. Doesn't drink. Doesn't mess around with other men. Has a great job.'

'You seemed okay. Happy. What happened?'

'Nothing really. Well, some stuff happened, okay? But mainly just the same old story as everyone else. The old cliché. You know. And I got busted.'

'Jesus,' said Jack. 'That's just plain dumb.'

'Fuck sake, Dad, you can talk.'

81

'Why'd you have to go and get caught? At least I never got caught.'

'Liar.'

'Well, okay, obviously, me and your mother. But at least I married someone who could forgive a little... peccadillo.'

'Thanks. Peccadillo. Love to hear my entire existence summed up that way. Anyway, *did* you marry someone who could forgive?'

'She's still here.'

'Like she had a choice, Dad.'

'That's mean.'

'Sorry.' Beer drinking pause. 'What would you do if she ever stepped out?'

'What?'

'If Milly ever found someone else. Fell in love with someone else.'

'As if!'

'What, you don't think other men have been attracted to her? Your wife is gorgeous.'

Another beer drinking pause.

'She did, actually, step out once. Or wanted to, anyway. I don't actually know.'

'Seriously? No! Seriously?'

'She's human. She met some guy at college. He was in a wheelchair, believe it or not.'

'You saying crippled people aren't attractive?'

'Give me a break. Anyway, we'd been married a long time. I hated it, but it didn't mean the end. In fact, when the day came I realised it was over, I felt so sorry for her I took her to Monterey for a weekend. Without kids. It was like a second honeymoon. Or a better first one.'

'Well, you know what I think? I think you are pretty damn lucky she's still with you. No offence, Dad, but you are kind of a dick.'

Another pause while they both drank beer, and watched the barmaid. Jack turned to his son with a smirk. August frowned, then they both laughed in their usual way. Loud, helpless, irreverent laughter, drawing looks from others in the bar. Then a winding down.

'Anyway, you're the one with another divorce on your hands, Augie. Me and Milly are still together.'

'Whoop-de-doo for you.'

Jack swigged more beer. 'You think *I'm happy?*'

August sighed, looking suddenly about twelve.

'Oh crap, August. I never liked whatsherface that much anyway. Kinda cold, wasn't she? Super efficient.'

'Not really. Why can't you ever remember her name? It's insulting.'

'It's not going to be easy now, Augie. You realise your new girlfriend's going to drive you insane too. Probably within six months. Insane. There'll be some little thing, like the way she starts to wear her hair, or some expression she gets when she's pissed off at you, or the way she votes. Then it'll be over. This phase, gone. Never get it back, that way you feel at the beginning. But you've got to hang in there anyway, because what's the alternative? New wife every five years? You listening to me?'

'Uh-huh.'

'Anyway, you've got those little girls in tow now. Nothing is going to be simple ever again.'

'Thanks, Dad. I was hoping you'd cheer me up.'

'Just think it's a shame, that's all. Not the smartest thing you've done.'

'Yeah. Keep it up. Like taking ecstasy, having a beer with you.'

August found his daughters covered in cookie crumbs on Milly's front porch.

'What are you doing?'

'Squishing ants. Look. There's the ant graveyard,' said one of his daughters proudly, while the other dispatched more ants.

'Milly?'

'I'm right here,' she called from the dim inside. 'I am watching them every minute. Thank God you're back safe and sound.'

'Milly, I've only been half an hour.'

'Safe and sound,' repeated Milly with genuine relief.

It was the best part of the day, still sunny but not hot, when Jack wandered back.

'Hi, honey. I got the milk and bread you wanted. How you doing?'

'Are August and Ah Lam really getting divorced?' blurted Milly. 'Is it true?'

'Ah Lam! That's her name!'

She was sitting in the shadows, her eyes bright, staring into his. And was that lipstick? She was wearing her yellow dress with red roses printed on it. It always reminded him of a dress she'd worn when young – a red dress with yellow roses. He couldn't help noticing she was actually very pretty at the moment. He felt a sweet ache start in his groin.

'There's nothing wrong with their marriage, Jack. I don't understand it.'

A silence, while Jack rinsed his face off at the kitchen

sink. The water came straight from the spring. Freezing and delicious.

'Maybe Augie is in love with someone else. It happens.' Slurring a bit.

'What's that got to do with anything?' Handsome big-nosed Harold flashed into her mind, and she blushed. 'They have children. You irritate me.'

'Want a beer, Milly?'

'What's wrong with August?'

'Where's the bottle opener?'

'You should talk to him.'

'Milly. Honey. Have a beer.'

'I'll have a Coke.'

And then, listening to the fly-buzzing, cricket-chirping evening grind down to darkness, and after the occasional interchange about the whereabouts of the matches and the potato chips, Jack and Milly subsided into their old silence. Their oldest silence, not of tension or animosity. There was no energy at all in this silence. This was the placid and private silence of this particular marriage when no one was looking. Jack had stopped noticing that his wife looked pretty in certain lights and in certain alert moods. He was thinking what he always thought about when not talking or working or reading a spy book. Women. For instance, that new novelist from New Jersey. He pictured Agata something-or-other, wrapping her long legs around his back. What if he bought her that turquoise necklace he'd seen her admiring? He never would, not in a million years, but what if he did? Lucky August, a free agent.

Milly was thinking about dinner, and mentally reviewing the ingredients in the cupboard, wondering how they'd combine into a meal. Strangely, those bags of groceries from United Markets seemed not to contain anything nutritious. Mostly junk food and beer. So dinner tonight – macaroni and ketchup? Under this was her eternal free-floating anxiety about…everything. She had to hold this base camp steady, or the world would implode. Silently, just a soft *whoomph* like when she fell and the dust rose, and soon it would be as if there'd never been a Mr and Mrs MacAlister.

'Jack!' she said, after an hour. They had not lit the lanterns yet, and sat in shadows. The heat finally seeped out of the day, and a semblance of energy trickled in.

'What is it, honey?'

'I'm fixing dinner now.'

She levered herself up, and started edging along the table like a non-swimmer holding on to the side of the pool. Extraordinary, she thought yet again, how pain-less her disability was. You'd think not being able to use your own legs properly would *hurt*. Then, for no reason, she decided it was time for another puppy. Company for Jaspy when Mackie was gone.

Jack opened a pack of bear claw pastries and reached for a John le Carré. He considered this: when you got to seventy, eating junk food took on a whole new dimension. Forget booze, forget Prozac. Forget Agata's long legs. When all else failed, when you were sunburned and you didn't give a shit about your waistline, and one of your sons had dumped yet another wife, and your own wife kept wanting to buy more puppies and she was a terrible cook – well, there was always bear claws.

Milly slowly lit the lantern on the table. Unlike most folk, they hadn't begun using battery lanterns yet.

'I *love* this,' she said.

'What?'

'This lamp. The hissing noise. And the smell. What is the smell anyway?'

'Kerosene. It stinks, Milly.'

'I know. I love it.'

TWO YEARS EARLIER

A Date with Lizbeth

❦

'Aren't you taking the dogs?'

She couldn't take them for walks any more, not with her leg so undependable.

'Not this time,' he answered. 'Going to the store, and you know how they hate being tied up. Anyway, Scout can hardly walk these days, and Mackie always poops in the middle of the damn sidewalk.'

'Well, okay. We need more milk.'

She was ironing. She still ironed his shirts as if he was going to the office every day. She ironed each one, and hung them neatly in a row in the part of the closet that was his.

'Okay. Actually, I might go round to see Ernie and Bernice on the way back.' Jack paused in the door frame, then stepped back into the house, made himself act relaxed. 'Might be a while, honey.'

'Okay. That's fine.'

'You know Bernice.' He made the yackety-yack sign with his fingers, and she smiled.

'Uh-huh.'

'So, see you when I see you.'

'Toilet paper. We need toilet paper too, Jack! And canned dog food, not that dry stuff.'

Off he went. The sky was a clear winter blue, and the air was deliciously clean and cold on the back of his throat. Walking without leashes felt strange. Like when he gave up smoking but kept feeling the ghost of a butt between his fingers. He replayed a memory: Lizbeth and himself, dancing to a Benny Goodman song played by a local band at the Fairmount. She was wearing a green silk dress that left her shoulders bare, so he hardly knew where to put his hands. On the slippery fabric? Her skin? She was short, very slender, very young looking – eighteen, but looked about fifteen. Her breasts pushed up from the dress like very sexy marshmallows. He was only twenty-one, but he'd been a soldier for two years. Dancing with her, he felt older but still inexperienced. If only he could dance. It was nerve-wracking, concentrating on where to put his hands, as well as where to put his feet.

Her hair was red, the kind of red people stared at. It had a fancy name. Titian blonde. It fell in soft waves down her bare back, and a part of him wondered if she was aware of it. Did it feel nice to have one's own hair caressing one's back? Did it tickle? Someone asked them to smile, took their picture (which was the photograph that still resided in his desk drawer), and when the shutter clicked, he magically forgot to be clumsy, and off they'd danced in each other's arms. He had one arm around her tiny waist and she had one arm around his back, and pulled him in close, close, till he could feel her heart beating and he blushed but did not pull away. Their free hands were entwined and raised, and her head nestled into that indent below his shoulder, so he felt tall. This was the most exciting thing to happen to Jacko MacAlister to date, including the war, including that wild camping trip with Ernie, including winning the cross-country that hot August in '44. Her head right there, just below his chin, and her body curling into his. Damn! He could still taste the vermouth, smell her perfume. Something heady, and mixed up with her own sweet perspiration. The windows had been open, to let in the summer evening breeze. Acacias? No, more like gardenias.

And now, after all these years, after all those imaginings, he was going to see her. A postcard with a black-and-white picture of Market Street after the 1906 earthquake. *Hey, stranger! Am in town for a funeral (old aunt Bethany), let's meet up for lunch at Marin Yacht Club.*

Milly was beautiful still, and he loved her, damn it, but she couldn't make him feel like this. Same with Colette. They'd both seen all his less flattering selves too many times. They knew him. It almost made him hate them some days. And so Lizbeth remained the most beautiful girl in the world. (And the reason his daughter was called Elisabeth, but no one knew that but Jack.) Lizbeth was the original love of his life.

He suddenly felt his bowels clench. He ordered his intestines to freeze. To not even fart till given permission. The closer he got to the arranged rendezvous the faster his heart raced. It was not pleasant. Goddammit! This was why he'd decided to walk – walking always calmed him. He made himself slow down. A cloud scooted in

90

front of the sun, and it was almost frightening. In less than ten minutes, he'd see her.

The first time was a September morning in 1947. They were both in freshman year. The GI Bill had given him an escape route from his past; he was the first MacAlister to attend college. (His father would have felt threatened, but his mother was proud. His sister, Ivy, too. She sent cards saying so. *You are a genius!*) Lizbeth been sitting behind him in English Lit I. He'd heard her laughter first. If laughter could sound intelligent and sexy, hers did. When she responded to the lecturer's question about Dickens, he'd had an excuse to turn around and look at her. He'd only dated a few times in high school. Then there'd been the oddly moving prostitute in Japan. That had felt like a kind of love too. Her numb responses to his kisses, her blank face, had touched him, and he'd left her un-touched (and kept his money). But turning and seeing Lizbeth was the first time his heart had ever stopped. Then resumed like a marching band.

The last time he saw her, they'd met at the Larkspur Half Moon Hotel for a drink. She'd persuaded him not to pick her up at her parents' house, and she rushed in twenty minutes late. He'd been on his second beer, half listening to the football game, nibbling on popcorn though he had no appetite. For three years, they'd been…well, Jack had called it *going steady* but Lizbeth called it *just going places with a friend*. Because she was also going places with other men, and she was a straightforward kind of girl. No secrets. No shame. They went dancing, walking, to parties, movies, picnics. There'd been kissing and holding hands and hours and hours spent simply clinging to each other, fully clothed. A time of blissful torture. An intensity of yearning that felt like it must culminate one day, *must,* and yet Jack had been strangely content with this limbo. It drove him wild sometimes, thinking of her with other men. But whenever she was with him, he felt utterly convinced he was the only one who mattered. None of the others would be able to bring out this confiding, cuddly side of Lizbeth. She was the most exciting girl he had ever met. But something had shifted, and all week she'd sounded different on the phone. Evasive. Now here she was.

'Sorry, Jacko. Sorry, I couldn't get here any sooner.'

'No problem.' He kissed her on the mouth, noticing her lips were slack. She tasted of garlic. She often did, but it never bothered him.

'Smoke?'

'Sure.'

He lit her cigarette and she sucked hard, pursed her mouth and blew a perfect smoke ring above his head.

'Show off,' he said.

'Jealous.'

'Drink?'

'Coke. Oh, hell, a screwdriver.'

'You okay?' he asked.

'Sure.'

'Good.'

'Actually, not okay.'

Then she blurted it out, before their drinks came. She was going to Paris. One of her less respectable, less discreet male friends frightened her father. He'd enrolled her on an art course at the Sorbonne. She'd take a year break from Cal.

'He can't do that. Just say no. Tell him about me. I'm every father's dream boyfriend for their daughter.'

'Ah, Jacko. I want to go, actually. I mean, imagine. Paris!'

Some team scored a touchdown on the radio, and as she stopped talking, the bar crowd cheered. Then the announcer started shouting about how incredible some footballer was. Jack could hear the crowd going wild, behind the announcer, behind this bar with Lizbeth perched on the bar stool next to him.

'Sure.' He inhaled his cigarette so hard, it burned his throat like scalding coffee. 'I get it. Paris. Wow! When?'

'Next week. I'll miss you, Jacko. Will you write?'

'I don't know. Maybe.'

'Please! I'll die of loneliness if you don't write.'

'Sure, I'll write.'

'And I'll be back before you know it.'

He'd taken her home early, feeling sober, despite four beers. Usually when they walked, she fitted perfectly under his arm, with her arm around his waist and their footsteps falling into an easy rhythm. But tonight he kept having to slow or speed up; he couldn't get it right. They walked towards the lit windows of her house, which was set way back from the sidewalk. A tall Victorian house, with a wraparound veranda and turrets over the windows. The shadows of her family were moving from room to room like they always seemed to be doing, always doing one thing or another, and he suddenly understood this might be it. This time, when they parted, they might never meet again.

'We'll have so much fun when I get back, Jacko,' she said, as if reading his mind. 'I just know we will. Imagine how amazing it's going to be, to see each other after not seeing each other for so long. It'll be a gas, Jacko. Really.'

Had it really been a simple as that? Mutual love, cruelly thwarted by protective parents? Now he sensed something less romantically tragic. He'd looked up to

93

Lizbeth, but had she merely adored him the way one adores an affectionate, loyal puppy? She'd always found excuses to not meet his mother, whereas he was a frequent visitor to her parents' much grander house. He remembered her mother's charming manner, and his own complete submission to it. He'd eaten his first oyster in that house, and pretended it wasn't. Denied his own class. So what mixed-up class were he and Milly now? Not working class any more, but not solidly middle class either. If class was a language, they'd become fairly fluent in middle class, but working class was still their first language. Perhaps it held them close; bound by a common class in a middle- and upper-class enclave? No doubt, they would always dream in the language they'd grown up with.

Suddenly he realised he would always dream about Lizbeth. In fact, he didn't think he could manage life without those memories. No matter how wonderful she still might be, she would never compare to his dreams of her.

When he walked back into the house, Milly was killing ants. She sprayed them with Windex, then wiped them away with paper towels. It was her annual winter campaign, but the miniature armies kept finding ways into her domain. No matter how many she killed, long trails of them appeared every day in the bathroom and kitchen.

'Is that you, honey?'

'Yeah.'

'You weren't very long at all. Wasn't Ernie in?'

'Huh? No. He wasn't. What's for dinner?'

'Hamburgers. Where's the toilet paper? And the dog food?'

'What? Store was out of the kind you like. I'll go into town tomorrow. You want a drink?'

'No, thanks.'

He almost always drank on his own, and he always asked her anyway.

'Okay, hon. I'm going to make a drink.'

She looked up from her ant massacre, frowning. Then as he turned to go, she said: 'Oh, why not. I'll have a beer.' It seemed to be a special occasion, and she didn't want to be a wet blanket.

THREE YEARS EARLIER

A Spanish Bus

Aug 14th, 1992, San Miguel and Madrid.
noon

Jack was putting their suitcases in the trunk, mentally checking he had everything. Tickets. American Express checks. Wallet. Milly's first passport and his battered, multi-stamped one.

'Milly!' he shouted. 'We're going to be late, Goddammit.'

'I am coming. We are not going to be late.' Every syllable enunciated clearly and calmly. She limped down the hall.

'Jesus, Milly, what are you, a crip?'

This was their private joke. It was such a terrible thing to say, to hear out loud, it always made Milly laugh. But not this time.

'I am coming as fast as I can, jackass.'

'Hey, no need for that,' snapped Jack. A swearing woman was just plain trashy.

Jack took a wrong turn at the airport, and couldn't get back to the long-term parking lot.

'Godfuckingdamnit.'

Milly giggled.

'What's so damn funny?'

'You. Your face.'

More giggling. A very girlish giggle.

'Shut up, Milly. It's not funny.'

There was silence for a few minutes, while they made the journey to the freeway so they could come off it at the correct exit.

'Jack, remember when you were Jacko and I was Billie?'

'What? Yeah.'

'When did we stop calling each other that?'

'What?'

'Remember? We used to be Billie and Jacko, and now we aren't. When did that happen?'

'Oh Christ, Milly. You really don't remember? You changed back to Milly so Willy could be Billy.'

Pause, while Milly frowned out the window.

'Jeez, it sounds so stupid when you put it like that.'

'And I went back to Jack when I got that new job at Golden Gate Freight, remember? Anyway, we were born Milly and Jack. Not such a big deal. We were kids when we were Billie and Jacko. It was a phase.'

He signalled for the on-ramp, and they merged into the commuter traffic.

'When we were married, we were Billie and Jacko to everyone. Even on our wedding invitations. Were we kids then?'

'I'm trying to concentrate, Milly. Can you please just be quiet for now?'

'Sorry. It's just I was thinking about Louise and Chuck's wedding. And then about when we got married. Forty years ago! And I remember you rushing me that day, just like this morning. Well, later that day, after the reception, we were off to the hotel. You kept worrying about the traffic. You said: *Hurry up, Billie, for Christ sake, will you please hurry up!* I remember it because I hadn't ever heard you talk like that before, like I really irritated you. Like you didn't like me one bit any more, and couldn't wait to get the honeymoon over with.'

'Can you look out for the right exit? Is that it?'

'You seemed like someone I didn't know at all. Just for a few minutes.'

Jack negotiated the turning, and headed over the overpass to re-enter the freeway.

'It seems like yesterday,' said Milly. 'I can still hear you, and see you, exactly as you were. You were so darn cute. And then you scared me.'

'How many exits back to the airport, do you remember? Is the long-term parking lot the first exit?'

'In fact, I seriously wondered if it was all a big mistake.'

Jack sighed heavily. He still flew for Dulcinea business – book fairs in London, New York, Frankfurt, Sydney, Ontario. He didn't understand how all these new roads had appeared so quickly.

'Did you hear me? I wondered if I'd made a big mistake in marrying you.'

'Uh-huh,' he grunted.

'It was a really beautiful wedding, though, our wedding, wasn't it? I still think about it.'

'Is that it? No, must be the next one.'

'But it hardly seems like you and me who were in it. Like Billie and Jacko were other people.'

'It was a long time ago, Milly. Why do you always get in talky moods when I can't listen? Now, can you please look out for the sign that says long-term parking lot?'

The car ahead braked. Jack didn't notice the brake lights because just then Milly shouted:

'Oh my God! I didn't turn the iron off! I don't think I did, you know. Do you remember me checking?'

Jack hit his brakes, but too late, and they both watched as they slid into the rear of the car in front. So slow there was no surprise, just their own faces cringing in anticipation of the crunching noise.

'Godfuckingdamnit, Milly!'

They missed their plane and were given seats on a later one. They used the pay phone and called Sam, who lived a few hours from Madrid. No one answered.

'It's the middle of the night there right now. He'll be asleep,' said Jack.

Settled in a plane at last, Jack ordered two gin and tonics from the stewardess. Poured both gin bottles into his own glass, and gave the tonics to Milly.

'It's all right,' he said to the staring stewardess. 'I'm an alcoholic.'

'I don't want tonic,' said Milly.

The stewardess asked her if she'd like anything else, and she said no even though she was actually very thirsty. She sat in silence, staring occasionally out the window, but mostly at the back of the seat in front of her. When they were somewhere over Utah, Jack said to her, without looking at her:

'Cut it out, Milly. You can cut it out now.'

'What are you talking about?'

'You can stop sulking.'

'I am not sulking.'

'Knock it off. You can talk now.'

'I am talking.'

'You know what I mean.'

She did not reply. A small smile played on her lips. It took six hours, but well worth it.

'I said,' in a slow patronising tone, 'you know what I mean.'

She coughed, in a fake way, and yawned. Also in a fake way.

Then she calculated how long it had been since she last urinated. It was almost seven hours, back in the airport. She could feel her bladder like a hard balloon. The collapsible cane Jack made her bring was under her seat. She'd been watching people walk back and forth to the bathroom, and imagining the journey herself. A few times she got up the courage, but then the plane juddered and her determination failed her. This was her first flight. So far, she was more daunted by prospect of falling in the bathroom than the plane falling to the earth.

'Milly, I am asking you a question.'

'Are you? What is it?'

'Well, not exactly a question. But I want you to quit this.'

'Yes, Jack.'

'I'm getting tired of it now. You win.'

'Are you saying you apologise for blaming me for the accident?'

'Goddammit, Milly, you always go too far.'

'Excuse me?'

'When will it be your turn to apologise? Everything is always my fault.'

'Fine! I love you, goodnight,' she said, flicking her hands in a dismissive gesture. As if she'd now washed Jack out of the seat next to her, and he was not there. She closed her eyes, willing herself not to fall asleep, afraid of peeing herself. Aside from that, flying was a piece of cake.

'Oh great. Typical. Good to know you haven't changed since you were…three.'

'I am tired,' she said with eyes closed.

'Why exactly are you tired?' He finished his drink and signalled to the stewardess for another. 'What do you do all day, every day?'

Since Billy left home, about three years ago, he was always thinking this, often asking this, so did not expect an answer now. She opened her eyes and looked at the ceiling.

'Well, since you ask, for one thing, aside from the grocery shopping, cooking, doing the laundry, vacuuming, mopping, and making sure there's always milk and toilet paper, I buy presents and cards for the kids. And the grandkids. And your sister, even though we never see her. And my sister too, even though we never see her either. And Ernie. And Bernice. I even remember the birthdates of your cousins. I choose gifts, gifts that show I know them. I wrap them and send them. You think that's easy?' She counted on her fingers, three times. 'That's twenty-nine birthdays. Not to mention Christmas, anniversaries, Easter, Halloween, July 4th, New Years.'

'You are joking. You call that work?' He snorted.

'I also fret. I worry about everyone. That takes time and energy too. Did you know that since Easter, Elisabeth has been getting headaches that make her throw up? Her son was diagnosed with asthma and she's not sure if it's allergies or just him. And Donald refuses to pay those parking fines, so he has to go to court now. Billy's Maria is pregnant again, and her youngest is only three months. Danny has another interview next week, and if they don't give him this job, I honestly think he might go back on the bottle. Sam is smoking too much grass, isn't he supposed to be outgrowing that now? He seems more addicted and spacier every time I talk to him. And August, well! Where do I start? I phone him every day now. Just to make sure he's still on this planet.'

'I know. Colette said.'

'Was she complaining?' She turned to look at Jack now. 'She doesn't have a leg to stand on, in that department.'

'No, just mentioned it. I think she likes it that you worry about Augie.'

'Good. She doesn't deserve such a nice kid. All the kids are nice. I like to talk to them every week. See how they are. Make sure they know I'm interested.'

'Jesus, Milly. I bet they love that.'

'And there's the dogs. I worry about Scout and Mackie a lot. San Pedro Road is getting so busy, and you know they have zero road sense.'

'That's easy. Let's get rid of them.'

'Ha. Ha.'

Jack laughed.

'You think worrying is fun,' accused Milly, ending the conversation by closing her eyes again.

Jack turned to look out the window. This trip to Spain to visit their son already felt like hell. He thought of the expense, the unlikelihood of there being any pleasure in it for himself. The likelihood that they would somehow manage to get lost, get sick, argue, not get on with his son's Spanish in-laws. Oh God – all the artificial smiling and small talk in a foreign language. The murderous boredom of pretending to have fun. All Milly's idea, this trip. These days it felt like every day was just one compromise after another. An endless exhausting delay of his own gratifications. The thought running through his mind most often was: *As soon as I finish blahblahblah, I will get to do what I want finally. Alone!* Some days he felt like he was cracking up, and the only thing holding him together was the routine of work and the morally doubtful hope for widowerhood. He was sixty-five and should be selling the business soon. It didn't look like the kids wanted it.

And then he thought of some of his colleagues who'd already had heart attacks. This made his heart pound till he remembered what a pounding heart could cause and he calmed himself down. Ernie just had a pacemaker put in. Lucky bastard, still married to Bernice – who was not ageing well, not like Milly who still looked about thirty-five. But by God Bernice could cook, and talk too. Very good at conversation, old Bernice. Maybe at the end of the day, that mattered more.

Then Jack started to think of Rachel, as was his current habit, but she'd recently turned nasty, so even this source of consolation had been spoiled. Hell. What were Rachel's parting words?

'You're a first-class prick, Jack MacAlister.' She'd looked at him like he was dirt. Worse than dirt. Dirty dirt, just because he'd stood firm about not leaving Milly for her. Oh, and there'd been other words too. Once shy Rachel got up her steam, she'd been like a demented duchess, lording over him. He'd been shocked and hurt. None of it felt deserved. He'd treated her well and been honest from the start. He'd told her he'd never leave

103

Milly. That had not seemed to trouble her at first. In fact, the impossibility of their dalliance becoming more added to the romance. Till last week.

'And you know what else?' she'd said. 'You're a crap lover. Your back pimples are like...like, like purple mountain ranges, you look unbelievably ridiculous naked. I always try to avoid looking at your body. And oral sex! Slurp, slurp, slurp, but in the wrong places. You wouldn't know a clitoris if it looked you in the face.'

She'd lisped *clitoris* as if it was one syllable. Clthrs. Of course, all her accusations were humiliating and untrue, but mostly he'd wanted to defend his back, which was certainly not pimply. It had started out such a promising evening. He'd told Milly it was a late work meeting, and he might even need to stay overnight. While showering and dressing earlier, he'd anticipated hours of fun. And loving words too, of course. Rachel was always so gratifying in that respect. A lover who was not in love with him was hardly worth the trouble, and in reality, he was a little in love with her too. She was pretty and extremely well read. Such a relief to talk to someone who was not trying to write a novel about their childhood or coming of age.

'You are adorable,' he'd assured her, after the dinner and wine, when they were back in her apartment with the wonderful view of the bay. Secretly, Jack liked single women's apartments as much as the women themselves. Their beds were always freshly made, and their bathrooms had fresh towels. Yes, his deepest secret might be that it was their apartments entirely, and the sex itself was... initially sexy, but ultimately disappointing. Depressing. Boring. In fact, he had no idea why on earth he still did it; it pretty much drove him crazy. In his teens, he'd spent

104

years fearing girls' rejections, but these days it seemed the world was heaving with welcoming vaginas. It made him yawn.

To make matters worse, Milly had given him a hard time the next day. So ironic! He'd gotten away with dozens of liaisons previously, and then she punished him for a sex-less event, because bitter Rachel had phoned Milly and told her everything. Then she'd phoned him, to say she'd told Milly everything, because she respected other women enough to warn them about the deceptions of wankers like himself. She'd said this in a prim voice, like she was informing him of his cancelled dentist appointment, or an overdue library book.

And weirdly, since that few days of two women ranting at him, peace had reigned. No more calls from Rachel, and Milly had seemed content. Happy, in a busy, secretive way. The lousier he felt the happier she seemed. It was as if happiness was an actual substance, travelling between them – and some glitch prevented it from residing in both places simultaneously.

The stewardess asked him if he wanted another drink, and he said: 'Why not?'

He glanced at Milly, opened his mouth to make a comment on the chilly temperature of the cabin, just some small talk, but she was still pretending to be asleep. Damn her innocent face! What to think about, then? The stewardess's cleavage? He was sick to death of women and his own responses to their body parts. He should make a start on his novel. He could draft the outline right now. He'd write about Lizbeth. Back to innocence. Lizbeth at eighteen. He closed his eyes and summoned his muse up, instantly feeling calmer. She was sitting under that tree on campus, a eucalyptus tree. She was wearing that red mohair sweater, and her breasts were practically shouting to his hands – *Come on! What are you waiting for?*

Yes, this was where Jack felt most like his real self. The world always felt right when he was not Milly's husband. Not anybody's husband. He farted long and loud, enjoyably. Airplanes were great places to fart, by God.

He was snoring, and Milly opened her eyes and turned to look at him. The second before she turned, she was still filled with righteousness. It had been simmering since Rachel's phone call, and the car accident had just underscored it. He had forfeited the right to be angry with her. Didn't he know anything? His marital crime brought months of clemency for her side. Her indignation was tended to with old remembered grievances. The time the washing machine flooded, the time they missed that play. All her fault, according to Jack. Why was every wrong thing always her fault?

But the second she turned and saw him, saw his open mouth and the way his head was flopped against the seat, all her anger turned to steam. Boiling water – that's what her anger was, and now it dissipated into the air. His snoring was ludicrously loud, even over the engine noise. She kissed him immediately, hard till it hurt and he said: 'Ow.'

She bit his lip.

'What? What'd you do that for?'

'I'm starving.'

Eight hours later they rode into the arrivals area on an electric cart driven by a man called Jose. This was an old person thing to do and embarrassed them both. Milly was concerned about Jack's grey face, and the fact that although the signs were bilingual, the English words were ambiguous and foreign feeling.

'How are you, honey?'

'Fine,' snapped Jack.

They scanned the crowd for their son's face. Oh, was his face ever as lovable as on these occasions, when it felt like he was rescuing them? There were a dozen men, all short, holding signs with Spanish names. Families in ragged clumps, and lovers and spouses and friends, all looking through Jack and Milly.

'Do you see him?'

Silence.

'Jack, are you deaf? I said, do you see him?'

'No, Milly.' Big sigh. 'I do not see him.'

'No need to be cranky. I only asked. I bet he was here earlier and gave up. We should have phoned him from San Francisco to say we'd missed the flight.'

'We did. He didn't answer.'

Jose helped them out of the cart, and they slowly made their way to a McDonalds. Fished out their traveller's checks, bought two cheeseburgers.

'You going to eat that?'

'No, guess not. Thought I was hungry, but. You have it.'

'Thanks.' Jack wolfed down his second burger.

'Do you want his phone number again?' asked Milly.

'No. He'll be here any minute. We'll see him from here.'

A very long thirty minutes passed, then a quicker hour, then a long hour. Hours seemed to be taking turns being slow and fast. Milly felt light-headed and Jack felt constipated.

'I'll try phoning him,' said Jack.

107

'Good idea. You're a genius.'

Milly's heart squeezed, remembering how Sam's voice always sounded on the phone, in her San Miguel kitchen. Tinny and disembodied. An ocean away was *too far*. Every time they took him to the airport, it felt like she'd never see him again. A sense of dying that happened over and over. But they were about to see him today. Incredibly.

Jack spent fifteen minutes trying to understand the Spanish pay phone, while Milly guarded their luggage at McDonalds. When he finally heard the ringtone and a voice answered, he lacked the correct change to insert. Or thought he did. He crammed some coins in, which did not trickle back down as refund. He hung up in a temper.

'Where are we going?'

'To Santa Margarita. Sam's town.'

'But, Jack—'

'It's all right, Milly. I have his address.'

From a large timetable on a screen, they figured out which bus was theirs and what time it left. After several false starts, they figured out where to catch the bus. It was hot outside, but after the cloying air of the plane and the airport, the heat felt energising. And despite little sleep the night before, they both began to feel recharged. At first they waited alone, sitting on their suitcases, then a line formed behind them and they stood, to not lose their place. By the time their bus rolled in and they climbed on, they'd stopped looking for Sam. They forgot they hated each other. Milly felt un-crippled, as if finding their own way in a foreign country had blessed her in some pilgrimage way. Jack glanced at his face reflected in the bus window. Thought: handsome bastard.

They were surrounded by Spaniards and tourists. A

boy sat across the aisle from them, pulled off his shirt and began talking in German to his seatmate, who turned away and ignored him. A large Nigerian woman with her three small daughters spread across the seats behind them. An attractive young English woman two rows ahead climbed onto her boyfriend's lap, giggled softly and whispered to him. The driver started the engine, and as soon as the bus began to move, Milly and Jack fell into a trance. Nowhere near sleep, but not exactly awake. They felt young; calm and excited at the same time. Like children who had evaded their sensible elders. Out in the world, free! No one knew where they were right now. In the whole world, not a soul. Like their wedding day, driving away from the church and all their friends and families with their moist farewells, and heading north on Highway One.

Jack stared out the window, and Milly found herself staring at the young couple. She could only see the tops of their heads now. First the girl's head was higher, then the boy's head. As if they were taking turns leading a dance.

Outside, cars and trucks and other buses flowed past. And beyond that, half-constructed hotels with iron girders pointing to the sky like parched plants reaching for the sun, or maybe the rain. On the horizon, strange mountains shimmered. Jack's hand squeezed her knee, just a quick squeeze, but it was like a thunder bolt on a humid day.

THREE YEARS EARLIER

Meatloaf in Marin

Tuesday Oct 17th, 1989, San Francisco and San Miguel
5:04pm

Walking down Market, at first he thought something
was happening to his equilibrium again. He'd had a
terrible ear infection in the summer that had lasted till
September, and the vertigo and nausea from that had
been terrifying. Reduced him to a kitten. It had been a
hellish day at work today, and that last meeting had been
a killer. What was wrong with Mark friggin Fiordinski?
Mark had ceased speaking to Jack the minute his deadline was mentioned. His bottom lip had protruded in
classic pout, his cheeks flushed, then his face had creased
up and Jack had turned away, convinced he was about
to sneeze. But it turned into a hiccupy wail full of tears.
Like a baby.

'How. Can. You. Expect. Me. To. Write. On. Demand?'
Jack had found a box of Kleenex and passed it over.

110

'Um. Because you agreed to? When we paid you $125,000 last year?'

'I. Am. Not. A. Machine.'

Oh, some days Jack hated writers. Hated books. Hated the whole shebang. He could not wait to get on the ferry, take that first sip of cold Chardonnay out on the back deck, and light up a cigarette. Even while he was worried about getting vertigo again, he wondered if Cheryl would be there, wearing that beige dress with the zip down the front. Sure, she was popular, but it must be obvious to everyone, she preferred Jack's company. They shared a love of hiking and Jack London.

Then the sidewalk beneath his feet rolled – he felt it, a wave starting from his toes to his heels. People were stopping, looking up with startled faces at the buildings either side of Market Street. Embarcadero and the harbour were only a few blocks away, and people started running there. They wove between the slowly moving cars and Muni buses. When he understood it was an earthquake, a strange elation crept over him. A kind of tickling, drizzling through his body. By God, this was it! Something big, beyond anyone's control. Like when he was sailing and the wind suddenly changed direction, the sea began to boil in huge swells, and the tiller needed all his strength just to hold course. He instinctively moved off the sidewalk, away from the buildings, but didn't join the running crowds yet. Then, for no obvious reason, he remembered walking along Market Street more than forty years ago. Walking this very block, in his three-week-old army uniform, with Ernie walking alongside him, in his own three-week-old uniform. Did they look fine? Some pretty girls thought so. A group of giggling girls, in pencil skirts and frilly blouses, wolf-whistled them by the Geary intersection. Clear as day, he all at once saw himself and Ernie as those girls must have seen them. Young soldiers, off to fight the Huns and Nips. Slim-hipped boys, swaggering. No two ways about it, army uniforms were sexy, and green was his best colour. Where were the street photographers when you wanted them?

How strange, for that memory to be slicing into this particular moment. As if the quake had opened a crevice in his mind. Or this particular spot – yes, this might be the exact spot – had suddenly been exposed as layers of history, and naturally he had access to the slice of history that contained his own self.

All that took three seconds.

A woman slammed on her brakes right in front of him, jumped out of her car and started running towards the bay. Jack noticed she left her car door open and the engine running. Linda Ronstadt was playing loudly on her cassette player. *Love is a rose but you better not pick it, only grows when it's on the vine.*

'Well, will you look at that!' he said out loud. 'Hot dog!' Boy oh boy, he hadn't said *hot dog* in a long time. Goddammit, he hadn't said *boy oh boy* in a long time either. What the fuck was happening? Even as he found himself automatically following her, a part of his mind was trying to remember who did that song originally. The rolling seemed to be over. No Muni buses moving, which was eerie, and the sound of sirens and running footsteps, and of course, the sound of people panicking. Hard breathing, shouting, running footsteps. Not a lot of talking. The occasional female squeal. He didn't feel afraid, or much of anything. In fact, he felt quite detached, walking swiftly with the other workers.

These observations took seven seconds.

Irrelevantly, he thought about the meeting with Mark Fiordinski again, and what to tell them on Monday. As if his office would still be there, and his editors still preoccupied with such things as marketing targets and book launch dates. He hurried – worried he'd miss his ferry. As if there would still be a 5:20 ferry. As if all these commuters would be able to get on it.

He couldn't seem to catch up with what was happening. Most days, life felt like he was in the driver's seat, driving himself and his family to a chosen destination, and all the road signs matched the map. And other days, like this one, he felt that life was something he was being yanked through, willy-nilly, and all he could do was keep breathing in and out, and squeeze his eyes tight shut when he had the chance. Like that day his dad had dropped him and Ernie off on the Russian River. It'd been late August, just before sophomore year. Armed with two old rubber tyres and dressed in nothing but their swimming trunks, the plan had been to float down the river half a mile, where they'd be met by friends. Within a half hour they'd realised they were nowhere near their destination. That in fact, they'd asked to be dropped off at the wrong point. The sun had been intense, but that hadn't been the main problem. The river itself was faster than they'd anticipated and sometimes their bottoms scraped jagged rocks just under the surface. They had no paddles, no control, and at first they'd caught each other's eyes and laughed – what an adventure! But soon, they'd grown weary and their bottoms had hurt. They spun round in sudden eddies, edged over small rapids, held on for dear life over bigger rapids. No time or chance to pee, and their stomachs had begun to growl. Around every bend, they'd looked hopefully for familiar sights. And that was what this day felt like. The world was tilting, and nothing was the same. He was sixty-two. Yes, he felt more alive now, but Goddammit he needed to pee again, and that made him cranky.

Three seconds had gone to the river memory.

By the time he got to the Embarcadero, he was telling himself: *So, it's not a normal Tuesday evening after all*, and all those plans for flirting with Cheryl over a glass of Chardonnay on the ferry had to be scuppered. He mentally shrugged. He reverted to anxiety about work. He'd have to remind Madge to check with Bookstop and Cody's, because he was betting nothing sent today would get delivered. He thought (calmly) that things would be in chaos for weeks. He'd need to make calls to Seattle and New York and London, reorganise things. Maybe look up Cheryl's name in the phone book, aim for the next phase. Get past this delicious and tortuous phase of accidental meetings? No, let it ride, he decided. The older he got the more time he had for innocence.

Two more seconds had passed. He was about to cross the road to the ferry building now.

He decided, while crossing, he needed to visit Colette soon. A heart to heart with Colette about August was overdue. What was wrong with that boy? His fifth arrest since he turned eighteen! The smoking grass part Jack could forgive, but the getting busted part – that was just dumb. And a heart to heart with Colette about Cheryl too, come to think of it. He'd already told her about the time Cheryl raised her arms too suddenly and her blouse buttons flew off. Things hadn't really happened till he'd told Colette; she understood everything. Especially she understood the humour. She was single again but sex was permanently off the agenda, thank God. No two ways about it: an unmarried woman one could not screw made the best friend.

Four seconds gone, and he reached the dock in time to watch his ferry leave. It was so loaded with people, it didn't look safe. But the ferry service had acted quickly and another ferry soon docked. He was swept on board with the crowd. He was wearing his usual khaki pants, yellow Brooks Brothers shirt and Rockport brogues, and he carried a battered leather briefcase. His hair was still thick and dark, the cowlicks still boyish, and his corduroy jacket was attractively loose. The ferry bar was open, but the lines were daunting. He scanned the crowd. Everyone seemed to be talking at the same time, squeezed up, everyone touching at least four other people. When he tuned in to the conversations, he noticed some people were talking about what just happened to them, but mostly people were wondering what was happening to their own homes. They'd heard rumours, ominous rumours of fires and collapsed buildings. As he listened, he thought of his own house and his wife inside it. Was she in the kitchen? Since their youngest had left home, dinner time was less sacrosanct. Milly had dinner on the table anytime between 6:00 and 9:00. There'd been a time when she'd change into something pretty for him, wear lipstick every evening, light candles at the table, but these days she seemed…well, a bit mopey. Oh for God's sake, he was not going to waste a second wondering about that.

What Milly was doing, in fact, was sitting in the living room watching the news. She always had the radio on in the kitchen, which was how she'd known to turn on the television news. San Miguel was not on the San

Andreas Fault, and she'd felt no tremors. The dogs had been acting a little restless, but then settled down again. She'd been about to make meatloaf, with bread crumbs and onions and egg, to stretch out the quarter-pound of ground beef she found in the freezer this morning. The week's grocery money ran out yesterday because she'd secretly sent money to August and Danny again. Budget night was Friday, in three days. This always made her angry even before Jack sat down with the checkbook stubs, and his pencil and paper. The third Friday of every month, they fought about money. Well, other times too, but this was a scheduled argument. A fight date.

But now she prayed her husband was not dead. The top tier of an Oakland freeway had just collapsed on to the lower, and the people who had not died immediately were screaming and begging the people below.

'Please! Help me!'

'Someone tell my husband the boys are still at Little League!'

A woman holding a small dog over the edge called out frantically: 'Catch my dog someone, please. His name is Lucky!'

Milly flinched; their pleas were so thin somehow, and hopeless. It seemed voyeuristic, *rude,* to be sitting safely in her chair watching dying strangers. Not actors, not a hundred years ago. Real people, crying for help, now. She tried phoning the children, but couldn't get a dial tone. Had the quake affected the phone? Her house suddenly felt isolated. She felt isolated. She wished the children were here, and were children again. They'd all moved out in such dribs and drabs. The boys had moved back every summer from college, till one summer she realised the boys' room only contained their least loved

116

clothes and shoes. Elisabeth had moved back home three times, when she was out of work or a relationship ended. Billy still came home on semester breaks, and sometimes the others came back to stay a few days or weeks, for a variety of reasons. Perhaps that was why she'd never been sure when a last time was a last time. Once, while visiting Elisabeth and eating lunch in a restaurant, her daughter suddenly leapt up, said: 'Oh! Late for work, got to dash, see you Mom!' She'd been so pretty, so happy, running back off to her life – and that was when Milly had finally realised (with a startling tearfulness) Elisabeth had really moved out for good.

She fed Scout and Mackie, and because her children were no longer children, and because she could not help the people on the collapsed freeway, and because Jack was late, she gave the dogs a whole can each. When they were finished, she stroked each of them and said good boy several times.

Her lapsed Catholic soul resurged. *Our Father, who art in Heaven, hallowed be thy name. Thy kingdom come, thy will be done, on earth as it is in Heaven. Give us this day, our daily bread. Give me Jack – bring him home safely.*

When had they stopped going to Sunday Mass? Sometime just before Billy left home. No discussion or major decision, the habit had just faded away. First missing one Mass a month, then a whole month of no Mass, then it became normal to do other things Sunday morning. Then they heard the priest they'd liked had moved parish, and somehow that liberated them from returning to church at all.

She went back to perching on the sofa arm, watching

television. A hand-held video recorder was cutting down Market Street. Panned down past the Hyatt Regency. Something echoed with Milly in this scene, and it came to her slowly – because this was one of those foggy days – that it was the corner where that book store used to be. Paul Elder's Books, with the arched doorway. Yes! Jack had loved it there, and spent hours choosing which book to buy, then they'd sit in a coffee shop or bar afterwards to talk and read. She remembered his yellow cashmere V-neck. He'd been so skinny, his pants had bunched up under his belt like a kid's.

She couldn't think of a single bad thing about Jack, because she had suddenly leapt to widowhood. She was wishing with all her grief-stricken heart that she could argue about the housekeeping money with her husband just one more time. She'd do anything to hear him say: Goddammit Milly! What do you mean, you don't remember what you spent $12.79 on at Macy's on September 27th? To have him throw open the front door and say: Just a joke, hon, here I am. Not dead at all.

Jack spotted someone he knew, who waved as if he was glad to see him. He made his way over to this man, and it turned out his whole ferry gang had made it on to this ferry too. Someone had bought two bottles of Chardonnay from the bar, and soon they were passing bottles around – no glasses – and laughing hysterically about nothing at all. In fact, the whole ferry had become an uninhibited party. And, oh sweet Jesus, was that Cheryl waving to him from the deck?

He felt as if he was finally getting into his stride. That up till now he'd been practising how to live, how to respond to things. Now he got it. All you had to do was not care.

Tears, prayers and the meatloaf mixture sat on the kitchen counter, with the flies having a heyday. This was one of the best days of Jack MacAlister's late middle-aged life, and Milly was rehearsing her eulogy for him. Also, choosing what to wear. Her black linen with the narrow black belt? Her brown tweed two-piece, if it was a cold day. With that cream silk blouse. Where was that blouse? Been ages since she'd seen it. She turned off the television, to go look for it. He'd better not have given it to Goodwill. Gosh darn that man for always getting rid of her stuff.

FOUR YEARS EARLIER

Glen Miller Died Too

<hr>

May 2nd, 1985, San Miguel, Marin County
2:10pm

At twenty-five, even forty, Jack regarded people in their sixties as an inferior race. Getting that old was just plain rude, he often joked. Loose skin around the ear lobes was never going to happen to him, Goddammit it.

But he must have taken his eye off the ball a few minutes, because: bingo! Jack MacAlister was now fiftyfuckingnine, and life expectancy for an American man was now seventy-four. That was sixteen more years. Christ. Without his glasses, in the bedroom mirror lit only by the flattering low lamp, he was still okay. Just. When he was out on his bike, heading down the grade towards China Camp with the bay sparkling and the warm euca-lyptus air rushing around him like...like a beautiful sexy madness (he'd been reading Kerouac again), well then, he was no age at all. Just his own self, the self he'd been since he could remember. *Jacko MacAlister.* And the whole world was as drunk on its own beauty and stupidity as it'd always been. But when he caught a glimpse of himself in the rear-view mirror while driving on a sunny day – well! *Fuck off,* he told his reflection. And usually refused to glance again, preferring the side mirror. Often drove faster in this mood. Passed on curves. *Death, you asshole, come get me!*

Then, as if mortality wasn't already breathing its nasty breath down his neck, Elisabeth, who was thirty-three, announced she was six months pregnant and two days later his mother fell, broke her hip and within days developed pneumonia.

Perfect.

Elisabeth was not married, of course, nothing as sensible as that. And his widowed mother – silly old woman! What was she doing, still walking around outside at her age, with her joints? The whole point of her moving closer to them had been to keep her safe, but she hadn't kept her part of the bargain. What did mother and daughter expect from him now? Endless hospital visits, flowers, money, babysitting? Milly was already the millstoniest wife in the county, with her limp and her lack of driving licence and her refusal to divorce him on the grounds that she still loved him. When was *his* time going to come? He had a life too, Goddammit, and he was tired of thinking of other people all the time. He was fiftyfuckingnine, for fuck's sake.

'So, Dad, you'll be a grandpa. Pretty cool, eh?'
   'No one's calling me grandpa.'

'Okay. What do you want to be called?'

'Oh, I don't know.' His eyes fell on a mouldy baseball, forgotten under the hedge. He had a soft spot for baseball. It was easy to understand.

'Baseball. He can call me Baseball.'

'It might be a girl.'

'I've got to warn you, honey. Kids are a mixed blessing.'

'Not exactly what I want to hear at this stage, Dad.'

'Break your heart, kids.'

He sighed dramatically. She had a biology degree from Cal. She used to talk about becoming a doctor. He'd always visualised her marrying and raising a family in a house on the Bay, maybe in Tiburon or leafy Ross. Last he heard, she didn't even have a boyfriend, just rented a room on Miracle Mile and worked in Peet's. But he'd always enjoyed confiding in Elizabeth because, while her choices puzzled him, he sensed a rapport with her. She didn't judge. If they'd been drinking, he became expansive and told her all his secrets. It felt great. Though Milly felt excluded and once said, 'Goodness sake, Jack!' when he told her he'd more in common with Elisabeth than he did with her. 'Why are you surprised?' he'd asked. 'We are blood related, after all. You and I are merely married.'

Though now things were shifting. Pregnancy seemed to take Elisabeth over. Overnight, she lost her edgy, intelligent look. He could see the matronly, literal-minded woman she would be become, just like he could sometimes see the cranky old woman Milly would become. Especially first thing in the morning, when her face was wrinkled from sleeping on her side. Those pillow lines used to last a minute – now sometimes she kept them till lunch. He supposed his face was going the same way. His rear-view mirror had certainly given him a shock earlier today.

They went to the hospital to visit his mother. Milly, Jack, and pregnant unmarried Elisabeth. She brought a Hallmark Get Well card, a *Chicken Soup* novel, and some home-made oatmeal cookies. Jack and Milly agreed on this: nice though the cookies tasted, it was hard not to prefer the old selfish, wise-cracking daughter. They'd not agreed on anything for so long, it was a surprising aphrodisiac. They exchanged vomiting mimicry behind Elisabeth's back, while she was propping up her grandmother's pillows and combing her hair.

'There you go, Gran!' Holding the mirror for her. 'Prettiest girl in the...ward. I know, will we say a prayer together? You'll be missing Mass, won't you. Let's say the Lord's Prayer together.'

Jack and Milly froze, not looking at each other. But when she brought her nicotine-stained fingers together to pray, it was too much.

'What're you two laughing about?'

They couldn't answer. In fact, they could hardly breathe. They wheezed and sprayed spittle and rocked on their chairs.

'I think that's enough prayer,' said Grandma MacAlister. 'Thank you very much. Bit tired now, do you mind, Elisabeth?' But her mouth was twitching with a bewildered smile too, as if she was thinking: was every family as odd as hers? How wonderful!

'Tell your sister to come home, Jack. It's time.'

'I phoned her. She said she'd try to come next week.'

'Huh! I'll believe it when I see it. Ivy hasn't been home in...I can't remember how long.'

'She's never been back, Mom.'

'Huh!'

'My sister's never been back either,' said Milly.

'What's wrong with these girls?' said the old lady. 'It's like they've slipped into other orbits or something.'

'I blame men,' said Milly.

'You would,' said Jack. 'See you tomorrow, Mom.'

'Sure. If I'm still alive.'

'Stop it, Mom.'

'What? I know it's a cliché, but life goes just like that!' She clicked her fingers, once, twice, three times. 'It's fast! Short! Over, just when you're getting the hang of it.'

And out they trooped, after planting a row of kisses on her thin dry skin. They took Elisabeth home to her purple hippie house, which she shared with five Sufi dancers. They were often silent with each other, Milly and Jack. Often, there was a tension to their silence. A grudging thick silence, like stale hard fudge. But now, the silence was exquisite. Full of suppressed mirth and more. An unexpected intimacy. Reluctant to drop anything remotely unpleasant into it – they'd both forgotten how to be friendly to each other in the normal way, and the old mechanics of flirtation were long gone – they prolonged the silence. Then:

'Can we go to Bolinas Beach on the way home?'

'Yeah. Great idea,' said Jack instantly, and signalled to take the coastal route. It was not on the way home at all, but he didn't point that out.

It was not a beautiful day. The sky was hazy, the light flat. The world looked jaded. They entered the town, passed the church where they got married, the café selling oysters in the shell, Smiley's Bar, weather-beaten houses and sheds. No traffic at all today. Once at the beach, parked directly facing the surf, Jack pulled on the hand-brake and they both sighed at the same time. Because there it still was. That old Pacific. Serious, freezing, noisy. Often impatient, churning, but right now ebbing, and the smaller waves lapped quickly, unevenly. Just beyond the breakers, the rip tide was clearly visible, a fault line of choppy water. The twice daily argument it had with itself. In or out? Make up your mind! Milly rolled her window down.

'Well! Beautiful,' she declared softly. 'Wish we'd brought Scout. Truman used to love this beach, remember? Scout's never even been.'

'Well, he's only a few months old. Do you want to get out of the car?'

'No.'

'You do, though. Don't you?'

'Of course.' Eyebrow began to cock.

'Well, come on then. I'll help you.'

'I can't walk on sand any more, Jack. You know that.' Lips pressed together.

'Of course you can. You just don't want to limp in public. You're too vain.'

He got out, walked round to her side and opened her door. This was so out of character for Jack, it was almost as funny as their daughter praying. But Milly did not laugh, or even smile. She sombrely took his hand, and let him lever her out of the car and down to the sand. One step, then another.

'Your mom.'

'Yeah?' he asked.

'She's all right, you know.' More slow steps. Step, stop. Step, stop.

'Is she? She never bought me Levis when I was a kid. Always the J.C. Penny jeans.'

'Levis, Schmevis. That was a hundred years ago. I like her. I can't walk any further.' He had one hand clasped under her elbow, the other arm cradling her back.

'Want to sit down for a while? Watch the surfers?'

She made a scoffing noise. 'I can't sit. I'd never get up.' Saying this aloud brought a large lump to her throat. The forbidden self-pity. They never talked about her increasing disability. Easier for everyone. Then without warning, Jack scooped up his wife in both arms and carried her to the smooth rock near the high-tide mark.

'Stop giggling, for Christ sake, you think this is easy? Stop it, Milly.'

But she couldn't stop. Unanticipated joy. She had no defence against this.

He plonked her down on the rock, embarrassed. Stood with hands on hips, looking out to sea.

'Go!' she commanded, swallowing her laughter. 'Have a walk. I am fine here.'

'Really?'

'Go!'

He took his shoes and socks off, rolled up his pants to his knees and set off at a brisk pace, letting the waves wash over his feet and rush up his legs. Every footfall proclaiming he was not fiftyfuckingnine. Strange to be beach-walking without Truman wanting a stick to be thrown over and over, then running off with other dogs and peeing on people's picnics. It was great not having a dog. How had she tricked him into getting a puppy again?

'Thank you, honey,' she called after him, but he pretended he didn't hear.

He felt young now, far younger than he'd felt this morning in the rear-view mirror. He didn't glance back

126

at his crippled wife perched on the rock, but he had a clear mental picture of her and his heart swelled thinking of it. Out of sight, he always fell for her. Goddammit, if she was still a honey, then so was he. So was he! The beach was almost empty, just some surfers and a few dog walkers. Not a sunbathing picnic kind of day. He decided that when he got home, he'd phone Ernie. Ernie had been a grandfather for years now, and lost both his folks. So had Bernice; they were a pair of orphans. This was immensely cheering. Ernie had paved the damn road. Milly had no parents any more either, but somehow that didn't help in the same way.

Watching her husband, Milly felt a swift series of familiar emotions. Attraction (ancient, careworn, hardly recognisable), romantic (in a black comedy way), melancholy (because his posture was slightly stooped and his cowlicks were beginning to grey and thin), and last of all, a raging jealousy. How she yearned to be walking in the surf, just like that. Jack didn't know how lucky he was. She suffered an attack of deep nostalgia for her own fitness. Ten, no, twelve years ago. To just walk on the beach without effort. To dance, to run, to skip. Oh heavens, it would be bliss to simply take her husband's hand by the sea. Squeeze it, as an equal. To be a fellow walker.

They'd had wonderfulness and not even known it, and now here they were. Him striding down the beach, and her bottom freezing on a damp rock. But had the imbalance really started with the accident?

Jack looked back from the curve of the bay and waved, and she waved brightly back as if they were an ordinary couple. She knew just how they appeared – a confident husband protecting his demure contented wife – and she willed herself to believe it. They were normal and happy. Good heavens to Betsy! He disappeared around the headland and her heart sank. The truth was, she had always been trying to catch up with Jack. The phrase *wait up, wait for me!* was never far from her lips, yet rarely uttered. An unwritten rule. What wife in her right mind admitted to wanting what a man had? Competitiveness was not feminine, unless it was sisterly rivalry, like Louise and herself, the way they used to argue and shadow each other through life. But there was no denying, there had also been competition between Jack and Milly from the very first day. When he'd asked her out, she'd rejected him, and he strode away pretending that he cared less than two figs. Darn him! It was so complicated. She was jealous of him, of course, while knowing at the same time he must at least have the appearance of superiority – of being the richer, smarter, taller, older, faster, funnier, best-loved spouse – in order for the whole shebang not to come cascading down around their heads. Bless his little boy heart. Bless all their little boy hearts – Sam, Billy, Danny, Donald, August.

It was all about being a winner, and she wanted to be a winner too. But if she was, she'd lose him. It had been touch and go when her mother died and she inherited a surprisingly large sum – even after she'd sent some to disinherited Louise. A tetchy few months, till she'd planted the idea of a small publishing house. Just a few casual remarks dropped into conversation, not pursued. *Oh, honey, that boss of yours is just crazy. You know tons more than him about writers.*

'I have a brilliant idea, Milly.' One morning over coffee, still in their robes. Their teenagers milling around.

'Yeah?'

'I've been thinking and thinking. You know how City Lights Books is small but still a huge success? And look at Ten Speed Press – just a couple long-haired kids with an idea and the right timing.'

'Uh-huh?'

'Well, here's an idea. We use your mother's money and I quit my job.'

'Uh-huh?'

'We could start our own business. A better publishing house. I'm sure I could take some of our best writers with me. Everyone's fed up with the new regime. Golden Gate Freight is too big for its boots now. So high and mighty.'

Pause. Best to act surprised. Not agree too quickly.

'What would we call it?'

'I'm calling it Dulcinea Press.'

'Dulcinea?'

'Dulcinea. The homely woman Don Quixote thinks is beautiful. I've always loved that. Beauty is in the eye.'

'Hm. Where would it be?'

'The city. Some cheap offices going around Columbus Street.'

'Goodness, you *have* been thinking about it.'

'I'm going to buy a big old oak desk, and have it right by the window. I need a decent view. And everyone in my office is going to be happy because I know exactly what kind of boss to be. And how to treat writers.' Then he'd leaned forward and whispered urgently:

'Taking care of writers is my specialty, Milly.'

She'd noted the shift from *our* to *my*, and smiled.

Women's Libbers made such a song and dance about everything. Elisabeth had given her *The Women's Room* and Milly had hated every page. If a woman agrees to a certain role, then she is not being exploited. The plain facts were: a single woman was the bane of society; a barren woman would go to her grave wishing she'd had kids. And a married woman had to be…be less than a man was, outwardly anyway. Less wealthy, less confident, less ambitious. Preferably less old, less tall. It was not fair, obviously, but it was no good pretending otherwise.

So, two options. Who would prefer to be a divorcee or an old maid, living alone on a tiny budget in a spotless man-less apartment? No, sir, not Milly MacAlister! But she couldn't help wishing he would wait for her, and more. She wished with all her heart she was independent. Truly independent, like Jack was. With a career, with respect. With working legs. Her bottom was getting so numb, she shifted a bit and wrapped her arms around herself. Where was that man now? Darn him. What if the tide came in and she was stranded on this rock? Then suddenly he was behind her, wrapping his arms around her too, so her arms were pinned by his arms, which felt young and strong. Thought evaporated. All those wishes for a tad of her husband's freedom flew away.

Nothing in this moment told her mind, or his, that they were fifty-nine and fifty-seven years old. His mouth nuzzled her neck, till she swivelled her face and they kissed in a way they'd never kissed before. A kiss that surpassed all those other kisses. Those dozens of first week kisses, those hundreds of early married kisses, those thousands of old married kisses. This was the kiss of two grown-ups who had just met. As if recent events had scraped away their personal history.

Two months later, two big things happened on the same day.

'This is Tom. Tom, this is my dad and mom. Jack and

Milly. Actually, you've met already, ages ago. At that Fourth of July barbecue, remember?'

Silence. Tom was five foot two to Elisabeth's five foot seven. He was wearing a track suit.

'Close your mouth, Dad. He's cool about this.' She patted her enormous bump.

'I'm not into genetic vanities,' explained Tom in a low voice. 'I don't look for immortality that way.'

And then the phone call interrupting the celebratory toast.

After Jack's mother's funeral, the family, which now had thirty-six-year-old Tom grafted on to it, ate lunch at Arrivederci. It was a rowdy lunch, and no one observing them would think it was post-funeral. Lots of red wine, loud chatter and laughter. Toasts galore. And under the table, some knees were touching, and some hands were entwined occasionally. At least four, including Ernie and Bernice. *Look at them*, thought Jack – *still at it obviously*. And Sam had brought his new girlfriend. A loud girl in a red turtleneck, obviously synthetic. As a rule, MacAlisters never wore turtlenecks or anything synthetic, but Jack was polite to her anyway. Danny and Donald seemed to be flirting with her, but then they always wanted what Sam had. Colette had brought fourteen-year-old August then discreetly left, promising to return later to pick him up. August, oddly, had loved his grandmother, and his eyes were still red. This puzzled Jack. Had he got his mother wrong? Had she been lovable? The other children didn't seem bothered much by her absence, not even Elisabeth really. Grandma MacAlister had been a crusty cold figure in their lives, not unlike Grandma Molinelli. He'd not had any time to think about her since she died. All the arrangements had fallen to him. Hardly even time to get his suit cleaned. Ivy had sent a card. *Wanted to come to the funeral, Jacko, but think it's been too long now. Think going home might finish me off. I am so sorry you got to do this thing all on your own.*

When Jack returned to the table after paying, there was only his wife left. Billy must have gone off with one of his siblings. Or maybe his girlfriend's mother had picked him up. Maria and Billy rarely spent a whole day apart. Jack didn't care. Billy was seventeen and annoying.

'Well,' Milly said.

He couldn't decipher her expression. He was a little drunk and worried about driving. Something else to stop the mom thoughts. Was his wife about to cry? To throw up?

'Let's go, Milly. Let me help you.'

'No, thank you. I can get up myself. You go to the car, I'll be there in a minute.'

'I'll walk with you, honey.'

Pause. He stood and stared at her. She sat and stared back, then said:

'I said I am fine. I'll meet you at the car.'

'Christ,' he said under his breath. Got the car and pulled it up to the front door. For two cents, he'd drive off right now and leave her. Stubborn woman! He spotted her wobbling a little at the entrance, and a young man rose from his table and opened the door for her. The man glared at Jack. Jack had the window down and he could clearly hear his wife's tinkling laughter and her flirty voice: 'Why, aren't you kind! I was hoping someone would open the door.'

'Oh, for crying out loud,' he said to himself. 'Get in the car,' he told her through the open window.

'Did you see that nice man over there?'

'Get in the car, Milly.'

And off they drove, into the afternoon of his mother's funeral day. Everything was increasingly surreal. He thought of the cinnamon banana cake his mother often baked. Always underdone, so it was dark and easier to eat with a spoon in a bowl. And that box of Christmas ornaments she'd kept in her cupboard under the stairs. Couldn't recall, for the moment, if she'd even had a tree the last few years. There was a reindeer ornament he'd always liked, even as a teen. It had gems on each antler point.

'Isn't it wonderful about the wedding?'

'What wedding?'

'Weren't you listening?'

Nothing in this day irritated him more than her knowing some family news that he did not.

'Of course I was listening,' he bluffed. 'You mean the fact they're tying the knot seconds before the baby pops out? Hardly call that a wedding to be excited about. Not in the ordinary sense, more like a marriage of convenience.'

'He is a nice boy, Jack.'

'Sure, sure. He's very nice.'

'You say nice like it's a bad thing. He told her she was the only woman he'd ever really loved.'

'And she believed him?'

'Oh! To hell with you Jack MacAlister. I suppose you think you know everything about marriage.'

'Well, I'd say it probably has a better chance when there's no baby on the way.'

'They know that! Of course they do.'

'I bet they'd never get married at all, if she wasn't pregnant.'

133

'And that would be good? You don't think strong marriages can come from weak beginnings?'

Oh, Milly was exasperating. That day at Bolinas, the day of that kiss – it might have never happened. Nothing had changed.

Once home, he took a walk to clear his head of wine, then did a bit of editing on Fiordinski's new manuscript. Made a note about an invoice for his secretary to type up. Made notes for a speech he had to give on Saturday, for the Dulcinea Short Story Prize, and better get it right this year after the last fiasco. He'd stood there in a room of 500 people, praising the winning author's ability to convey profound loss without sentimentality, while the author had stood by him frowning, tilting her head, puzzled. How was he to know her story had been a comedy about getting on the wrong train? Was he expected to have read the damn thing? Was it so unrealistic to think the conveying-profound-loss-without-sentimentality was a phrase that could apply to 99% of literary fiction? But this time he was prepared. Even read the stupid story.

He took a phone call from Billy.

'Staying the night at Maria's, okay?'

'But it's a school night.'

'We're going to study. It's cool, Dad.'

'No, it's not,' said Jack. 'It's not, technically, cool at all.'

Maria was on the pill now, so at least there wasn't *that* to worry about. At least Billy had said she was on the pill. Something about her Catholicism had been part of that sentence, but Jack hadn't really listened. Now he could hear Maria giggling and some record playing in the background. Elvis Costello singing about an aim that was true. Well, to hell with Billy. But still, he suddenly

134

wished he would come home. And next year, no kids would live at home. He'd yearned for that day, and yet now he dreaded it.

'Pick me up tomorrow after school, Dad? Got football practice till six.'

'Okay. Goodnight.'

Jack went back to his editing. Secretly he thought what the writers did, and what he did too, was a kind of magic. It made him smile. A man took his thoughts and emotions, and without opening his mouth, transferred them via black scribbles on paper into the minds and hearts of people he'd never meet. Strangers. A silent miracle every time, but everyone was so used to it, the miracle was unnoticed. Aside from perceptive people like himself, of course. Now and then, he appreciated the miracle of writing.

Jack and Milly ate dinner in silence. Scrambled eggs on toast. Not-hot eggs on soggy bread.

9:00. Time for the news and a brandy. They settled in their usual places and watched the news. At a commercial, he turned the volume off and said, looking at the television screen:

'You remember when Glen Miller disappeared?'

'Jack, what are you talking about? Glen Miller was killed.'

'No one knows that, Milly.'

'Well, he's dead. Died years ago.'

'Well, I wasn't saying he was alive *now*. I was just asking...'

'Of course I remember when he died,' she said with contempt. 'You think I'm stupid?'

Oh, his heart was so heavy. It was so unfair. He sighed,

and she heard it and turned to him with her old dispelling smile. Melted things a little.

'Sorry, honey. What about Glen Miller?'

'Nothing.'

'Come on. You brought it up.'

'It's nothing, forget I mentioned it. It's just, I was thinking. It was pretty damn sad, wasn't it?'

'I suppose. I was only a....a sophomore in high school, I think.'

'Did you cry?'

'Yes, I think I probably did. All the girls cried.'

'Yeah. Same at my school.'

'Did you cry, Jack?' she asked with a laugh in her voice.

'What do you think?'

'No. Yes. I don't know. I didn't know you then. Maybe you were soft when you were eighteen.'

'I did not cry.'

'Of course not.'

Jack stood up and poured himself another large brandy. He said from the kitchen:

'But that doesn't mean my heart wasn't broken.'

'What? I can't hear you.'

'Nothing.'

'Hey, didn't your dad die that same year? When you were a senior?'

'About six months earlier, when I was a junior.'

'Terrible.'

Milly watched the TV a few minutes, then said:

'Must have been tough on your mom. First her daughter jumps ship, then her husband dies, then you head off to war.'

'Huh. Yeah, I suppose. Never thought about it, to tell the truth.'

'Are you sad about your mom?'

'What a question.'

'Well, you haven't said anything. Or acted sad. Have you cried? I haven't seen you cry.'

'It was just before Christmas.' A second brandy was finally hitting that particular spot behind his ribs.

'What was?'

'When his plane disappeared. Over the English Channel.'

'Oh, for heaven's sake. You are nuts. Where's the remote? What are you doing now? Hey, I wanted to watch that!'

'Oh shut up, Milly. Just shut the hell up, okay?' Jack put on a record, lowering the needle carefully.

Milly opened her mouth, then closed it. Then opened it.

'She was my mother-in-law for thirty-one years. I miss her too, you know.'

The opening notes of 'In the Mood' purred into their living room. And with it, those dark green shoes he bought to wear to the spring hop, and that girl's perfume – like no flower on earth, just a sweet smell on a sixteen-year-old girl named…Doris! Doris Smithers was her name, and when he asked her to dance, her face lit up like a firework display spelling out YES. God, when was the last time a girl looked at him with such undisguised, wholehearted admiration? Well, aside from Colette of course. He'd stepped on Doris's toes repeatedly, and each time he apologised, she giggled. Giggled as if she'd drunk a whole bottle of gin.

My throat hurts, he wanted to say. The words were in his mouth, as solid and sour tasting as lemon-flavoured hard candy, or unripe plums. If he could speak he would say: My throat is so swollen I cannot swallow. Everything hurts. My eyes burn, my chest hurts with every breath, and my stomach. My stomach has something hard and sharp and painful stuck right in here, just above my belly button. Why aren't we able to really talk to each other? Tell each other how we really feel? That hurts too. I'm lonely.

He turned the volume up.

'Fine!' said his wife. 'I don't care. I am going to bed.'

He stood by the stereo, and stared at the record as if it needed him looking to keep going. He rocked on his feet a little, to the music.

'Darn dog!' she said, as she tripped over Scout. 'Darn stupid leg!' she yelled at her lame leg.

'I agree. Stupid leg.'

'What do you mean? I haven't noticed you tripping over the dog. Haven't seen you take ten minutes to walk up the hall to bed.'

'You think your lameness has just affected you? It happened to me too, you know. Your being crippled happened to both of us.'

'Oh, good night!' she shouted.

He waved one hand a little.

Then from the hall, her hard flat tone: 'I love you!'

Jack pretended he hadn't heard. He was wondering why, despite his dad dying, losing Glen had felt like the first proper death of his life. It had been crushing to think that there would never be another Miller record to line up to buy. That all there would ever be of Glen Miller was already here. Christmas had been ruined.

'Jacko-honey, what on earth's the matter? You haven't touched your turkey.' His mom's voice, a little thick with sherry, but well meaning, warm. She'd even tried to touch

138

him. The old mom hug, and he'd almost fallen into it, but then he caught her eyes and there was a definite laugh hiding there. Mocking him and his sadness! He'd pushed her aside and left the house, slamming the door. He took a long walk, that long ago Christmas evening, every step in time to the Miller songs in his head. Over and over again, 'Moonlight Serenade', 'In the Mood', 'Everybody Loves My Baby'. Till he felt a humming personal connection. Glen was right there, walking beside him – only him, because in this neighbourhood, only Jacko MacAlister understood and truly loved him. Jacko was walking his wake.

Till he suddenly stopped under a dripping sycamore – it was drizzling, of course – and remembered that Glen Miller was missing over the English Channel, presumed dead. Not definitely dead. He could be alive! And this thought cheered him up so much, he dived into it with everything he had. Not a walking wake any more, he practically skipped back home. Alive! Somewhere in Europe, in his Army uniform. God, Glen looked damned good in that khaki. Someone somewhere was probably cooking something nice for him right now. Maybe it was all a government plot to keep it secret. Maybe Glen was being used as a spy now, or maybe he'd been injured by his own army, and they were so embarrassed they were nursing him back to health in secrecy. Or maybe Glen had been kidnapped, or taken prisoner, or maybe he just had enough and bailed out himself. Met a cute French girl, and he wanted to be a normal guy for a while. No wife, no fans, no fame. Yeah, that would be like him. Had enough of all the fuss. Back to basics.

Just before high school graduation, Jack signed up with the army. All the way to the recruiting office, and all the way home, Jack kept beat with the music. His feet took the rhythm, and his head and shoulders took the brass, threading its sexual, sassy way through. War come get me!

When the record was finished, Jack tried to turn it over but he was too drunk and his hand was clumsy. The needle fell on the record and the noise was so awful, tears finally came. And because he was alone and drunk, and because there would never be another Glen Miller record or cinnamon banana cake baked by his mother, and because his father was finally someone he missed, and because his wife was someone he could French kiss on the beach but could not confide in, he did not bother wiping the tears or blowing his nose. Just lay down on the sofa, fell asleep and carried on crying in his sleep. Deep shuddering breaths, snot and tears on the sofa pillows. Scout, who at six months was already a lumbering Labrador, contentedly licked Jack's face.

A month later, into the world came the first grand-child. Not a dramatic entrance, more like the quiet departure of his mother. Just the usual sequence of small ordinary events, leading to a push in a darkened hospital room and another human, luckily with all the usual number of digits. Milly set about buying blankets and teddies. She felt the world turning on its axis, and everything was exactly as it should be. Her family was expanding finally. This was why she married, why she had children.

Jack didn't give the baby a minute's thought. He spent more emotional energy on wooing that young Asian lesbian novelist who won the Baker Prize for her unpublished novel. She had everything the critics would love. They'd eat her up. He had to sign her up before anyone else noticed her. And there was Ike, one of Milly's dogs – he was twelve now and needed to be taken to the vet again about that alarming skin condition. And he had to get his mother's house valued and on the market. Paint it first? Might get their own house painted while they were at it.

No, Jack did not open one of the bottles he'd set aside years ago for special occasions, but when this first grandchild was presented to him, at a week old, he smiled absent-mindedly and said:

'Well, hello you.'

The symmetry was pleasing. Mother gone, grandchild born. And a boy too! Well, this was pretty good, really. And it was good, too, that he didn't miss his old mother much, wasn't it? She'd been alive, and now – incredibly, silently – she was not. His life seemed to have swallowed up her passing, quite painlessly. Her house had been cleared out in a day, a surprisingly easy task. She'd already shed so much. But instead of being relieved, her empty house had made his heart flutter in a mild panic. He would die one day and his having been alive would amount to nothing too. He would be missed only occasionally and then not at all, and everything that mattered to him would be regarded with the same cynicism and ignorance that he brought to bear on his mother's belongings. Consigned to the Goodwill or the garbage.

He looked at his new grandson. A whole human being who recently was not, and now he was. He looked at the baby's hands all curled up, and his downy eyebrows, his scrunched up face.

'Has he got a name yet?' he suddenly asked, looking up at his daughter.

'No. We had lots of girl names ready, but.'

'Well, how about...'

'Jack? Forget it, Dad. No offence.'

'No! How about Glen?'

THREE YEARS EARLIER

Cooking with Leftovers

Oct 3rd, 1982, Berkeley
1:31pm

'But what's wrong with her?' Jack asked his nephew Donald.

'Nothing. I just don't think she's the right one, Jack. I don't want any doubts when I walk up that aisle.'

Pause, while Jack frowned and poured himself some red wine.

'You think people marry without doubts?'

They were sitting at a restaurant table in Berkeley. This was the lunch to mark Donald's graduation, albeit four months later. Finally! He'd done all kinds of things his aunt and uncle disapproved of. His mother would have torn her hair out if she'd known. Milly's letters to her sister were always brief, edited versions of the truth. Just the highlights, with some fiction thrown in for good measure. If Louise became worried she might

143

want to reclaim her sons, instead of just sending them birthday and Christmas gifts. (For three years running, she'd sent them each crystals with instructions on their magical properties.) Donald's father would have...well, Chuck's reaction was difficult to imagine. In fact, no one remembered him very well any more. An unremarkable man, even his facial features had failed to register in his sons' memories. Danny said their dad wore wire glasses and smoked a pipe, but Donald swore he did no such thing. Chuck had phoned once or twice and said he might visit if he was passing through Marin, but he never had. No one seemed to mind much.

In the ten years since he left high school, Donald had tended dozens of bars, put his thumb out on hundreds of freeway on-ramps and tried most drugs including heroin once. Married young, divorced young. Primarily, up till now and this English degree, he'd not given Milly and Jack a thing to brag about to their friends. It was a nice restaurant, but no one really wanted to be here. It was a symbolic gesture, and no one could think of much to say. It was only Donald, Jack and Milly. Danny had sent his excuses that morning – a dentist appointment he'd forgotten. Elisabeth was in Mexico volunteering on a clean water project. Sam was living in Santa Barbara with his plump Bible-thumping girlfriend and using his engineering degree to work at Taco Bell. Billy was a sophomore in high school and a quarterback – today he was off with his team to play a game in Eureka. August was only eleven and lived with his mother and new stepdad, in Stockton of all places. Though he did join them for some family occasions.

Donald sighed, looked out the window. His uncle said: 'Hmph!' As if he'd just thought of something.

144

'Did you get your ring back?'

'No. But it was her ring, Jack. I mean, she'd bought it. She'd bought both our rings.'

'Huh.'

Pause.

'Did she ask for your ring back?'

'Yeah, Jack. I gave her back the fancy ring.'

'You could have said you'd lost it.'

'What?'

Jack poured the rest of the bottle into his glass. 'Aren't you drinking anything?'

'Water. I'm drinking water.'

'Am I the only one drinking? Christ.'

It had been a bad year for Jack. His glorious new publishing house, Dulcinea Press, was in its second year – it should have been a fantastic year. The IRS letter had been very upsetting, and their audit terrifying. What about the American dream? he'd felt like shouting. Why are you making this difficult, when I've lived by the rules (sort of) and am already working my butt off? Where's my reward? He'd had to find a partner for financial reasons. An intelligent pretty woman, very pert breasts, very wealthy east coast family. He thought he'd been flirting with her, but as it turned out, she'd seduced him, then dumped him like a sack of potatoes. Moved on to his new editor. Plus the Republicans were in again, that greasy Reagan and that racist Bush. The world was going to hell.

'Where the hell's Milly?'

'Bathroom?' said Donald.

'Stay single. Best way. Your life's your own. She's been too long.'

'I'll look for her.'

He found Milly deep in conversation with a waitress

145

in the entrance hall. Her face was animated. When Milly saw her nephew, she said:

'Donald!' As if it was an amazing coincidence to see him here, of all places.

She introduced him to the waitress, who eyed him sympathetically.

'No one wants to marry me either,' she confided.

'No? Well, nice to meet you.'

He took Milly's arm.

'You don't get out much, do you Milly?' he whispered.

'What, honey?'

It was a long limp back to the table. Donald found himself limping a little in sympathy.

'Oh, Donald, you are going to have to bite the bullet one day, if you want a family.'

'Excuse me?' He could see Jack ordering another bottle in the distance.

'You've had so many girlfriends, nice girls, every one.'

'Yeah. Wish I could make up my mind.'

'Silly boy!' Milly stopped walking, to say this. She waited till he was looking right at her, then said sternly:

'Don't you realise, it doesn't matter who you choose, it just matters that you choose.'

'That's bullshit. Sorry, Milly.'

She shrugged off the apology. 'Like jumping off a bridge into a river.'

'Sounds like suicide.'

'I mean a river you can swim in, honey. Scary, and probably freezing. But if you don't get in there, you'll end up standing and watching it flow away to the sea without you. You'll be high and dry!'

'So you think it's random. I just have to randomly grab a girl.'

'Not just any girl. A nice girl. You had a good wife and you threw her away, Donald. That little girl you married adored you like a puppy! And now this fiancée. You give up too easily. Marriage is like a job. You've got to put in the hours.'

Donald hated this. He hated this snobby restaurant, he hated his aunt's advice, he hated his uncle's assumption that he'd be better off single. Most of all, he hated the fact that in an hour he would be back in his quiet, messy apartment, with the beautiful summer evening empty before him. Since he stopped drinking, beauty just made him want to cry.

'Oh, Milly,' he whined. 'You have no idea what my life is like.'

'What is your life like?'

Pause.

'I know,' she blurted, when he didn't answer. 'I know it's not easy.'

'My life is fine. I'm fine, okay?'

Jack and Milly drove Donald back to his apartment. He had no car, no job, no money, and now no fiancée. He soaked the full humiliation of sitting in the back while his uncle drove and his aunt asked him if he was still taking vitamin C. The expensive lunch formed a hard bitter ball in his gut.

'So what's your plan now?' asked Jack, rather belatedly as Donald opened the door to get out.

'I'm going to travel again. I told you.'

'No you didn't.'

'I'm leaving next week. South America.'

An afterthought of kissing Milly – he turned back from his front steps, indicated she should roll down the window, leaned in and kissed her soft cheek. He shook Jack's hand across her chest.

'Thanks again. Great lunch. Take care,' he said.

His voice was heavy with emotion. What kind of emotion was difficult for them to tell. Jack decided Donald sounded defensive. Milly thought he sounded tired, overwrought, like he needed a glass of milk and an early night. Donald had always needed sleep to cope.

'Bye then,' said Donald.

'Goodbye,' said Jack, looking in the rear-view mirror to check traffic.

'Be careful, Donald. Write! Phone us anytime!' called Milly. 'No hitchhiking!'

'Yup!' He mumbled something else, smiled, and then he was walking away, and Jack and Milly were driving in silence.

'Did you hear that last thing he said, Jack?'

'Nope.'

'I think he said he loves us.'

'Yeah, right.'

Milly remembered the day her sister left. They'd both been hung-over from Jack's fortieth birthday party. Louise's voice on the phone from some service station, rushed and nervous:

Got to get away awhile, Billie. Give me a chance, yeah? Bob's a good man, but I can't drag the boys with me this time in case it doesn't work out. The boys will be better off with you and Jack. I'm crap at everything. I'll be back one day real soon, I promise. Counting on you sis. This is not about enemas. Or astrology. I love him.

Milly remembered the drive to her sister's apartment, and gathering up the boys. The grabbing of sweatshirts and pyjamas, T-shirts and jeans. Randomly stuffing them in grocery bags, then pulling the boys out to her car. They'd been twelve and thirteen; small for their age, shorter than Milly. A pair of skinny adolescents with croaky voices and gawky walks. They'd shaken her hand off, politely, proudly, and followed her to the car. They'd known, by then. They had read the note left on the kitchen table. Unbelievably, they were not crying or acting traumatised. At one point they even had an argument about who was going to carry Hammy's cage. Apparently the hamster belonged to them both.

'Come on, come on. It'll be okay,' she kept repeating. She had left Billy strapped in his car seat all this while, counting on him not waking. Then back home, she ordered pizza and everyone ate it standing up in the kitchen, then later watched *Bewitched* in silence. All five children had piled on the sofa, Billy sucking his thumb on Elisabeth's lap. Jack and she had sat in their usual arm chairs, and she remembered him knocking his ashtray to the floor twice, swearing, and she'd scolded him in a whisper. As if everything was normal and swearing was still not allowed. She'd set up two camp cots in Sam's room with sleeping bags.

Donald wet the bed. In the morning, he apologised to her for spilling a glass of water, but he couldn't find the glass. Then he accused his big brother of spilling water – Danny was always teasing him. When he realised it was his own urine, his face darkened. She hadn't been able to decide whether to take the boys to school or not. She had to get Sam and Elisabeth off to school first. In the end, she took her nephews and Billy to the International House of Pancakes, and the boys finished their tall stacks of blueberry pancakes and link sausages and hash browns. They ate as if they were starving, and even giggled when the waitress teased them about playing hooky. High-pitched, girlish giggles.

The boys later asked when they could go home, and she told them she hoped they felt at home in her own house. That she loved them, the whole family did. They shyly reminded her they each had their own room at home. They spoke in a confidential tone, with trust, as if she could arrange for the same privacy. As if she was Samantha Stevens in *Bewitched*, and could wrinkle her pretty nose and magic two more rooms. It was a three-bedroom house. Elisabeth was the only one with her own room now; Billy was still in his parents' room.

'Here's the plan,' she said over the maple-syrupy plates. 'I'll get bunk beds, and I'll mark territory in the room. So you'll each have a bit that's only yours. It'll be great. You can give your bit a name, like a country name. Or a football team. And no one will be allowed unless you invite them, right?'

They both stared at her.

'Who gets to keep Hammy?'

'You can take turns. I'll make a rota.' Still not a minute to think of her sister. Her head had squeezed with not thinking of her. Louise taking that dawn Greyhound heading to Texas, her shabby yellow suitcase in hand, her sons still in their beds.

'Jack, Jack! Stop the car!' she commanded now, after a few blocks. The panic had been building up, filling her chest like a liquid.

He slammed on the brakes. The car behind him honked, so did the car behind that car.

'Jesus, Milly. What is it?'

'We have to go back.'

'Goddammit, why?'

'Something's wrong. We have to turn around, Jack.'

'Are you insane? You are insane.'

'Jack. Please. Please, Jack.'

'Donald is twenty-seven years old. If he's in trouble, he'll have to deal with it. Did we go running to our parents when we were twenty-seven?'

'We had each other, Jack. It wasn't the same thing.'

He indicated to go on the freeway.

'Oh, Jack. Don't you care?'

'Actually, no, not at this very moment. I don't care, okay? We've given him money, love, advice. He's never starved or had to sleep rough. Up to him now.'

Silence.

'Goddammit, Milly, do you know what that meal cost?'

Jack merged too early and a car flashed lights at him. 'Goddammit,' he said again, and they drove home.

Milly did not speak to her husband until dinner was ready. Billy ate in his bedroom. Since the other kids had left home, he often refused to come out of his room. His father assumed he masturbated a lot. His mother thought he missed his siblings. Or was ashamed of his parents.

'Jack! Dinner's ready.'

'What is it?'

'It is what it is.'

'Hamburger. Thanks. My favourite.' He barely ate, half expecting poison.

'Where's yours?'

'I am not hungry,' she said and left the room. Strangely, her limp was less at times like this. Ike followed her, his toenails clicking on the hardwood.

151

'We're getting another dog, by the way,' her voice trailed down the hall.

'Are we?'

'I need another dog,' she said. 'Another Lab.'

He looked at his hamburger, then sniffed it.

She'd get another dog (dogs needed dog company) and she'd leave Jack. It was obvious he was a terrible person. A heartless parent and a philanderer and mean with money and a dog-hater. She sat alone in the bedroom, arms round herself. She imagined leaving, but she couldn't get past the practical difficulties. Where to go, and with what money? What would Harold say if she knocked on his door, bag in hand? His wife would certainly be concerned, and her own children horrified. In any case, there seemed to be no residue of love for Harold in her heart, so what would be the point? She had no idea where all that intensity had gone. Perhaps it had evaporated over Monterey Bay, in her husband's arms, her physical fidelity still intact. She was either shallow, or she'd not been in love with Harold after all, merely lonely and susceptible to flattery. She'd been a fool, a lucky fool. Like that time with her neighbour Jeff, when she'd flirted with him and he'd assumed an attempted rape was the correct response. Terrifying at first, but after a short while she'd felt entirely unscathed by the event. Hadn't most women fought off unwelcome advances? And hadn't most wives had crushes? It all made her feel worldly.

But not worldly enough for independence. If she left this house, somehow, without money, would Billy come with her? Would the older children still respect her, want to visit her? Would she end up like her sister, Louise? Mentally unstable, impoverished, vulnerable? No real home, a transient? Or like her mother – coping with singleness by being manly, tough, aggressively competent? She couldn't even remember if they had enough suitcases, or if over the years Jack had taken over the suitcase department. What had happened to those powder blue cases from her single life? She used to live without Jack. A long time ago she'd been a feisty secretary who escaped from the valley. She'd spent her own money and never had to account to anyone. How many times had she decided to leave him? And each time she had not, she felt her marriage settle more heavily around her shoulders. Somehow she'd become paralysed, both literally and metaphorically.

Slowly the day dimmed and she still sat, ignoring her hunger pangs and her shivers. She'd get up in a minute, turn on the heating and cook something for herself. She mentally listed all the possible solutions to her dilemmas. Leave Jack? Not possible. Mend her shattered femur bone and pelvis? Not possible. So, she did what she always did when feeling helpless. She thought of Jackie Kennedy, throwing herself through the barrage of nurses and orderlies to get to her philandering husband bleeding to death on the operating table.

'*Get out of my way! I want to be with him when he dies.*'

She thought of darling Charlie. She thought of who he might have become, and of finding Jack alone in the dark hallway that funeral night, blubbering. The way she'd loved Jack for blubbering.

She thought of Grace Kelly, of her beautiful face going through the windscreen as her car tumbled down a hill last month. Life was precious and it was lucky to be alive at all.

Her day began to look better. She replayed that scene of Jackie in her bloodstained pink Chanel suit, forcing those doctors and nurses to allow her to hold her husband's hand as he died.

Eventually Milly rose, switched on lights and the heating, and headed to the kitchen for some food. When she got there, instead of food, she decided to write a quick note to Donald. Better than a phone call, and in any case she didn't want to be overheard by Jack and she needed to do something right this minute. She found some paper.

Darling Donald – It was great seeing you today, you looked GREAT.

Milly had a weakness for capital letters, and all her letters were extra large, loopy and long hand.

I am sending you this (began to write the word *letter*, then crossed out the *let*) *check for your trip.*

We are so proud of you. The world is your oyster. (Underlined the word *oyster* three times.)

She found the checkbook, wrote a check for $100, inserted it in the envelope, already construing the justification she would give to Jack, come budget night. She sealed and stamped the envelope.

'Milly!'

'What is it, Jack?' She had heard the television, and noticed he was watching the news, but it must be commercial time now because he'd turned off the volume. She could see his body stretched out on the sofa and his neck craning round to call to her, but he couldn't see her. She was on the other side of the refrigerator, slipping the letter into her pocket.

'What are you doing in there, honey?' His brandy-warmed voice.

'Just getting something to eat.'

'I'd skip the hamburger. Think it's gone bad.'

This made her smile. She'd forgotten the undercooked hamburger she'd slapped in front of him earlier. She had excavated it from under some old ice cream, hoping it tasted as old and disgusting as it looked, in its ancient freezer bag. Probably the cow had died more than a decade ago.

'Do you, honey? Thanks for letting me know.'

'So what are you making?'

'Oh, some pasta, I think.'

'With pesto?'

'Probably. I think there's half a jar in the fridge. Should still be okay.'

'And black olives?'

'If there are any. Think I put some in a bowl some-where.'

'You could heat up that French bread, maybe. Sprinkle some water on it first, wrap it in foil. Press some garlic.'

'Suppose I could do that,' she said, not reminding him she knew very well how to freshen stale bread. 'Aren't you watching the news?'

'There's a bottle of red left, I think.'

'Oh yes, there is. Thanks, Jack, but you can watch the news now, I'm fine.' In her prim cold voice. 'I'm still getting another dog, Jack. I mean it. I'm thinking maybe a spaniel this time.'

'Uh-huh.'

'Another male.'

'Huh?'

She boiled the water, pressed garlic, sliced some chorizo from a few days ago. It was pleasing, this using up of old things. It made her happy – to watch a nutritious meal emerge from what could easily have ended up in the garbage. It harked back to their more frugal days, the best days. Food really had tasted better then, when she'd make the best of what she found lurking in corners.

Marriage could be like that, she thought. Taking what was, and rather than tossing it all away in a fit of temper, finding a use for it. Economy, that was the answer. When the water boiled, she automatically put in enough pasta for two. *Out of my way,* she said to all the forces and temptations of divorce. *I want to be with him when he dies.*

FOUR YEARS EARLIER

The Advent of the Big-Nosed Man

❦

Nov 28th, 1978, College of Marin, Kentfield
10:21am

Milly kept coming back to the image of those American mothers in that small settlement on the north coast of South America. Jonestown. Last week, those women gave toxic Kool-Aid to their children. Put it in their baby bottles and plastic cups, and then what...put them to bed? Read them stories, sang last lullabies? Then those mothers drank their own Kool-Aid and curled up with their children. She kept thinking of the people who entered Jonestown afterwards. They must have thought everyone was asleep at first. Almost a thousand people in a very still, deep sleep. And before she could get used to that idea, just yesterday, councillor Harvey Milk was gunned down in the middle of a normal working day in his office in San Francisco. The two disasters were connected in her mind.

The world!

The world!

Life seemed to knot into messy disasters, in between trundling through spells of routine bad news. 1968, for instance. She hadn't thought about it at the time, but that had been a messy knot of a year too. Martin Luther King and Robert Kennedy – both killed. Then losing Louise and gaining her boys, with their good manners and wan faces. All within seven weeks. She looked back now, and saw that it took a decade to properly appreciate the size of that catastrophe. World leaders being gunned down; hard to get the right perspective on her sister's departure.

And now, Harvey Milk and Jonestown. Mayor Moscone too, she reminded herself guiltily. It worried her that no one seemed to think his death was as tragic.

It all put her in a certain mood. Anything at all might happen now. She felt a little raw, a little ragged. Not quite herself. And it had to be said: she felt a little more alive than she had last week, when life had been less frightening.

She noticed things more. Different things.

For instance, she noticed Harold's wheelchair. She made an effort to open the door for him when he came to class, and immediately felt less disabled and therefore less depressed. As if he was obese, and she'd been worrying about her little paunch. (Aha! Not so fat after all!) Her left leg visibly dragged all the time now – she was a lopsided ship, always trying to correct the list. There was no pain if she let her right leg take her weight when walking, but excruciating pain if she forgot. And twice now she had fallen. She'd been angry and not wanted any help getting up. Unsuspected depths of stubbornness had risen up, without her summoning them. She was surprised by her

158

own determination. Apparently, Milly MacAlister would not be crippled. She would not.

The second thing Milly noticed was that Harold had an extremely large nose. A beak, leaning over his Roman mouth. Olive skin, high intelligent forehead, lazy-lidded dark eyes, and that nose – enormous. Fascinating. And strangely attractive, the more she looked at it. She was sitting to the left of him, one row back, so she could gaze at his profile anytime she liked. A curiously compulsive habit.

The teacher was talking about the symbolism in *The Heart of Darkness*, and possible influences on Conrad at the time, particularly related to the political upheaval in...Poland? Maybe Milly was not listening carefully enough. Her pen slid over the notebook, making doodles of daisies. Outside, blue jays were yammering away in the acacia trees, as if they knew the winter blossoms were weeks away. There was no heating and the room was chilly. Despite her new fisherman's sweater, she was cold. Not being able to move quickly affected her circulation, and she often felt cold. The teacher had moved on to Conrad's family history, and his publishers. The public's reaction. Milly tried for a full ten minutes to focus, and made a page of neat notes. Rewarded herself with a glance at Harold's nose. But he turned just then and their eyes snagged. She was too slow to look away, and blushed.

'Did you manage to make notes?' he asked when she opened the door for him later.

'Oh! I tried, but I could hardly concentrate. Too cold. And I need this class to get my degree.'

'Is it your last one? Me too.'

'Really? That's amazing!' she gushed.

'Yeah.'

'How long have you been going?'

'Three years.' He held up three fingers.

'That's amazing.'

'Three years for you, too?'

'Yes! Well, ten, actually,' she admitted. 'One class a semester.'

'Excuse me,' said the teacher, trying to squeeze around them and leave the classroom. Then he turned and said: 'Have you two entered the short-story competition? Deadline is tomorrow you know.'

'Yeah,' said Harold. Then in a low voice to Milly: 'Got to admit, I think it has a chance. Best thing I've ever done.'

'Me too,' said Milly, and laughed. 'Actually mine's pretty awful, but who knows. Thought I'd give it a whirl.'

Then Harold and Milly found themselves in the hall. Light poured through the glass doors at the end, white and hard. Classroom doors opened and shut, and students chattered around them. About Jonestown, about Harvey Milk, about the Huichol Indian exhibit at the de Young museum, guitar practice times, dates for the movies, sales at the Gap, bands playing at the Fillmore this weekend. Two ponytailed boys shouted to each other down the hall:

'Dude! Free concert tomorrow at Golden Gate Park, want a ride?'

'Cool, man. I'll bring my bong.'

This – just this – was why she was here. To be a college student! Well, not really *one of them,* but to be immersed in their world for a few hours a week. And to eventually join the elite tribe her husband belonged to: of college graduates. Milly stood straight, balancing on her right leg, left foot hardly touching the ground, her backpack nonchalantly over one shoulder like all the younger students. She noticed that her right hand had found its way to the back of Harold's chair.

'It's electric,' he said. 'I don't need pushing.'

'Oh! Of course. I probably couldn't really, anyway.'

'Let's have a coffee,' he said abruptly. 'Do you have time? Let's go to Café Olé, my treat.'

His chair began to whir down the hall, towards the ramped doors, but then the doors flew open and a group of boys in identical athletic shirts rushed in. So many robust bodies! Harold looked up at her – he had to look up at her – and smiled.

'You okay? They'll be gone in a minute. Hold on to my chair if you like.' He swivelled to provide a protective barrier.

She felt them rush past, all that youth and carelessness, and she shivered because she was about to sit in a cafe with a man not her husband. She looked round at the boys, and they were good looking, of course, but all their noses were small.

'Right,' said Harold. 'You ready? Let's go.'

'Yeah, let's go,' she echoed.

And just like that, aged fifty, with her oestrogen ebbing daily and rogue hairs appearing on her chin, and her breasts finally grown large, Milly MacAlister was smitten. Like a sudden bee sting, or a clap of thunder. She felt nauseous and stunned. It turned out that loving Jack had not inoculated her from loving another man after all. It must be a different kind of virus, she found herself thinking, having spent years charting her children's cold and flu bugs. She knew you didn't catch the same virus twice, but the world was heaving with other viruses, and the same viruses mutating. It was inevitable to be infected again. Wasn't it?

Jack didn't seem to care about avoiding infection. You think he would, after Colette. Her husband, the philanderer. But unlike him, she'd never go that far. Goodness me, how foolish that would be! No one could help getting a crush, but there was no excuse for acting on it. None whatsoever. Wives who had affairs were just plain tacky. These thoughts took two seconds, while she walked lopsidedly to the cafe. During the second cup of coffee – and she didn't even like coffee – Harold brought her thumping to the ground with:

'My wife likes to bake muffins. Chocolate chip. But she's begun putting all sorts of weird healthy stuff in them. Seeds. Wheat germ. Brewer's yeast. Yech. You ever tasted carob? Disgusting.'

Wife! Of course, but why did he have to say it?

'I like muffins to be sweet and fattening, myself,' she said. She gobbled up the last of her muffin, to demonstrate her sensual appetite.

'Ditto.'

'My kids all have sweet tooths,' she said. 'That doesn't sound right, does it? Sweet teeth? No, not right either.'

Harold smiled, then he waved the waitress over and ordered two more muffins.

'My husband likes muffins too,' said Milly, lobbing the word husband casually. Well, it was only fair. A spouse for a spouse.

'Is he a student here too?'

She laughed. 'Jack? No! He graduated twenty-five years ago. Four of our kids are away at college. Well, our son and daughter and our two nephews, who've lived with us for years. They're all over the state, no one chose the same college.'

'Goodness. Four.'

'Still have one at home. Billy. He's ten.'

'Five!'

Milly considered mentioning seven-year-old August. They were seeing quite a lot of him these days, since Colette got remarried.

'Do you have kids?'

'Nope!' he said with gusto. Then a quieter, 'No.'

'Oh. Smart thinking.' Floundering. She wished she could shirk the kids immediately, join Harold in his childfree world.

'Well, we did have one, but she was stillborn.'

'Oh, no! I'm so sorry. We had a baby that died too,' she rushed in, relieved.

He looked out the window at the traffic in the drizzle. She did too. A woman crossed the road pushing a shopping cart full of what looked like wet rags. She wore three coats over a pair of jeans, and a headband with rain-sodden feathers. Others quickly walked round her, with umbrellas and rain coats. Milly sighed and felt guilty for using poor Charlie as a social lubricant. She hadn't mentioned him to a stranger in years. What kind of woman was she? She pictured his dinosaur sleep suit, which instantly invoked genuine grief.

'Do you have a degree already, or is this your first?'

'My first,' she said, heavily.

'Want to catch up, eh?'

'Sort of. At first I just thought it would...'

'Be fun?'

'Improve things.'

Jack had not stopped her, but he hadn't exactly encouraged her either. He treated her classes like a cute housewifely hobby. College of Marin was not a university, and everyone knew an Associate degree was a nothing degree. Last night, when he called to her from the sofa asking if there was any beer, she'd answered in her preoccupied voice: 'I'll check as soon as I finish this.' He'd walked into their bedroom, and there she'd been, her forehead wrinkled in concentration, her right hand scribbling notes. He'd blinked and left.

'I just wanted to...to improve myself,' Milly said to Harold. 'See if I could do it. Sounds silly, doesn't it?'

'Not at all. I want to, as well. Learn. Go on learning. But I keep daydreaming in class, and I'm not finding it very easy to study at home either.'

Milly was dying to ask why it was not easy at home. As they left, she blurted out:

'Why don't you come for dinner some time?'

Oh my God! Who said that? She felt possessed. Maybe just noticing a man's nose was enough to open the door to that kind of thing.

'I mean, you and your wife, of course. Come this Saturday.'

It was the first time in her life Milly had initiated a date with a man, even though technically she was just inviting another married couple for dinner. Their social life was usually of Jack's making, since that incident with Margery. Women friends had now been excised from Milly's world. Hard enough not be able to trust her husband, and she couldn't make him disappear. But friends who engaged in hanky-panky with her husband – well, they were easy to dispose of. The people at their dinner parties were Jack's friends. The main criteria, as far as Milly could make out, was that they were funny, intelligent and Democrats. A lot of authors and editors. Mostly men, without children or wives. They smoked, drank and swore a lot, and sometimes stayed the night on the sofa. Ernie and Bernice still visited, of course, though come to think of it, she hadn't seen Bernice for a while.

There had been a time, before Jack worked in publishing and they moved back to the Bay Area, when there'd been no single people in their crowd. Milly remembered how they used to meet – always two by two. To drink, dine, flirt of course, and rehash their daily lives for the immense comfort of hearing echoes. My daughter, she's so slow at her reading, I worry. Me too! My plumber, he wants more money, doesn't do half the work he promised to, doesn't do shit. I know, you can't trust them these days. My boss, well, I'm seriously thinking of just telling him he can go screw himself. Me, too! My husband is such a slob, leaves his stuff all over the house like a baby, and he never cooks, not even a hot dog. Terrible!

Milly would never admit this to Jack, but sometimes she felt nostalgic for those days. She had much in common with those other housewives. Somehow housewives had gone out of fashion, and their new friends hardly made eye contact with her. They were always laughing hysterically at things she didn't understand. She kept the peanut and potato chip bowls full, the ashtrays empty, and let Jack's friends pull her on their laps sometimes, or give her a good-natured squeeze around her shoulders. Millymoo, some of them called her, and she pretended to like it.

'Well, dinner would be really nice,' answered a surprised Harold, as if whatever he had in mind had to be rejigged. But his smile was genuine, even humble. He was blushing, she was blushing, they were adorably pink, both of them. And the world tilted and tilted and tilted. Why weren't the buildings crashing to the ground? Had she ever felt this sensation before? As if the normal boundaries which contained everything were suddenly gone, and she unravelled into eternity. On and on! Expanding, body and soul, into newness. No wonder Jack gave in to Colette, to Margery, to the Susans and Lindas.

The morning of the dinner party, Milly gave herself a facial. Egg yolk with a bit of olive oil, and while this was drying on her face, she scoured *The Joy of Cooking* for something new. She'd have time to go to the store, clean the house, put some flowers in vases, shower and give her hair a vinegar rinse to make it shine. She'd wear that new Indian print wraparound skirt and peasant blouse. Would Billy be a nightmare? Rude, sulky? Possible. Send him to stay with a friend? And what about Ike and Truman? What if they jumped up on Harold's wheelchair? Well, they'd be bound to; they always egged each other on, and loved all visitors pathetically. Harold might even be allergic to dogs. Maybe send both dogs off with Billy. Yes.

The day went like clockwork. Facial pores tightened, menu decided upon, ingredients purchased and cooked to perfection, house tidied – well, floor vacuumed and table wiped – and white daisies and bluebells in vases, fresh as the sea. Billy and dogs escorted off the premises. Harold and his wife pulled up in a red Saab, peering doubtfully at the front door, where the house number used to be bolted. Milly spied them from the kitchen window and hobbled to the door, but Jack got there first.

'Come in, come in! Milly's new college friends! You must be…sorry, what're your names?'

She'd forgotten the rogue element, her husband. He'd had a few beers. They wouldn't realise it, but they were being mocked already. Her heart sank, because she could

166

see how the evening would go. All the way to making fun of them after they'd left. She felt her romantic love shift into a protective blanket she wanted to toss around Harold and his nose.

But wait. Another rogue element: Harold's wife. She was chic, petite, with a knowing smile outlined with red lipstick. Smiling right now, ready for an adventure. And was Jack taking the bait? Would he down weapons in order to pursue? Sneer or seduce? She glanced down at Harold. He was looking up at her with such open tenderness, that both Jack and the wife disappeared. Just like that! First a room crowded with question marks, then just Harold.

It rained and rained all weekend; a thin windless rain that flooded the gutters and thrummed on the roof at night while Milly lay in the dark, replaying scenes with Harold. On Monday morning, they met in the college hallway before class.

'Done your homework?' she asked shyly. His nose looked downright aristocratic today. A nobleman.

'Let's skip class,' he said. 'Can you? Let's go for a coffee.'

'Oh, yes, please. Let's.'

They sat in the same cafe, in the same seats, and Milly could not help thinking of that song. *We meet every day, in the same cafe. Me and Mrs Jones, we've got a thing going on.* That was her, here and now. Terrifying. And, oh my, wonderful too.

'Milly, do you mind if I ask what's wrong with your leg?'

'Oh, not much really. A car accident, five, no – six years ago.'

'Bummer. What happened? Drunk driver?'

'No, no, nothing like that. It was my fault. Hit a car head on, passing without looking.'

'God, Milly. Was anyone else hurt?'

'Luckily not. It wasn't literally head on, it was more side on. I was speeding because my son had hurt himself, and I was taking him to the hospital. He'd fallen from a tree, you see. But it turned out he was hardly hurt at all, just knocked unconscious. Not a single broken bone, whereas stupid me completely wrecked herself.' She shrugged and giggled and smacked her own forehead softly.

'You must have been worried to death about your son. No wonder you took a chance.'

'Oh, I was worried all right, even before he fell.' Should she tell him about reading Sam's diary? Would that bore a childless man? 'But everything's fine now. I don't mind my leg. Well, I do mind, actually, but I'm just so lucky it's not worse. Lucky it's my left leg, so I can still drive. It doesn't hurt unless I use it. Can I ask why you...?'

'Need this chair? Multiple sclerosis.'

'Oh, dear!'

'Yeah. Tough, eh?' He laughed a little, and shrugged. 'Fuck-all anyone can do about it.'

Pause. Then he said: 'Have you read *The Joy of Sex*?'

'Of course, hasn't everyone?' She commanded herself not to blush, to keep her voice even. She'd been mortified when Sam found it in his dad's dresser drawer, under some T-shirts. It'd been bookmarked on the page with the Viennese Oyster position, and Sam had laughed so hard he almost cried. Even now, if anyone in the house wanted to make everyone else laugh hysterically, all they had to say was: *Viennese oysters, anyone?*

'Perfect example of a bestseller that was over rated,' said Harold. 'Popular because it was popular.'

'Oh, I know. Yeah. *Women's Room*, too. I hated it.'

'So, you're not a libber?'

'It's not just that. I just think it's badly written. More propaganda, than literature.' She was quoting Jack, which felt disloyal.

Harold was wearing brown corduroy pants and a white T-shirt. His arms were very muscular, as if the chair was not electric and he was always propelling his own body with his arms.

Why had he brought up *The Joy of Sex*?

That night, as soon as Jack came home from work, Milly announced:

'I won! I won! My story won the competition!'

Her voice was soft, but Jack flinched slightly, as if she'd shouted.

'Did you?' His mouth formed a wide, stiff smile. 'That's wonderful, sweetheart! Is that the one I helped you with?'

'No.'

'Oh.'

'It was another one.'

'Oh.'

Two weeks later, twelve cups of coffee later, Milly and Harold admitted they didn't really like coffee and decided to see a movie instead. *Midnight Cowboy* at the Tamalpais. She drove them in the family station wagon, tossing shoes, candy wrappers and dog leashes onto the back seat. The windscreen wipers beat time to her heart, as the car sluiced through puddles. Neither knew what the movie was about, only that it starred that new short guy, Dustin Hoffman. They sat near the front, where a seat had been removed to make room for Harold's chair. Milly's seat was much lower than his chair, and she had to reach up for the popcorn he held on his lap. The theatre was warm and full of people. It didn't feel like the afternoon. It felt like 9:00 in the evening, and for whole minutes she couldn't recall where she kept her maple syrup, which of Jack's teeth was false, how old exactly her children were. All the answers existed, of course, but just beyond her ken. There they orbited, the essential minutiae of her life, about three inches from her skull.

By the time Ratso and Joe Buck were on the bus heading out of freezing New York, Harold and Milly were holding hands. Ratso coughed and grew quiet and then he died, slumped against his friend, who did not know what to do. The bus driver said nothing could be done till they got there, so it was best to just carry on. Big, dumb Joe Buck sat and looked out the bus window as Florida came into view, palm trees, oranges and tiny pastel houses. Their big dream, come true. He put his arm around Ratso who was not breathing, whose stink of urine had begun to draw disgust from fellow passengers. Joe Buck looked like a little kid trying to pretend he was brave, and Milly felt her throat tighten. Oh, why did a young man's distress tug at her so? Boys were so stupid, so reckless, they could break your heart. Joe Buck's arm around Ratso tightened, not confidently, but as if he couldn't think what else to do.

Milly suddenly thought of all those children and babies in Jonestown, trustfully accepting their Kool-Aid. 'Drink up,' their mothers would have said, but surely some of them would not have been able to keep their voices normal. Some of those children must have sensed something, and paused a second before swallowing. And then slumped against their mothers – who, for all their

170

wickedness, would not have been able to drink their own cyanide till their loved ones were safely dispatched. They had never been rich or lucky people. They had all been desperate, with nothing to lose. Jonestown was supposed to have been their heaven on earth. Their Florida.

The lights went on and Harold and Milly still sat. Sadness swamped her, muted her in a delicious choking wave. They didn't look at each other, and their hands remained clasped in a sweaty embrace as the song finished and Ratso and Joe Buck rode into the glare of a Florida day.

I'm going where the sun keeps shining, through the falling rain. Going where the weather suits my clothes.

SIX YEARS EARLIER

Cleaning the House

Oct 8th, 1972, San Miguel, Marin County
11:17am

'Ah, honey, I'm going to really miss you,' Jack said, and instantly felt his heart lift.

'You look like one of the dogs,' she replied. 'When they've been digging up the garden. Happy – guilty.'

He didn't answer, but looked down to his open suitcase on the bed. After three years, they'd both become accustomed to the extra weight of the word *guilt*. It could never just be said any more. Billie was standing in the bedroom doorway. Willy clung to her leg, blank-faced, his nose running into his mouth. *What is wrong with that boy?* thought Jack, then calmly recommenced packing. He was good at travelling; in fact, it might be his finest skill. If they offered degrees in travelling, he would have a doctorate. Doctor Travel.

'I want to come to Frankfurt,' she said. 'I've never been

to a book fair. Take me with you. Take me away from this nuthouse.'

Down the hall behind her, the usual chaos of voices bickering and loud music and the dogs were barking. Truman was three months old, a golden ball of fluff with no sense at all; Ike seemed mature by comparison – even by Labrador standards. Nevertheless, Jack hated them both.

'What's the problem with your dogs?'

'No problem, Jack. Your kids are just teasing them as usual.'

Suddenly Elisabeth's treble squeal cut through the boys' broken bass notes and the barking:

'*Mom!* Tell them to leave the dogs alone!'

'You cannot leave me with four teenagers and a puppy. It's inhuman, Jack.'

'Stop exaggerating.'

'It's probably a mortal sin.'

'Well, I don't know. Kill them?' He rolled a pair of khaki pants and wedged them tightly into the case.

'Okay.' Frowning. 'But then Willy would be an only child. You'd have to give me another baby.'

Jack wondered yet again: should he tell her about August? If she knew about August, she'd never want another baby. Infant from hell, if ever there was one.

'What's the matter with him? He's eating his own snot. Willy, use a Kleenex.'

'He's upset because the boys are calling him Penis Head again.'

'Idiots.'

'Maybe Willy isn't such a good name after all. Maybe kids will bully him at school. Maybe all little boys call their penis a willy.'

'I definitely never called mine a willy. Think it's a British affectation. Anyway, a little late for renaming him,' he said, choosing a paperback from his bedside table. *Rabbit Redux* by John Updike. He slid it into the outside pocket, along with a comb. 'Ah Willy, cheer up, son. Anyway, nothing wrong with being called Penis. I'd be proud if Penis was my name. Penis MacAlister.'

'How about the name…Billy?' asked Billie.

'Don't be stupid.'

'We could spell it different. Billy with a y. The boy way.'

'Have you seen my cuff links?'

She sighed and Willy sniffed. Jack kept packing. His flight was a mere three hours away, but he was not panicking. He rolled four pairs of light socks into his spare shoes, then slipped them in sideways, one shoe to each side. The case was the largest size allowed in the overhead luggage rack. It was not one of those new cases with wheels. Those were for old ladies and amateur tourists. His case was soft canvas, with a leather handle that extended so he could swing it over one shoulder leaving both hands free. He zipped his case closed, and began emptying his jacket pockets of old receipts, then slipped his passport, tickets and wallet into the inside pocket. He imagined that packing minimally was paring back to his original self. The real Jack. *Jacko*. Get out of my way, here I come world. But then he admitted to himself, he didn't really want to be the original Jacko again. He'd been so shy, not a born charmer. In fact, he had clear recall of loneliness. But all those years of learning how to be funny and confident had paid off. He surveyed his bag and briefcase and smiled vaguely. Well, will you look at me now!

'Look at you – already half gone, aren't you?'

174

'What?'
'Nothing.'

He took the shortcut to the long-term parking lot, glided through the check-in process, and sat in the same seat he always sat in, with the best view in the departure lounge. He enjoyed being surrounded by people who didn't know him and didn't want to talk to him. He took out his book, but didn't read it. Watched the mini-skirted stewardesses, wiggling and giggling, marching behind the two pilots. The pilots' uniforms always reminded him of the army, in a reassuring way. The men would drive and the women would bring him his dry martinis, with those little bags of fish-shaped salty crackers.

Then he was on the plane, lighting up a cigarette, sipping gin and falling in love with Billie again. Wanted to instantly tell her so. Write a letter, phone her. The thought of their reunion in a week shimmered romantically. Jack never loved her more than when he was leaving her. But what was more curious: after a day or two in Frankfurt, she seemed to dissolve altogether. Truly, Billie began to seem like someone he made up, and all those teenagers and babies too. Even Colette. *Puff!* All gone. The only real people were the ones in front of him. The dark-eyed French woman who was considering buying one of Golden Gate Freight's novels for translation – she was intensely clear. And the young man from Prague, trying to sell him the rights to a Polish novel. His own wife's face, not so clear. Each time, each trip, he was caught by surprise. Stunned at his own shallowness. Here I am again. *This place.* Then his Catholic upbringing paid off, because he forgave himself this flaw, and commenced to enjoy what life was throwing in front of him. Life was good and must not be wasted.

The week passed. For Jack, it felt like a month. *La vie est très, très intéressant et le monde est beau! Die Welt ist schön!* No one wanted to buy the rights for their big seller, oddly, but he sold *If I Touched You* to seven European countries, and to Canada and Australia as well. The French buyer seemed to have triggered a landslide of popularity. In turn, he negotiated a deal with a Swedish publisher to buy and translate a literary thriller. A very good deal, if it sold at home all right. He did not phone home. He never did.

For Billie, the week had been strange because it felt both too slow and too fast. If asked, she might have said she enjoyed the break. But now she was pushing Ike off the sofa again. Damn hair everywhere. She squinted at the calendar, sucked in a horrified breath, then grabbed both morning papers to read the date. Within a minute, she rallied the children to the kitchen and commandeered her troops.

'This is important. Listen. He's home tonight. Elisabeth, you do the hall and bathroom, and vacuum the living room please. Donald, you help Elisabeth. Mop! Remember to mop the bathroom with disinfectant, especially around the toilet. And then mop the kitchen floor. Danny, you can go through the refrigerator. Check the dates, throw away everything out of date. Give the shelves a wipe. Make sure the oven is empty. I found the dog dishes in there yesterday, and you know plastic melts. Sam, you— you— you clean out the bedroom. And deal with the dog doo in the yard. Must be a ton.'

'It's dog *shit*, Mom. I'm not five years old.'

Sam had just turned nineteen. Remote and secretive, tall and skinny. His fair hair was pulled back in a long stringy ponytail. He looked at his mother with jaded eyes – but only half-jaded, as if he deeply aspired to the bored look but still had to practise. Even his voice had slowed and slurred recently. It drove Milly crazy to hear him sometimes, talking to his friends. His loose laugh, his drawn out *Far out man! Allllllriiiight!* Even so, and even though he had barely graduated from high school and hadn't got into any college or found a job, he was currently her favourite child. All he had to do was be present and she was happier.

Eighteen-year-old Danny was the quiet one, permanent dark circles under his eyes. He was biddable, but often made her uneasy. If she'd raised him from a baby it might have been different, she told herself. As if changing a person's diapers predisposed one to a deeper understanding of someone's nature. But he was a darling, and that's why she'd given him the refrigerator chore. By far the easiest and most rewarding.

At seventeen, Elisabeth puzzled her: a pretty girl, taking after Jack's mother. If only she'd make something of her assets. But no, there she was, in her oversized pair of denim overalls again, her uncombed hair hanging limply either side of her unmade-up face. Which, in Billie's opinion, was an over-serious face. So unflattering, her chosen style. Why? But she could and would help her clean the house today. What was the point of a daughter, if she didn't lighten the domestic load sometimes?

Donald at sixteen, well! Trouble ahead, no doubt. The number of parent teacher conferences he'd caused. Drinking, driving before he passed his test, smoking joints in school. But who could blame him, really, considering.

And strange, she thought, how she actually felt closer to the difficult ones, like Sam and Donald.

And Willy. Well, Willy was only four, bless his freckled face. He was a bit dreamy, a bit slow, a bit messy and lazy. A bit inclined to sulk when his siblings and cousins teased him, or called him Penis Head. Often he just ignored his mother's requests, like drink your milk or brush your teeth, but somehow Billie could never get angry at Willy. All he had to do was look at her. *Oh come on, Mom. I know you love me best.* Actually, now she thought of it, she had two current favourites.

Billie belonged to the concealment school of house-keeping. Carpets were for sweeping under. She started shoving toys into closets, throwing dirty clothes into baskets, dirty dishes into the dishwasher, and everything else into the older boys' bedrooms, because they never put anything away and wouldn't notice extra mess. They seemed to possess everything under the sun, aside from bras and make-up. Three hoarders. Elisabeth's room was neat as a pin. On her desk, her pens were in a pen holder and their caps were on. Took after her dad, thought Billie.

She caught a glimpse of herself in the hall mirror and had one of her moments. As if a Martian had suddenly materialised, tapped her on the shoulder and asked: *So, is this it? This is your life? Really? One thing happening, then another thing happening, and then something that's happened before happening again?* Her life seemed to be eaten up in waves. Or contractions. Sometimes quickly, sometimes slowly. Sometimes painlessly, sometimes not, but there was always a rhythm. Some days it felt like her sprawling future was being fed into a greedy indifferent processing machine, like a meat grinder, so that second by second her lived life was turned into something uniformly

178

grey. Dispatched to a place of cold dead minutiae. Old shopping lists, dried-up dog faeces, out-of-date television guides. The days and minutes of her one and only life amounting to not much at all. She'd never thought life would be like this, at forty-four. So bitty. So fragmented. When she was thirteen and imagining her future, she'd seen it as a whole entity. Well shaped. Not perfect, but logical and rewarding. A life worth waiting for, worth working towards. And a few times, for instance, her wedding day and the births of her children, she'd felt well and truly ensconced in that imagined future. But here she was, smack dab in the middle of her life, and she still had the sensation, deep down, that she was waiting for it to properly begin. Everyone told her time went quicker the older you got, but Billie didn't find this to be true. Most days, she seemed mired in mud, and the clock and calendar told lies. Afternoons especially, were often drenched in disappointment. Soft, surprised, disappointment. This husband? These children?

Suddenly, still in front of the mirror, she thought of one solution. She'd been mulling this dilemma for weeks now. Wasn't it brilliant the way problems found solutions while you were having existential thoughts? Billie, no, *Milly*, felt like a genius.

'Willy, sweetie.'

'Uh-huh?'

'You know how you hate being called Willy these days? And being called Penis Head?'

'Uh-huh.'

'Why don't we call you Billy instead. My real name is Milly, and I'll go back to that.'

He stared at her, thumb halfway to mouth.

'I like the name Milly,' she said. 'It's what my parents

called me. I am giving you the name Billy. You can be Billy now. It's a boy's name really, and it's short for William. Which is your full name.'

He stared at her blankly. She didn't like it when he looked dumb, so she shook him gently by the shoulders, and kissed his forehead.

'You'll be okay with Billy. It's a great name. Suits you, honey.'

'Billy. Billy, Billy, Billy.'

'That's right. Billy boy. My handsome Billy boy.'

She called the children again, held Billy's hand.

'From now on, your brother is Billy. Not Willy, right?'

'Yeah, yeah.'

'Far out. Love it that you can just change names like that. Can I be Cassidy instead of Donald? I love that name.'

'No. And no more joking. Willy is now Billy. Please try to remember. No more Penis Head.'

'What's he going to piss from then?'

'Enough. And I am Milly now, in case you're interested. My birth name. Though I'll still answer to Mom.'

'Does Dad know?'

'Yeah, did he say you could?'

'Of course. We agreed before he left, I just forgot to mention it.'

'Mom, you're a crap liar.'

'Stop swearing. Go back to cleaning, please. Now.'

'Why? Why all this hassle?' whined Donald and Danny.

'Why do we need to impress him? While he's been off in Timbuktu, probably sunning himself on a beach,' said Sam.

'Stop talking like that! He's been working in Germany. Doing important, difficult...stuff. Book sales

180

and stuff. Do as you're told. Your father is...Jack is...'
And here, her voice gave way to a high note, denoting
irreverence.

'He is...the king!' She waved her hands upwards and
curtsied.

At this, they all scoffed and laughed, aside from Willy/
Billy, who began to cry softly. Billie/Milly heaved him up
and cuddled him. Was this name switch going to work?
His legs dangled down, and Ike affectionately licked his
bare feet while Truman tried to chew Ike's tail.

'Where are your shoes, Billy?'

'Doo doo,' he mumbled.

Milly put him down and sniffed the air. Yep, definite
dog excrement. She moved to the other rooms, sniffing.
Hell! Only three hours to go. While she tracked down the
smell by putting her nose to several places on the floor,
she admitted to herself it had been a blissful week. No
cooking real meals, no having to justify where the money
went, or why there were no peppercorns in the grinder,
or constantly telling the kids to play their records at a
lower volume. No arguments. But she'd missed Jack, *she
had*. She always did, but it was such a mishmash kind of
missing. Living without him was possible, of course she
knew that now, but if he for instance suddenly ceased to
exist, well! It did not bear thinking about.

Darn, where was the disinfectant? There was dog poop
stuck to the new rug, where Billy (already it was becoming
more natural to say Billy instead of Willy) was walking
earlier. Darn dog! Darn Willy! (So, not so quickly after
all. It would take time, of course it would.)

Half an hour later, from the living room record player
came that song again: *This could be the last time, maybe
the last time, I don't know. Oh no, oh no.* Donald was

pretending to be Mick Jagger, prancing about, his fingers plucking air. Elisabeth was sitting, eyes closed and cross-legged, on the floor and appeared to be mouthing words. Sam was watching *Sesame Street* with the sound off, and Billy/Willy was on his lap, sucking his thumb. Danny was reading Herb Caen with a smile on his face, oblivious to everyone. Billie/Milly noticed, not for the first time, that they all looked related. Each completely different too, of course – but there was a thread of Molinelli running through them all, so now, arranged around the room, they looked like a tribe. All four boys had the Molinelli almost-white hair, which was really Anderson hair from her mother's side. Elisabeth had her father's dark hair and blue eyes, but her mother's heart-shaped face and, it had to be said, her perfect legs. Not that she ever showed them. There was something self-contained about them all, thought Milly/Billie. Something almost insular. They were, she realised for the first time, essentially antisocial. Hardly ever invited friends round. Hardly ever went out, actually.

There were at least half a dozen empty cans of Shasta on the floor, empty Fritos bags and candy wrappers eddying at the room's edge, not to mention shoes absolutely everywhere. How did six people acquire so many pairs of shoes? But she had to admire their skill, negotiating around the house without constantly tripping. Really, it was not easy living happily in a pigsty. People underestimated slobs.

In her mind, she said sternly: *Turn that down please! I asked you to help clean up this house!* But what was the point? If Jack was here and shouted at them, they'd swear under their breath but obey. Since his job changed to publishing, their lives had become patterned around his absences. Dad-at-home meant rules, clean rooms, proper

182

meal times, proper meals, twice-daily dog walks. Dad-away meant unmade beds with unfresh sheets, dog sloth, French toast for dinner three nights running, Grateful Dead on the living room record player instead of in their rooms, records left out of sleeves, and no shouting at all.

'Children!' she said softly during a pause between tracks.

'What?' They turned to look at her with identical expressions. The next track began, and Donald turned the volume down.

'Can you please help me finish cleaning the house. Your father is, Jack is...'

'We know! The king is on his way! Don't sweat it.'

'Geez! The house is fine, Mom. I've vacuumed the hall, and the bathroom's clean.'

'All we have to do is pick up in here. It'll take two minutes.'

'Mommy?'

'Yes, Wil...Billy?'

He giggled at this, so she repeated herself.

'What do you want, WilBilly?'

'I can't hear *Sesame Street*.'

'Turn the music off, Donald. And turn up the television, Sam.'

'Sure thing...*Milly*.' Sarcastically.

Milly again, she thought. It was the perfect solution. But how strange. Was being *Billie* really gone for ever? Quite fundamental, yet it had happened so easily. She felt more grown up, not in a pleasant way. *Milly* felt more... conventional than *Billie*. Also childish, because the last time she was Milly, she'd been living with her mother and sister. She'd had a favourite outfit, the summer she declared herself Billie, not Milly. A red nylon dress, with white polka dots and a tiny black belt. Billie had sounded so snazzy. So modern, so not valley. And now, she was back to meek Milly. Just how much would a mother sacrifice for her child? She sighed as she took an armful of clothes belonging to Sam to the room he shared with Danny and Donald. It used to be the master bedroom – but that seemed like ancient history now. Willy/Billy was in the smallest room, Elisabeth had the converted garage, and she and Jack slept in the middle room. Somehow, over the years, the small house had expanded to accommodate them all. If another child magically appeared, she had no doubt the house would at first groan, then stretch out till a suitable corner was found.

She kicked open a storage drawer at the base of Sam's closet, and dumped in his clothes. Bending to push the drawer closed, she spotted his diary. The one she gave him for Christmas a few years ago, which was why she felt entitled now to have a quick read. Also there was the way her son's eyes looked last night when he went to bed at the unprecedented hour of 8:30, after being dropped off by that new friend. And actually, now she thought of it, he'd been avoiding her eyes all day. So she squatted by the open drawer and quickly flicked through the diary. She was impressed – almost every page was full. Some even had scribbling going up the margin, with arrows. Peace signs appeared in various sizes, as did doodles of naked girls. The dates had been crossed out, new ones scribbled in, and some entries were longer than one page. One entry, about a year old, in messy handwriting:

I love Frances. This is it. Destiny. I gave her a necklace tonight for her birthday and told her I love her. She didn't say she loved me too, but so what.

184

How sweet! Sam was a romantic. She'd always thought he was different.

Now I get all those love songs. It's like when I finally started to inhale, after months of smoking doobies and wondering what the fuck everyone was talking about.

Sam smoked pot? Well, of course he did. So did Jack, actually.

Wonder if she'll let me fuck her now.

What? Oh well.

She flicked to the final page. Yesterday's date. The handwriting was different. The pen had not been pressed hard enough, and at times almost faded into transparency. But there were the words still, loud as a smoke alarm.

On acid. Flying. I can hardly feel this pen, and Che Guevara is winking at me from the wall. Henry said it lasts for at least 8 hours, which means I have 3 hours to go. Fuck. But this will pass. All things must pass, as the song says. All things must pass away.

Milly shut the diary quickly, replaced it and closed the drawer. Her heart raced as if a train had mysteriously derailed from that rarely visited side of downtown, and was heading straight for her home. And in a way, that was exactly what had happened. She had been so relaxed all week, but here was life, rushing to meet her again.

Finally, with thirty minutes till his father's return, Sam was out in the backyard scooping up dog poop with an old spoon into a brown paper bag. Eight, nine, ten, eleven, twelve. Thirteen, under the steps. Fourteen and fifteen, behind the barbecue. Most were dry, odourless, but some were soft and fresh. The dogs were following him around, sniffing their own excrement as if they'd never seen it before. Billy, who was increasingly less a Willy, was playing hide-and-seek with Elisabeth in the house. Elisabeth was actually reading *Seventeen* magazine, but every few minutes shouting numbers, and *Ready or not, here I come! Where's that Billy who used to be Willy?* Danny and Donald were playing Pong, sitting on the floor in front of the television with their remote controls in their laps. There was a hollow *ping!* every time one of their paddles hit the ball. Milly, who was less Billie already, surveyed her house. It looked a little sneaky, a little false, with a shoe toe peeping out from under a sofa, and the kitchen junk drawer refusing to shut. The kitchen floor was still wet, highlighting the corners that the mop had missed. Jack was on his way home, the house was superficially clean, and the kids were all present. Tick, tick, tick.

But Sam had taken acid.

She watched him in the yard, from the kitchen window. Milly often let her eyes linger on her first born; of all the children, he resembled her most. As for taking drugs, however, he got that from his father. Loving intoxication from whatever source. Which reminded her, had she dusted his water pipe recently? He might be wanting that when he got home. Grass was not scary, but acid was. While Milly was considering what to do, she noticed Sam pulling himself up the tree in the backyard. He hadn't climbed a tree in years, what was he doing? Up and up he climbed, and Milly felt a coldness creep over her skin, despite the sun. Sam paused on a branch about forty, maybe fifty feet up. She stared at him but did not go outside, because she had to keep her eyes on him in order to will him down safely. He hardly looked like Sam, way up there. She imagined him looking down, seeing the yard and the dogs, and maybe even her own worried face looking out the kitchen window. He started swinging down quickly, holding onto branches with his hands, not stopping to find proper footholds. Like a monkey, she thought. Then she watched as he missed a branch and hung by one hand, his other grappling in air for another place to grip. The bark was smooth and he was a big boy. It was obvious to Milly he couldn't hold his own weight long, and she watched as his hand slid off the branch. He fell quickly, but her own reactions seemed to happen in excruciating slow motion. She opened doors and ran out of the house, but it didn't feel like running. Tried to scoop up her son as if he was six again, his gangly legs and arms spilling awkwardly. He moaned a little but didn't open his eyes.

'Shush now, you'll be fine,' she ordered softly over and over. Danny carried his feet while Milly held him under his arms. He swung heavily between them. Elizabeth opened the back seat door and helped them slide Sam's body across the seat.

'Want me to come?' asked Elisabeth.

'Stay!' Milly commanded, as if she was a puppy. The adrenalin still pumping, her arms and legs trembling.

'Look after...him.' Pointing at Billy/Willy, and blank about his name. 'Everyone stay put till I get back.' Even her voice was shaking now. She was one big shake.

'Is he okay? Is Sam hurt bad?'

'I don't know. Your father will be here soon. Tell him.'

Then she got in the car and burned rubber for the first time in her life. The acrid smell seeped into her panic, even as she hurtled the old station wagon down China Camp Road, the shortcut to Marin General Hospital. She had never felt this afraid. She'd never driven this danger-ously. She figured (in some calm, calculating room in her mind) that since she'd driven twenty-six years without breaking any traffic laws, she was due a little leeway and would get away with this. She had the perfect excuse, the only excuse really. This was an emergency, and she wanted to scream at the Volkswagen puttering along at thirty. She hit her horn, then swerved out to see if it was clear for her to pass.

By the time Milly registered that her car was no longer moving, people were running up to her. She heard an odd grating noise, and it turned out to be her own cries. She knew because her throat hurt. So did every other part of her body. Especially her left leg. Someone opened her door and reached across to release her belt. When they pulled her out she immediately fell down. She sat on the roadside and as if she'd just come out of an elocution lesson, explained to the stranger leaning over her:

'Excuse me. I need to get to the hospital immediately. Immediately, do you understand? My son is hurt. He is in the back seat.'

Perfectly crisp and clear.

'Excuse me. I said, excuse me. Did you hear me? And my name is Milly. No longer Billie. Mill. Ee.'

Jack was Jack, meanwhile, and sitting eighteen miles away in the living room of the poet from Nebraska, Betty Lou Schmidt. In his left hand was a Manhattan that might just be the best cocktail he'd had in his life. In his right hand was a cigarette. Screw those Gauloises and Gitanes. Screw those huge tankards of *schwarzbier*. He'd meant to drive straight home, but his plane had landed early and Billie wouldn't be expecting him for another hour. Why rush? He needed this. The flight was murder.

'Tell me all about it,' said Betty Lou, stretching out the word *all*. She sat next to him. Close enough so he could smell perfume, but not touching.

He'd head home in a half hour. He wished he didn't feel this way, but the truth was, he didn't want to go home. Billie would be dressed up for him, and she'd skip back and forth to the table serving his favourite steak and salad with Thousand Island dressing. Oh, that sweetness and servitude could drive him crazy sometimes. It could feel accusatory, and he'd done nothing to feel guilty about. This was an innocent situation right now, him and Betty Lou.

'And how did the publisher justify that?' Betty Lou was saying softly. 'Bastard! When you'd come all that way! Well, their loss.'

'Krauts. They always have to win.'

Pause, while he lit her cigarette. More perfume wafting.

'Actually Jack, that is not a word people use any more. *Kraut*. You know that, right?'

Pause. Jack chuckled indulgently, as if she was a child. He noticed, suddenly, his own odour. That particular sour airplane stink. His head hurt and his skin felt greasy. He wanted a very hot shower and bed. He remembered a few nights ago in Frankfurt: drinking too much and getting lost walking around. Those prostitutes had started following him – giggling at him, it had seemed. He hadn't been able to remember the name of his hotel to tell the taxi driver. He'd just wanted to be home then, with his

Billie frying hamburgers, wearing that old denim shirt-dress, her hair tied back in that cowgirl scarf. The kids all bickering about something trivial. Willy's broken fire truck. Danny's new record being scratched by someone. That cold Frankfurt night, Jack had wanted nothing more than to lie on his bean bag in front of the television, his feet up on the hearth, a cold can of Hams by his side, and to watch *The Mary Tyler Moore Show*. Secretly, he loved that show.

TWO YEARS EARLIER

Lemonade on the Deck

October 4th, 1970, Billie's house and Colette's house
10:12am

All the terrible things Billie had expected to happen actually happened. She'd watched *Peyton Place*; by the time they happened to her, adultery and separation were old hat. She'd almost ticked them off a list. Less money – tick! Loneliness – tick! Social exclusion – tick! Despite the presence of four teenagers and a toddler, there'd been the unsurprising emptiness in her home. And her bed was cold and too large. She'd huddled up on one side – at first her side, then his side. She bought a floral bedspread Jack would have hated, but still huddled and shivered, especially around 3am. She'd noted the absence of invitations and didn't mind, curiously. Though she was shocked when Bernice dropped away. It turned out she was part of a package with Ernie, and Ernie belonged to Jack.

Actually, had Bernice ever really been her friend? Did

191

she have any friends left at all? Any real friends? There was that Irene from across the street. She kept making overtures, since her son and Willy were the same age, and she was single too. She seemed to think she and Billie were soulmates, but Billie was not been drawn to her. Her sister, Louise, Bernice and Jack were the only people she actually liked, and they'd all jumped ship. The image was particularly apt in Louise's case, since her most recent postcard was from a cruise ship, where she had a temporary job working in the kitchen. *The gallie!!!* she'd called it. Her sister's spelling mistake and exclamation marks had made Billie weep. It was so like her. She missed her sister. The missing of Jack was expected and justified; it sat smack dab in the middle of the kitchen table every night at dinner. But over the fourteen months since Jack's departure, missing her sister had become visceral and obsessive. A chronic pulling down in the area just above her abdomen, and couldn't be explained with words like grief or love or even sister. It ached all the time. Sometimes Billie rubbed her belly absent-mindedly, as if trying to loosen it.

Then very early morning in October, suddenly, Louise was back. Her maddening sister was following her around again with her caustic comments. Why now? Had she been biding her time till Billie's life calmed, emptied? Or till Billie could no longer do without her? Heavens to Betsy, it hardly mattered. And it certainly didn't matter that Louise was just a manifestation of Billie's own desperate need, because the relief of her was so very… relieving.

Louise had been forty-one when she disappeared with Coffee Enema Bob, but she seemed to be about twenty now. At dawn, and later at breakfast, it was just her voice – her spirited younger voice intruding into Billie's thoughts. Just little grunts of agreement or dispute, sometimes a comment on the way her sons were changing. On how Billie was raising them. Sometimes she just grunted her approval. Then she got louder and louder until, while Billie was in the shower, Louise contradicted her in person. Billie dropped her soap.

I should have worn micro-minis and fishnets, Billie had been thinking. Shouldn't have been such a prude. Should have learned how to give a decent blow job. What a stupid thing to call it, anyway. No blowing involved at all, sadly – blowing would have been easy. But if I'd been serious, and really loved Jack properly...

Don't be stupid! Stop blaming yourself! Louise was on the other side of the shower curtain, sitting on the toilet, lazily filing her nails. You are such a sissy, Billie. You always were. Time to buck up, gal.

Louise was full to the brim of encouragement, in her bullying way. And Billie's heart didn't skip a beat, seeing her sister when she knew for a fact she must be hallucinating. It was too wonderful to worry about, and the ache in her abdomen dissolved. But after a few days, Louise became annoying in the old way.

'You're not really here, Loulou,' reminded Billie politely. She said this out loud. She always talked to Louise out loud when she was on her own, or with just Willy. He never noticed because he often chattered away to his imaginary friend, a four-foot squirrel called Alfredo. Louise was her Alfredo. 'You're a figment of my imagination.'

Your point?

'And anyway, Jack's leaving is partially your fault. I forgot all about being a wife, after you left and your boys moved in. It was all I could do, to keep...'

Louise yawned, and for a second was her ten-year-old self. It was that kind of wholehearted melodramatic yawn.

Uh-huh. Blame it on me, if it helps.

'It's true, though. I took my eyes off the ball, and *whoop*! In walked cute Colette.'

Colette Schmet! What a pretentious loser name. Collettey Spaghetti.

'That's how I talk.'

Your point?

Then one morning, Billie was woken by Louise sitting on her bed; in fact, right on top of her feet, which now had pins and needles. They'd shared a bed growing up, so in her first waking moments this felt entirely normal.

'Gee, Loulou. What is it now? What do you want? It's not getting-up time yet.' She whispered, because all the kids were still asleep. It was hours before get up time.

I was thinking, when you are you going to get rid of all his stuff?

Billie shrugged, avoiding eye contact. Then she got up and went to the kitchen to eat a yoghurt. She often did this because yoghurt seemed to make her sleepy again. She glanced around the dim living room, and down the hall with the bedroom doors shut. The house felt full of kids, in a muffled way. Adolescent boy sweat and the cotton-candy-scented hairspray Elisabeth used on her back-combed hair. (Ratted hair, she called it.)

Jack had taken a suitcase, a few grocery bags full of clothes and shoes, a pile of manuscripts, his file of important papers and his two work briefcases. He'd not expressed interest in claiming anything else. Not even his collection of hardback Everyman Library novels, or his Glen Miller albums. Evidence of Jack was still everywhere she looked, as if he intended to keep his territory well marked.

As she finished the yoghurt, she pictured packing all his things up. She smiled a little. But what about every-thing else? Each piece of furniture was soaked with Jack memories. Even the wallpaper (grass) and the kitchen tiles (terracotta). Even the pair of slippers she was wearing right now. They belonged to her, but they were not completely devoid of Jack. They'd argued over the blank checkbook stub which should have said *slippers – Macy's 9/10*.

Ditch it. Ditch it all. You're a divorced woman now, said Louise. She appeared suddenly, perched on the kitchen counter, reading the fashion section of the *Chronicle*.

'Louise Molinelli! I am not divorced!' she whispered.

Hey, it's not a dirty word.

'Says you. Anyway, easy for you to say. Jack's stuff is all mixed up with my stuff. It's our stuff.'

Is it? Either a thing is yours or his. Nothing belongs to you both any more. Looks to me like you're hoping he's going to walk back in that door one day.

Louise was briefly her much older self, chewing her fingernails, then reverted to her unlined younger self. She got out her compact and preened in the mirror. Billie bristled. Louise could be so smug, it made her want to spit. To flounce out and slam the door. 'No, I do not! And if he did, why, I'd tell him to…to just get lost. Git, I'd say. Take your suitcase right out of here, and go back to Miss Slutsville.'

A pause, as she noted the photograph above the phone, from that trip to Disneyland just before Willy. The kids had been too old to admit to having fun with their parents, and they were not smiling. And yet, now she thought of it, they really had been happy that day. She was convinced of it.

'Jack is not welcome in this house any more. Unless he's here to visit the kids, of course. Which he has to do. Which I want him to do. But let him try and move back, well, no siree!'

Uh-huh, said Louise, then she squinted at her sister. Hey, you going to do something with your hair?

'What's wrong with my hair?'

And your face. You look like death.

'You can talk. You keep morphing.'

Billie yawned, threw the empty yoghurt pot in the garbage bag and walked back to her bedroom. It was strangely comforting to bicker with Louise. Since Jack left, she really missed arguing.

Men are all cheating lying bastards, said Louise in a reasonable tone, as she followed Billie down the hall. You know Mom always considered Dad a prime example of bastardly-ness. Of course Jack was going to be one too.

'How dare you lump Jack in with Dad.' Billie slipped back between the sheets.

Oh, come on. You still think he's different?

'Of course.'

Billie Molinelli. You always did think you were special.

'My name is Mrs Jack MacAlister,' she whispered, adjusting the quilt around her toes.

La di fucking da.

'Anyway, anyone can be special, Loulou. Nothing special about being special, it's just that not many people really want to be. You could have been special, if you'd wanted.'

Who says I'm not? I just don't think you are, not as much as you think you are.

'Goodnight.'

Listen, Billie. I've got an idea. Who needs a man? Get a puppy!

'Are you nuts?'

Remember Sally? You loved Sally. She was your shadow all through high school, that mutt.

'Jack hates dogs.'

Jack Schmack, said Louise.

Then Louise was gone and Billie could hear blue jays, and other birds she didn't know the names of, and a dog was barking to be let out for a pee. A puppy popped into her mind. One puppy in particular, and this changed from labrador to spaniel several times as she pictured the way it would follow her around the house, toenails clicking on the wood floor. It would curl up at her feet wherever she sat, and she'd make new friends. Dog people. She let her head fall back on the pillow. It was still too early to get up and she felt her being, made up of whatever it is that made her Billie and not anyone else, drift away from her body. She wondered if this was what dying felt like. If so, then it wasn't so bad after all. This lifting sensation, this liberating of her truest self from everything that… everything that fretted it. And darling little Charlie – well, what separated her from him didn't feel so very substantial after all.

No Jack! she'd been crying into her pillow for more than a year. In fear, sadness, regret. *No Jack!* she silently sang now as she went back into sleep, puppies bouncing around in a pink clouded backyard. For a second, she pictured a Louise-like guardian angel hovering over her, edging her drowsy heart in the direction of joy.

When Billie woke again, she felt odd. Almost drug-sedated. Was something wrong with her? Should she go

197

to the doctor? She smiled, imagining that. Of course, she wouldn't go to the doctor. She'd find a puppy! She slowly rose, put on her robe and walked down the hall to check on Willy. Still sound asleep, bum in the air, thumb planted in mouth. The room smelled of pee and Johnson's talcum powder. In the kitchen, she asked her teenagers the questions she did every weekday morning. Had they done their homework, remembered to put it in their school bags, did they need lunch money? None replied further than the reflex: 'Yeah, yeah.' And: 'Nah.'

'Elisabeth, is that my cashmere sweater you're wearing?'

'You said I could have it if I wanted. Don't you remember anything? Pathetic.'

'Danny, you need a haircut again. Take a tenner out of my bag. Go to Supercuts.'

'Mom, I told you I'm growing my hair, remember?'

'Donald, that shirt needs to be ironed. Take it off, I can do it right now.'

'It's supposed to look like that, Aunt.' He said *aunt* in his new sarcastic way, as if he was making little quote marks in the air with his fingers. Was he going to mock her for the rest of his life?

'Sam, those jeans are way too long, the hem's all frayed. Why you don't trip over, I've no idea. And listen, what time are you coming home? I need you to be home when you say you'll be home.'

He'd been late every day this week, and she felt the need to exert some authority over at least one child. He complied with a long mumble. Impossible to decipher, but this didn't bother her. In fact, it pretty much met her expectations. More mumbling, arguing, shuffling up and down the hall. Then, in dribs and drabs over ten minutes,

198

they all took turns slamming the front door on their way out, and each time Billie said:

'Shush! Willy is still asleep! Have a nice day at school!' Then she made herself some toast, whistling softly and perfectly in tune. Outside it rained the thin warm rain of October, and the drum of it on the roof gave her peace, not the usual agitation. She considered phoning someone – perhaps Irene? Willy might like to play with her son. The edge of loneliness that might impel her was absent, but nevertheless it was good to know Irene was available if needed. Like a loaf of bread in the freezer, poised for defrosting. Billie leafed through the new *Sunset* magazine, aware that Louise was loitering nearby, plucking her eyebrows again. Jiminy cricket, life was sweet when your vanished sister had begun hanging around and you were on the verge of a puppy.

She'd spend the day puppy-hunting with Willy. He'd adore a dog. They all would. A dog would distract them, bring them closer, might make home a place to love again. She looked at her watch. Six hours and twenty-two minutes till the older children poured back through the front door, smelling of hormones and cheap deodorant.

Better get a move on, lazy bones, said Louise, passing by and going out the door without opening or closing it. She was about seventeen today.

Willy woke. He came into the kitchen, pyjamas drooping, yawning, scratching his head, fine hair all fluffed up above his sleepy blue eyes.

'Hey Willy Wonka. Hungry?'

He smiled but said nothing. A toddler of few words. He pulled off his diaper in the kitchen, dumped it on the floor and trundled to the bathroom. While Billie listened to the steady stream, she poured him a bowl of Lucky Charms.

Lucky boy indeed – his siblings had grown up eating lumpy oatmeal every morning. Somehow, worrying about junk food had tailed off. After he'd finished eating, she decided that instead of her usual quick shower, they could take a bath together. Willy loved baths. She put on a record, *Sounds of Silence*, and filled the bath while Willy tossed his bath toys in. She added bubble bath, then cold water till it was just right. She undressed them both, lifted him up and they both sank into the water. His skin was smooth, slipping against her own skin. She soaped him gently, washed his hair, rinsed it by tipping his head back over her chest and scooping water over it. Normally Willy hated having his hair washed, but today he just chuckled. Then she lifted him out of the bath, got out herself and towelled him dry. She pulled clean clothes on his wriggling body, popped a bottle into his mouth, grabbed his bunny and his blanket just in time for *Mister Roger's Neighbourhood*. *It's a beautiful day in the neighbourhood, a beautiful day for a neighbour, would you be mine? Could you be mine?* Willy sat on the beanbag and sucked, trancelike.

Well? You call this looking for a puppy?

'Shut up, Loulou. Loads of time.'

Billie sat on the sofa, still wrapped in her robe, and attempted to imagine Mister Rogers being married. Or even kissing. The more she looked at him the more he seemed like an overgrown sexless child. She'd bundle Willy into the car after the show and head to the pet store. Lots of puppy ads on the bulletin board there.

A knock on the door, damn it! She looked around – she could see the door from the sofa. She tightened her robe around her, but before she could get to the door, it opened. And there he stood. Jeff, from number 23.

'Hey, Billie.' That embarrassed smile he always seemed

to have these days. 'Sorry, it's so early – didn't mean to… want me to come back?'

'That's okay, Jeff. Just having a lazy morning. Want some coffee?'

Why are you encouraging him? hissed Louise. You don't even like him, do you?

'Well, sure,' said Jeff. 'That would be great.'

'Let's have it on the back deck. Willy's addicted to Mister Rogers, he'll be fine for another twenty minutes.'

'It's raining.'

'We can sit under the sun shade. I love to sit there when it's raining.'

'Oh, me too,' he replied seriously in a low voice, as if they'd both confessed to a strange and intimate affinity. 'In fact, I was just thinking we could talk about that decking repair you mentioned needing.'

'Uh-huh,' she said nonchalantly, while yawning. Oh! To have a man flirt with you even before you brushed your hair or put on your lipstick! Also, his wife, Shirley, was so superior, with her tiny waist and university degree, lording it over all the other moms at the PTA. Billie felt a little thrill, imagining Jeff preferring her uneducated self.

'Let's have lemonade instead of coffee,' she said softly, smiling.

'Jack! Why are you drinking lemonade? I bought more gin yesterday. And tonic. And green olives and vermouth.'

'Did you?'

He was only seventeen miles from his old home, but it was not raining here. He was sitting by the pool, enjoying Indian summer and reading a John le Carré. Jack and Billie lived in different universes. He lived in Colette's clutter-free beige house with three bathrooms (each with a shower that worked), a colour television, and a record player with two speakers (stereo!). Which reminded him. He needed space to put his records and books, and they'd need another dresser. And more shelves. And maybe he could take over one of those spare rooms as an office. And the room with the big windows could be his studio, for painting.

'Yes,' said Colette. 'Why not have a drink? You're on vacation.'

'Silly me.'

He was sick of getting drunk in the morning. What's more, he was sick of getting drunk with her. But she was standing in the doorway in her bikini, smoking a cigarette with that pout, so he repeated:

'Silly me. Limes? Did you get more limes?'

'Of course, honey pie.'

This was wrong too. Honey pie belonged to Billie. Colette used to call him lover, sex God, hottie. But how could he complain? He didn't pay rent, and she offered him amazing sex any time he wanted it. Even better, she offered decent conversation about politics, literature, life in general. There were no awkward silences or sulky ones either. They were soulmates and life was good. No nagging, no sneaking around, no guilt.

Ernie had been wrong-wrong-wrong yesterday. They'd been eating pastrami sandwiches on the deck of Ernie's sailboat. Not out in the bay, just a lazy lunch at the dock. Since he and Bernice had finally moved to Marin six months ago, this had become a weekly ritual. Always on the boat, away from wives and girlfriends. After the third beer, Ernie had burst out laughing.

'What's so funny?'

'You. You're so funny, Jack. I mean, Colette's nice, but look at you. Forty-two years old and you're acting like a kid. Why didn't you get all this hanky-panky stuff out of your system when you were young?'

'Well. I'm a late bloomer. What's wrong with that?'

'But why, Jack? Why bother at all? I mean, your wife's gorgeous. And sweet natured.'

'I know.'

'She doesn't smoke or drink. Take my Bernice, now. She gets so she can hardly walk to the bedroom. You're lucky.'

'Huh.'

'Billie doesn't even flirt. Bernice flirts with other men all the time. It drives me a bit crazy, to be honest. But Billie, well. You have a wife you can count on, there. She's got eyes for no one else.'

'Jesus, Ernie, I know all that. But.'

'But what.'

'Oh, I don't know. I felt...cheated. Billie didn't keep to the deal. I know it sounds dumb, but the original deal was that we were supposed to be like this.' He clasped his hands together. 'That's what I thought was going to happen. Laughing at the same stuff. Billie has no humour. She thinks jokes are funny.'

'Jokes *are* funny, Jack.'

'You're joking, right? Anyway, I figured we'd talk all the time about everything, like you and me do. Understand each other.'

'I think you're overrating conversation, Jack. Sure, Bernice can talk the hind legs off a donkey. I can hardly finish a single darn thought, some days.'

'You don't get it. You and Bernice play guitar together, for Christ sake. It's all working out how you planned it to. You suit each other. Me and Billie, well. It's not her fault, but she's not really my type.' He'd meant this to sound sophisticated and funny, but hearing it out loud he instantly knew it wasn't.

Pause, while they'd opened more beers. Then Jack sighed. 'I missed first kisses. I love first kisses. And first looks. When I look at Colette, something still changes in her eyes. Like I'm switching on the Goddamn Christmas tree lights.'

'Aha! That's it. I know what your problem is, Jack.'

'Oh crap, here we go.'

'Jack MacAlister. You're a fucking romantic and always have been.' (Jack had smirked and lit a cigarette, flattered.) 'You want what's out of reach, and imagine it's perfect. But when you get it, you find fault with that too. God, poor Billie. Poor Colette! Who next?'

'I never chase women, Ernie. Colette chased me. I am not a predator.'

'I did not say that. That would be sleazy. You are not sleazy, Jack.'

'Correct, I am not sleazy. I am...reluctant to hurt a girls feelings, that's what.'

'I'll tell you something for nothing, Jack.' He'd begun slurring. Shomething for noshing.

'What?'

'Sometimes I wish I was married to Billie.'

'No. Really? No.' He could see two Ernies now. Amazing. Two entirely separate Ernies preaching to him. How was he going to drive home?

'Do not ever remind me I said that. I want that erased from your memory right this very minute.'

'Gone.'

'But it's true, Jack. Bernice can be very annoying. You have to stay on your toes all the time, because she's so fucking smart. She's a fucking mind reader. At least with Billie, your thoughts are your own. Your life is your

204

own. I almost wish I was doing it too. Getting some extra marital, while I still can.'

'Jesus, Ernie, aren't you?'

'Are you kidding? She'd know instantly and then she'd kill me. The whole thing would be over in a day, and I would be dead.'

That was yesterday, blind drunk at midday. Ernie had to make do with what he had, but Jack – well, Jack now had exactly what he wanted. In addition to a hangover. He got up, but Colette pushed him back down onto his sunlounger. Her crotch was inches from his mouth.

'You stay right where you are, Jack. I'll get you a nice tall drink.'

'Here you are,' said Billie, and as she handed Jeff his glass, her robe briefly opened enough for a glimpse of white thighs, and three-quarters of one milky white breast. Jeff took the glass but didn't drink. Billie started to feel the beginnings of uneasiness. Was Jeff asthmatic? Then Jeff put his glass down, pulled her to him so quickly, so clumsily, so adolescently, that at first she was not frightened. She was amused and angered in equal measure. As if it was sweet Mister Rogers who was groping her by mistake. He'd just meant to button up his sweater and got confused. 'Stop it,' she scolded. 'Knock it off!' she said with more seriousness, when his hands slid inside her robe.

Kick him in the balls, screamed Louise from the roof. Poke his eyes out!

But Billie was not prepared for this. She could not fabricate aggression quickly enough, and found her polite self, her protective mother self, still in operation. Willy was in the other room, and must not be alarmed. This was her own fault, her own dilemma and she must solve it quietly. His hands on her body were so strange, a part of herself detached and noticed that his skin was not as rough as Jack's, but his fingers were more insistent, and there was an odour emanating from him now. Unpleasant, but she couldn't think what it was. She had time, while he pulled at her robe and she held tight to it, to wonder if he smelled of rotten eggs mixed with deodorant, or was this the essential smell of male horniness? She kept saying: 'Stop it!' in a low hissing voice. 'It's all right,' he kept saying. 'Calm down.' His face was ugly now. He smiled. Then they fell to the deck, and he pinned both her hands together above her head before she had a chance to struggle. With his other hand, he fumbled with his jeans. His body had a density she had not guessed at. He was stronger than Jack. She went limp and told herself: this is what men do to women sometimes. What bodies do to other bodies. How extraordinary it's happening to me. Then she wondered if she was getting splinters on her bottom. The deck was redwood and terrible for splinters.

Even Louise gave up and whispered in a practical tone: Hold still, sis. He's a cunt, but he won't hurt you. Just ignore him and let him finish before Willy comes looking for you.

Then Willy cried out from the living room, a sudden sharp whelp as if he'd fallen, and Billie found she had strength after all. She squirmed hard sideways and freed herself while Jeff was still trying to open his jeans.

Jack swallowed his morning martini and felt a bit flat. Maybe a blow job would cheer him up. It was weird to be home on a weekday. Weird to call this place home. Maybe Ernie was right, and soon Colette would drive

206

him crazy too. Watching Colette swim back and forth in the turquoise pool put him in a trance, which melted into a nap. When the phone rang, at first he thought it was part of his dream.

'Billie? What is it?'

'Slow down. What?'

'What the fuck? Jeff from number 23?'

'Who is it?' called Colette, emerging from the pool like Venus – the body of an eighteen-year-old, not a stretch mark on her.

Jack didn't reply. Hurtled out of the house with his car keys. If he married Colette tomorrow, if they never argued, if they had endless stimulating conversations, incredible sex, it would still only ever be a secondary marriage. A perfectly formed, easily executed but trivial, shallow marriage. The real thing, the primary connection, would always be with his sweet-kneed, cock-eyebrowed, stubborn Billie. He imagined the space he used to take up, that space exactly his body shape, patiently waiting for him to resume his old rightful life. He pressed harder on the accelerator, hit eighty-five.

But there was someone else at his old home, a vaguely familiar woman, and it looked like her kid was playing with Willy, pushing little cars and making engine noises. And this stranger had an arm around Billie, like they were old friends. They turned to stare at him, and he suddenly remembered he was supposed to knock on the door first. That was their agreement.

'Jack, remember Irene? From across the road.' Billie did not meet his eyes.

'Nice to see you again, Jack.'

He ignored Irene. 'Billie? You okay?'

'Well, yes.'

'She'll be fine,' said Irene. Then: 'Can I make you a coffee, Jack?'

'No,' he answered, his eyes still on his wife. How dare this Irene offer him coffee in his own house! He bought those stupid mugs. He fumed and fussed, and checked that the plants on windowsill had been watered and that the kitchen taps weren't leaking again. Then the kids came home early from school because of a power cut. The boys grunted their hellos and disappeared into their rooms. Elisabeth said hello, then loitered awhile, making herself a sandwich.

Nothing had been said about Jeff. No one had remarked on the fact Jack was here on an unscheduled visit, and Billie seemed to be having a very lazy day, still in her bathrobe. Even Willy seemed oblivious. Now he was methodically emptying out alphabet blocks from one dumper truck to another, while the other toddler rolled playdough into tiny balls then squashed them together again. Jack could not get near Billie. His old home conspired to make him feel unwelcome; no Jack-shaped vacuum waiting for his return after all. It seemed recent history had entirely removed his right to protect his wife. But she'd phoned him first. Not Irene.

'What are you doing here, anyway? It's not your visit day,' snarled Elisabeth, halfway through a peanut butter sandwich. He flinched and declined to answer. Traitor daughter! He'd talk her round, next time. She belonged to him; they were buddies, Goddammit.

'Anything I can do, Billie?' He tried to catch her eyes. She was wearing a baggy sweater over her robe. His sweater. He remembered opening the gift box containing that sweater, one of those Christmases that had now blurred into one morning of pine-scented chaos. 'You don't like it, do you?' she'd accurately guessed. 'I'll return it,' she'd promised, but evidently never had.

She turned from her half-whispered conversation with Irene, looked at him wandering slowly in the kitchen, and for a brief second there was her old look. Half giddy, half knowing. His heart lurched. But:

'Thank you for coming, Jack. I was upset when I rang, but I'm all right now.' In a low voice.

Irene said, 'Nice to see you, Jack.' Dismissively.

He looked away, towards Elisabeth, who was watching *Gidget* on television now. 'Hey, you got a colour TV!' His voice sounded peevish to his own ears.

'Yeah,' said Billie guiltily. 'Mom gave me some birthday money.'

'Where's the black-and-white?'

'Our bedroom. The bedroom.'

He was momentarily confused. He felt oddly pleased about the new colour television, as if it was his too. He had to stop himself from going over and inspecting it. Then Sam loped into the room, with his usual mixture of gangling cockiness and deference. Turned to his father, and said so maturely, it made Jack's heart stop:

'Nice to see you, Dad. But I guess it's time for you to head out, yeah?' He remained standing, as if waiting to escort his father to the door. A distant politeness in his face, more upsetting than all their heated arguments to date. Jack looked around at the living room with the framed family photos and the stain on the rug where the kids spilled orange Shasta one hot August day. The rug he remembered buying and laying while the Shangri-Las sang 'Leader of the Pack'. And there was nothing for him to do now but leave. Move, he told his legs. *Walk*, he told his feet. *Go!* Jack had never properly noticed gravity before.

209

'All right, Billie,' he said thickly. 'Let me know...' He didn't know how to end this sentence, and so opened his hands in a helpless gesture instead. And managed to move finally, with the kitchen clock ticking very loudly, and the rain outside dropping very slowly.

When Jeff heard the knock at the door, perhaps he imagined it was her. Perhaps he thought: that was women for you. No meant yes, and no matter what anyone said, women loved to be dominated. He could hear his wife vacuuming the staircase; she was always vacuuming those damn stairs. He stepped over a toy fire engine, opened the door, and *pow!* Jack knocked him flat on his back.

TWO YEARS EARLIER

Stepping Out

December 31st, 1968, San Miguel, Marin County
11:02pm

Jack was a little drunk, walking down the stairs from the bathroom. He could hear voices of course, and laughter, but mainly it felt like he was descending into a pool of jazz. It was one of his favourite records from the old days. 'Cry Me a River', with the Harry James band. Nothing but noise, the music these days. Then before he reached the last step, it changed to a dance tune, and he had to pause because the room had become a throbbing mass of bodies, all dancing away like they were teenagers again. He sat on the middle step and watched. Maybe they *were* young again. He was still holding the high ball glass that he'd carried upstairs to the bathroom without spilling. 100% gin. He understood everything in the world now. He saw himself joining the dancers in a while. He'd join in clumsily at first, then he'd become one of them. He knew he wasn't a good dancer, but no one would notice. He decided music made the life force audible: an energetic pulsing stream, and musicians and dancers and anyone who lived intuitively could join in. Himself after a few drinks, for instance.

Then 'Chattanooga Choo Choo' came on, and Jack kept sipping his gin. He started thinking that maybe life was more like a moving train, than music. If you had enough nerve, or equally if you did not give a damn, you ran alongside it till you could leap on, and then you too were part of the action, part of the world, you were going somewhere with a bunch of people who were also holding on tight and going somewhere. But if you couldn't run fast enough, if you were too old, or tired, or sad, or drunk, then you would have to sit back and watch it all happening without you. Feel the wind of its passing, and sigh. He was lonely suddenly. If only Ernie and Bernice would move to Marin. If only they could afford it. They met a few times a year, not nearly often enough for Jack. He'd never admit it, but he only really felt like himself, his true self, with them. And of course, with Billie. But she got his less fun true self. The simple truth was, Billie was not the wife he'd hoped for. In the beginning they'd had similarities in abundance, but now he only noticed their differences. She didn't get drunk with him, didn't share his love of oysters or mussels or scallops, didn't read literature, didn't like the same movies, didn't laugh at the same things that made him laugh. It was hilarious, when you considered it. It turned out it was possible to love a woman who was not your type. He shook his head in drunken wonderment. Who would have thought?

Then he rose and glided down into the dancers. When the song ended, he found himself next to Colette, who

212

asked what his resolutions were. He immediately said: 'Get divorced.'

'Jack! He's just kidding, Colette,' said Billie, who appeared by his side looking stunningly sober.

As soon as Billie walked away, he gave an exaggerated shrug and lifted eyebrows. Colette gave him a quick tight hug as if he had just done something too adorable to respond to verbally.

'How are your kids?' She had to shout over the music.

'Nightmare. Sam's become impossible. Billie doesn't see it, but he's a complete pain in the ass. And Danny and Donald – well, of course, I feel sorry for them, who wouldn't? But they hardly ever wash, they won't even get haircuts. Plus, they all hate me.'

'Crap, Jack.'

'I don't get it. They're so lucky, compared to how we grew up. But they're rejecting all the good stuff. Everything's gone to hell.'

It was true. The boys were breaking his heart, so was Elisabeth. She used to be the one who always laughed at the same things he did. And since Willy, they were back to sticky surfaces and the smell of sour milk.

'Never mind. Well, better mingle,' Colette said, giving his hand a squeeze.

They'd known each other for years. He'd always liked her slightly gauche way of acting, especially when drinking. And her amorality – she was single again now, with two wealthy ex-husbands supporting her life style. Plus she never wore a bra. He could see her nipples clearly outlined in her dress. Those have never had a baby sucking on them, he thought. Women without kids were sexier. When midnight came, he conspired to be next to Colette.

213

'Happy New Year,' and he kissed her long and daringly hard, on closed lips. He thought Billie was in the kitchen somewhere, still sober. She'd be talking to the host's father, a doddery man who drooled and adored Billie. Jack remembered hearing Billie describe Colette as *fast*. Kissing Colette felt numb at first, the loose kiss of drunkenness. But when he pulled away, she grabbed his head and pulled him in for a deeper kiss. For a second, she parted her lips and he felt the quick flick of her tongue. Suddenly, it was as if they were alone. Did a police siren begin and people hose them off, and shout: *Stop! That kind of kissing is dangerous and life threatening and terribly against the law!* Nope. So they kissed again, parted to kiss others and shouted Happy New Year! Then moved to a dark hallway and dived straight back into it, mouths open, tongues deeper and deeper till Jack was afraid finally.

'Billie, honey, ready to go home?'

She turned to him and smiled beatifically. God, she was something. The only un-blurry person in the house, and she was his wife.

'Yes, ready when you are honey.'

That would have been that, but Colette was determined to call his bluff. And a devil in him wanted his bluff called. It took another seven days of ambiguous phone conversations, and a bad mood brought on by his wife's extravagance in I. Magnin. Damnit! Did she think money grew on trees? She was such a child in some ways. Not like the independent Colette. Colette was a woman, all right. She knew what a man wanted. And she had his number in every way possible. As he drove to her house, he was stone cold sober, telling himself with every mile this was not a mad impulse.

As soon as entered his own house again, he knew life would never be the same. Everything was different. Of course his own body felt different, and it should, given where it'd been recently, but why did his furniture look odd, and the children's voices seem thin somehow, and his wife's expression seem…well, so unsuspicious? Didn't she know him at all? Couldn't she see the imprint of Colette on him? It was glaring, Goddammit; it was blinding. Another reason to betray her. His own wife was virtually a stranger, but a stranger he was tied to, someone he had to support financially. Not to mention the life's sentence of eating, sleeping and watching television with her. God! It was only just now dawning on him, what marriage was. To literally *be* with a specific other person until you were dead. Dead. The price was quite simply, quite obviously, too high.

And then, of course, all his life Jack had been dishonest regularly in small ways. He and Ernie had stolen Hershey bars from the corner store all one summer. And it was a fact that Jack neglected to inform the checkout girl when she undercharged him, he parked illegally in the staff-only slots behind the courthouse, he told fibs about being sick when he was just hung-over, and he cheated annually on his income tax. He even lied to the IRS about that money Louise sent once, when she'd had a lucky day at the races. Doing these things diminished some kind of vague resentment; evened things up. This thing with Colette was not like that at first, it was too big. But as with the stolen Hershey bars, when he wasn't caught, he became accustomed to not paying and kept stealing. A bit more each time. Three Reese's Peanut Butter Cups, a Snickers, ten Milky Ways. Once, a whole carton of Milk Duds. After a while, it hadn't even felt like stealing, or cheating. Anyway, didn't everyone do it? Hadn't John Kennedy, bless him, done it too? It was human nature to want to get away with things. Jack told himself he was not a bad man, just a man trying to find a way to make his existence bearable without hurting anyone. His first affair felt like getting drunk for the first time. Discovering that intoxication made nonsense of his worries, and realizing that while a bit naughty, it was also something pretty much everyone else already knew about. Opening a door to a room he hadn't really believed was accessible, and finding no need for even a key. It was unlocked and inside, a big crowd of partying people. *Hey, Jack! Where the hell you been?*

Probably faithful spouses were just spouses without choices. Anyone in their right mind would be an adulterer, if the right temptation came knocking on their door. Within a month, he convinced himself he was actually a kind of saint. That Colette was doing his marriage a huge favour. That, given his wife's extravagance, the sudden burden of his nephews, his sinless marital track record and human nature itself, he was entitled to Colette.

Billie didn't know about the New Year's Eve kiss, but she knew about Colette. She hadn't noticed much since Louise had left – it'd been a teary blur of a year – but of course she noticed. She knew her own husband, didn't she? He was in love, it was as clear as day. It began with the phone calls. His animated voice, the giggling. Jack was not a giggler, not unless she was tickling him. But all this wouldn't have given the game away, if he hadn't lied so badly.

'Who was that?' she had asked after he hung up the phone.

'Who?' A second's beat. 'It was Peter.'

With those two syllables, Billie had felt herself slip into a fearful place.

'Peter? What did he want?'

'Oh, nothing. Just the time of the meeting tomorrow. You know Peter, so forgetful.'

Then he walked away, and a minute later she heard him whistling in the garage. He was converting it to a bedroom for Elisabeth, and always hammering or drilling. But now, that traitorous whistle! He was not a whistler; that's who *she* was. Though weirdly, she'd stopped whistling since Louise left. As if without Louise to witness her, the whistling side of Billie did not exist. Sometimes she hummed, but not the whistling any more. Jack's whistle was traitorous, and anyway, Peter would never have elicited a whistle or a giggle. And if it wasn't Peter, why lie about it?

While her husband learned new ways to deceive, she did too. Furtively, she went through his pockets, letters, the credit card bill. She did not confront him, though at first she almost did. Louise certainly would have, she thought, then bit down hard on the thought. Where had Louise's methods got her? Or indeed, her mother's? Instead, she rehearsed the confrontation.

Jack, I know, she'd say calmly.

Know what?

Don't play the fool with me. I know about...her.

She'd get her hair cut, wear her Chanel red lipstick, her new jean skirt, her powder blue sweater with the ivory buttons. Gird herself with the only real weapons she had. She'd shave her legs, to tell her husband she knew he was unfaithful. But something stopped her, and it took a whole week to realize what. She overheard him on the phone again, when he thought she was in the shower.

(She'd left the water on – part of her new devious system.) The tone of his voice, liquid with sex, was pouring into the ear of the invisible recipient. She stood just out of sight, frightened. Indeed, this felt like a battle for her very life. For her children's lives too. Just imagining them the children of divorce was enough to make her weep. Removing her wedding ring, not signing her name Mrs J. MacAlister – unimaginable tragedy. So she surreptitiously watched her husband, to not lose him. She often watched him watching something else. Television. The newspaper. She was so aware of him, the children and their demands became an unwelcome static, which she batted away impatiently. *Yes, yes, yes*, she said to sixteen-year-old Sam, fifteen-year-old Danny, fourteen-year-old Elisabeth, thirteen-year-old Donald, and her baby son, Willy – *whatever you want, fine by me, just please shut up, okay? Can't you see I'm busy?*

Yes, she was distracted, but she *had* noticed that Danny had tacked a photo of his mother and himself to the wall above his bed. His little brother didn't ask about his mother any more, and seemed almost defiantly cheerful whenever she was mentioned. Billie had been reading Louise's occasional letters to the boys, and sometimes pinned them to the kitchen bulletin board, but they rarely elicited comment, aside from grunts and nods. She didn't allow herself to think about Louise much, but she sometimes wore one of the sweaters she found when she cleared out her apartment. Red with large green glass buttons and a floppy collar. It was big and saggy, and perfect for certain moods. It had a coffee stain down one sleeve; she'd not washed it, nor she did she intend to. It was a staying-home sweater.

Sometimes she caught Jack staring out the window, but

it wasn't like him to look at the view. She made a careful note of his decreased appetite, but made no comment on his half-eaten dinners. She was losing weight too. She noted the extra time he took in the bathroom, and the way he'd begun to grow his hair a bit longer. He did daily Canadian Air Force exercises and spent weekend afternoons painting abstracts with vivid colours and jagged shapes, or working on the sailboat alone. He played records full blast, an eclectic mixture – Ella Fitzgerald, Kingston Trio, Harry James, *West Side Story*, Simon and Garfunkel. He appeared home with shopping bags full of new shirts and boxer shorts, and she bit her tongue when she wanted to remind him she usually bought his boxers.

One day, she was suddenly inspired.

'Jack! I've got a great idea. Let's invite Ernie and Bernice for the weekend. It's been ages.'

Billie had often been jealous of Jack's devotion to Ernie, but now she saw him as a possible ally. Jack respected Ernie. If Ernie disapproved of this dalliance, if he scoffed at it, Jack would drop it instantly. Wouldn't he? But:

'Not now, Billie. Maybe next month. Got too much on.'

Further proof of Jack's affair. He was afraid of seeing his best friend. Billie was now convinced Ernie would be shocked. Disgusted. In fact, she was on the verge of phoning him herself, when she was derailed by an urgent need to know who she was. Who was this other woman? Really, it shouldn't matter, but it preyed on her. Sometimes she felt quite nauseous with jealousy. It made her stomach clench and her brain stop. She forgot to buy milk, forgot to meet the school bus, forgot to flip over the pancakes when the bubbles stopped filling in. She didn't have many close women friends these days – her husband, she'd hoped, was her best friend – but this was the point at which she began to look at them differently. Was Margery really just wanting to come for a cup of coffee, or was that a suspiciously happy smile she gave Jack when he walked into the kitchen? And newly divorced Karen, with her sexy walk and nice clothes. Divorced women were dangerous, everyone knew that. She phoned her mother.

'Oh, baby,' she said.

'What, Mom? You think I'm just imagining it?' She couldn't read her tone, but some small hope rose.

'No, no. I believe you.' Pause. 'I believe you.'

'You do?'

'Oh, Billieboo. Of course I do. He's a good-looking man, and you're tied to all those fucking kids.'

Billie slumped inside, but also felt irritated. And why did her mother always have to swear?

'Does he hit you?'

'Of course not! No!'

'Is he a binge drinker?'

'No. He drinks every day.'

'Well, that's something. Has he joined some kind of cult?'

'Don't be ridiculous.'

'Then what's the problem?'

Then came the announcement:

'Honey, I'll be away next Friday night, all right? We don't have anything planned, do we?'

'What do you mean, away?'

'Oh, some silly staff training session down in Santa Barbara. I really don't want to go, but it's compulsory. All the editors and marketing people. Team-training garbage.'

'Can I come? Just for the evening?'

'Afraid not, sweetie. Wish you could. No spouses allowed.'

He smiled at her and gave her a hug, but now it didn't mean a thing. Worse, it felt insulting. A patronizing hug. She was a fool, an undesired woman, and he felt sorry for her. She wanted to kill him and felt tears welling up. Darn it! Here they were, pouring down. She felt incontinent with self-pity.

'Billie honey, what's the matter? It's only for a night. I'll phone and kiss you goodnight, okay?'

He looked so sincere. Maybe she was wrong. Wouldn't it just spoil things to tell him her suspicions?

'Okay. I'm being silly. Sorry.'

'Anyway, you'll be busy with the kids.'

'True,' she said, sniffing. Willy was teething again; she couldn't even leave him with a babysitter.

'Go get yourself a Kleenex. Come on, my girl.'

He never called her *my girl*, but it had come out so naturally, as if he said it all the time. Maybe that's what he called *her*. The evening petered out unmemorably, except it was the night his fling was spelled out in the air for her to read and reread. When she pictured her life a few years ago – contentedly married with two children, and a sister she loved and hated – well, that seemed like a very faded postcard now. She was on an overloaded boat with a dead engine, and the rip tide was pulling them further and further away from that place in the postcard. She was seasick.

Time passed. Elisabeth moved into her new bedroom in the garage. Willy moved out of his parents' bedroom, into Elisabeth's old room. The three boys grumbled that they still shared a room, so they moved into the larger master

221

bedroom. A man walked on the moon and everyone sat on the sofa and floor to watch it, while Billie stood by the set, twiddling the vertical knob and wriggling the aerial whenever the picture started flipping up. Three weeks later, a music festival happened on a farm on the east coast. The older children talked of nothing else and began wearing headbands, and making the peace sign whenever possible. Hellos and goodbyes were fingers flipping V's, and for days Billie thought they meant victory over something. Everything seemed to be happening at once, fastfastfast, and meanwhile her husband was loving some other woman. She could hardly pay attention to it all, and still get dinner on the table every night, still keep clean socks in drawers and spare toilet rolls in the bathroom cupboard. The world made a rushing noise in her head, and she hunkered down inside herself. Focused on the essentials of day to day life.

Soon Billie could not remember a time when she was not aware of the affair. She lived with this invisible third party always present. For Jack, it was the same, so each of them – separately and secretly – had more in common than they'd ever had before. They were each living a double life. Jack with Colette, and Billie with the idea of Colette. But all affairs have their lifespan, their own plot line, and finally came the climatic night. Billie had been sensing an increasing urgency, coupled with an increasing carelessness. Did Jack want her to find out? It seemed like it, with his openly flirtatious phone conversations, his coldness in bed, his transparent excuses for everything from a late night home to yet another overnight meeting in Santa Barbara. It was a Saturday night, a night that still had some of the heat of the day, and flies were buzzing in circles in the kitchen. No one noticed them usually but tonight Jack ran around with a fly swat, cussing and slapping. He tried to mend the screen door, but it still wouldn't close all the way.

The phone rang. Billie was standing right next to it, but before she could answer it, he grabbed it, covered the mouthpiece and hissed to his wife:

'Do you mind? This is private.'

'What do you mean? Who do you need to be private with?'

'Work! It's Bob from work, about the new writer he signed up. He gets pissed off if he thinks anyone's listening.'

'It's not a work day. It's Saturday night,' she answered limply.

She left the room, and two minutes later he went out too, saying offhandedly:

'I'll be back later honey, don't wait up.'

Impossible to be forty years old and feel this way, but here he was, driving like a teenager, heart pounding, head bursting, to his lover's house. She'd given him an ultimatum.

Leave Billie.

Leave her and live with me.

Do you love me? You said you loved me.

He might never again in his life have such great sex, and he could easily die of this deprivation. He knew this sounded melodramatic, but he couldn't help it. If he said no to Colette, he'd be saying no to life. Imagine if he'd never slept with Colette! He'd never have discovered how amazing it felt to do *this* to a woman, and have *that* done to him. And he used to scoff at D.H. Lawrence, think nothing was really that horny. People didn't really act like animals, not in his experience. It was all pretty hot, especially in the honeymoon period, but even then there'd been no torn clothes, no begging for it in coarse vocabulary, and certainly no anal sex. Colette called it love. He didn't have a word for it. Sex with Colette was like being stunned by gunshot. Violent, thought-stopping, cutting to the bone every time. He slammed on the brakes in her driveway, hurtled to her door, which was locked. Knocked loudly, indifferent to the neighbours. At first he thought he was too late. He stood there and called her name, with a world of wretchedness in his voice.

Six thirty in the morning, and Billie heard the car. Without thinking, she got up and pulled on a coat – his raincoat, because she was too upset to see what she was wearing – and slipped out the back door onto the deck. Huddled in the dawn, behind the barbecue. She heard him walk in, switch lights on, use the bathroom. Then through the closed door, she heard his voice call her name. She heard her name in his voice, and it was like an executioner's voice, cajoling the prisoner to place his head in the noose. Indifferent. Impatient, even. It was a midsummer morning, not a cloud in the sky. It was going to be hot later, hot enough for a swim, she thought. She thought of that time she and Louise dared each other to jump off the bridge into the Sacramento River, and they'd held hands and jumped together.

Her bare feet were wet from the dew, and all she had on under the raincoat was her thin nightgown. A mourning dove in the lemon tree sang those elegiac notes, high for one count, then low for four counts. LA la-la-la-la. LA la-la-la-la.

'Billie? Billie!'

She shivered. Held her breath. Inside the house was her life, her old life. There it waited, and she would not go in to say goodbye to it. She would not. More footsteps, more doors opening and closing. He'd wake the baby if he wasn't careful. Then she'd have to breathe again. Finally, he called in a tone she recognized from way back. From those days by the Bay. Her red dress with the yellow roses, and his Old Spice cologne. It was as if layers had been stripped off him during the catastrophic night and dawn, and here he was again at last. A skinny, shy kid who hated to be alone in the house.

'Billie? Hon?'

LA la-la-la-la.

EIGHTEEN MONTHS EARLIER

If You Come to San Francisco

July 8th, 1967, San Miguel, Marin County
5:32pm

Early evening, but still in the low nineties. The blinds had been closed all day, the windows all wide open. Jack sat in the living room in his white T-shirt and khaki shorts while she cooked. He drank a cold martini, an especially strong one, and watched the news. Viet Nam was heating up again. The world was going to hell. Did Johnson know what he was doing or not? Jack was a loyal democrat; hated these doubts. Yesterday, six reported American casualties, forty-two Viet Cong casualties. Helluva word for it, *casualties*. Euphemisms made him cranky.

He went into the kitchen and made another drink. He carefully peeled the lime, added one green olive to the glass, measured the gin and vermouth in a tiny silver cup, then poured it and added two ice cubes. Tasted it. Added another dollop of gin. Tasted again. Yes! Absent-mindedly

226

he kissed the back of Billie's head as she peeled potatoes for mash. This made him happy too. He loved mashed potatoes. Then he went back to his chair and watched a clip of an anti-war demonstration in San Francisco. Thousands marching down Market Street, then up Powell to Union Square. Disjointed chanting and singing, and under the words, steady drumming on something metallic. *And it's one, two, three, what are we fighting for? Don't ask me, I don't give a damn. We're off to Viet Nam.* It was amazing how many pretty girls were marching – and even without his glasses he could see they were not wearing bras, most of them. Unbelievable. Nipples just out there, poking through tight T-shirts for anyone to see. Sure, the war was upsetting folk, but look at them – all the marchers had happy faces. These days the world was a fun place all right, and San Francisco in summer was the centre of the universe. Everyone said so. Lots of songs did, anyway. *If you're going to San Francisco, be sure to wear some flowers in your hair.* From all over the country, everyone was coming here for a...*love-in?* He could hardly think the phrase without smirking. Jack had smelled patchouli dozens of times before he heard the word patchouli, and it was another three months before he knew how the word looked on the page. He imagined Union Square now in a patchouli cloud. It reminded him of sex somehow.

'Billie!' he called.

She drifted into the living room, wiping her hands on her jeans. She owned several aprons given to her by his mother, but thought them very unflattering.

'What is it honey?'

'Where are the kids?'

'In their rooms. Homework. You told them, remember? No TV.'

'Oh, yeah. Right. Good.'

'Uh-huh. Why?'

'Oh, nothing. Just wondered.'

'Okay. Dinner in half an hour.'

Something about the way they interacted these days made passion difficult to initiate. Were they too familiar to each other? Too self-conscious? Had they become like competitive siblings? Goddammit. He nursed his martini, felt the lust fade in a sweetly melancholy way.

Ah, Life!

In some ways, he felt he was still at the beginning, still making his plans, but here he was already: almost forty. The life expectancy for a man was seventy, which left him thirty more years – assuming the final decade was not spent as a dithering idiot. He felt panicky.

He'd begun painting last year because his latest great novel was stalled in chapter three as usual, and it depressed him. He'd never got beyond a third chapter. Sailing had become a bore too. All that preparation, and later all the putting away of sails and hosing down the decks. Plus Elisabeth and Billie whined whenever it got windy. No one talked to him when he was painting, and a painting could be finished in a day. He'd fallen in love with the smell of linseed oil, and the image of himself as an artist. At first he'd copied the masters: Leonardo, Van Gogh, Picasso. Then he tried painting from life, from photographs. His own house, the children, the beach, sailboats under the Golden Gate. But it was abstract expressionism that really caught his imagination. The challenge of expressing emotion about a thing, without painting the thing itself. To strip all effort at contrivance away, and rely on shapes and colours alone. Surely this was the epitome of art. Pollack, Motherwell, de Kooning had become his idols.

He sat in front of the television, and while the presenter interviewed a local politician, Jack imagined the challenge of putting his whole life into one painting. Taking his nebulous mass of memories and somehow summing them up with oil on a single canvas. How satisfying it would be, to frame it, hang it on the wall, step back and look at it and say, *Well, there it all is!* It might make some sense then.

'Jack?'

'Yes honey?'

'Where are the peppercorns?'

'I have no idea.'

'Okay.'

Seemed like he just filled that pepper grinder! Which perfectly illustrated his point. So – the painting of his life:

Birth. Dot.

Childhood. The twelve years of his mostly unremembered childhood would become a three-inch line of cobalt and chrome yellow. Hot dusty days of boredom. He remembered years of feeling shy, not at home but at school. Lonely. Add some dabs of transparent viridian for each trout he caught while fishing alone on the Sacramento River. Riding his bike home with the fish in a bag hanging from the handlebars. Pretending to go to church with his sister, then sneaking off to the park instead – that would deserve a dollop of chartreuse. Meeting their parents later in front of the church, and making up lies about the service. Being bad with Ivy had been great. Listening to his parents bicker had not been great. They bickered continually, with real venom. Mostly about money. Blue and yellow to make irritating green strokes.

High school. A horizontal line less than an inch, like a dash. Squiggles of burnt sienna and cadmium red would

229

burst from it like a fountain, with patches of deep French ultramarine. Blissful days of swimming and sunbathing and walking for hundreds of hours with Ernie, back and forth to see movies at the Sebastiani Theatre. Talking about nothing and everything. Laughing their heads off. Girls, well, they'd been okay to date, sure, but he'd enjoyed those long walks with Ernie more. And Ivy taking off with that young husband of hers. Oh! That would be deepest darkest indigo, and moist from all those tears he did not cry. Then his dad died, aged forty-eight, and six months later Glen Miller died too. Black smudges, grey at the edges.

Army. Fewer splotches of paint than high school. Some zinc white in there, which would be grey where it mixed with black, in between an inch or two of horizontal blue. That nameless girl in Japan. He could honour her now, with a shape that was both sensual and dignified. Perhaps tones of pure ivory. And though he remembered laughing a lot with all those other soldiers, it hadn't been real laughter. Not the kind he had with Ernie. He'd not kept in touch with a single army friend.

College. An oddly shaped ellipse of time, with no horizontal lines at all. It would be an alizarin crimson explosion, running vertically right off the canvas. Yards and yards of Lizbeth's breasts! Hemingway! Harry James! So many discoveries, so many firsts, it was as if those times had been too large somehow to fit into their allotted minutes and hours. Had leaked into another, more eternal, dimension. That must be what timelessness meant. Literally unattached to time in the normal sense. Defying the laws of physics. Most of all, he remembered consciously refining his own personality. By the time he graduated, Jacko MacAlister was solid, both inside and out. Witty, assured, sexy. Or at least he was under the impression he was, he now realised.

Billie. First week knowing her had lasted about three years – probably an excitable orange, with the oil so thick it would dry in spikes. But that romance had disappeared in a whirlwind gust, and since marriage, the years had gone by without leaving a week's worth of trace, really. More like the transparency of watercolours – mostly green and pale blue. Sure, the babies came, and that had been exciting in a way, little wriggly splodges each of them, but in memorable terms, overall it had been blurry. Losing Charlie would be magenta jabbing into deepest blue. Jab jab jab. But then that too had been absorbed into smoother, more forgettable days. And forgettable days didn't count. Their shape was nowhere near the size it ought to be.

Every change stretched time, but only initially. Like walking the same route every day through the field to the beach, thought Jack. Initially it felt like a long walk, but eventually a path was created. And soon the path was walked in a daydream, feet carving deep ruts. Probably the same as everybody's life, he thought with a sigh. Not so special after all, damn it.

Four years ago they'd stopped moving house. Perhaps that would explain his building restlessness. The sense that something would have to give soon. Like a fault that was due for a quake. If there were to be no more adrenalin-charged house moves, or new jobs, or more babies, or more wives – then what else could change? He told himself that tomorrow he'd attack his great novel again, or start that great painting depicting his life. Quit his job and find a way to start his own publishing house. Make a stance against time passing. Against death itself.

He closed his eyes and let his daily routine run through him. Get up, do a few push-ups, grab some coffee, read the paper, drive down San Pedro, passing the same old man jogging at 4th & Heatherton. And the lady with the three babies in the giant stroller. And the tattooed teenage boy hitching. It always seemed like just five minutes since he last saw them.

He focused on the television again. The hippies were still marching. Was this live news? It seemed so. Life was happening elsewhere, to other people. And it seemed to have happened overnight, all these social changes. He and Billie had been holding steady at young, young, youngish, then suddenly wham! *Not young.* Ponytailed boys and long-haired girls were having sex all the time and laughing at guys like himself. Uptight dudes in suits. Squares. The world was full of undulating copulating bodies, humping away right in plain view.

Free love.

Jealous? Oh yes, he admitted it. Jack was bitterly, passionately jealous. It was so unfair. When he'd been their age, he'd been in Japan wearing an army uniform. And then studying, then working to support a family. Not having an entirely unpleasant time (who said army food was terrible? Jack had loved K-rations), but still. Rewards were supposed to come from hard work and discipline; hippies were cheating. They didn't pay their dues to sing the blues; they didn't even *want* to sing the blues. Dreadful racket, their music. Grateful Dead, Jefferson Airplane, Country Joe and the Fish. But what really annoyed him was the way hippies called themselves freaks and rebels. They were spoiled babies; nothing radical about them at all. Even his own kids pissed him off. Sam, who was nearly fifteen, was about to join the peaceandloveman club, he could tell.

'Stop being such a drag, man.'

'Don't you call *me* man,' Jack had scolded his son.

'Okay, Jack.'

'And don't call me Jack either. Dad. You call me Dad.'

Fledgling flower child, with his tie-dye shirts and KMPX blaring on the radio.

1967 was laughing at Jack, all right. And San Francisco was a party he had not been invited to. He was forty years old during the summer of love and pissed as hell. He could hear his wife whistling in the kitchen, as she clattered pots and pans.

'Billie!'

'What is it now, honey?'

Wiping her hands on her jeans again. Her roots were showing. This was made more obvious because she'd pulled her shoulder length blond hair into a tight ponytail high on her head, fifties-style. Her bangs were about an inch above her eyebrows. Those sexy caterpillars. Looking at her, even while irritated at absolutely everything, he still couldn't help thinking: *Damn fine figure of a woman, my wife.*

'Any more nuts?' He offered up the empty nut dish.

'I'll have a look.'

She took the dish, and he took a Viceroy from the bronze turtle cigarette holder. Lit it for something to put in his mouth, watched Billie return to the kitchen. He could do this from his living room chair. Did other men still check out their wives, after sixteen years? It felt a bit furtive, watching her lean over to find the bag of nuts in the bottom cupboard.

She brought the nuts and sat on the arm of his chair, trying to sense his thoughts. He was in a bad mood, she knew that for certain, and whenever he was tense, he did seem to get more...affectionate.

'Oh, look, Jack, isn't that Union Square?'

To Billie, it seemed innocent – a whole generation of kids had cottoned on to the war-is-bad idea, as if they'd just discovered the wheel. Bless! Just look at them flash each other the peace sign, like a tribal code. They all seemed adorable. Like Sam and Elisabeth. Silly, soft kids, doing silly semi-dangerous things. Half the time she wanted to walk right up to them, scold them for their own good. Give the girls baggy shirts to cover up their nipples. Pass out bus tickets to the boys hitching on the on-ramps. Overall, she preferred hippies to the beatniks. The Beat movement had never really interested her; black was unflattering, unless you were fat. Loners and show offs and pretentious queer poets were beatniks. Oh, well. She guessed everyone had to belong to some group when they were young. But wait, had *she* ever belonged to a group? She'd been a cheerleader once.

She thought of her mother's world, and her grand-mother's. All those silent movies, the Buster Keatons and Laurel & Hardys. The rattling little black cars that needed to be crank started, the stiff corsets and eternal gloves, the way every man and woman had worn a hat. How those things must, in their own day, have seemed so exciting, so modern compared to what had come before. And now look at them. People just laughed at their old-fashioned ways. As for the clothes – well, it had recently occurred to her that the outfits her mom wore, were simply the clothes she'd always worn. And her grandmother hadn't suddenly started wearing flowery dresses when she'd turned seventy; she'd always favoured floral. No doubt, the Levi jeans and L.L. Bean polo shirt that felt youthful to her right now, would one day be perceived as old lady clothes too. She thought it strange and amusing, that

234

every generation felt superior to the previous one. Not only superior, but less innocent. She'd often wondered when it would apply to her own generation, and here it was. Happening right before her still-young eyes.

Billie was secretly enchanted by hippies. They reminded her of the travelling show that used to come to the county fairground every spring. The rides, the costumes, the exoticness, the way all her friends and family would become slightly exotic that weekend too. Stuffing pink cotton candy into their mouths, addicted to the sensation of melting-to-sweet-nothingness on their tongues. Drinking too much beer, laughing hard, shooting plastic rifles for lurid stuffed pandas. The late sixties, so far, had that same glorious anarchy. So shamelessly raunchy! She'd never forget her sister, Louise, screaming from the top of the Ferris wheel, that she loved Johnny Tib, who was, of course, still married to that tramp he got pregnant in sophomore year. Betsy Snodgrass, with her pointy bra and kohl eyeliner.

Johnny, on the ground, shouting up to Louise: 'Run away with me then!'

And Louise screaming back: 'Yes! Yes!'

By Monday he'd finished with Louise, and she'd consoled herself with bespectacled sweet Chuck, who'd always been too shy to ask her out, and now, in her humiliation, saw his chance at last. Billie remembered her sister clinging to him as if he'd rescued her from a burning building, but for years now, Louise had done nothing but complain that Chuck was boring. His hair was still a crew cut, he liked his jeans ironed and his mealtimes regular, while she'd let her hair grow long, wore headbands, and begun meditation classes. Come to think of it, she'd stopped shaving her legs too. God only knew what was going on with her armpits.

The sixties was a travelling show her sister might be joining, but Billie didn't have an admission ticket for it. There it was, just the other side of the chain-link fence. Visible, audible, smellable. Once, alone in the bathroom, she'd made the peace sign to herself in the mirror. Smiled the way she'd seen some of the long-haired bare-faced girls smile: sleepily, carelessly, sexily. Eyes half shut. Did being Mrs Jack MacAlister, mother of two, driver of a station wagon, mean she was forever banned from summers of love? And how had this happened so quickly? She'd thought *they* were the hip ones. Even the word hip was not hip any more.

She was still on the arm of his chair, and they were both still watching the news. Weather now. Tomorrow would be in the nineties again. Crazy-making headachy heat.

'Jack, the kids are on vacation.'

'So?'

'So how can they do homework?'

'Jesus, Billie. I don't know. I just meant...*go to your rooms!* The homework bit just came out automatically. They were both rude.'

'Can I tell them they can come out now?'

Pause. Jack looked up at Billie, a silly smile creeping out. He loved it when she kowtowed to him like this. So what if it was just her ploy.

'Nah,' he said, and slid an arm around her waist. 'Not yet.'

She knew he loved her. These quiet moments were the best. The news program cut to a commercial. *Rice-A-Roni! The San Francisco treat! Rice-A-Roni! Everybody's got the beat!* She made a mental note to buy some, then yawned, raised her arms up high, let her breasts rise

236

too, till Jack had to stop pretending he was watching television. He pulled her onto his lap, and she giggled her little-girl giggle. In this moment of forgetfulness, they slipped into their old selves, and every single thing in the world – even the children – disappeared.

Then the phone rang.

Jack tried to hold on to her, but Billie sprang up to answer it. It was sufficient that he'd pulled her onto his lap. Anticipation, for her, was the best part. But Jack's spirits dipped immediately. She never wanted sex.

'Jack, it's the boy about the Volkswagen you saw in the paper.'

He took the phone, and Billie danced a little and sang softly. *Sugar! Honey, honey! You are my candy girl, and you got me wanting you.* One thing about Billie, she'd always been light on her feet. Jack could hike, play tennis, sail a boat, ride a ten speed, but could he dance? Billie danced around him now like a nymphet, as he talked on the phone about mileage and air-cooled engines.

After the boy had been paid and the VW Beetle parked in his garage, Jack did a territorial inventory. Emptied out the glove compartment, peeked inside the trunk, under the seats. The boy had been just another spoiled brat driving a car his dad bought him, and there was lots of junk left behind. Hershey wrappers, beer cans, butts. Jack threw all these out onto the floor of the garage, with disgust. Then, in the little pocket on the back of the driver's seat, he found a sandwich baggie full of green...what the hell?

A week later, Sam was rummaging in his dad's sock drawer for a pair to wear to school, as usual. Why were his dad's socks so much nicer? They just were. And there it was, nearly an ounce of marijuana in his father's sock drawer. Jiminyfuckencricket! He'd only just begun smoking joints himself, and felt both proud and sinful about it. Now he frowned. Was there no way to rebel against this man?

They decided to go for a walk in the woods, not too far from home. The neighbour's dog followed them, a red setter. It was a delicious day, and the sun filtered down through the eucalyptus trees. The air was a warm fug of tree menthol and dust raised from their hiking boots. After a while they stopped, sat on a log, and Sam rolled a joint. Jack loved to smoke, and he sucked the joint down like the first cigarette of the day. The dog wandered off. There she went, her tail thwacking the underbrush.

'Lady!' called Jack. 'Lady, come here!'

'Just leave it, Dad. Not our dog.'

'We didn't stop her following us.'

Jack kept calling, and the dog kept walking. Then his voice dissolved. He couldn't even finish saying her name without giggling so hard he fell off the log.

'La…deeee!'

'La…! Dee…!'

'La…la….la…! Dee…deee…dee!'

'You okay, Dad? Guess you're feeling it now, eh?'

'Where's she gone? The damn dog's gone!' This was the funniest sentence Jack had ever uttered or heard, and he was speechless for a good five minutes. Tears were rolling down his cheeks, and his son laughed too. In a surprised, conspiratorial way. Then Jack stood up slowly, smiled goofily and meandered off. This way, that way, an aimless gait till he was out of sight.

'Lady!'

His voice trailed through the shadows under the trees, interspersed with low warm laughter.

'Lady!'

He returned with the dog and an anxious face, and sat down beside Sam. He noticed his son's knees still had scabs, just like a seven-year-old. Did he still fall off his bike? And what was he doing smoking this stuff, at his age? He was just a kid. Gin was tons better. You knew where you were with a martini. Must explain that to him. As soon as talking became possible.

'How are you Dad?'

'Not. Good.' He leaned closer and whispered: 'I'm screwed. How can I go home to your mother like this?'

So they walked around a bit, till things seemed less scary for Jack, talking about football scores and camping plans. His eyes were bloodshot and the pupils dilated. By the time they headed back to the house, Jack's heart had stopped pounding quite so fast, and light and sound had almost reverted to normal intensity.

'Thanks, Sam,' he said as they approached home. 'Really.'

'No problemo. Hey, don't look in the mirror for a while, okay?'

'Okay.'

'It's far out, isn't it? Getting high.'

Jack imagined replying that, yes, it was far out getting high, but the phrase made him cringe, would sound affected in his mouth. In any case, talking was still difficult.

It was only 4pm, but Jack went straight to his bedroom to lie down. And there she was. There was his wife. He really did have an actual wife, an entire female human being who belonged to him. Sorting laundry out on the

239

waterbed, neat piles of shirts and shorts and pyjamas – their children's clothes. Imagine that – they had two children! Children who wore clothes! One of whom just got his old dad stoned. His whole life was a Goddamn miracle.

Billie was her usual dreamy self. The summer months, with the kids home, seemed to be an endless round of interruptions and domestic chores. She was never alone, and missed her solitude a bit but didn't dwell on it. Most days she moved from one activity to another, and hummed songs from her youth. A bit of hair had fallen out of her ponytail, so it curled up on her neck. That was what he noticed first, as her face was turned away. That curl, that part of her neck. And a relief she wasn't looking at him.

'Not feeling that great, hon. Going to lie down for a while,' he said as naturally as he could, then moved some clothes, lay down on his side and closed his eyes. The water in the bed sloshed loudly. He stayed still and waited for the turbulence to subside. How had he never noticed how noisy it was? But still, it was warm at night when he got in, and also proved they were not valley fuddy-duddies. All in all, a great way to sleep. But what was that smell? Jesus, since when had clean clothes smelled like this? He wanted to bury his face in the neat pile next to him. He wanted to open his mouth and eat those shirts. He was very conscious that everything was wonderful, but what he really wanted was to feel normal again. He sighed. His old self, that oblivious being, hovered just beyond the bed. Oh, blessed unselfconsciousness!

He heard the door close softly, and the water sloshing of Billie on the bed beside him. She lifted one of his arms and placed it around her chest, as she manoeuvred

240

herself backwards into the curve of his body. For a few minutes Jack slipped into a deep sleep, as if her presence had unlocked him somehow, returned him to his relaxed self. Wife as antidote to marijuana-induced paranoia. But when she moved slightly, he instantly rose to the surface. Trying to ape normality, he slid a hand up her leg. Then scooped her breast inside her bra, recorded how moist it felt. He didn't feel inside his own body – instead, he watched himself. She was a stranger, really. He was a stranger too. And hell – what he was doing was just bizarre, wasn't it? Wanting to literally slot into this being. This woman. He carried on regardless, but while fiddling with the condom, was humiliated to find there was nothing to make one necessary.

'It's okay, honey,' she said casually, as if this was not an entirely new experience. 'I've got to take Elisabeth and Sam to the mall now anyway.'

He got up after he heard the front door slam, and went to his desk. Tried to work, then decided to do chores instead. Nothing that required thought. Tightened the hinges on the basement door. Paid some bills. All the while thinking: *To hell with marijuana.* Goddammit, what if it's ruined him permanently?

Then he stopped suddenly and phoned Ernie.

'So, Ernie, you know about grass, right? Joints.'

'I know, but have you tried any?'

'Really! Both of you?'

'Me too! Yeah, yeah. A while ago. Well, earlier today, actually.'

'To be honest, I liked it, but then I hated it.'

'But yeah, me too. Nah, nah.'

'No, not Billie. Not yet. Maybe never, to be honest. She doesn't even drink, much.'

And though nothing they said was particularly funny, he laughed his old laugh. His old Ernie-laugh. Thank God for Ernie.

Then, while he was thinking of something else, he was delivered back to his old frame of mind. Whew! And yet, within seconds, he was remembering being stoned as a pleasurable experience. Scary, sure, but like a roller-coaster ride. Adrenalin washing the pettiness of daily life out of him, and now he felt like a new man. A different man, but with a connection to his youngest, truest self. The Jacko he'd thought he'd lost for ever. That cocky boy. He said to himself, parenthood and marriage clipped my wings, but I am back in the saddle now. (Automatically he noted his mixed metaphor, as if he was editing some manuscript. Some days, he couldn't say or hear anything without mentally editing it. Every time someone said *Have a nice day!* he marked it with a red pen. *Cliché*. Unless it was meant ironically, of course.)

All evening, he took covert looks at Billie, while she was scolding the children, filling the dishwasher, picking her nose when she thought no one could see her. Later in bed, he told her to leave the light on, and she did, reluctantly. Asked her to take her pyjamas off slowly. And she did.

'Wait, honey,' she said. 'Wait till I get a thing for you.'

But suddenly things had gone too far, and he thought: Oh well, what harm can one time without do? Also thought: when was the last time he'd felt like this? The last time she'd kissed him back like this? In fact, had they ever kissed like this before? The waterbed sloshed noisily for fifteen minutes.

Two months passed. Billie was on a grapefruit diet, but it was a disaster. She'd been eating nothing but grapefruit for almost seven weeks, and all she had was indigestion. In fact, she'd put on weight! Billie was thirty-eight and in search of her eighteen-inch waist. She blamed her children. Three delivered by caesarean, after stretching her poor belly skin to smithereens. The memory of Charlie flicked through her with its habitual jagged bite, then her thoughts moved on, she always made them move on. He was the flicker that shadowed her days. A silence that took up space, rising and then falling back again. *She would wear that grey dress again.* It cost a fortune, and she would not give it to the Goodwill. It hung at the front of her closet, a daily taunt. Wasn't it pretty, with its fine embroidery on the yoke, and the three-quarter-length sleeves? The narrow grey belt? Sophisticated, that's what it was. Something a valley girl would wear, it was not. Every time Billie thought of her childhood, she shuddered. Milly Mae Molinelli grew up in a hick town. Billie MacAlister, or Mrs Jack MacAlister as she preferred to be called, lived in her own house in Marin County, the wife of a very successful publishing executive. (So what if his business card called him editor; he was an executive, really. She told everyone so.) Her children – a girl and a boy, yes, how lucky! – attended a good school and played with the children of psychiatrists and doctors and lawyers. Mrs Jack MacAlister dressed with understated flair. She was classy. Very. She wore real Levis, not cheap imitation Levis. She bought expensive (on sale) dresses from I. Magnins, if proof was needed.

Every day, she sent her young husband off to work in his Brooks Brothers yellow or pink shirt. Well, Jack was not young, but to Billie he was still exactly the same boy with extraordinary cowlicks who'd walked into her office that day. In her mind, the fact she'd married him was entirely down to her determination, born that first day, to catch that cocky boy as he was walking away from her down Pine Street. Cupid with his arrow poised had Billie's face and her steady aim. She'd arranged her own marriage. And if it wasn't always perfect, well – *c'est la vie!* Also, *que sera sera!* It was perfectly normal to feel life was one step forward, two steps back. Or was it two steps forward, one step back? Some days felt like one step forward, six steps back.

Maybe she should quit the grapefruit diet, she was starting to feel sick. Car sick, all day. Or maybe she really was sick. A stomach bug. Or food poisoning. Then one day, a Monday, her shopping day, she vomited in the cold cereal aisle. It was that sudden – no warning, no time to get to the bathroom. Her children were disgusted. Billie was embarrassed, but also worried now. She made a doctor's appointment.

'How long have you been feeling nauseous?'

'Oh, a few months.' She wouldn't tell him about the grapefruit diet. He'd scold her.

'Could you be expecting?'

She looked at him blankly, waiting for him to finish his sentence. Expecting what? For it to rain at last? For her waist to return and the grey dress to fit?

Eating normally again was bliss. Now that she knew the reason, the sick feeling was ignorable. As soon as Jack got home, she'd tell him. Except that when he got home, he was in a lousy mood for some reason to do with his boss, and a writer whose name was misspelled on the book cover. So she decided to wait. Billie had more respect for her husband and his career than most people had for the president. Well, this president, anyway.

Besides, he'd said many times that two was the perfect number. (Charlie had been an accident too.) Their house only had three bedrooms. Their family was complete, and other challenges were occupying him now. While rehearsing how to tell him, she cooked his favourite dinner: meatloaf. She poured a lot of ketchup into the meat mixture, and used white bread crumbs, a few spoons of sugar and an egg. Squished it all between her fingers till it was gluey enough to form a loaf. Three strips of bacon over the top, for that salty crispy flavour. Ah! Nothing like meatloaf. They both liked it, though it was valley food, so a private liking. She'd tell him tonight. After dinner.

She glanced at him occasionally while she was peeling potatoes. He sat in the living room and frowned over a checkbook. Oh dear. Budget night again already. How could she have forgotten? She'd wait till tomorrow to tell him. Or the weekend. He was always more relaxed on the weekend. Maybe they'd have a dinner party, with some of Jack's work friends. It was kind of cute the way he got out his brass water pipe when they had company. Everyone was wanting to try it these days. Their crowd had been invited to join the party after all. Personally, she didn't care for marijuana. She had enough trouble holding her thoughts in a useful way, as it was. And besides, smoking anything these days made her cough. At the same time, she was proud her husband smoked the occasional joint or pipe. They were a modern liberal family. She was still doing things her mother would not approve of.

'Hooray!' she said softly to herself, breaking up the syllables to make two words. Hoo. Ray.

Meanwhile, the kitchen radio played KFRC's hit

parade. The new hit by the Bee Gees, 'To Love Some-body'. And while the meatloaf sizzled in the oven, Billie's feet did a graceful little dance between the sink and the counters. She didn't even notice – she was that anxious about her secret. Her breasts were hot and heavy already, but the rest of her, her feet and legs, her arms and hands, was blissfully unaware of the change, while she slow danced with herself.

She sang along.

There's a light, a nanana of light, that shines on me. Nananananana. If I ain't got you. If I ain't got you. You don't know what it's like, you don't know what it's like, to love nanana, to love nanana. The way that I love you.

She didn't know all the words; she never did and she didn't care.

TWO YEARS EARLIER

Home on the Road

April 10th, 1965, Highway Five
8:42am

They were driving up the valley highway. Elisabeth and Sam were sitting in the back seat of the old green Hillman. Billie looked out the front window, but the low morning sun flickering dark-bright dark-bright through the straight rows of olive trees hurt her eyes, so she turned to look out the side window. Concentrated on looking down each long row of trees. Focus, blur, focus again; a row a second. In and out. It was hard work but it kept her busy and it was not as confusing. She was very tired. Then her eye caught the first sign. It was a wooden placard of a fat Italian-looking woman, her black hair in a red spotted kerchief and a frying pan in her hand. And though Billie was nearly thirty-six, she still felt the old excitement. She forgot the rows of trees and sat forward to look for the next sign. Her mouth started to water in anticipation, and there it was – a thin wooden man in a blue striped apron, his hands on his hips and a string of sausages dangling around his neck. Yes. Then the sign with the single word. *Bill*. Then the sign saying *and Kathy's*.

She turned around to see if the kids had noticed. For a millisecond, she saw Charlie between them, his chubby cheeks and his wild infant hair, then he was gone. Sam and Elisabeth's eyes were not shut, but they looked asleep. Slack, pale. She couldn't help but notice again how they'd lost their cuteness. In fact, at twelve and ten, they were both, in different ways, quite funny looking. Sam was still very blond and Elisabeth's dark hair was pretty, but they were both too skinny, too freckled and pale, with sticky-out ears and gangly hands and large bony feet. She and Jack had discussed this and laughed. How could two beautiful people make such funny-looking kids? Maybe it would skip a generation. Maybe their granddaughters would have feminine feet and their grandsons not have sticky out ears. Meanwhile, even as it puzzled her, she felt an extra protectiveness towards Sam and Elisabeth. To begin life with such a disadvantage.

'Anyone awake yet? No?' shouted Jack. 'Then we'll forget Bill and Kathy's and keep going.'

'Stop the car! Pancakes!' both the children cried, shedding years and yelling like six-year-olds.

On the horizon, across from twin silver silos and surrounded by flat fields, was the familiar building – log cabin style, with old covered-wagon wheels fencing in ice plants.

'Nah, let's go on to the Red Top. It's only thirty miles.'

'Daddy! Stop the car! Put on your blinker, put on your brakes!'

'What? Did you hear something, honey?' No slowing down.

'Jack, cut it out. They'll be hysterical. She'll throw up.'

'Mom's right. I'm going to be sick, I'm going to vomit all over the seat, stop the car!'

'You always go too far, Jack.'

He smiled as if this was a compliment. Sprinklers sprayed them lightly as they walked up the path to the restaurant, the kids running ahead. Bacon and coffee beckoned, but it was the pancakes they came for. Short stacks, tall stacks, five inches across, melting whipped butter and hot maple syrup. Sometimes the blueberry syrup. Every Easter and every Thanksgiving – the long drive up the valley to Billie's mother in Redding. They always had early morning starts, and in the beginning Jack and Billie would carry the limp pretending-to-be-asleep bodies of their children out to the car, and bundle them into the back seat. Pancakes at Bill and Kathy's was part of the ritual.

Back in the car, heading north again, the second phase of the journey began. Four hours to go. The Sacramento valley was flat as Kathy's pancakes. The straight road disappeared in a shimmering heat haze. Jack fiddled with the radio dial, scooting past country-and-western singers singing about dead dogs, preachers preaching about Judgment Day, commercials for manure and cheap vacations in Reno. Billie squinted her eyes and tried to see mirages. The watery waves rising from the highway, then vanishing as they got closer. By eleven o'clock both children were bare-chested and the windows were all the way down and the dust of the farms was coating everyone inside and out. Up ahead, it would all be washed away in the shower in the cool basement, but for now it felt permanent. A dust-coated family.

Jack pulled over at a rest stop and they switched places; Billie drove and Jack tried to snooze. And as they approached the heart of the trip, Billie realized she was waiting. There was always a fight – she couldn't remember a trip up the valley that did not include bickering, then loud hurled words, then hours of silence. The core of the day. Awareness didn't ever seem to prevent it, and she was listening for its beginning.

'Billie! Pull back, you can't pass that truck now.'

'Darn it Jack, you made me jump – don't do that! You almost caused an accident.'

'Stopped one, you mean.'

'Do you want to drive?'

'No. I'm going to sleep,' he said, and closed his eyes.

'Because if you can't trust me to drive, maybe you'd better.'

'I'm not listening. You just want to argue.'

'I just want to be treated with some respect. When you're driving, do I continually criticize you?'

'Shut up, Billie.'

'No, I will not. When you drive, I trust you, I relax.'

'I'm tired, Billie.'

'I don't know why. It wasn't you that stayed up till midnight packing.'

'I loaded the car.' He opened his eyes and yawned.

'Which took five minutes.'

'Jesus, that Chevy's right on our ass. Get back in the slow lane.'

'That's it. You can drive.' Brakes squealing, more dust rising, more cars honking angrily.

'Fine.'

'And we're getting a dog, Jack. We all want a dog.'

'We are not getting a dog.'

This part of the fight went on so long and was so familiar, Sam and Elisabeth ignored it and waved to strangers in other cars. Sometimes people waved back, which made them laugh hysterically, as if they'd played a trick. Sometimes teenage boys flipped their middle finger, which was not as funny. When a truck was alongside, they tried to catch the driver's eye and pump their right arms, and sometimes the driver obliged by pulling his horn. More giggles.

'Aren't you two getting a little old for that?'

'Oh, leave them alone, Jack. They're bored.'

After a while, they played a languid game of naming the fifty states. They had fifteen more to go. Billie half listened and tried to visualize a map of the United States. What were the names of all those little states up in the right-hand corner? Eventually, Sam fell asleep and Elisabeth dozed off too, her mouth hanging open and her head jerking on the sticky seat back. When she woke an hour later, she said:

'Stop the car, I'm going to be sick.'

'Jack, did you hear her? Stop the car.'

'I can't right now. There's no shoulder. She'll have to wait.'

'Can you wait a minute, honey?' said Billie. 'Put your head out the window. Breathe deeply.'

Elisabeth couldn't even open her mouth to answer, the sick was so imminent. She swallowed convulsively.

'Jack, you'd better pull over.'

'Goddammit!' as he swerved onto a rough embankment and someone honked. Elisabeth got out of the car, leaned over and retched dryly. Nothing. Billie stood just behind her, thinking: Oh no, not again.

'Has she been sick yet?'

'No. Come on, honey, hurry up and throw up. Your dad wants to get going.'

251

'I can't.'

'What do you mean you can't. Just do it.'

Elisabeth leaned over and tried to trick her stomach into emptying by making the noises of vomiting.

'I can't, Mom. I don't want to any more. I feel fine.'

'Are you sure? We aren't stopping again for a while.'

'I'm sure.'

They both got back in the car and Jack turned back on the highway. Billie felt good now, but couldn't trace the source at first. Her daughter's carsickness? Why would that lift her heart? But there was something about the familiarity of what had just occurred. The way it instantly dissolved tension between herself and Jack. They seemed to nip at each other all the time now; it was background music. Bickering and then noticing an absence of bickering. When had the habit started? She reflected, not for the first time, that if they hadn't married so quickly, so romantically, if they'd waited till they'd really *known* each other, they might never have married. Maybe the whole point of marriage was to make those promises before you really knew the other person. Maybe marriage had to be undertaken while sedated with lust.

Well! So be it. Probably every new wife woke up one day and suddenly noticed her husband didn't much resemble the man she married. That he was really very annoying, that he farted loudly and all the time, and slurped his cereal repulsively. And this was where married love really came into its own, she thought. Love, while he farted long and loud and accused you of bad driving again. While your daughter tried and failed to vomit by the roadside, again. Not getting dizzy, while going round and round the same old circles.

Billie half smiled, not at Jack, but out the side window.

She felt wise. And superior to her sister, who just last week had said about her husband: 'I'm not saying I'm leaving him today, I'm just saying – I ain't waiting till the cows come home to do it. Every day, I wake up and feel ready to roll, then I go to the grocery store instead. I'm going stir crazy.' Clearly Loulou did not have sticking power, and was never going to discover what Billie had discovered. That a veteran marriage could be hell, but it could also have shiny moments like this.

'Mom.'

'What?'

'Nothing.'

'She's not about to throw up, is she?' asked Jack.

'Do you feel sick again, Elisabeth?'

'No. Yes. A little.'

'We'll stop at the next rest area. Ten miles,' said Jack. 'Can you wait ten minutes, honey?'

She nodded and closed her eyes.

'Don't close your eyes. Look straight ahead and – oh my God. Stop the car, Jack.'

'Goddammit.' More cars honking. 'Did she do it in the bag?'

'No.'

'Why not – oh Christ, it's everywhere.'

'I didn't have a bag. Sorry.'

'Why didn't she have a bag, Billie?'

'Because she didn't, that's why. Just shut up and give her your handkerchief.'

'Jesus, why am I always the only one to ever have a handkerchief in this family?'

'Because you're so darn perfect, of course.'

Aside from the car overheating twice in the afternoon, and Sam being caught cheating on naming the states by looking at the out of state licence plates, the rest of the trip passed uneventfully. It took eight hours instead of six, but so what. Jack and Billie had used all the usual words with each other and subsided into dulled silence. Sam half read an Archie comic, while Elisabeth half stared at the road. All day she'd kept some distance from Sam, but now she was splayed out so her legs rested against his. The ghost, or idea, of their missing brother skirted round the edges of Billie's thoughts, but not theirs. No one talked to them about Charlie any more.

By five o'clock, it was not a lot cooler but it was not as glaringly bright and everyone felt more human. Jack especially felt good. He kept thinking about his new twenty-foot sailboat, and wondered which varnish to buy for the decking – the cheap one or the expensive one. And what to call it. *Dream Come True*? No, that was corny. How about something classier like *Nora*, from *Ulysses*? Or Epiphany. God, he loved James Joyce. He'd call his boat *Epiphany*. You couldn't get more Joycean than *Epiphany*, and anyone who didn't get it, well, that'd be their problem. And he'd get the expensive varnish. Home seemed very far away and the world had shrunk up to the size of his family and thoughts about varnish brands. The drive, which always seemed interminable, now had an end in sight. On the horizon were the minuscule buildings of his mother-in-law's town.

'At last,' said Billie, brushing her hair.

'At last,' echoed Sam. 'I can't wait.'

'Huh,' grunted Elisabeth, stretching her arms above her head. 'Well, I can. I can wait just fine. I kind of like this right now.'

'You numbskull,' said Sam. 'You just puked your guts out, and now you're saying you want to keep going?'

'Well, yeah.'

Jack looked at his daughter in the rear-view mirror. She caught his eyes, stared blankly, then abruptly smiled. He smiled back, and it felt as if there was an adult secret between them.

'I don't get you,' mumbled Sam. 'You're nuts.'

'Ah, leave her alone,' said Jack, because all of a sudden he felt the same way she did. That actually, he *could* wait too. The wheels of the car were bumping over the heat cracks in the highway and the air rushing in his window smelled of exhaust fumes and overripe fruit. For the first time this spring, he noticed the poppies; they dotted the verges along the highway, humble wisps of orange. It was good to see them again. His family was safe and near him and quiet, and soon he'd teach them all how to sail. Ernie had been showing him; it was easy. His body felt relaxed and alert now, the same way he'd felt after that first day sailing. Tension and nausea, then a wonderful loosening and energy. Behind him was home, the office, daily commuting, friends; ahead lay white bread salami sandwiches with the crusts cut off like Billie never made them, Easter Sunday Mass, endless sports on television, his mother-in-law bringing him cold beer and the house full of those marshmallow eggs no one ever ate. But right now, just driving the car at dusk, just letting his thoughts float in the haze and *not arriving yet*, well – this would feel fine for ever.

Billie and Jackie

❦

Oct 2nd, 1963, Sacramento
10:29am

After the kids had gone to school, Billie sat at the kitchen table and made a list. Making lists was something Jacko had taught her to do. At first she hadn't seen the point, but now she was addicted. At the top, in big loopy letters, she neatly wrote:

Things Me & Jackie Kennedy Have in Common
(Then underlined it.)

Things Me & Jackie Kennedy Have in Common

- Names – 2 syllables. Both names end in eee sound. Billeee. Jackeee.
- 2 kids, boy & girl
- Kids are two years apart

- Caesarean both times
- My Charlie. Jackie's Patrick.
- Catholic Church
- *Camelot* – Fav musical
- Fathers absent since we were seven. (Jackie's due to divorce, mine to death.)
- One full sibling, a sister (like Jacko too)
- Birthdays – 10 months apart, same year
- Same patent leather purse. Almost.
- Me – Homecoming Queen '46. Jackie – Debutante of the Year '47.
- Profile. Same chin. Forehead. (well, everyone *says* so!)
- Hair style. Left parting.
- Hair texture. Different colour, but same depth of colour, the same thickness.

On the front page of the *Sacramento Bee*, Jackie Kennedy was wearing a hair clip which was exactly like the one Billie was wearing right this very instant. Clipped to the right side of her head, holding her hair off her forehead.

- Same hair clip!

Sixteen similarities. Uncanny, that's what it was. So not surprising, really, that they were both married to charismatic powerful men. Jacko and John. And wasn't John sometimes called Jack? Mr MacAlister and President Kennedy. Mrs J. MacAlister and the First Lady. Billie and Jackie!

Okay, so their backgrounds were not similar. And their income. And the Kennedys, it had to be said, were a well-established American dynasty, whereas the MacAlister dynasty was still being created. But the affinity was there, and Billie knew, *just knew,* that if she and Jackie were to ever meet, they would be instant friends. She felt closer to her than she did to her own sister. Louise, well, of course Billie loved her…but let's face it, Louise lacked class. Not only did she not aspire to it, she made fun of it!

In the two years since the Kennedys moved into the White House, Billie's personal style had changed from timidly garish to confidently muted. Corduroy featured a lot now, and 100% cotton had become something to look for on labels. Cotton madras was her new interest, as well as seersucker for hot weather. And if she ever had any more babies (and here, Billie stopped and sighed), she'd name them Caroline and John. And it was a fine time to be Catholic! To sit in a pew every Sunday, with healthy children and a handsome successful husband. Weren't lots of people on their block the same – solid Catholic families with names like Gilotti and O'Reilly and Cincotta. Okay, MacAlister wasn't exactly Catholic sounding, but everyone knew Scotland and Ireland were practically the same island. And anyway, her maiden name was Molinelli – very Catholic. The bottom line was, if she wasn't in the life she was, she would be insanely jealous of herself. Goodness me, she thought giddily, I would hate myself.

A photograph of John Kennedy on his sailboat had been pinned to the kitchen bulletin board for six months. She'd cut it out of *Life* magazine and Jacko had teased her. Said she had a crush on the President. But now he wanted to get a sailboat too. Not a motorboat, they were tacky. A wooden sailboat, to take his children out on. And Billie would go too, with her Brownie box camera, and take lots of photographs of them all, with the wind filling the sails and their sunburnt freckled faces all beautiful with smiles. God bless families. God bless Catholic families. God bless Catholic families in America.

The MG Jacko drove when Sam was a baby was gone. They had one car again, a green four-year-old Hillman which Jacko used to commute to his new job as subeditor at the *Bee*. Oh! Another similarity.

- John Kennedy and Jacko – both wore white collars to work.

But unlike John, Jacko's job involved quite a lot of typing on his Remington, and phoning. And unlike Jackie, Billie did not have servants to clean her house and provide clean clothes for her family. Actually, she didn't even have a washing machine or a dryer. Ah, the price of living beyond one's means. But didn't they own the sweetest little white house on Cherry Blossom Way, at the centre of the coveted Land Park neighbourhood?

- White houses

But life behind the facade was hot dogs for dinner, home-sewn dresses and a drawer full of Blue Chip stamps all carefully pasted in books. The *Blue Chip Catalogue* was her most frequently read book. Their vacations were either trips to her mother's in Redding, or camping. Camping! Arriving with tired children, everyone cranky from the hot drive and from packing up, and then having to put up the tent and unpack before you did anything else. All that scrabbling around in dirt, picking insects out of food, hearing mosquitoes like jet planes inside the tent.

259

It suddenly occurred to her that marriage was a bit like their tent. When Jacko brought it home, it had nestled neatly in a shiny clean bag. After the first use, they couldn't fit the tent back in, no matter how hard they tried. It would not go! And by the fourth use, they'd lost seven pegs, the zip stuck sometimes, and there was a little mould growing in the corner where they'd all slept in a familial heap. Nope! No matter how closely they read the instructions, that darn tent was never true to its promise. And she'd never be able to squeeze the days of her marriage back into that neat orderly way she'd imagined them.

• Acceptance of imperfect marriage.

Billie slipped the list into the Blue Chip stamp drawer. Jacko never looked in there.

Twice a week, while the kids were at school, Billie filled a suitcase with dirty clothes and headed to Sunny Suds Laundromat. They'd only lived in this neighbourhood six months; routines like this made it seem much longer. The suitcase was awkward and heavy. She switched hands now and then, so each leg had bruises. Today was hot. Hotter than Piggleston, where they'd been living this time last year. The two apartments they'd briefly rented before buying this house had been much less convenient for the laundromat. It had been a forty-five-minute hike from the first one. She'd hated that apartment. Snot-green stucco, with their apartment on the fifth floor. No elevator and no air conditioning, just a ceiling fan that made an irritating whine. All their boxes had still been in storage, and for months they'd lived out of the suitcases they'd driven down with. Like camping.

Most of those mornings Jacko would shower, while

she ironed the shirt she'd washed the night before in the bath. Then she'd serve up eggs and bacon for them all. He'd kiss her goodbye, ruffle the kids' heads, and go off to his air-conditioned adult world, briefcase swinging to beat the band. He never complained, and she always complained. The kids kept asking for the toys which were still in storage, she had no friends, and Jacko was often out.

The lease had been short – it was more a boarding house really – and they'd moved to a better apartment for a few months, and now they were in their own house, 1910 Cherry Blossom Way. All the boxes had been unpacked and friends had been made. Well, Jacko had some friends at the office, and they'd been to three cocktail parties, at which she'd been able to finally wear that empire waist dress with the poppies, spitting image of the dress Jackie wore to her nephew's christening. Robert and Ethel's eighth child. The Robert Kennedys were classy too, but Ethel couldn't hold a candle to Jackie. It was Billie's feeling that Ethel was holding Robert back from the political success of his brother. Her eyes were…too small, and she'd let her figure go. She had the look of, not exactly trailer trash, but definitely housing tract. Not that there was anything innately bad about housing tracts. In fact, Billie and Jacko were living in one right now. But at least it was an old one, and the houses had long ceased to be clones of each other. In fact, Billie had fallen in love with 1910 Cherry Blossom Way because it was different from the other houses on the street. For one thing, it had a huge sycamore tree in the front yard, and the attic had been converted into a tiny bedroom with a multi-paned window peeking out to the sycamore branches. There were lemon and orange trees in the small backyard, with

261

grey squirrels continually leaping from branch to house roof to branch. Yes, it had cost too much, barely enough for groceries after the mortgage, but it was worth every penny, every sacrifice.

She was nearly at Sunny Suds, and her arm couldn't wait to let go of the suitcase. She passed Vic's Ice-Cream Parlour, and out drifted that song. She paused here, putting down the suitcase. Suddenly, no other songs were on the radio. *I want to hold your hand!* Just kids, the Beatles. Cute, though, she had to admit. Jackie had admitted to liking them too, just recently. Paul McCartney was twenty-one years old, over a dozen years younger than Billie. This made her feel old. She sighed. The sky was a flat white, too polluted and windless to be blue. She thought the sky looked unwashed. A rush of vanilla-scented cold air hit her from the open door of Vic's Ice-Cream Parlour. She was accustomed to constantly telling herself: *No, not yet.* She walked on, her mouth tasting the Jamaican almond fudge she loved, and she didn't miss a beat, the sweat staining her pretty pink blouse. So self-sacrificing! So mature! So thin and classy! Well, wouldn't Jackie do the exactly the same? She'd suffered so much, had Jackie, but did you ever hear her moaning about her lost babies? All the miscarriages, the stillborn daughter, the son who died at three days old? Not a word. Always the bright smile, the controlled serenity. Jackie knew how to endure, how to not let life get you down. Darn it, there was no two ways about it: Jackie Kennedy had style.

Since Charlie, Billie had struggled with style.

At first she'd howled like a demented thing, even in public places. When the crying became more controlled, she stopped having sex. She felt crazy. One day she put all the photographs of Charlie, all his newborn sleepers, the teething toys and teddies still brand new, away in a box. Then she took them out again, talked about him too much with strangers, upset Elisabeth and Sam with her afternoons on the sofa and a box of Kleenex. She never drank, which was a good thing, but Jack still said she was embarrassing herself. And embarrassing him. So she put Charlie's things away again, aside from a brown teddy bear and three framed photos, which she did not display in the living room. They were on her bedside table. Charlie at one day old, asleep; she could smell his newborn skin just looking at that picture. Another from the park, when he was just two weeks old, sleeping in that new buggy she'd coveted. And one a week later, just before the terrible night: Charlie naked in the bath. This one was her favourite, because she was in it too. She could see her own arm cradling his back, and her hand scooping water over his belly. She loved the way his skinny legs and arms seemed to keep moving, even in the photograph. She never got tired of looking at the photographs, but she rationed herself. Her guilty treat. She avoided times when Jacko was home – he didn't like to talk about Charlie any more.

'It's not that I don't miss him,' he explained to her one evening when he'd been drinking. 'It's just that talking about him doesn't help. If it doesn't help, what is the point? It's…it's uneconomical.'

He was right. It was an inefficient use of time, to talk about Charlie, to think about him, to picture him. And yet. It had been just over two years now. He'd only been a month old when it happened, but the nine months of pregnancy made her feel she'd known him longer than a month. Some days just after she woke, the family felt like a family of five, a completely different shape in her mind than a family of four. Five was asymmetrical but rounder, four was equal but angular and sharp pointed. Then she remembered, and it was like her family reversed, sucked in on itself, and going backwards had never felt right to her. It never felt the same. It turned out that once someone took up space, the space didn't disappear just because they were gone.

Jackie would understand this. Her son Patrick had died two days after birth, and Arabella had been still-born. There had been miscarriages too. She probably never bothered her husband with her moods. With her nostalgia, and this awful feeling of...permanent wrong-ness. No, no. She'd continue getting her hair done, her nails painted, her leg hair removed. She'd be ever-ready in bed, pliable, melting, a proper lover. Billie could remember behaving this way, but she couldn't summon the actual feeling. Jackie would be hiding all her sorrows, but Billie imagined that somewhere in the White House, perhaps in some small closet or cubby hole, she had built a little shrine to her lost babies. Photographs, unworn baby shoes, a birth certificate. She imagined Jackie slipping away from some state dinner or cocktail party, maybe slipping out of her post-coital bed, to take solace alone with her mementoes. To just sit with them, and somehow *inhale* proof that once she'd had other children. She adored her Caroline and John-John of course, but when alone she might sometimes whisper the names of the others.

Weird, how occasionally thinking that Charlie was still alive when she first woke, made her so happy she hardly minded the shocking dip straight afterwards. So secretly, sometimes in the afternoon in the empty house, she'd begun pretending that he was just in the other room, having a nap or playing with his Matchbox cars. He'd be just over two now. Maybe he'd be looking at a picture book, pretending to read, trying to copy his siblings. On one level she always understood it was a game, but, oh, the second's worth of joy it brought her anyway. And to think he began life as an accident! The night Kennedy won, they'd drunk expensive wine, made love, and she'd fallen asleep before douching. How could such random carelessness lead to someone so sweet, so specific – the surprise of Charlie had made him more precious somehow than the two planned children. He so nearly wasn't. With that amount of luck, it seemed illogical that he didn't get to have his full life as well.

Some days she got irritated, thinking of the way she'd taken him for granted, almost from his first day. The older children and Jacko had still absorbed her; her own appearance had still absorbed her. For long periods when he napped, she'd focused on other things. That dress she was sewing for Elisabeth. Helping Sam with his arithmetic. She revisited memories, just daily routines like changing Charlie's diaper, or tilting his head back in her hands to rinse the shampoo out, or putting him in his crib and covering him with that yellow blanket. This time she infused the occasion with the proper enthusiasm. As if appreciation could be effective, retrospectively.

Sunny Suds was steamy and smelled of Tide. The powdery, chemical sensation burned the back of her throat as she loaded up the three machines. Whites, coloureds, delicates. As usual, she briefly remembered days when she did one load of wash a week. Sometimes not even that. Hard to believe that had been her, suiting herself every minute of every day. That lavender silk lingerie she'd been so proud of and hand-washed. The fine lace on the trim of each piece. Nowadays, all her underwear was greyish cotton. But then Jackie probably didn't place much importance on fancy underwear either. In fact, it seemed vain now. Serviceable good quality underwear, that was classy, wasn't it? 100% cotton. Breathable. Something a little trashy, a little desperate, a little unwholesome, about sexy lingerie. Anyway, her Jacko certainly didn't need encouragement. Mores the pity, she often felt.

She sat down to watch the clothes tumble in the machine, wishing she'd brought a magazine. *Good Housekeeping* was out now, maybe she could pop out and buy a copy. She swung her purse over her arm, and set off to the corner store. Instead found her feet taking her – without so much as a nod to her brain – to Vic's Ice-Cream Parlour.

Jacko was ninety miles away, in a downtown San Francisco restaurant. He was sitting with two men in white T-shirts and Levis. Their corduroy jackets were slung over the backs of their chairs. They were drinking German beer and making Martin Luther King jokes. *I had a wet dream.* They knew it was in bad taste; that's why it was so funny. The beer was stronger than the beer Jacko was used to. He listened to them snorting with laughter at something he didn't understand, but you wouldn't guess it to hear him respond with a burst of laughter. Not a fake laugh, either. Jacko was laughing because he was so happy, he might burst into song if he didn't laugh. Look at him – Jacko MacAlister, the winery worker's son, the skinny kid who hadn't kissed a girl till he was sixteen, eating pastrami on rye and drinking fancy beer with two Golden Gate Freight Press editors! And they hadn't even asked him questions about his employment history, which was a huge relief. He'd sent them a partially fictionalised CV, just on a whim, never expecting to be invited for an interview. Crazy impulse, but here he was. He made a mental note to ask Billie to buy him some good quality white T-shirts. His own button down shirt suddenly felt boring. His shoes seemed too polished, and his hair a smidgen too short. And also, maybe buy a case of this stuff, what was it again? Boy oh boy, it tasted fine! He was living the American Dream now, Goddammit.

The waitress cleared their plates, brought coffees, and they all lit up cigarettes with Jacko's Zippo. A moment passed, while they inhaled and puffed.

'So, Jack!' said one of the men. Jacko considered reminding him again that his name was Jacko, not Jack. Then did not. No one liked to be corrected, right?

'Jack, I may as well tell you now.' He looked at his colleague, who smiled his approval. 'We want you.'

'Boy oh boy!' was all Jacko could think to say, but inside he was saying *Fuck!!* They couldn't have checked any of his references.

'You'll be assistant editor for half a year or so, then maybe commissioning editor. You're going to fit right in, Jack.'

Both men shook his hand vigorously, and Jacko suddenly saw himself as they must see him. A reliable, unpretentious *Jack*. Not the wild card, Jacko. Was the name Jacko a bit silly?

'Very now place, the city. Your family will love it.'

Jacko/Jack knew exactly how now and how wow the Bay Area was. Back to base camp. San Francisco, the sweetest town in the world.

All the rest of the day, while he sobered up driving

home, he kept calling himself Jack. With the new beer, the new job, the prospect of a new house, the new name easily jostled into the big picture. New life, new name. Jack MacAlister, one of the Golden Gate Freight guys. He imagined cocktail parties in apartments with views of Coit Tower, Alcatraz, the bridge.

'You're not *the* Jack MacAlister, are you? Golden Gate Freight's Jack?'

'Well, yes, actually,' he'd reply, acting mildly surprised. They'd smile and mention that they were writers, albeit unpublished. They'd tell him what a genius he was, to have discovered so and so, who was their favourite all-time writer. And could he maybe take a look at their poems one day? Or their novel?

Golden Gate Freight wouldn't have strict work hours. There'd be long mornings in Café Trieste with his notebook and black coffee, making notes, surrounded by poets, artists, musicians, not to mention all those inhabitants of North Beach that made it North Beach. The strippers, the out-of-work longshoremen, the fat old Italian women in black, sweeping their door steps. In his mind, San Francisco took on the shape of a vaguely familiar once-loved woman he was now determined to get to know again. To woo. No, not just one familiar once-loved woman: a dozen women. San Francisco was a room full of beautiful women, all desperate to seduce him.

By the time he was driving onto Cherry Blossom Way, the name *Jacko* seemed juvenile, show-offy. *Jack* was serious. People took a Jack seriously. Jack Kennedy. Jack Kerouac. Jack London. Jack, Jack, Jack. Jack MacAlister, editor at the best publishing house on the west coast. Life could not be better.

So when he told Billie later, over a late dinner of French toast, bacon and maple syrup, he was not prepared for her tears. She wasn't either. Why was she crying like this? Her tears were hot and fierce.

'Why didn't you tell me, Jacko?'

'I was sure I wouldn't get the job.'

'Isn't Golden Gate Freight that same place you applied to before?'

'Yeah! You remembered. I've been applying for jobs there since I left college. Couldn't believe it when they finally shortlisted me. I had to go, Billie.'

Pause, while she found some tissues. Blew her nose.

'You could have mentioned you were driving to the city.'

'I should have. Sorry, sweetie.'

'I don't know why you have to be so darn secretive.'

'I don't either. But just think – we're moving to San Francisco!'

She missed this house already. The lemon and orange trees, the squirrels and the attic bedroom with tiny-paned windows and cut-glass doorknobs. The coolness of the living room, with its white walls and curved door arch. And missing 1910 Cherry Blossom Lane was immediately clumped with everything that she had ever missed, starting with that falling-in-love feeling that faded one afternoon in 1955. The view from every kitchen window since they'd married, which amounted to eight kitchen windows. She missed the way she used to fit into her grey honeymoon dress, with the narrow grey belt. And Charlie – there he was, adding his infant poignancy, and the smell of sick in his hair. Darn it! She opened her mouth to speak, but cried louder instead.

'Aw, what's the matter, honey?'

She blew her nose again. 'Sorry. I'm just so tired, Jacko.'

'I know. This heat. San Francisco will be so much cooler.'

She wasn't being honest with him, but still – his ignorance of her was infuriating. She glared at him, sitting across from her, and he seemed not just miles away, but an entirely different species. It was not classy, not a Jackie thing to do, but she pushed her plate away, then stood up and scraped her dinner into the garbage.

'What? For Christ sake, Billie, what the hell?'

At least the children were already in bed.

'You announce we have to move. Pack everything up again, pull the kids out of school, find a new place to live, new friends, new everything and you wonder why, why, why I am not dancing for joy? Darn it, are you...nuts?'

Billie could not swear out loud. It was like a speech impediment. Her mind was screaming *Goddammit you fucking selfish asshole*, but out came the ineffective *nuts* and *darn it* again.

'Billie. Honey. You've always coped so well before.'

'No. No! I have never coped well. It's been hard each time. I love this house! It's the best house yet!'

'You never said you minded moving. Am I a mind reader?'

Another nose-blowing pause. He kept his eyes on her. Fork poised above cooling French toast.

'What's the date?'

'It is *not* my period,' she lied.

'It's the middle of the month.'

'Stop changing the subject. I hate moving.'

'You should have said something before.'

'Well, I've been proud of you,' snuffled Billie. 'And I

270

just got on with it, put everything in boxes yet again, but it's so hard. You have no idea.'

Jacko felt her misery drift towards him, like a threatening thundercloud. And he'd been so happy all afternoon, so excited. Damn it, why should she ruin this? She had an instinct for ruining things. He was reminded briefly of something much more unpleasant, disconnected but somehow similar. Billie had said *You have no idea* in just that same accusatory and triumphant tone repeatedly the year Charlie died. Over and over. Charlie flashed through his thoughts right now, like he sometimes did. Sometimes just the memory of holding him; now and then, his whole face. Just the sight of his still body in the crib, this time. Followed by a second's memory of Billie's wild crying jags and his own detachment – well, someone had to stay calm. Elisabeth and Sam had been frightened enough. Billie could be so selfish. A child, really.

'You. Have. No. Idea,' she'd said, hatred filling her eyes.

Had she any idea whatsoever what it cost him to stay on top of things then? What did she imagine would happen to the world if every grief stricken person just upped and lay on the sofa for a year? All right for her, she didn't need to support a family, Goddammit.

She called him The King, deferred to him, then pulled this garbage. Screw her! But he felt his joy leak away anyway, and a huge tiredness descended.

'Did you hear me? Are you listening to anything I say?'

She heard her own shrillness. Jackie would never behave like this. Smoothing her hair off her forehead, she raised her chin and looked him straight in the eye. She looked around. The table, the curtains, the whole dining room was already changing – she could now imagine looking at a faded photograph of it one day. Oh yeah, she'd think. That room, that house. That time we lived in Sacramento for a year. Suddenly the whole house felt insubstantial. This was just another interlude. Not part of her proper, permanent life. This would all be packed up into yellow Mayfair boxes. She took a big breath. Let it out.

'I'm sorry. I know I shouldn't get so upset, Jacko.'

'It'll be fine. Ernie says they plan on moving to Marin too one day. And we'll be closer to Louise. You could see her all the time.'

'Yeah, that would be good. Those poor boys of hers. Maybe they could stay with us sometime.' Despite herself, she felt better. In fact, she began to feel the tiniest tentacles of excitement. Jackie Kennedy moved often too. Heavens, you had to follow your man.

'All right, Jacko. I'll start looking for houses in the Bay Area tomorrow.'

'That's my girl.'

He wanted to start eating again, finish his French toast. French toast was no good cold.

They went to bed, kissed good night and hunkered down in their usual positions. Jack on his back at first, then turning on to his right side. Billie on her side, facing him, one arm over his waist. An hour passed, then another. Jack removed her arm, rolled over and faced her. It was light enough from the hall light to see her face. Her mouth was slightly open, a slight frown in that eyebrow. Maybe she was dreaming about packing boxes already.

'Billie,' he whispered.

'Hey, Billie.'

'Billie, you awake?'

'Jiminy, Jacko. Can't you see I'm asleep?'

272

'Listen, can you call me Jack now?'

'I just did.'

'No, you called me Jacko. I want to be Jack from now on, okay honey?'

'Oh, for heaven's sake. What time is it?'

'About two. Can you please do that? Call me Jack?'

'Two o'clock in the morning? Why did you wake me up?'

'I was just thinking. I can't sleep. I'm excited, I guess. So, do you think you can call me Jack?'

'Why?'

'I don't know. I feel more like a Jack now.'

'All right. Can I go to sleep now?'

'Say it.'

Big sigh and moan from Billie. 'Jack! Jack, Jack, Jack. All right?'

'Thank you. I love you.'

'I'm not promising to remember this in the morning.'

'Okay.'

Ten minutes passed. They'd turned away from each other.

'Jacko,' she whispered.

'Jacko, you awake?

'I mean, Jack! Jack, all right?'

'What is it?'

'I can't sleep now. You've ruined my sleep.'

'Say *I love you, Jack*, and I'll rock you to sleep.'

She giggled. Jackie Kennedy probably had just kind of conversation sometimes with John.

'I love you very much, Jack MacAlister,' she fibbed, but the saying of it made it real. And she did.

Billie Obeys the Book

Nov 8th, 1960, Piggleston, Oregon
9:31pm

As always, they watched the Huntley-Brinkley report till the end.

'Goodnight, Chet.'

'Goodnight, David.'

'And good night for NBC news. Stay tuned for more election coverage.'

Billie had not been listening, or really even watching. She was knitting Christmas stockings for Elisabeth and Sam, who were in bed. Sam was getting a Santa going down a chimney and Elisabeth's stocking would have a snowman. It was the hardest thing she'd ever knitted, and needed all her concentration. She frowned when Jacko spoke, because she'd been silently counting stitches.

'What?'

'I said, let's celebrate.'

'Why?'

He ignored her and opened a bottle of Zinfandel from Buena Vista. He'd bought it in a nostalgic mood; his dad had been entitled to discounts, and Zinfandel had often been on the table at home.

'Here's to our saviour,' Jacko said, touching her glass with his own. 'Kennedy almost certainly won,' he prompted. 'Skin of his teeth, but it looks like he's got it in the bag. Thank God for the electoral college.'

'The what college?'

'Never mind. Cheers!'

'Cheers,' said Billie, automatically, and put her glass down without drinking. She resumed knitting. It had been a long day. Martha from the PTA had phoned to scold her about forgetting to bake three cakes for the school sale as, apparently, she'd promised. Then Elisabeth had wet herself at kindergarten again. Twice, so she'd had to wear the kindergarten underpants and skirt home. Elisabeth had whined all the way home, not because of her humiliation, but because the underpants were blue, and she hated the colour blue. Sam had brought home a note from school asking Billie to arrange for a parent-teacher meeting soon, to discuss Sam's ongoing problems with reading. What problems with reading? There was nothing wrong with Sam's reading ability. Now, this. Christmas stockings beyond her knitting ability. Why had she begun? They were 50¢ at Woolworths, for heaven's sake. In August Billie loved the idea of Christmas, but although it was still only November, it had already begun to feel like something that loomed.

Jacko drank and smoked. Squatted in front of the set and turned the channels till he found another program about the election results. Such a close race, still counting till this morning and the result not confirmed till now. It was incredible, because Nixon actually won the popular vote. He wanted to race outside and find other people who also thought it was incredible. He wanted to drink a Goddamn case of this stuff.

'Can we get a puppy? The kids would love one.'

'No,' he said distractedly, and lit another cigarette.

'What if it was one like Lassie? I can't believe you don't want a dog. I thought all men liked dogs.'

'Billie. Listen, honey.' He spoke very slowly. 'The Republicans damn near won, but they lost.'

'I heard. So what?'

'So it's important. It's very good news.'

'I know! Your face looks funny. Are you drunk?'

He'd been feeling old lately, and hating his job. He hated this town too. And the neighbours in the apartment below. They had a dog that barked continually, and the wife never said hello unless Jacko said hello first. He'd apply to Golden Gate Freight Press again. Why not? Hell, he'd look for jobs anywhere in California; Oregon was not for him. He was thirty-three years old already, for Christ sake. According to the news yesterday, he only had thirty-six more years. If he was lucky. And here he was, stalled in some podunk town, with a valley wife who didn't know the difference between a Republican and a Democrat. In fact, who the hell was she? He didn't have a clue what she was thinking. In the back of his mind, that very small cool room, he wondered: So then, is *this* what my marriage is? This daily, constant getting to know a person you thought you already knew. Was it just that, plus a slow accumulation of joint memories? Surely marriage must be more, could be better than this…this business of thinking he knew her, and then not. Estrangement and intimacy, round and round. In the beginning it had been thrilling not really knowing her, but the best bits now were the times Billie felt familiar and comprehensible. It was so cosy, then. He wanted that feeling back.

'Oh come here, Billieboo.' He patted the place next to him on the sofa and smiled his old self-mocking leer. That used to break the ice.

'Get lost.' Then, softly: 'I'm all comfy here.'

'I'll rub your feet.'

'Are you spilling ash on the rug again?'

Billie scolded herself silently for nagging. Rule number three in How to Keep your Husband Happy: *Do not criticise him*. She stood up and took him an ashtray.

'Here you go, sweetie. Sorry.'

'That's okay. Take your shoes off and sit down.'

'Just going to finish this row.'

She went back to her seat. I'd be happy if he never touched me again, she thought. She crossed her legs, smoothed her hair back and argued with herself while still managing to knit. Rule number two taunted her. *Make him feel valued and attractive. He needs to feel you respect and love him.*

Oh, just go sit on his lap, she chided herself. Go on, it's what he'd love.

Why? I don't want to. (She had a few sips of wine.)

Go on, just do it. He's your husband. He's not a bad man.

I didn't say he was.

Well? You read the book.

Billie drank more wine.

Chapter two. *Please Your Husband. His home is his refuge from the world of work.*

Billie imagined herself doing just this, so a second later when she put down her knitting, rose and walked over to her husband, she felt distant from herself. False. She stood in front of him, then leaned over, stroked his head softly, enjoying the feel of his feathery cowlicks. He looked up, eyebrows raised.

Sit, she commanded herself. That's what wives are supposed to do. Don't think about it.

So Billie curled up on his lap like a little girl. Like Shirley Temple, who her five-year-old daughter loved. Nothing sexual in this yet. Nothing that would require rinsing out her douche bag, anyway. She burrowed into his chest near his armpits, prolonging this part. Quite enjoying this part, actually. It was so relaxing, just cuddling. Soporific. Then she told herself: No man is as wonderful as my Jacko. No man is as handsome – look at those cowlicks! His smart eyes! He's my King Arthur. Where would I be without him?'

Exactly. Where would you be? Like your mother. Alone and poor. You are very lucky he married you.

Still burrowed into his chest, Billie slowly and softly sang in her Marilyn Monroe voice: *Don't let it be forgot, that once there was a spot, for one brief shining moment that was known as Camelot.*

He needs me, she told herself, putting her arms up to his neck, and wriggling her body tighter into his. *Do not undermine him. Do not challenge him, or ask why he is late. He needs you.*

You think so? she asked herself.

Oh yes, she answered. He doesn't know how much. I won't ever let him know how much.

Are you sure?

Yes. Oh yes.

She felt his muscles relax, his skin heat. Her muscles relaxed, her skin heated.

Then he started unhooking her bullet bra, and she let him.

Half an hour later in their bedroom, she was staring at the ceiling and asking herself: I don't have to do that for another week, right?

That's right, she answered herself, yawning deeply. Not unless he wants to.

Then, just as she was telling herself to get up and douche before she fell asleep, she fell asleep.

Two Women and Three Breasts

February 14th, 1957, Piggleston, Oregon
10:04am

He sat in the office he shared with five other men, recalling the squeamish face she'd made last night when he'd suggested beef teriyaki for dinner sometime.

'What's the matter?' he'd asked ingenuously, hoping she wasn't really that provincial, and yet also willing her to confirm it out loud.

'Nothing. Only it sounds foreign.'

This had both pleased him and depressed him. Was part of him actually happy when she displeased him? His parents had always seemed at odds – perhaps he felt more at home in a marriage that was not harmonious. Not a good thought. He put it aside and took a look at the secretaries. They sat outside his office, but were visible to him because the wall was mostly glass. The three women sat typing, almost continually. They never seemed to look at their typewriters, just the scribbled shorthand on the yellow pads. Two of the women were unattractive, but one was a pretty blond, about twenty years old. The office reminded him of his first job in San Francisco, Perkins Petroleum Products, where he'd met Billie. That sweet-legged, red-lipped blonde bombshell, though it was getting harder and harder to associate that Billie with his wife.

On his desk was a photo of her. She watched him all day. He didn't normally notice, but he kept glancing at her today. The thing was, they'd fought again last night, and right now, as far as Jacko was concerned, Billie was an ungrateful brat with the taste of a three-year-old. Maybe it was having children that had changed her, made her greedy and stupid. And no sense of humour at all these days. She used to tease him sometimes, and giggle, and whistle, and dance around the apartment in her underpants and bra. She used to say she was going to start reading so they could discuss novels, but she'd not mentioned that in a long time. She watched reruns and ate Tollhouse cookies, while he read Penguins and sipped Chardonnay. Was this difference down to his relative proximity to San Francisco while growing up? He felt he'd been married at least twenty-five years, not five years. He'd tried teasing her about ageing before her time, about her figure becoming more womanly, but she'd just stared at him and burst into tears. Of course, he'd read about wives like her, he'd listened to husbands in the office complain about their wives too. How they never did anything but complain and nag and they hated sex. But he never thought it would happen to his darling Billie.

Bottom line? Billie was not much fun any more.

And this job was not much fun any more either. He thought he'd love working for a newspaper and he didn't. The hours were a joke. Either up before dawn, or home after midnight, and every Goddamn weekend and holiday. The only good thing was that he saw a lot of his kids. Though when they started school, that'd change.

In principle, reporting should feed into his fiction writing, but sadly rarely did. Piggleston was worse than Smithton, their last town. Another dull newspaper in another dull town. What was wrong with him? Jacko sighed. With each new job, he'd been convinced his life was vastly improving, that he was moving up. And none of it was good for his writing. He spent an hour a day scribbling out the story of Josh McCoy, womanizing longshoreman living in the Tenderloin. But lately it had gone so flat. He reached for Josh in his mind, tried to get a grip of him again, but Josh seemed to have deflated like a balloon filled with fart. Just an unpleasant smell lingering.

The only inspiration in Piggleston was the lack of inspiring people and events. He considered dropping the novel for now. Writing short stories like *The Dubliners*, where people went about their mundane lives and became aware change was possible but then didn't change. Yes, he should definitely try that. That's what writers did, wasn't it? Tap into whatever was there. He could write a collection and title it after one of the short stories. *Epiphanies in...Tiffany's*. He'd have to explain that the small town jeweller named his store Tiffany's ironically. Or not. Maybe the jeweller would be genuinely convinced his store was as elegant as the New York version. A sad delusional main character. Maybe he could be a lonely

Jewish homosexual like the blind man in *The Heart is a Lonely Hunter*. Or would that be too derivative? Damn, damn, damn other writers and their books. Especially damn successful writers still in their twenties!

The phone rang and he answered.

'*Piggleston Journal.*'

'Yes, speaking.'

'No, I remembered, I'm covering that. The meeting starts at five pm tomorrow, right?'

'No. Yes. I said yes, we understand the vote will be very close.'

'Uh-huh. Uh-huh. Uh-huh.' He held the phone away from him, made a face at it.

'Yeah. Yeah. Don't worry.'

'I know, I know.' He faked a laugh.

'Oh no. We take littering very seriously.'

'That cartoon was a joke. That's what cartoons are.'

'An apology? For a satirical cartoon?'

'No, no, satire means....oh, listen, I've got to go now, a breaking story coming in.'

Jacko felt vastly underused. Stalled at the starting gate again. Like his Morris Minor, which was now dying at intersections and probably needed a new choke. Very irritating. British cars were great, but insanely expensive to fix. He should make some notes for that article about stray dogs scaring children in the park, but picked up his fountain pen instead and began making a list of chores and projects.

- shelves – buy wood, bricks
- varnish – buy
- Fix bed-frame. Nails? Screws?

- Billie – $. Allowance? Cash only?
- Car – service
- Write Ernie. Ivy.

His handwriting was clear and bold. He took pleasure in quality pens, and he admired his own writing. It made him feel like someone who was in control, and not a fraud. Which was good, because of course now and then he remembered that he was a fraud. That he'd been fired from Perkins Petroleum Products for pretending to carefully research products and update their description in the wholesale catalogue, but in fact had made most of it up. But the worst slip up had come not from his creative wording, but from some carelessly placed zeros. In the famous peach plastic toilet seat episode, by the time it had been discovered, almost 100,000 had been sold at a huge loss. He was not ashamed of lying, but he remembered keenly the humiliation of being caught.

His colleagues sat close by, writing or talking on the phone. Occasionally talking to each other. He was lucky to have a desk by the window. He looked out at downtown Piggleston. Foggy again, though not much foggier than in this office where everyone had a cigarette lit. He watched the men below, in suits and hats, looking like they knew where they were going. And women too; serious faces, purposeful strides through the grey. He was thirty years old, Goddammit, but they seemed like the real grownups. Then something happened to his perspective, and he saw them all as versions of himself. Just guessing, getting it wrong sometimes, and bumbling through their days. Faking it. Year after year, decade after decade, generation after generation. Everyone dying with loose ends, like…like unsatisfying novels. Or worse – like unfinished novels.

He smiled. Must write that down.

It always cheered him when he got a glimpse of the bigger melancholic picture. It reminded him of working on his novel. The way he'd disappear. Even the fight with Billie now evaporated – out the window it went. He stood up to get a better look out the window, as if the fight really was visible. He stood there awhile. No one noticed, but he pretended to be loosening the catch to open the window and let some smoke out.

The world was operated by a changing shift of amateurs like himself, all making lists when they felt at a loss. Or their equivalent of lists. Each overlapping generation was just passing on the baton of taking life seriously, of being productive citizens and acting as if life was worth persevering. Aside from the God he wasn't sure he believed in any more, there was no one who was overall and permanently in charge of the world. No one alive had enough hindsight to get it completely right. (Damn, that was clever. Must write that down too, he thought.) It was a miracle the world kept running as smoothly as it did. A miracle that most people would wait in lines and pay their bills and brush their teeth and park legally and show up for doctors' appointments and say please and thank you. Just a small per cent doing the bad stuff: stealing, killing, going bananas. Everyone else, imperfect of course, but still getting up every day and doing their best. Goddammit! It turned out good manners and timidity might be the glue that held the whole shebang together. But he reckoned it was a nebulous kind of glue that breathed and congealed and sometimes dissolved without warning. After all, he thought, what was the war all about, if not a total dissolving of that glue? That reminded him.

- Buy glue

A cup of black coffee, that's what he needed. Or a martini. He looked at the clock – only 10:45. An hour and fifteen minutes, and he'd put on his coat, go to the park with Billie's dry bologna sandwich. Or would it have a smear of mayonnaise? Maybe even the crusts cut off? He could read her moods through her sandwiches. How much did she love him today? Crust-less roast chicken sandwiches on white, with lots of pepper and mayonnaise wrapped carefully in foil was code for *I love you madly*. Dry bologna wrapped in wax paper – well! He'd choose a park bench that his colleagues would not walk past on their way to popular cafes and bars. The trouble was, he had no friends in the office. In fact, he had no real friends in Piggleston at all. What were they doing here? Was it still necessary to live this far from the Perkins Petroleum Products scandal? These were not his people. He missed Ernie. He even missed bossy Bernice. Friends were everything, they made time fly, and not a single man here was his kind of guy. They wore polyester suits, made stupid lewd jokes, talked about pension plans, property prices, golfing vacations in Pebble Beach. They complained about their wives being frigid. About being nags. About being neurotic. They bragged about conquests, some from the typing pool.

Their contempt for their wives suddenly made him feel loyal towards Billie. He'd never cheat on her. Never! And he never trotted her out to join in their wife-trashing sessions. His Billie was many irritating things, but by

God she was a class act compared to their wives. He was proud of her.

He looked at his list and picked up his pencil. Anything could be fixed, if you just thought hard enough.

- Alternatives to Piggleston – Quit job, apply for other jobs, move back to Calif, live with parents. Go back to college?
- Alternatives to no friends. Join a club. Tennis? Find a decent bar. Near college?

Sometimes all it took was writing a list. The day's deadline was in an hour, but his work had been finished an hour ago and tomorrow's copy wouldn't come in till later in the afternoon. To hone the appearance of working, that was the trick. He opened and shut his desk drawers, sharpened his pencil, scrabbled in files, fiddled with paper clips. He didn't look up to see if anyone saw him because another trick was to look preoccupied. Genuinely concerned about word count and the way the Piggleston mayor's wife's name was spelled. Meanwhile, he returned to fret at his central problem. He was sure it was just a matter of thinking hard enough. Mistakes could be fixed, damn it.

- Alternatives to marriage

Divorce was unthinkable. Not that he hadn't already cast his eyes over their joint possessions, imagining how they'd be divided. He had friends who were already divorced; he knew it was an option which did not end in certain death. If she kept the sofa and television, he could have that expensive oak kitchen table and chairs. He'd spent hours sanding and varnishing them; he deserved them. The record player was his. And the records and the books (They were all going to look great, once he built his brick-and-plank shelves.) He'd keep his MG and she'd have the Morris Minor, and hell, he'd let her keep the set of china that had been a wedding present from his mother. He began to feel less ruthless when he thought about the wedding photos, and the letters from those premarital months, when he'd been up here missing her and she'd been in the Bay Area, planning their wedding. Those lonely nights he drank too much and poured it all into letters, rewritten them ten times, then walked at midnight to the corner mailbox. He'd never been any good on his own. All his daring words of love! And she'd written back once to his three times, and almost no words of love. He'd loved her harder than she'd loved him.

And now, some days he didn't even like her.

What a fix. What a jam. Jesus Christ, what was he going to do?

He screwed up some paper he didn't need and tossed it, missing the wastepaper basket. Swearing, he retrieved it and put it in. Lit a cigarette, looked at his watch.

He suddenly thought of his son, of Sam, the image of himself (according to his mother), only blond. And he thought of baby Elisabeth too. How would they be divided? He started to visualise himself picking them up on a Saturday morning, taking them to the zoo, but his chest hurt when he did this. No, no, no. Absolutely not. Jacko sighed, impatient already to turn Billie into the kind of wife he needed and deserved.

Improving Billie:

- College evening classes? English lit?
- Money – back to work part-time? Kelly Girl – temping in an office?

- Budget. Evening classes on finances?
- Food. Get her to try one new thing a week. Smoked salmon?

In the same way a rich man was more careful with his money than a poor man, a beautiful woman was more careful of her appearance than a plain woman. More rode on it. Jacko teased Billie about letting herself go a bit, and this upset her because she was trying so hard not to let herself go. He had no idea the daily effort she still made, even at home with the kids. Sometimes she practised smiling in the mirror. Just to check no flaws were advancing, like crow's feet or turkey neck. Any kind of bird resemblance at all.

There she was right now, sitting in the park, squinting into her compact mirror. Four-year-old Sam was digging elaborate roads in the sandpit while two-year-old Elisabeth hovered near him, scooping sand randomly over the edge onto the paving. She had a cold, and there were shiny streaks running from her nose like snail tracks. It was so foggy, Billie could hardly see her children, even though her bench was only a few feet away. So foggy, her own reflection looked ghostly, her blond hair almost greyish-white. She licked her lips and applied lipstick over them, baring her teeth to do so. She frowned when she noticed a rogue eyebrow hair, quickly grabbed hold of it between thumb and finger and yanked hard. She smoothed her hair down with her hand and re-pinned the hair clip, which kept her forehead free of bangs.

Last night was terrible. She tried to replay his accusations, to think of better replies, but the children kept intruding.

'Mommy! Wanna play with Sam!' An early talker, her enunciation was perfect.

'Well, but he's a big boy Elisabeth. You don't care about cars and roads, do you? Why don't you make a sand cupcake, like we did yesterday.'

'Sam, play with me!'

She was a serious little girl, stubborn and jealous. She moved closer to her brother but looked away from him. Began patting the damp sand into little humped shapes. Sam happily ignored her.

Billie sighed deeply. She loved her children, of course she did. One of each, a boy and a girl, both healthy – what more could anyone want? But she did not love them continually, and that was the problem. Right now, for instance, she felt nothing at all for them but impatience. Probably by lunch her heart would swell again, but right now she felt as separate and critical as if she'd just glanced at some stranger's children. It was just plain annoying, the way they both interrupted her own thoughts all the time, till she had trouble remembering the most basic information. What was in the fridge for dinner? Would she ever again fit into that skirt she'd worn on their first date? When did Jacko say he'd be home? After midnight, or afternoon? If it was not mid-afternoon, maybe she could watch *Days of Our Lives*. Or *Queen for a Day* – she loved that show. It would be great if he had to do a triple shift.

From this distance, she looked back and saw that being in love had been like…joining some kind of fanatic religion, where you were not allowed time to think, or sleep, or to be private. Attraction had just been an enormous and cruel bluff. Kisses like wine were just to trick a person. And even now, she often felt a little sedated, not quite herself, as if the edges of her personality were blurring. Because he liked camping, she now spent some weekends on her knees, heating up cans of stew outside their tent. Because he only liked some of her new friends, she'd let some friendships drift. Loud-laughing Brenda kept turning up regardless, but the rest seemed to have taken the hint. Her sister, Louise, married finally to Chuck, was coming for a visit, but Jacko was not crazy about Chuck, so she'd have to discourage them from staying too long. Because Jacko didn't like beans, she'd given up one of her favourite foods. Because he was the only one earning, she couldn't buy a pretty dress on impulse. Who was she now, really? If she wasn't a tent-hating, bean-loving, Brenda-friend, impulse dress-buyer, who was she? Some days it felt like her younger, pre-Jacko self was struggling to keep her mouth above the water, gasping for air.

'Mom! Tell her to shove off! She's ruining my tunnel!'

'Elisabeth honey, come here.'

'No.'

'Look at her! Stop her!'

'Lizzy, look what I've got in my bag! Cheetos! Sam, stop it. Stop shoving your sister.'

Elisabeth fell backwards onto the hard paving and howled. Snot ran into her mouth. Billie scooped her up, wiped her face with a Kleenex while managing to protect her own blouse from snot and dust. She carried her back to the bench, searched for and found the bottle of milk she'd told herself just that morning to stop giving Elisabeth, she was way too old. Popped it into her mouth, till her lips closed round the teat and began to suck.

'Sorry, Sam. It's a wonderful road system you're making.'

'You always give her what she wants.' He pouted for a second, but his pride was soothed. Billie could tell by the way his eyes lit up, and he tilted his head. He was such a quick forgiver. Vain, but big hearted too. Oh, she may not continually feel love for her children, but, my goodness, she knew them inside out.

You always give her what she wants.

Last night's fight finally came back, and her one good line. After he'd shouted, she'd gone quiet to collect her thoughts, then hissed:

'The trouble with you, Jacko, is simple. You want everything your own way, but you don't want to live alone. Do you? No, you do not. Sure, you hate me, but you wouldn't know where to start without me.'

Oh! How good that had felt! Like hitting a target.

What could he say? What could he do? Except storm out and slam the door so hard, the Van Gogh chair picture toppled off the wall. Of course, he'd been back within the hour. Not many places to go in Piggleston, aside from Lacey's Lounge, and that was the other side of town.

Usually she let Jacko decide when they made love. But last night, to try and make up, and because it was Valentine's Day, she ran her hand up under his T-shirt and gently run her fingers across his back and shoulder. Then around to the front, further down. But his breathing had slowed and eventually a snorting snore commenced. She'd blushed with shame in the dark. Sleep came eventually, but fitfully.

She rubbed her eyes now, remembering. Sam was making car noises, and Elisabeth was drifting off to sleep on her lap. She should really get them home, make some lunch, do some housework. Maybe if she got out the play-dough, they'd let her watch *As the World Turns*. Getting a television had changed her life. Yes, she'd relax on the sofa, in front of the television. No point in fretting over Jacko. This morning, he'd seemed normal enough. He had accepted the brown bag lunch she'd packed for him: boloney sandwich, apple, potato chips. She'd slipped in a home-made Valentine, written in crayon. *Billie & Jacko forever*. He wouldn't see it till he opened the sandwich bag.

They were on a budget, a very tight budget which was checked monthly, painstakingly, by Jacko. Last night had been budget night, hence the fight. In the beginning, when they had both been working and before the babies, they'd happily eked out their pennies, rewarding themselves with occasional bottles of bubbly and nights at the movies. Their frugality had made them a team, but these days it underlined their very different teams. She spent, Jacko earned. He interrogated and reprimanded her, if he felt that (for instance) artichoke hearts were an extravagance, or she had no real need for a new bra when the old ones were still in her top drawer. Buying him a present was doubly dangerous. Impossible to predict exactly what he'd like, and equally risky to gauge how much to spend, since he regarded the money as his. It was all a little humiliating.

'Why haven't you filled in all these check stubs? Must be half a dozen blank, I have no idea what you spent, or on what. How do you expect me to balance the budget?'

She'd meant to, she'd shoved the receipts in her bag meaning to do it later, but then she'd forgotten. She'd shouted back:

'What difference does it make? The money is spent! Don't you trust me to spend it wisely? Don't you respect me? You should respect my judgment.'

The kids had been asleep. She'd shouted and he'd shouted, but a subdued, controlled shouting because waking the children was the number one sin.

Then his voice had become very quiet. He spoke as if speaking to a very young child.

'You cannot spend it if we do not have it. That's how it works, Billie. The bank charges me money every time you spend more than I have.'

Pause.

'Billie?'

Pause.

She had no idea what he earned. It was not a wife's business to know that.

'I can't live this way,' she'd told him at last, quietly. 'I will not live like we're poor, counting every penny, always getting the cheapest things. It isn't necessary. We are not poor. Anyway, it isn't like you deprive yourself of the luxuries. Look at your shirt, Brooks Brothers isn't the cheapest, is it? And your darn car. That MG.'

'I thought you loved that car.'

'I do, Jacko. For goodness sake, that's not my point. Why do you get to be extravagant but never me?'

'Why?' For a second he'd smiled his silly, naughty smile. 'Because I get up and go to a job I hate every day. Because I work hard, Goddammit. What do you do? It isn't fair. Look at this place! A pigsty. I work my butt off while you do nothing but watch daytime television.'

Then she'd had her inspiration, her moment of clarity, and shot him with the line about him always wanting everything his way but being unable to live alone. He had kicked Elisabeth's building blocks and left the house, slamming the door, while all her outrage swelled up and had no place to go. It clogged her throat. She'd been unable to eat anything for hours. Oh, it made her blood boil even now. If the roles were reversed, how would he feel if she shouted at him for…for buying a tie he liked? She decided the problem was he didn't know her any more. But she didn't really know him any more either. She felt this knowledge hover, recognising it as an older feeling. It had been coming, she'd just been too tired and busy to say hello to it.

So, as she bundled her children back to the warm house to make lunch, she accepted the new equation. What else could she do? Adrenalin coursed through her; it felt like an emergency. How could her marriage feel in such danger, when it was only five years old?

'Mom! Slow down! Wait for me.'

She looked back guiltily at Sam, skinny legs running to catch up. She stopped the stroller and waited, though Elisabeth wakened and began to cry. She automatically checked to make sure she had her purse, the baby bottle, Sam's green teddy that came everywhere. The check she did a dozen times a day. Yep, all accounted for. Both children also accounted for. Off they go!

By the time the hot dogs were on the table, she'd made up her mind. She would get to know this stranger. This moody critical husband of hers. She'd get to know him and she'd seduce him, darn him! Her marriage *would* be a success. She had an urge to…what was this feeling? It was so familiar, but felt unusual, like an item of once loved clothing suddenly come across at the back of the closet. Oh yeah. She wanted to talk to her sister, Louise. Tell her about Jacko being so unreasonable. She began to dial, but then stopped. No, no, this would not do. Billie was not going to admit her failure to Louise, though she had a sudden lurch of homesickness. For California, for San Fransisco Bay, for the proximity of her family.

Only 1:20. Was this afternoon *ever* going to end?

Her mother arrived the following week. The children hid behind the sofa when she walked in.

'Helluva place to live,' she announced. 'Ugliest town

I ever saw. The streets ain't got no signs! Been driving around for an hour.'

'What a surprise!' said Jacko. 'If I'd known you were coming, I'd have met you downtown so you could follow me back.'

'Would you like some iced tea, Mom?' Billie asked, taking her suitcase.

'Beer,' she grunted. 'No, make that bourbon. Jeez, I'm tuckered out.'

She plopped herself on the sofa, kicked off her shoes, and the hidden children sniggered.

'I can see you two, so you may as well come out right now and give me a hug and kiss, seeing as how I've just spent an entire lifetime getting to you.'

Sam and Elisabeth froze, looked at each other, then raced around the sofa and jumped on her, kissing her wildly.

'What brings you here?' asked Jacko, slightly awkward. The children never kissed him like that.

'Eh?'

'Mom's going to look after the kids this weekend, so we can get a break. Isn't that sweet of her?'

'Really? Wow. That is fantastic. Thank you! You're wonderful.'

'I friggin know that,' she said over the children's heads.

'Did you call her?' he whispered when his mother-in-law left the room for a minute.

'No. Well, I kinda did. I wrote her.'

'You sure your mother can cope?'

'My mom could cope with Al Capone.'

He smiled and gave her shoulders a squeeze.

They packed small bags, and the next morning off they went. Billie and Jacko, their first trip alone in four years.

They took the MG and headed south-west, towards highway 101, retracing their honeymoon drive. The weather was good, for the time of year. Clear, but not warm enough to take the top down. The sky remained a solid blue all day, and the Pacific was also blue, only darker. In the end, they found a small hotel outside Gold Beach. It looked idyllic, but the woman who answered the door was sharp tongued and the room smelled of mildew. Still, they were alone.

He opened the champagne her mother had given them, and poured it into the glasses she'd insisted they take.

'Here's to your coarse-mouthed mother.'

'Here's to my darling mom. Who swears too much'

Jacko sat on the bed, while Billie sat in a chair.

'We can make as much noise as we want! Come here, you.' He wanted sex of course, right away, before dinner, and she had hoped this would happen, yet she found herself assenting tiredly.

The drive home the next day was quiet, but they told each other it had been a great break.

'Just what the doctor ordered. Tell your mother to come more often.' They took their time, stopped at a beach, then a restaurant for a late lunch. There was very little traffic on the road. About an hour from home, the red sports car ahead of them tried to pass a truck, and was hit by an oncoming station wagon. Before Jacko even had time to brake, they watched the much higher station wagon flick the sports car into the air like a Dinky toy. Jacko finally stopped, about the same time the station wagon screeched to a stop down the road. The driver, a man in his fifties, jumped out of his car and ran up towards them, saying:

'Jesus fuck, I never saw it coming. Out of the fucking blue...'

'Stay here,' said Jacko firmly to Billie, as he got out of the car.

She was making disapproving noises with her mouth shut. The kind of noise she made when the children injured themselves, half anxious, half angry that they'd been so careless with their bodies. The noise from the accident had been horrific; there was still an occasional metallic clanging. The truck had stopped up ahead too, and the driver was running down the highway to the accident. A few other cars had slowed to a stop, and people were running and shouting. Jacko ran back and Billie asked:

'What did you see?'

'The driver's unconscious. Went through the windscreen. Don't think anyone else was in the car.'

He frowned and started the car, not looking at her.

'Unconscious? But will he be all right, do you think?'

'Uh, maybe. Tell you the truth, Billie, probably not.'

'Where are we going?'

'Got to find a phone.'

His voice sounded odd. Billie saw the driver of the sports car, flung on the tarmac like a rag doll. He was a young man, thin, maybe a teenager, his features invisible, too bloody. He was on his back, arms flopped out, motionless. Jacko had to slow down here, to get around the upside-down car, and she noted that the boy was wearing a suit. A nice suit. The white shirt was a mess, but the jacket seemed fine. A nice blazer, probably wool. There were three or four people, the drivers of other stopped cars, leaning towards him, talking to each other. One looked up and gave Jacko some kind of signal with his hand, and Jacko nodded. A woman, middle-aged,

298

was crouching down next to the boy, her head bowed, crossing herself. Jacko shifted up a gear.

'Maybe he was on his way somewhere fancy. His suit.'

'Uh-huh.'

The first lit-up house they came to, Jacko slammed on the brakes, ran up to the door, and without knocking, pushed it open and shouted:

'Need to use your phone. Been an accident down the road. A bad one.' Billie had followed, but stayed behind him, silent. She felt her old respect for him ebb back. Men really were wonderful at times like this. Jacko was wonderful. The old couple in the house acted unfriendly at first, wary, then suddenly changed. They switched off their television and offered coffee, whisky, anything at all. But Jacko and Billie got back in the car and headed north again, and outwardly it was as if nothing had changed.

'Don't we need to be witnesses or something?'

'They have our number and address. The others are witnesses too. An ambulance is on the way now.'

'Oh.'

Time passed.

'How much longer, Jacko?'

'Don't know. Half an hour?'

Pause. Billie fiddled with the radio dial and tuned into half a dozen stations, static-ridden snatches of song, news, weather, a talk show about crop diseases, and then an interview with Elizabeth Taylor. She clicked the radio off and sighed.

'Hey, remember that time I had Elisabeth, and you brought Sam to the hospital to visit us?'

'What? Oh yeah. It was Thanksgiving. We had a terrible meal in the cafeteria, after we saw you. Turkey like leather.'

'Did you? You never said.'

'Well. Guess you had enough on your mind.'

'Don't know why, but I often remember that time. I was so sore, so tired. All those stitches, I was afraid to even look down there, much less touch it. Elisabeth wouldn't suck, remember? All I wanted to do was sleep, anyway. I felt sore and ugly and strange. Then you and Sam walked in.'

'Sam threw up later, after the terrible dinner.'

'He did?' she said after a second, very softly and slowly. As if his voice was like one of the radio stations, briefly cutting into the air. 'Did he get food poisoning from the turkey?'

'Think it was just the excitement.'

'Yeah, he was so thrilled about the baby, wasn't he?'

'No, I mean the other kind of excitement. You know. I mean, there he was, going along in his own little world, two whole adults at his beck and call, when suddenly you disappear, and when he next sees you, you're all gloopy over some squally baby. He was upset. He wasn't happy-excited, Billie. He was jealous. Sick-to-his-stomach jealous.'

'Funny. That isn't how I remember it at all.'

'No. Well.'

Billie yawned. 'I just remember how awful I felt before you walked in. The anaesthetic was wearing off, I guess. I felt….brittle. My head had broken off from my body. But the minute I saw you.' She stopped here. Looked away from him, out the window. 'The minute you came in, it was like all the bits joined up, and I was me again. I remember I felt...'

'Great?'

'Normal. I felt normal again.'

'Huh,' said Jacko, quickly glancing at his wife. 'All I

300

remember is cleaning the puke out of the car later. Stunk for months.'

She didn't reply, but that seemed okay. After a while she started singing softly: '*All of me, why not take all of me. Can't you see, I'm no good without you.*' She couldn't hold a note, but she told herself it didn't matter. Jacko probably thought it was a sweet lopsided way of singing.

'Damn right,' said Jacko, who liked her singing some days, but not today. 'Let's see what's on the radio. Might be something about that accident.'

There wasn't, and he turned it off. Ten minutes passed. The mountains had given way to a valley, and it was dark now. Winter dark.

'I keep thinking of how someone's waiting for him right now to turn up and wondering why he's so late. Someone who loves him. His mother maybe.' Pause. 'His dinner's in the oven, getting all dry.' Pause. 'I was talking about that poor boy,' she said.

'I know you meant the boy.'

The house was dark when they got home and they tiptoed into their bedroom. The room was freezing, the sheets almost damp.

'Doesn't your mother ever put the heating on?'

'Shush. She'll hear you.'

They spooned closely for warmth, Jacko around Billie, then he rolled over, so they were back to back. Billie thought that nothing had changed. The extravagant and inconvenient rekindle experiment had not changed a darn thing. Her eyes were open, and she looked at the Gauguin print on the wall. Two women, baring three breasts. She remembered the day they bought it. Before the kids, because she'd been wearing that blue skirt she'd not been able to fit in since. A summer day, and a shopping list with items like wine glasses and pineapples, limes and gin, a wicker laundry basket. Still nest-building. They'd been holding hands all day, and had gone to an art gallery. Billie had never been before. She'd liked it very much, it made her feel calm and reverent, as if she was in church. But she didn't really know what to say about anything, aside from *I like that*. In the gift shop, Jacko had spotted *Two Tahitian Women* by Gauguin, and had been so enthusiastic, she'd cried: 'Well, let's buy it then!'

Putting it on their bedroom wall had made her feel very much not like her mother. Jacko and her, well, they were very cultured. So what if they didn't have much in common, she suddenly thought now. She wanted to make him happy – wasn't that bigger than compatibility? They'd lived through two house moves, had two children and endured countless sleepless nights with infant colic, not to mention changing hairstyles, changing presidents and changing states. They'd fought, made up, fought, made up. Gone away alone for a weekend to a hotel! They really had done that. Already, she was remembering it with nostalgia, though last night she'd felt disappointed. Was there something perversely romantic about it being unromantic? It seemed now that she'd been happy in that mildew-smelling room. Why hadn't she known it at the time?

She closed her eyes, pictured the bedroom they were lying in right now, inside their own apartment, in their neighbourhood, their town, their state, their country, and the whole indifferent world orbiting through cold space. Really, there was just their bedroom and the rest of the world. Us and them.

302

Five minutes passed.

'Jacko.

'*Jacko.*

'Jacko, are you asleep?' An accusing tone.

'Yeah.'

'I love you. *I love you, darn it.*'

'I know.'

'I know you know.'

'Well, shut up then.'

'You shut up.'

'I said it first.'

Then he turned round, so he was facing her. Eyes closed. She noticed the scar on his chin from the champagne disaster. Not a good start to the honeymoon, but hadn't it been wonderful later? She traced the scar tenderly with one finger.

'I was just kidding. I hate you, really.' She whispered this.

'I know, honey,' he whispered back. 'I hate you too. Like crazy. Did I ever thank you for that Valentine in my lunch bag?'

'No.'

'Well, thank you.' Then he began kissing her with his eyes still closed, and his lips tasted good to her. She'd forgotten how good he could taste. Imagine if he should suddenly disappear. It was always like this, after a spell of hating him. Like they were new people, like she was in love all over again. But even so, she couldn't shake the person who was waiting for the boy to arrive. This time, it was the lover. A girl who for months had not been able to concentrate on anything, because she loved this boy so much. She was all dressed up, but because it was very late now, her dress was a little wrinkled and her lipstick had worn off. He was never this late, where was he? She happened to be looking out the window again when a police car pulled up. Two policemen got out and walked up the porch steps. Billie tightened her arms around Jacko. She kept thinking about all the terrible things that could happen to a person.

To Begin at the Beginning

Jan 28th, 1954, Smithton, Oregon
2:32am

Sam cried. He cried a lot. Also, his poops were green sometimes, and this made Billie worry that something was wrong. When she thought of something being wrong with Sam, her stomach hurt and she felt like crying. She tried to take him out for a walk every day, but it was the middle of winter. The good news was she could fit into most of her old clothes already. She got her haircut in a bob, chin length, and it curled up perfectly in front of her ears. It was still very blond – she'd worried when they moved to the dark north. It was her belief the sun kept it fair.

Tonight Sam woke her at 2:30. He was almost one; this should be unusual, but sadly was not. His crib was in their bedroom, so she didn't have far to go. She lifted his damp hot body, carried him to the bed and guided his mouth to her nipple. It was engorged – had been hardening since his cries had woken her. It was a second before he properly latched, and a relief when he did. They both entered a trance as he sucked.

'You need to wean Sam,' Jacko had said earlier. 'He's getting too old for that. Try that bottle we bought.'

'I know, I will,' she'd said. And she did plan to, as soon as she got the energy to not breastfeed. Bottle-fed babies must have more energetic mothers. She was bucking the trend, breastfeeding. When Sam cried to be fed and she was in a store or park or coffee shop, it was a problem. Mostly she ended up in a toilet cubicle, nursing him. She didn't go out much these days.

She noticed the apartment was extra quiet, a muffled quiet, and looked to the window. The blinds had not been closed because they lived on the fifth floor and privacy was not a problem. It was snowing. Large fluffy flakes. Some of them sticking to the window, as if they were not frozen water but a gluey substance.

'Jacko.

'Jacko!'

'What.'

'It's snowing.'

'Huh.'

Then he turned over and began snoring. This was their second winter in Oregon, but Billie was still not used to snow. It felt magical. She tried to put Sam down in his crib, but he woke again. She carried him to the living room and stood looking out at the snow, rocking him and singing very softly and slowly. *I've been working on the railroad, all the live-long day. I've been working on the railroad, just to pass the time of day. Can't you hear the whistle blowing? Dinah, won't you blow,*

Dinah, won't you blow, Dinah, won't you blow your horn, horn, horn? Outside, the world turned white and rounded. Car became humps and trees branches bowed down. She stared and stared, and could not imagine ever getting used to it. But it was cold in the living room, and after a while she went back to bed and put the sleeping Sam in his crib. The bedroom felt cosy, especially now she knew the world outside was coated in snow. She fell asleep within seconds.

Jacko woke up. His wife was snoring gently, her hair across her face. She was on her side, with her face tilted up and one arm above her head as if she was reaching for something. He told himself he loved her very much; it caught at his throat. She seemed so young. The room smelled of Sam. Jacko tried for a minute to describe it. He smelled like a cotton sheet, just taken in from the line on a breezy warm day, with something else added – what was it? Something food-like. Toast? He gave up. He got out of bed, noting the snow and wondering if it would be possible to drive today. He was not sure how often the road was ploughed. It would be a nuisance if he couldn't get out. Today was Saturday, and they usually went shopping on Saturdays. Especially, they needed coffee. He tiptoed around, careful not to wake Billie or Sam. It was great to have the place to himself for a bit. He was wearing a tartan robe over his boxers and T-shirt, with hiking socks to keep his feet warm. He put the kettle on the stove and lit a cigarette on the burner. Since Billie gave up smoking, he was always having to do this. She'd been the one to always keep the Zippo filled, and a book of matches on the table. That was marriage for you. You get used to one new way of doing things, then bam! You had to get unused to it.

The wind was picking up; the snow made thwacking sounds against the window. There was also a shrilling sound. Jacko looked outside and decided it must be the wind and the telephone wires. It was spooky, but in an exciting way. Suddenly, a gust hit the window and rattled the panes. A draft crept through, metallically cold. This made him very glad to be right here, inside his apartment with the door locked and bread and milk and cans of soup and a nice bottle of Pinot Noir in the cupboard. Not to mention his wife and his baby. The gust became a gale, and the whole wooden building seemed to shudder and even sway. He made his coffee, leaving enough for one more cup, and smoked his cigarette. They probably wouldn't get out today. But his family was safe; they were all under the same roof and this struck him as wonderful. His family. The phrase was still a novelty.

To begin at the beginning. He remembered the radio program a few days ago, and Richard Burton in that strange and powerful play *Under Milkweed*. Or was it *Over Milkwood*? *To begin at the beginning.* Apparently poor Dylan Thomas died just recently. Pity. He made a mental note to buy the book, if such a thing existed. At first he'd just half listened while sanding the oak table, then found himself pausing before finally sitting down and giving his full attention to the Bakelite radio sitting on the counter. The little dark Welsh village slowly emerging, and all the queer and quirky inhabitants populating his living room. He remembered the line that went something like: *as we tumble into bed, little Willy Wee who is dead, dead, dead,* because it was repeated a few times. A story and a poem and a song. I want to be a writer too, thought Jacko suddenly. That's what I want to do in my life. He imagined this for a while, then decided he also wanted to be Welsh, or at least some kind of British. Well, it was something to aspire to anyway. Maybe he'd buy a tweed jacket. And next car – a Hillman. And an MG? No more Fords, anyway.

Eventually Sam woke again, and Billie stumbled through to the living room with him. 'It's like *White Christmas*,' she said sleepily. 'Say, wasn't that a swell movie?'

'I preferred *It's a Wonderful Life*.'

'Me too, actually.'

They took turns with Sam. Feeding him, bathing him, changing his diaper, dressing him, trying to give him a bottle, changing his diaper again. 'You know what I was thinking earlier?' He wanted to tell her he'd decided to be a great writer. It filled him up, this new yearning. But he couldn't say it out loud. 'I was thinking we might have another baby one day.'

'Oh, sure, Jacko! I was thinking exactly the same thing. Someone to keep Sam company.'

Christmas was a month ago. A nutcracker ornament that somehow never made it back into the ornament box was hanging from the window above the sink. It was their second Christmas as a couple, and the nutcracker was new. Billie had made some ornaments. Clowns, constructed of cotton spools with yarn for hair and sequins for eyes. Small fairies made of felt and pipe cleaners, with small wooden balls for heads. She'd made these while Jacko was at work and Sam was napping. She had also baked gingerbread men.

'I miss Christmas,' she now said. 'I loved it.'

'Me too,' said Jacko, though he clearly recalled inedible turkey and glutinous gravy. He'd given her a Timex watch and a bottle of Hypnotique perfume which she thought smelled like cheap candy, and she'd given him a subscription to *National Geographic* and a tie he thought made him look like a used car salesman. Neither admitted disappointment.

When Sam fell asleep again, Billie yawned and said she might go back to bed too. Jacko joined her, but didn't fall asleep. While his son slept close by and the world outside became mysterious, he reached for his wife, gently pulled off her clothes and they made love silently and tenderly. As if they'd died and become ghosts, still in love with each other. Afterwards, when she had rolled away from him, he stroked her back. Softly; hardly touching her skin. He thought of the time she'd asked him about the war, and whether it had been scary for him. He'd wanted to say yes, because then it would make him seem brave. He couldn't remember what he answered, but he remembered wanting to say he'd been in danger, and been scared shitless. She'd looked at him with such admiration.

'Jacko?' she said, turning back to him after a while. She smelled of coffee and breast milk and sex.

'Sorry. Did you want to sleep?'

'Not really. Or maybe yes. Do you mind? I'm so tired.' They lay, spooned into each other. Just before Jacko drifted off, he whispered:

'Shush now,' though she hadn't said anything at all.

TWO YEARS EARLIER

Honeymoon

July 24th, 1952, Highway One
2:43pm

My goodness, her waist had never been so tiny – look at it, in her honeymoon outfit, the belted grey dress swinging just below her knee. Jacko could almost put his fingers around her waist, and she often guided his hands to do just that. He was looking thin too, in his cream khakis and white T-shirt under an unbuttoned flannel shirt. Just right for the drive north, in his dark green Singer 8 with the top down. There they were now, taking the turn off to Highway One at Olema, swooping down towards Stinson on an absolute peach of a summer day. This dark-haired boy in dark glasses and this Marilyn Monroe wearing a red Liberty scarf. Not talking, not laughing. They'd been married for nearly thirty-two hours now, and hadn't a lot left to say. Or maybe it was just too noisy with the wind.

Behind was their wedding day, that chaotic whirlwind

of kisses, hugs, flowers, dancing, feeding each other cake, laughing, posing for the photographer. Those vows finally spoken, no words forgotten. The wedding had been imagined so many times, the event itself had seemed déjà vu. But they'd carried it off. Planned, paid for, executed – all by themselves, no parental help. What a team! They even remembered the names of all those relatives. Jacko and Billie had a great time. Or not – it didn't matter, did it? It was over.

Behind also, were those years of being other people, unaware of each other's existence.

Almost impossible to remember what it was like to not know each other now, but there you go. Those years had been lived, and they were part of the past now. No need even to look at them, if they didn't want to. Goodness me, who would want to look at Redding or Sonoma, or anywhere at all in the whole damn valley?

Okay, it was a fact that Jacko had been fooled by Billie at first – thought by her clothes, her shoes, her attitude, she was a Marin girl, or at least a Bay Area girl. But by the time her lowly birth had been revealed, it was too late, he was a goner. Oh, the plunge his heart had taken, as they drove up her mother's street the first time. She'd directed him through leafy downtown Redding, then an avenue lined with large houses and wraparound porches, then told him to turn left at Sugar Street. A mean street, with car carcasses in most yards, skinny stray dogs and barefoot kids kicking a can. There was no sidewalk. Her mother lived in a wooden one-story, with yellowing grass growing right up to the door. He'd not said anything, just closed down his face.

'So,' she'd said, snorting with giggles. 'So, tell me. Did you think you were marrying...*up*?' Then she'd giggled harder as if this was the funniest thing she'd ever heard. Which in a way, it was. She'd been fooled by him too, but not minded.

'Who said we were getting married?' he'd replied.

'Why, you did, Jacko MacAlister! Last night, don't you remember?'

'I did no such thing.'

'Did so.'

'Did not.'

'So.'

'Not. And stop laughing like a hyena.'

'But it *is* pretty funny, Jacko. I mean, here we are,' she'd said, as he pulled into the driveway, crunching over something he hoped had not been alive. 'Both trying to... well, to better ourselves, and who do we fall for? Why, practically our next door neighbour in disguise!'

'Sonoma is not next door to Redding.'

'It's still valley. You're not better.'

'It's in the north Bay Area,' he said primly.

Billie put her hand on his knee and stared him in the eye.

'Okay,' said Jacko. 'It's valley. But not as valley as Redding, you've got to admit. We grow grapes for wine. You grow...what?'

'Almonds? Some cattle ranches outside of Red Bluff. We grow hamburgers.'

'My point exactly.'

'Oh, come on. We each thought we were other people. Serves us right for being snobs.'

But Jacko hadn't seen it that way. And his disappointment had not entirely dissolved, because she might never allow him to totally reinvent himself.

Oh, what did it really matter? Now they were going

to a place where no one knew them, and they could be whoever they wanted. If he was lucky, no one there would find out he'd been fired. For Christ sake, how could any man spend his days describing plastic roses and toilet seats, and still respect himself? It had been a silly, boring job – vastly demeaning. Ahead was their new life. Their bright and shining brand-new life! It waited for them 600 miles away in Smithton, a small industrial city in Oregon. Jacko had already rented and furnished an apartment. Well, just the bed, really. He wanted them to choose the rest together. He'd been dreaming of this shopping trip for weeks. He liked simple lines, lots of beige and white, or just unvarnished pine. No more of that dark colonial furniture favoured by his mother. No patterned wallpaper. And please, no collections of china animals! He already had his eye on a certain dining table and chairs. Would Billie want them too? He snuck a glimpse at her profile – she was so damnably sexy. Like a doll, with her red lipstick and heart-shaped face. Even her knees, just poking out of her skirt, were adorable miniature knees. The most feminine knees he had ever seen, and they were attached to his very own wife. Imagine that! It did seem a kind of dream or miracle. They'd need shelves for his Modern Library books, and Penguins too – but he'd make those himself some weekend soon. He'd draw up some plans.

The road opened up, flat and straight for five miles, and Jacko accelerated till the engine made that satisfying sound he called the Singer scream. It would break his heart to be in the passenger seat.

'Billie?'

'What is it, my Jacko pie?'

'Nothing. I love you.'

'You'd better.' She smiled.

'Oh, I've got it bad,' he said, focusing on the road so she couldn't see him smiling too.

'And bad ain't good.'

'Oh yeah.'

The lines were song lyrics and an old joke now, but they giggled anyway as if they were hearing them for the first time. Boy oh boy, life was good. Jacko squeezed Billie's knee, and she covered his hand with her own, while leaning just close enough so her left shoulder brushed his right shoulder, closing the circuit, amplifying whatever erotic music played in each of their pounding hearts. To their left was the Pacific Ocean, wild and empty. The road was empty too, and they each thought to themselves:

Whew! It's over, thank God. Lucky us.

The way they looked at it, they'd accidentally discovered a new country, one that millions of innocent people never got a chance to see. No matter what happened from now on, no matter what horrible things life threw at them, they would be behind this buffer of...well, a happy marriage. Corny but true. What if they had missed this? As long as they could access this current that was travelling down his arm and hand, into her knee and leg and entire being, nothing could hurt them. Not really.

Last night had been their wedding night, but they'd been too overwrought to treat it as such. In any case, he'd been making love to her whenever he could, sometimes both of them falling off her single bed. He rarely slept all night with her, but hadn't minded. He'd quite liked those solo journeys back over the Golden Gate Bridge, then

315

slipping into his own single bed, the cool sheets keeping him awake till he drifted off to the memories of what had just occurred in Billie's bed. Strange, how it kept feeling new; every damn time seemed different, almost like a first time. Strange also, how much he'd missed her at night, those three months prior to the wedding when he'd been working in Oregon. He'd written, and so had she. He wrote with a fountain pen. She'd sent letters typed at work.

Marcus Whitman Hotel
Beaufort, Oregon
June 3rd, 1952

Darling –
I love you. I miss you! Drove over from Smithton this a.m. Will be working with O.L. Bloomer for a few days on the Philpott murder case. He is a very bitter, profane little man who thinks that no one at the paper is any good unless they are about to quit, or even better, have just quit, or best of all, been fired. I was tempted to tell him the truth about me and Perkins PP, but decided it was too risky. Clean start, that's what we need.

Did I mention I love you? I will love you forever and ever and be the best husband on earth. I still can't believe you want to marry me. I can't believe how much I miss you! I've rented us the sexiest apartment you ever saw. I wish you were here right now. I wish you were here, and wearing that yellow dress with the roses and all the buttons so I could unbutton them slowly. You wouldn't have to do a thing. Then I would get you under the covers and keep you warm. I love you. I miss you! Oh yeah, I already mentioned that, didn't I. See, missing you is making me BORING.

316

J'amour tu boucoup,
Mon cherie,
Jacko

Ps If you think Redding is bad, you should see some of
these hick towns.

Perkins's Petroleum Products
22 Battery Street San Francisco 6, California
June 15th, 1952

My Dearest –
Have so many things to tell you, I don't know where
to begin. First of all, Mr Corey received a memo from Mr
Richmond about me leaving and in turn Mr Corey wrote
head office, and the company is giving me a send-off office
party on the 25th, and a wedding present! So, Darling, I
guess that's their way of apologising. Didn't I tell you
they'd be sorry? Fools, firing the best man they had, just
because you made a few mistakes anyone could make.
You'd think they couldn't afford to lose a few grand! But
they are all being so sweet to me, and therefore you. You
are missed! I told them about your new job, obviously –
and they are all very impressed you are now a reporter. I
fibbed a bit and said you were the crime reporter. Well,
you kind of are sometimes, right?

Last night Louise got home about 2:00 in the morning,
so of course we stayed up and talked until about 4:00.
She had a wonderful, wonderful time, but darn Chuck, he
never committed himself.

I dreamt about our apartment. Know the address by
heart. To be truthful, am scared to death to start cooking
for you for fear none of my recipes turn out. Please have
patience with me and pretend I've never cooked before
and am just learning. (Which is the truth almost.)

317

Received wedding invitation from your college friend Stan for the 16th or 17th of October to a girl of the name DeLang. I do not know what to get them so will leave it up to you.

Made an appointment for our blood test on Wednesday as that takes 24 hours to get the results and we have to have that before we apply for a licence. What red tape, huh!

Mom will be down a week from this Friday.

Hurry home,

Billie

PS. Am taking car to the garage tomorrow for a lube job and new oil filter.

And now here they were, about to live together. An hour later, they pulled into the hotel Jacko had booked: Agie's Guesthouse in Jenner. He figured they'd take their time going to Oregon, like a proper honeymoon.

'Name please?' asked the landlady primly.

'Mr and Mrs MacAlister,' said Billie, feeling her face heat. '*My husband* made a reservation a while ago.'

'Yes, thank you, Mrs MacAlister.'

'*My husband* is just coming now. With our suitcases,' she said. 'We just got married,' she added quickly. 'Yesterday.'

'Yes, I was aware of that. Congratulations.' Then she smiled finally, handed her a key and said: 'There you go, *Mrs* MacAlister.'

Jacko had a bottle of champagne. The bottle was too warm, and the landlady brought a bucket of ice. It was not an ice bucket, but a normal bucket, and when he plunged the bottle in, the ice completely covered it. He hoped it chilled quickly so they could drink it quickly, get under the sheets quickly. A double bed! By God, marriage was a fantastic institution. They tested the bed, immediately fell into a clinch so tight each almost swooned. And yes, it felt different yet again. Were they different people now they were married? Would it just go on and on changing, or would it now solidify? They kissed deeply, legs scissoring, and Jacko's plans to do things in the proper order went out the window. Off came the clothes, and within seconds they'd set the springs to squeaking. They tasted of sweat and salt and of each other.

'Billie, why don't you have a bath first? Leave the water, and I'll get in after you.'

'Okay, honey. I do feel sticky.'

'You complaining?' in a cornball John Wayne voice.

Billie knew Jacko was teasing, that he was not really being vulgar, he was being ironic. But it was too convoluted, and she couldn't think of a witty reply. She hated this slowness, this literal mindedness in herself. She made a vow: Learn to be funny. Practise sarcasm. Meanwhile she overcompensated by being affectionate, and gave him three kisses.

She ran the bath, thinking all the while: This is how married people are, how they talk, how they take it for granted they'll share bath water. But she was modest still, and closed the door. She undressed and looked at herself in the mirror, thinking of the Sutro Baths with Jacko last summer. What a show off he was, with his fancy diving. Funny how when you loved someone, their showing off wasn't annoying. Wasn't it great, the way her red bathing suit fit her? Snug but not pinching. And she was pleased with the way her body looked now, as she slipped into the bath water. Ran her hands down her legs, feeling for bristles she might have missed. None. Good.

He was on his back, eyes closed. It was just them at last. Last night Billie's sister, some of her bridesmaids, her mother and his mother (widows, the pair of them), and Ernie and Bernice had all visited them in their hotel suite, as if it was an ordinary room on an ordinary night, and they'd come to admire the view and say goodnight. They'd even brought bottles and glasses. What a hoot! But not a second of privacy.

This place was so romantic, she thought. This night. This was the romance that the wedding night should have held. She got out of the bath, almost pulled the plug then remembered. Decided to make a few repairs before summoning that handsome husband of hers – creamed some lotion into her skin, and while waiting for it to soak in, brushed her hair. Applied some lipstick, sprayed some Evening in Paris. Wiggled her boyish hips to the song in her head, 'The Tennessee Waltz'.

Suddenly, a loud pop and glass breaking.

'Godfuckingdamnit! Billie! Billie, Billie!'

She stood there, naked and greasy, frozen at the sight of her new husband with blood pouring from his face.

'Bill. Hon. It's okay. The bottle exploded.'

'Golly! Let me see,' she said, coming closer.

'Don't! Put something on your feet first.'

He lowered the hand holding a pillow case to his chin. Billie's face told Jacko what he suspected.

'Okay, better find a doctor,' he said.

'I'll drive,' said Billie, as she pulled on underwear. She was worried, but she was also thinking that she'd never seen Jacko with quite this expression. He really was just a boy! Part of her wanted to giggle. And then the giggle really did sneak out. She coughed to cover it, and commanded herself not to look again till the giggle was gone.

320

Jacko's face was starting to throb, and as he felt for glass shards in his forehead, he couldn't help ogling his wife's breasts. There they were, struggling against her bra, which was so pointy it looked dangerous.

The drive to the doctor's office was fraught.

'Billie, shift down!'

'Okay.'

'Shift up, Billie.'

'Okay.'

'Speed up a little, honey, cars are behind us.'

'Okay.' And then: 'Sorry.' Tears spilled down her face.

'Oh come on. Nothing to cry about.'

'I. Am. A. Good. Driver,' she said softly, managing just a syllable at a time.

'What?'

'I drive all the time.'

'Not in this car, you don't,' he sulked. Handkerchief held to his head, blood-soaked.

'Whose fault is that?'

No answer. Was this their first fight? It was their honeymoon, and they were bickering and bloody. Ah, and there was the sun setting to their left. All that beauty wasted, because now they hated each other. Especially, there was nothing erotic between them with Jacko in the passenger seat. Billie thought: *Oh heck. Now what should I do?* Jacko wondered what Ernie would do, if Bernice drove his car like this. He couldn't imagine Ernie feeling this bad, or Bernice driving this badly.

And then they reached the little hospital, and they were talking to the nurse, then to the other people in the waiting room. Just small talk at first, then Billie listened while Jacko told the story of the exploding bottle for the first time. Everybody laughed. How funny, to be getting stitches

321

on the most passionately romantic night of their lives! How amusing to be arguing about her driving his car! But wasn't that life for you, one step forward, two steps back. Something had to go wrong, and it may as well be a bottle exploding. Everyone had their own stories about disastrous honeymoons. One fellow patient told a story about running out of gas on the way to his own wedding, and hitchhiking in his tux. Billie stopped thinking how wrong everything was, and started to be proud they had joined this fraternity of adults who took small catastrophes in their stride. Someone called it a hiccup. As if their smooth lives had literally jerked in a spasm. *Ouch! Oops!* Then normality and easy breathing again. Have a cup of coffee, and here, have a swig of this too. Need a smoke? Here's a light.

And then more time passed, and they were back in their lovely hotel room. What else could they do, but curl up to sleep like two overexcited, exhausted toddlers. Billie's last thought was one of wonder. So far, marriage was not what she'd anticipated. Not even a teensy bit. This didn't dismay her, though it did make the future feel like a bowl of Jell-O now. What on earth would happen tomorrow? And the day after that?

Jacko snored beside her, smelling of antiseptic, and looked for all the world like a sixteen-year-old. She curled up next to him, and fell sound asleep.

ONE YEAR EARLIER

Billie makes Coffee for Jacko

Friday February 12, 1950, San Francisco
8:12am

'Hurry up! You'll make us late again!'

'Coming! Sorry, Loulou. Ready now, let's go.'

'Jiminycrapcricket, Billie. That's my sweater, you know.'

'Yeah? So what? Whose heels are you wearing?'

'Oh, all right. *Come on!*'

'And are those my stockings?'

The two sisters run down the street, with five minutes to cover two blocks. They don't look at all alike, but there is something sisterly about them anyway. Something in their clumsy tandem run, and their laughter. They both laugh in a helpless way, as if even now – as they run – they have to surrender to a delicious, mysterious mirth. Don't ask them what's so funny, you'd never get it. They laugh because the very thought of themselves late for the bus

323

again, arguing about clothes again, tickles them. They're laughing at the very idea of themselves as friends, when the obvious truth is they can hardly stand each other.

The fog is dense, but they hardly notice. They live by the bay; it's foggy nearly every morning and every summer evening about five. But the fog horn is still exotic to them because they are from the valley. It makes San Francisco feel like a foreign country. Just plain better than Redding, that's all. Every darn thing is better here. Especially the boys.

The bus driver teases them by closing the door just as they reach it. It's part of the ritual. He's their age and flirty.

'You're just plain mean,' scolds Billie, dropping her dime in. Her voice is high and soft. Before they reach Market Street, the sun has broken through. A hard blue sky, no clouds.

People get on and off, and the air is full of cigarette smoke and *See you later alligator* and *In a while crocodile* and *Not if I see you first, sweet potato*. Just before Embarcadero, Billie and Louise get off the bus and join the throng of office workers. This is Billie's favourite time of the day. *Here we are, here I am*, she thinks. *Will you just look at me? A stylish young secretary, rushing to work*. Her face has shut down, despite her inner joy, because part of the joy is in blending in, and they are surrounded by workaday faces. They head up Post, and are in shadow. The sky scrapers block the sun. It's cold. Thinner crowds, and more serious. Still the seagulls, though. Like the fog horn, the sisters can never quite take a seagull for granted. They know seagulls are like pigeons here, pests, but they adore them. Adore all the different squawks they make,

324

like confused, emotional human cries. Nope, nothing melodic about a seagull.

Entering the Perkins Petroleum Products building, they quickly dash into the bathroom. Silently comb their hair again and reapply rouge with old soft brushes. Billie curls the ends of her page boy with fingers dampened in the sink, so her face is perfectly framed by two butter-yellow curly cues. A side part, so a hank of hair keeps falling across her face, till she clips it back with a red rose barrette. Louise yanks a brush through her kinky hair, shoulder length, then slides in two bobby pins on either side, so from the top of her ears it bunches straight out like, well, like the hair of that girl Talithia, who used to sweep the floor in their mother's hair salon. (*Looka you, with your nigga hair, you should be Talithia's child*, her mother used to croon affectionately.) In fact, it was Talithia who first showed Louise how to turn frizzy hair to her advantage. Billie would hate frizzy hair, but she's jealous watching her sister nonchalantly twisting her hair back. It should look ridiculous, ugly, but Louise carries it off. Billie feels uninteresting, next to her.

'Got that new lipstick on you, Loulou?'

She covets this lipstick, which costs $2.99 from I. Magnins. As soon as pay day comes, she's going to buy some. But wait – pay day is today. How absolutely wonderful. And tonight, Tommy White from Pacific Heights, if she remembers right. Her obligatory Friday night date. Billie has been in the city for three years now, since she was eighteen. She's had three Friday nights without a date. Louise has been seeing Chuck for almost five years now, but Billie's still shopping. She's looking forward to Tommy White. Or is his name Timmy?

'See you at five?'

'Nah, going home tonight, remember? Chuck's picking me up early to skip the traffic.'

'Nuts, Loulou! Driving all the way to Redding? Well, just remember the Alamo.'

'Oh, yeah,' Louise snorts. 'That had a happy ending, right?'

Louise often snorts, is often irritated or bored or sarcastic, but somehow her life remains something mysterious and glamorous to Billie. She frequently has to remind herself Louise is a year younger.

Jacko is drinking a cup of black coffee at Mike's Meals, his new leather briefcase leaning against his legs. He lights a Viceroy and gets a little light-headed. Love that first smoke of the day! He gives a quick thought to Lizbeth and the way she dumped him last year and ran off to Paris. Crazy girl. She'll be sorry one day, but it'll be too late then. He's decided to get married, start a family. Ernie and Bernice made it look so good. So easy. It's all waiting out there, he just has to grab it. Like aiming for a college degree and getting one. All a person has to do, really, is just put their mind to something.

Maybe Jacko looks too young to be smoking, because a middle-aged woman sitting nearby stares pointedly at his smoke. This reminds him of the way his mother used to make a face at him whenever he swore, even mildly. Even *Oh God*. He blows smoke her way, as if to say: What's it to you, lady?

'Cocky kid!' she says, with disgust, and looks away.

And then because he's noticed that she's not all that old, and she's wearing a low-cut sweater and now that she's blushing with anger, she actually looks kind of pretty – he smiles at her.

'Sorry,' he says. 'Just, I'm a bit nervous.'

'Oh! Okay, I get it. Trouble?'

'Nah. Just my first day at a new job.'

'Ah, but you'll be great. You will! Here, let me pay for your coffee. A good-luck gesture, yeah?'

That's how charming Jacko can be. And how much he needs even cranky ladies he'll never meet again, to like him.

Billie is sitting in front of her typewriter, clacking away a mile a minute. She is not in the typing pool with Louise and all the other girls, because she can type eighty words a minute *correctly*, take shorthand and has the sweetest legs in the office. Not too thin, not too short or muscular. And she has a way of whistling softly when she works.

'What's that you're whistling?' her boss asks now.

'Was I whistling? Well, I don't know. Probably 'Dream a little Dream for Me'. Was it?'

'Could be. Do it again, and I'll tell you.'

She whistles the song, a little self-consciously.

'Great song. Great whistle, too.'

'Oh, gee, thanks. I've always got a song going in my head,' she says. 'Always.'

'Yeah, I bet you do. I've noticed you humming a lot too.'

'Sorry.'

'No need. You hum and whistle away, honey. Just get those letters typed right, and you can dance too, if you want.'

Now she's humming a Glen Miller tune she's forgotten the name of. Her fingers fly over the keys, *clickety clack, clickety clack*, in time to the song. She daydreams while she hums and types. She wonders what to wear tonight, and remembers her birthday is next month and she'll be twenty-two. For heaven's sake, what kind of age is that for a single girl? Time she was choosing someone. Mentally, she reviews Andy, Harry, Jimmy and Larry. All swell guys, but nope, nope, nope and nope. Andy's a cook in a diner downtown, not good enough prospects. Too like her high-school quarterback boyfriend, who begged to marry her right up till the midnight before she moved to the city. Harry's an accountant, white-collar, but a little chubby and both his parents are very fat. Fat is not a good thing. Jimmy's not fat, and he has a noble career as a social worker, but he's just so…nice, so very nice. Billie, who never swears, always finds herself wanting to say something shocking in his presence. Larry's slender, well paid and white-collar, and also a good mixture of corruption and goodness, but – and this is a big but – the man cannot kiss to save his life. Dear me, she's tried enough times, but given up. A man sucking her tongue like a Popsicle is enough to make any girl run a mile. And tonight's guy. Tommy, or Timmy. Well, she summons his face, and it's an all right face, not too handsome or homely, just somewhere in between. He works at a high school in the Castro. They're supposed to go to a movie later, the Fillmore. She'll give him a whirl, she supposes.

Time's getting on; maybe she's too fussy. Her mother thinks so.

'You just find a man who doesn't drink or gamble or knock a girl around, and then you work on loving him. There ain't no Mister Perfect, Miss Milly Mae Molinelli.'

Her mother loved to use her full name like that. All those m's. No one else calls her Milly. She renamed herself during junior year in high school after reading novels by Carson MacCullers and Harper Lee. Sophisticated, artistic girls had boys' names, it was simple as that. Not that she actually enjoyed those novels; she loved them because they looked so marvellous, so out of place, sitting on her mother's kitchen table. They embodied the world she wanted to find, the life she wanted to live.

Clickety clack, clickety clack. All the time she's thinking, her fingers flying and the words appearing. *Clickety clack, clickety clack.*

She notices, not for the first time, how when you really think about it, typing sounds a bit like a train. Like one of those big old freight trains at home, rolling down the track. She and Louise hearing the whistle, then dropping everything and racing each other down to the tracks, long weeds scratching their bare legs, their old mongrel, Sally, following them through the vacant lot – just for the thrill of that big noise, that diesel smell, that black greasy smoke, the sight of the caboose man. Sally was used the trains, so she never barked, just sat patiently at a safe distance and watched the girls. They'd absent-mindedly grab some liquorice weed to chew – there was always plenty by the tracks. But, oh, the times their mother gave them each a hard slap up the sides of their heads.

'You gals! When you gonna learn? Tracks ain't no place for nice gals.'

Still, they could never resist, right up to the time they left home. The whistle sounding all mournful and excited at the same time. The dust rising and the clickety-clacking filling them up as it whooshed three feet from them. The caboose man, with red handkerchief round his neck, smiling and waving.

Now, Billie pretends that her true love is the caboose man, and when he spots her, he makes the train slow down so he can leap off and sweep her up. He is Clark

Gable. No, he's actually James Stewart. And he doesn't so much as glance at Louise.

Billie is cursed with a vivid imagination. It leads her into all sorts of difficulties, mostly to do with imagining scary things, or impossibly exciting things. She doesn't sleep well. A constant movie in her head, and the soundtrack too – always the soundtrack. She occupies two realities. Her imagined reality gives the world a pretty good run for its money. She assumes everyone is basically like herself. She has to. There are limits to even her imagination.

Jacko is being introduced to his colleagues. They are all older. Salesmen in suits, with slicked-back hair. Copywriters in rolled-up sleeves. Boozy red noses, and old man's aftershave. Not much like his pals from college. He bets none of them read Penguins or shop at Brooks Brothers or listen to real jazz.

'What do you think, so far?' asks one of these colleagues, a man with bad breath and a stained shirt.

'Fine, fine,' says Jacko, offhand. 'What time is lunch?'

This job is a mistake. His real job is elsewhere, somewhere intellectual and cultured. He sighs and his tour of the building continues.

'The bathrooms are down the hall to your right,' explains his boss. 'And the cafeteria is on the third floor. And here, this is your desk.'

This is the best news he's had all day. The desk is right by a window, and it is a big desk, with a pencil organiser full of sharp pencils, and a cut-glass ashtray. There's even a file drawer. He can see a chance of being happy here. Jacko MacAlister, star copywriter: a sudden upsurge in sales since his arrival. Yeah.

'Sorry it's so far from our offices,' his boss is saying. 'My office is on the fifteenth floor.'

He'll be unobserved, in his own little kingdom, right here, within the perimeters of this desk. Jacko-land. Truth is, Jacko is not crazy about having a boss at all.

'You won't mind being down here, will you?'

'Not a problem.'

'Good. Good, I thought you seemed an independent type. Now, you might see Mr Tidmarsh from personnel later. Usually makes a point of introducing himself to the new folk.'

'Okay.'

'And if you need anything typed, or a cup of coffee, just about anything, just ask Billie. Her desk is over there. Guess she's away now, but you'll see her later. Nice gal.'

Billie is delivering her typed letters to the mail department in the basement. This is one of her favourite things to do. So satisfying, to interpret a man's rambling dictation, condense it with her shorthand, reproduce it on her Remington till it's a tidy black-and-white document, then see it on its journey. Louise is there, at the new Xerox machine.

'Loulou, I swear those heels look better on you than me. I hate you. *Hate you.*'

'I know. I'm pretty darn gorgeous, aren't I? I'd hate me too. I mean, if I was as ugly as you.'

'What you doing tomorrow? Want to go shopping?'

'Nah, can't. Going to Redding tonight. I told you! Don't you ever listen to a word I say?'

'Oh, yeah. Gosh, Lou, it's such a long drive. Weren't you home last weekend?'

'Yeah. Well. Mom's saying it's an emergency again.'

331

'Tell her you're busy. That's what I do. You've got be firm.'

'Oh, you know I can't. She needs me. And Chuck's muscles.'

'You know she'll try and make you feel bad about moving here again.'

'Yeah, well. Maybe I should feel bad.'

'Oh, no! You better not move back, Loulou.'

'Oh, I like it here fine. But it ain't home, is it?'

'Well, no,' Billie says over her shoulder, as she hands her letters to the mail boy. She turns back to see her sister's face change. Now she looks young, half formed. It never fails to stun Billie, the way her sister can change in a second from cocky to weedy. It makes her think of Louise's insides as something nebulous and volatile; nothing solid inside that girl, just a bowl of mush.

'Do you think San Francisco will ever feel like home, Billie?' She keeps inserting memos to copy and a hot inky smell envelops the girls.

'Well, of course it will.'

'Tell the truth, even when I'm having fun with Chuck, I don't really feel like myself here. Not as much as I do back home. Know what I mean?'

Billie absent-mindedly strokes Louise's hair.

'I know. But seriously, Lou, I wasn't that crazy about the self I was back home.'

She's not had a moment's homesickness, not even a second's worth. But then she wonders – is she really so very brave? Here she is, in her new life, different routines and rituals, already fearing change. And her sister is a huge hunk of home. Maybe she has merely transplanted Redding to San Francisco.

'Please promise me, Loulala.'

'Hell, no. I like Redding. You're the one who was miserable there. You going give me my sweater back by Monday? Go great with my black taffeta.'

'Promise me! Don't move back!'

'Oh, silly Billie, how can I promise? Are you going to cry?'

She hadn't planned on it, but suddenly now she is.

'Golly, hon. I have no idea where I'm going to end up. Let's go powder our noses. I'm done here.'

So they link arms, fetch their bags and off they go.

Jacko leaves the building for lunch. He's peeked at the cafeteria and decided it's lousy. Old people, fat and ugly people, and it stinks like stale grease. In fact, now he thinks of it, the whole set up is a little stuffy. The furniture, the hair styles, the job itself – call it anything you like, the bottom line is writing stupid lies about stupid products, for the benefit of stupid buyers. Nothing and nobody with any taste at all. Not a soul he'd like to drink beer with. Oh, sure, it's good money, but for crying out loud, what's a man like himself to do? Bury himself in a place like this for years? He's walking swiftly, feeling lighter with every step he takes away from Perkins Petroleum Products. Maybe he won't go back.

He arrives in Chinatown, and decides to wander up Grant. He goes into the first restaurant he finds, and orders chop suey. He has a sudden need to use chopsticks, a newly acquired skill. A pretty Asian waitress silently serves him, with a shy smile, and he starts to feel all right again. He orders the strangest food he can find on the menu, just to counter his conventional workplace. In fact, to cancel out his whole rural upbringing too, with the little glass bowls of Jell-O and marshmallows, the polyester shirts, the dearth of bookstores and jazz. He looks around, noticing he is the only Caucasian. No wonder the food is so good. He suddenly decides to take a girl here. He orders another beer, then looks at his watch. Goddammit, he's going to be late from lunch on his first day.

Billie is back at her desk, having eaten the baloney sandwich she'd made the night before. In her head, she's singing 'I've Got a Crush on You'. She's stopped thinking about the possible disaster of Louise leaving, and the dresses, shoes and lipstick she wants to buy. She's back to thinking about boys. No, not boys. It's a man she wants, not a boy. She has a clear picture of what she wants to happen in the near future. Her imagination has honed this idea so often, it appears the instant it's summoned. Like a memory, not a wish. She has a baby in her arms, a pretty, pink, sleeping baby, and she's in a home that she owns, with walk-in closets and a full-length mirror in the master bedroom and everything is new. There's a backyard so their golden retriever can come and go. And somewhere near is her husband, faceless for now. This man is mad for her. And she makes him happy. She wants to be a wife with the same fervour other women dream of being famous movie stars, or missionaries in Africa. Making some man happy will be her vocation. She relaxes into her work, filing documents in the big metal cabinet. Humming very quietly, the tune to 'You Belong to Me'. It's so calming to know what you really want from life.

Jacko re-enters his new office, a little sweaty and a little drunk. He glances around the room, notes the young blonde woman with her back to him, filing manila folders in the old grey cabinet. Doesn't think much, except *I hope she won't report me being late.* He sets to his task, which on this first day, is the job of reviewing last season's catalogue, looking up the sales figures for each product, and making notes on possible ways to improve the copy on the slow sellers. Now he comes to think of it, this job isn't that different from being a psychologist. If he's good enough, he'll be able to intuit what makes people buy, and tap into those secret fears and desires. Milk them without them feeling a thing. He is a genius, after all, and this job is way below his capabilities. He'll knock their socks off, all those red-nosed oily-haired bosses.

Mr Tidmarsh comes round after lunch. Introduces himself to Jacko. Slaps him on the back, asks him how he's coping.

'Great to have you on board, soldier!'

Jacko bets he always gives the ex-service men the back-slap, never the other men.

Then he says: 'You've met Billie, yeah? No?'

'No.'

'Billie, come shake hands with Jack MacAlister,' he shouts across the room to her. 'Fresh out of college. First day copywriting. The new boy, eh, Jack?'

Another backslap, followed by an arm punch. Jacko flinches a little. His dad was Jack; he is not, and never will be, his dad. He is way more than *Jack*, Goddammit. At least another syllable. But the correction can wait till Monday.

'Find a nice place to eat lunch, Jack?'

'Yeah.'

And finally, over comes Billie from her desk, and she says: 'Hey.'

'Hi,' says Jacko.

They don't shake hands. Hardly look at each other. Both look, instead, at Mr Tidmarsh.

'Billie, make Jack a coffee, will you honey?'

'Oh, I don't want a coffee. Thanks anyway,' says Jacko.

'I don't mind,' says Billie coldly.

'Okay then,' he says. If she's not going to even smile, then she can damn well make him a cup of coffee. 'Black, with sugar.'

There's a line at the coffee maker and Mr Tidmarsh is gone when she gets back with Jacko's coffee.

'Thanks.'

'Okay.'

She returns to her desk slowly, with a wiggle in her walk he decides is for his benefit. He looks at her the way he looks at almost every girl. Checks her out. Just the right height. Small hands and feet, medium tits, darling legs with sweet knees peeking out when she sits. Interesting eyebrows. He didn't know eyebrows could be sexy. And hair, swear to God, just like Marilyn Monroe. That same butter yellow, that same way of falling over half her face. Her voice too, little-girl whispery. Then he goes about his business again. Arranges the pencils neatly, the pad with the lists of products. His ashtray, his Zippo lighter. He lights up a Viceroy and goes back to the minuscule photographs of the products in the catalogue. It's a huge volume with thin pages, like a phone book – as he flicks through he sees artificial legs, toilet seats, shower curtains, hula hoops. He tries to visualise them individually, be interested in them. Think of ways they could sound more enticing. It's hard because forcing himself to care is exhausting. Caring eventually trickles in, but then, ironically, for the sweet kneed Billie he pretends it's old hat. He yawns loudly and stretches between bouts of concentration, and of course, this results in genuine boredom again.

He's young and single; there's a girl with sexy eyebrows on the other side of the room. Caring about petroleum products would be unnatural. He makes a list of questions he needs to ask someone, which soon dwindles into a to-do list, then some sketches of the desk he wants to build this weekend, and finally, in the margin, a doodle of Lizbeth's breasts. They are anatomically accurate, though based on imagination only. She'd always teased him, then giggled like mad when he started unbuttoning or unzipping. Strangely this never made him fall out of love. Or perhaps, not so strangely. Bared breasts might have killed it. Anyway, Lizbeth is over. Though suddenly, now, sitting in his new office, he doesn't believe it will ever be over. Even if he never sees her again.

There sits Jacko, feeling a bit old at twenty-four, in a cloud of his own smoke, his mouth dry and his energy wilting. Life is not turning out the way he'd anticipated.

Billie's considered and dismissed half a dozen boys she knows, and she's still typing. *Clickety clack, clickety clack.* None of them will do for a serious boyfriend, much less a husband. How about that new boy, Jack MacAlister? Cocky, that's for sure. Actually, he reminds her a little of James Dean. Dangerous, even though he looks about twelve. Had she smelled beer? Bit daring, drinking at lunch on the first day of work. And no real smile for her. Just a smug look that said: *Oh yeah, I know. You want me.*

Not likely, thinks Billie Mae Molinelli. She's never had to chase a boy, there's always been a line of them just waiting for a chance with her. But he has nice eyes, blue and smart, and the cutest cowlicks. One on the crown of his head and one just above his forehead. (Not dark with cheap oil, thank goodness. Oily hair is what valley boys have.) She can't remember why, but Billie has always had a soft spot for boys with unruly hair. And is Jack's V-neck cashmere? It looks so soft hanging over the back of his chair, and as yellow as...well, as the Butterfinger sitting inside her bag right now. Gee whiz, she's hungry.

The rest of the afternoon passes, with Billie typing and Jacko scribbling. Suddenly, it's five o'clock.

'Okay?' Mr Tidmarsh asks Jacko, on his way out. 'See you Monday?'

'Yup. Monday.'

Jacko pulls on his V-neck. He's never seen the point in keeping good clothes for special occasions. His dad did that, and see where it got him. A life in slob clothes, and a brand-new suit for the coffin Billie finishes her typing, loops her sweater around her shoulders, and puts on some lipstick. She squints at herself in her compact, as if she's alone.

'Bye,' she says nonchalantly to Jacko, and sails past his desk.

'Bye.' He clicks his new briefcase shut carefully, as if there's something important inside, and follows her down the stairs to the street into the February sun. A wall of light and cool air. She stands on the sidewalk outside, putting a cigarette in her mouth. Without saying anything, as if they've known each other for years, Jacko pulls out his Zippo and flicks it under her cigarette. She smiles her thanks, and inhales. They are almost the same height, so their faces are near. They don't look at each other. She begins to walk away, giving him a little wave. He lights his own cigarette, heads in the other direction, then quickly swivels and follows her. He has to walk fast. When he is a little ahead, he turns to face her and walking backwards says:

'Hey, what you doing for dinner? You like Chinese?'

Billie doesn't stop walking, just half smiles, pityingly. He's spunky, have to give him that. Poor guy. Dumped last week, she bets. He reads her look, almost says: *Hey, just kidding.* Instead says:

'Could have a few drinks first. It's early. We could go to North Beach. Vesuvio. There's always some good music on Friday nights. Some great sax player's been there every Friday this month.'

'Oh, no thanks. I'm meeting someone.'

Something alerts him to something unpleasantly familiar. What is it? Her vowels? Her way of walking, slightly flat-footed? But she's wearing very classy shoes, and she's not wearing her hair in bangs. He notices things like this. No, she's not a bit like the farm girls he grew up with in Sonoma. There is nothing wrong with this girl.

'You got a date?'

'Yeah!' She laughs a little. *Of course a date!*

So he smiles crookedly, hoping his smile hints at a wealth of untold jokes. Jokes she'll never hear now, the stupid girl. He boldly gives her the once over and says:

'Well, have fun then!'

He turns on his heels and leaves her in his wake. As he strides down Market Street the sun is glinting off the sidewalk, even the bubble gum glows. The whole place is exploding in light. Billie's hair, glinting gold. Goddammit! If he was in private, he would hit himself hard. Damn, damn, damn. Nothing like starting a weekend by making

339

a fool of himself. He takes a deep breath and expels the humiliation. He's Jacko MacAlister, Goddammit. No girl is going to ruin his Friday night.

Billie, meanwhile, strides along a few more seconds, oblivious to everything but the loveliness of the evening, the prospect of her date later, the compliment of that new boy asking her out. Then she glances up to see him about to disappear round the corner of Pine Street, into the shadow of the Bank of America building. Lean, neat, an easy athletic gait, arms swinging like a man undefeated. Into the shadows he goes, and his shoulders are half gone, and his torso and legs too. A beat of a second more, and he will not be visible.

'Hey!' she shouts, but he is too far to hear her.

Then she begins to run because something inside is lurching towards him, as if the sight of him is something she cannot live without. No idea why, or what she'll say to him if she catches him. And when she opens her mouth to shout to him again, he turns around with a look of pure smart-ass delight.

'Wait up! Wait for me, Jack!'

Afterword

First off, let me confess to an obsession with marriage, and in particular the marriages of my parent's generation. Those post-war weddings, with all their American Dream optimism and frugality and grand plans. The class shifting, the reinventions! The way wives and husbands coped with finding the person they'd married wasn't remotely related to the stranger they'd begged to marry them. And what's more, how many of them stuck to their vows anyway. Of course, my parents figure in this obsession. It has been pure indulgence, thinking about them. It's felt wickedly fun; at other times, guiltily exploitative. What business is it of mine, why they stuck together, how they managed not to kill each other? Part of my motivation was to honour their tenacity, to pay tribute to their particular way of travelling six decades together. And to tell the truth, or at least one or two truths, not necessarily about their marriage, but about marriage in general. I have picked over but not always used the bare bones of their lives – for instance, it is true that their venetian blinds did not work for eighteen years, but the fictional Jack has dalliances, whereas my father, George only had infatuations. George loved his dogs, and Jack hates them. And my mother, Barbara, was not crippled from a road accident like the fictional Milly, but by early onset multiple sclerosis. Jack is a failed publisher; George was a successful economist. My parents never lost a child, unlike their counterparts, and they didn't separate, or inherit two children from a runaway aunt, or a love child from an ill-advised affair. But they did raise children, who gave them a great deal of worry.

There is a curious alchemy that happens when a writer begins with something true and then adds something untrue. With each invention, the characters of Milly and Jack became more their own selves and less my parents, until they stood completely apart – individuals in their own right. I have imagined what happened, how my parents felt during certain crises, but at times I have also simply fabricated events and emotions, not to mention landing an extra three kids on their doorstep. So, this is neither entirely memoir nor fiction, but a story of how a marriage like theirs may have panned out, over sixty years.

Finding love was never their problem; making love last even when it felt like hatred – now, that was the challenge. With great gratitude and respect, therefore, I raise my virtual glass of cold champagne: To my parents, George and Barbara, aka Mickey and Bobbie! And to their holding on to each other through some pretty rough terrain.